Berndt Sellheim is the author of the novel *Beyond the Frame's Edge* (Fourth Estate, 2013). He has a doctorate in philosophy, and his poetry collection *Awake at the Wheel* (Vagabond, 2016) won the Federation of Australian Writers' Anne Elder Poetry Award. Berndt lives in British Columbia, Canada, with his wife, their daughter and a household of other creatures. He works in photography and video production for a museum outside Vancouver.

The
Fatal Dance

Berndt Sellheim

HarperCollins*Publishers*

HarperCollins*Publishers*
Australia • Brazil • Canada • France • Germany • Holland • Hungary
India • Italy • Japan • Mexico • New Zealand • Poland • Spain • Sweden
Switzerland • United Kingdom • United States of America

First published in Australia in 2021
by HarperCollins*Publishers* Australia Pty Limited
Level 13, 201 Elizabeth Street, Sydney NSW 2000
ABN 36 009 913 517
harpercollins.com.au

A catalogue record for this book is available from the National Library of Australia

ISBN: 978 0 7322 9584 4 (paperback)
ISBN: 978 1 7430 9715 1 (ebook)

Cover design: gray318
Cover image by istockphoto.com
Author photograph by Tara Moss
Typeset in Bembo Std by Kelli Lonergan
Printed and bound in Australia by McPherson's Printing Group

MIX
Paper from
responsible sources
FSC® C001695

For my mother, Dorothy,
for my sister, Annelies,
and for all those
Women of the Land

Those the gods would torment
they first let glimpse the future

after Sophocles, *Antigone*

The Sea

Chapter 1

In the morning there is the sea, her first great love. Lori presses her forehead against the cool of the window glass, staring out at the earth's edge, that line where sky and water meet and hold. She could spend eternity watching that shifting horizon, past the streetlights and concrete and cars. She can sense it there, even when she isn't looking. Just as she knows this stretch of road by the brushbox, bloodwood and tuckeroo, knows how close she has come to the sea without needing to look – a deeper knowing, of heart before mind.

Here, the bitumen and earth beneath.

Out there, ever-shifting shadow.

The ocean, in all its moods, has always been Lori's home.

And now she will return to it.

The taxi slows to pull into the carpark, and she pours everything from her purse. She had a fifty folded up in there, she's sure enough of that, but the driver isn't ready for it and half the change goes clinking between the seatbelt clip and console. Not to worry. She pulls herself out using the handle over the door, and by the time the cabbie lifts his head Lori has already crossed the pavement. She can hear the waves. It's important not to be delayed. As she shambles over the grass she can hear the bloke calling, 'You want your change, love? Hey! You forgot your stuff. Hey lady! *Hey!*' But she doesn't turn and will not turn, his voice dwindling to wind-tossed half words lost in the surf, and by the time the sand is there she hears nothing but the sea.

The clouds have the merest hint of new-day light, all the world's colour freshly minted. A smoothly shadowed lawn leads down to the beach, the white lines of the break stretching headland to headland, dreamlike and slow. She stops for an instant, breathes it all in: the salty, granular air; the endless horizon, firming moment on moment with new light; the cliffs, and how they frame it all.

Her shoes she takes off on the edge of the grass, and walking down the ramp to where the dry sand begins, she places them the way she likes, side by side just so, then plonks herself beside them to wait.

Waiting for the sun.

How many mornings has this spot been hers? It *is* her spot, has been forever. It reminds her of the first place she kissed Mada's father, although that was in Byron, almost a thousand kilometres north. Something about the fall of early shadow taking her back to that other place. They spent the whole summer together, surfing and camping, making love.

Well, so be it. Lori breathes deep, tasting the salt, just like back then. Faint aromatic wafts come from the bakery past the lights. All that love, and she got pregnant, and he shot off like a startled rabbit, and that was that.

Where is her son now? she wonders. Still sleeping, no doubt, beside that gorgeous girl of his. He will be angry when he finds the note, and afraid. That much is certain. But he, more than anyone, will understand. He saw how things went with her dad.

She sits as still as she is able. One of her arms gives a small jerky leap, and she contemplates it as she pulls off her T-shirt. This body that is her. Looking it over and counting its parts: feet, shins, thighs, wrists. It is her body, but not. Its essence belongs to the universe and must one day be re-joined. The air is brisk and she is not in any hurry, but she would rather have the wind on her skin, to feel that she is alive. It will be better to wait for the light to turn. It's then that she will slip off her jeans. And in she will go.

Easy does it.

Not a care in the world.

The shore break is loud, she can feel it as much as see it. A real whopper, booming pale and diffuse along the dark runway of the beach, saltspray lifting fine mist into the air. Beneath her the sand is dry and cool and smooth. She builds curved mounds on the blue denim covering her legs, letting herself drift into the cadence of surf. The rhythmic suck and boom in the lift and fall of waves.

The whales will be out there this time of year, making a course back to Antarctica with their babies, born swimming, calves trailing along while their mothers sing: singing as only those viewing the world anew can sing. She imagines their song, how it fills that infinite underspace, the melody and pitch travelling through the deep. Out on the southern point, the headland is a sandstone pillar, falling sharp and certain to the early bright foam. There is something so complete about it, so perfect. The way the swell meets the constancy of rock. Steadfast. Immutable. To how many sunrises has that stone borne witness? To how many storms? Solid and unmoving before the ever-turning world.

It is starting to brighten now, she has timed it just right. Lines of cloud stretch in low purple bands, the sky sprinkled in pink salt. The beach is almost empty: a couple taking an early morning walk, down the far end; a few surfers rising and falling in the slow motion of the swell. The fear is there, but not as much as she'd anticipated. Mostly there's peace, a sense of victory. She will be the one who decides. The breeze is gentle, refreshing but not harsh, and Lori slips off her jeans, folding them on her shoes and shirt with her purse propped on top. With a determined breath, she gets to her feet and makes her way – slow, mostly steady – over the dimpled sand, shivering lightly in her frayed cotton knickers.

The shock of cold is butt-clenching as the water hits her belly, and then she throws herself, flailing just a little, into the fist of the wave. She's always felt more elegant in water than on land. Should have been born a seal, that's what her dad liked to say. Under the next wave she crouches, watching it pass over with all its brash turbulent shadow, then she pushes up from the seafloor to let the next one lift her high, and she is off completely, into the depths, and then she has to swim in earnest.

She plunges each hand into the water and draws herself onwards, freestyle; it's hard work the way her arms are now, but she gets through a set of waves and then the light is coming up fully and oh but her shoulders are aching. She has come level with the pillar, and she goes under the first wave of the next set, ducking to avoid a big dumper, swimming deep beneath the churning wash and coming up with her lungs on fire and coughing out salt. She has let herself be drawn too close to the rocks and swims with all her strength, cresting the next wave before it breaks.

One of the surfers rises into view and flicks back a wet mane of shaggy long hair, staring in her direction, frowning slightly. His face is chiselled, beautiful. Beside him a girl, still in her teens, rides a crest into vision, glancing over briefly at Lori before she falls away. The water pulls Lori down into the trough then gathers her aloft, and she floats high on the broad back of the next wave, the sun's first brilliance a glinting horizon, and all of it flashing the white and gold of nirvana. Then the swell drops steeply back, drawing her into that shining fire, and Lori flows down into the next wave, into the great Pacific, into her promised sea.

Red's Morning

Chapter 2

Redmond Campbell wakes with something hovering about his head, like a mosquito buzzing his ear, near-insensate vibration. The remnant of a foul dream dims and pales as he comes to. He's on the couch, on his back. Polo shirt, light blue; Y-fronts; white socks. His ankles are scored by the sock elastic, and as he lifts a foot to pull off a sock – *slowly slowly*, must be careful not to upset the equilibrium – he hears that buzz again.

Red shifts his head. Eyes right. No sign of the fucker.

He peels off the first sock, then raises it, stiff armed, and permits its release. Scanning the space above him. Still no mozzie. All the same, his whole system is now thrumming uncomfortably, as if the buzz and the discomfort and fragments of the dream are carried in the same malign air. Maybe it's the intercom, on the fritz and catching some static. His phone battery is dead, he made sure of that last night, so even half-asleep he knows it's not a call.

Red makes a valiant attempt to sit, but it's beyond him so he stops halfway to vertical and less than halfway in his body, and it's then he remembers about the dog – still in the garage fridge, he's going to have to deal with that – and the weight of the present pushes him heavily back upon the cushions.

Oh god. He needs water.

He raises both hands and presses his knuckles to his forehead, trying to pick the moment that led him here. Not so much here, now, this precise moment of head-bent purgatory on the couch. More the deeper, dispersed movements of fate, which have driven the currents of his life these last ... what? Thirteen months? Somewhere along the way, Red's shit has utterly derailed. What made his luck turn? It isn't just Bea, his wife, going to prison. Like some common crook. It's deeper than that. Personal.

Not that it isn't significant that Red's wife went into the slammer just three days past. Of course that was a lot for him to deal with. Even his shrink says as much. And although he maintains a sense of injustice in this regard, if he's going to be honest, his maudlin funk is more concerned with *him* than her. What did *he* do, in this life or another, to make it go so wrong?

How can it all shift so fast?

Oh, sweet Jesus, but his head aches fiercely.

The world is coming back into focus and the bulk of it is shoddy.

Red closes his eyes, gently, lightly, and attempts to push it all away. Simply breathe through it. In. Out. In. Out. But even as he settles into the rituals of relaxation – there is the beach, warm and gentle, the blue of the ocean, the white of the sand – Red's body betrays him, and into his consciousness floats the fact that he has a stonking hard-on.

Typical.

He grabs himself through his Y-fronts, just to confirm, get things straight. The thing is, even this bona fide fact leaves Red not so much excited as perplexed. Why does he always wake like this? It's not as if his dreamscape is a desert island harem, full of pussy and white sand. Red's dreams are weird and terrifying. He has the subconscious of an over-burdened morgue attendant, or so Bea, his wife, is fond of saying. *Was* fond, he corrects himself, before it all went to hell, before she got herself locked up. Nope, his dreams are ghastly, at least when he remembers them. Most of the time he wakes with little more than a feeling. A horror in his body as he confronts the corpulent, corporeal world. And a taste, as if death is in his mouth and he can't spit it out.

Dread. Disappointment. And a boner.

Life is weird, he thinks. And bodies, they're weird as fuck.

Red gives a snort. *Weird as fuck.* That's a good one.

He has to move. He has to do something about the volume of blood pulsing through the pressurised brainspace of his skull. Aspirin, paracetamol, ibuprofen. Any port in a storm. But up. Up and to the bathroom. Red scoots his left hand over the floor, trying to locate a solid anchor before the move to vertical. Working by feel, keeping his eyes closed so as not to explode his head. Golf pants, belt still looped. A pocketful of change jingling over the carpet as he pushes the trousers, inch by inch, along the couch front so he can swing his feet down unimpeded, and by the time he's done the coins are clanging church bells against his headache and he's beneath the tower. He stops to wait it out, and after a minute or so things begin to steady. Red sighs audibly. Maybe the payback won't be bad as he first thought.

TV's off. That's something.

Now all he has to do is kill that mosquito.

He's sure he can hear it again. Up in a shadowed corner. Yet even as the sound tickles the fine hairs deep inside his ears, Red doubts his senses. It's the residue of the dream, that's what it is. Still fading, even now. That same goddamn melted reality that sucked him in for a stretch of the night. Rats everywhere, walls closing in. He shakes his head, trying to push the vision away. Light explodes in his forehead, sharp and bright as a blade.

Red grips his temples, trying to contain the throb at the soft poles of his skull. He has to get up, there's nothing for it. He sucks in some air, gets ready, and then, in a pocket of silence, the buzz returns. He can almost see it. A mozzie after all. Red brings his hand up, scanning the space cautiously. He hates mosquitos, especially when he's trying to sleep. They can tell the moment your eyes are closed, the moment you're vulnerable. Then *bzzzzzz*, and before you know it, they've stung you on the fucking eyelid.

Goddamn freeloading bloodsuckers.

Nausea coheres at the edges of things, the objects in the room, then shrinks to a dot on the darkly mirrored television. Still, it's better to be out of that dream, even if it means being woken by a mosquito to a Defcon 3 hangover.

He gives a shudder.

Red's shrink has recommended he keep a dream diary. Even given him a notebook, a nice little Moleskine, to write them all down in. Madness. Who wants to recall that dross? The endless junk the psyche pukes out in that welcome oblivion of sleep. No thank you. It seemed a nice gift at the time, just before Christmas. But then, Red figures, he's put the bastard's kids through private schools, what with all his sessions this last year, and it's no less than he deserves. So the notebook's pages are empty. And anyway, you wake up, you pick up the pen, you look at the page and go to write something down and half the time all you've got is a feeling. A shapeless horror, fading as the pen hits the paper – thank god – accompanying the hard-on wrought by REM sleep.

Why, he ponders, does the body give you a boner in the midst of a nightmare?

He gives his cock a satisfying bend. God, it's been a while. But even if he had the energy to jerk off, he doesn't think his head could stand it. Red lies back, closes his eyes again, and stretches so his feet butt the armrests of the couch. Practising deep breathing, like the shrink told him. Counting the beats of his inhale: one, two, three, four, five, and out. He's just starting to drift off when the mozzie comes back. Red flicks his eyes open in readiness for the kill. Body still, preparing for the ambush. He'll slap his own face if it means killing those parasitic little pricks. He's done it before, made his own nose bleed. Mosquito was dead, though. Big bastard too. You lose, sucker.

He tenses his arm, so the slap can come in an instant, but the noise has gone. There is only his breathing. And a bus moving off from the kerbside, out on Glebe Point Road. And with the realisation that beyond this room there is the house, the street, the Anzac Bridge and the sky, that there is nothing to slap, for now at least, aside from himself, Red is fully awake. He might not have made it off the couch; he might not have moved much at all. He's still unwilling to commit to that. But he's pushed through the swell of nausea, and the objects about him are sliding into focus, rather than swelling and dwindling in the morning glare, as they were doing not five minutes earlier.

Perhaps it's not a hangover and he's coming down with something? There's a lot going around. It would be just his luck to come down with the flu on a day like today. He rests his hand on his forehead, testing for fever. It's hot all right. The shining crown of his head feels clammy and overcooked. Radiant. Then memory hits from the club toilet, him losing the oysters and much of the beer, and the pulse of his headache intensifies.

He thinks briefly about the word *headache* and says it out loud. His voice doesn't sound right. It's reedy. Nasal. Maybe his hearing is going.

'Mosquito,' he says, testing things again.

That was closer, but still weird. Red closes his eyes, squeezing so he feels the pressure in the sockets. His pulse throbs dull achy redness through his vision. And the same thin edge of noise, so he's not sure if it's really there. He keeps his eyes closed this time. It could be far-off machinery. Heavy equipment cutting through concrete, blocks and blocks down the street. A fly buzzing back and forth between the screen and the window glass. Far end of the house. Bouncing from one surface to the next until it finally stills, gives up, waits there to dry to a sun-bleached husk. Or is it, dread thought, the onset of tinnitus, the ringing in the inner ear that near-on drove his father mad, though right now he's not sure if there's a noise at all. But isn't that what they say about tinnitus? How it comes and goes at first? That you're not sure whether it's real? And right at this particular moment, it's less a noise than a feeling. The sound of a feeling, even, whatever the hell that might mean.

Red gathers his reserves.

He will get up, head to the kitchen and drink a litre of water. That's what he's going to do. Drink a litre of water, neck some pills, and resist the urge to put his head in the freezer. Or the oven. After the aspirin, he will begin the week anew. The day, the month, the year. Hell, the whole damn parade. After the aspirin, everything will be possible. After the aspirin, Redmond Campbell resolves, he *will* change his luck.

Red stands from the couch, legs wide, momentarily a-stagger, caught in a vapour cloud of breath, reeling from it, examining the man reflected in the flat screen of the television. The man in the polo and Y-fronts, the man with the hair, such as it is, on end. His vision wobbles in and out. He cannot make out the entirety of his gut, not in the dark-clouded image on the screen, but can discern a bulk and roundness that is dispiriting enough. His sports jacket is crumpled over the handrail of the stairs, the small flight that leads up from the sunken lounge, and he stumbles forward and grips the rail a minute as he steadies.

Five days have passed since he went into the office. The day before the final day of the trial, the final day, the two days after the trial, and yesterday. He wouldn't have left the house at all after the trial, but for Angelo coming by and dragging him to the golf course.

'No matter how bad things get, you can still play a round,'

Angelo declared. 'In fact, the worse they get, the more important it is.'

Eight thirty in the goddamn morning. Red was sleeping. Naturally. Only Angelo would be so insistent as to holler and buzz at the door until Red, eventually, emerged.

'Get your arse out here, you lazy bastard, the birds are out and the sun is shining!' He was dressed in Thom Browne golf pants, every abundant hair on his head lasered with Brylcreem, grinning like he didn't have a care in the world. They drove to the course in a car Red didn't recognise. Angelo owned a few dealerships, on top of a commercial real estate business, and there was always a different car. Yesterday it was a Lexus. Silver. Two doors. Red felt his bones creak as he folded himself within, and sure enough it was a terrible round. He sliced the first tee, ending up in the sand. Things slid downhill from there, the ball transformed into a hazard-seeking missile, finding the water twice. Still, the seven hours they spent in the clubhouse were a sight better. Angelo was in good form, which was saying a lot for Angelo, whose appetite and capacity for enjoyment were world-beating. He must have had a quiet word with the barmaid, as even Ice-Queen Mary was nice to him.

A bit too nice. His head is a mess. He gets a flash of memory, like a splinter: Angelo rounding on him, a grin to split his face. *He who dies with the most hangovers, wins!* Then dragging Red towards the toilet with the wave of a small white bag, slamming the cubicle door behind them.

God he needs coffee. Coffee and food.

He flicks on the espresso machine in the kitchen and drops a *robusta* cartridge in the slot. While he's waiting for it to warm up, Red sits a frypan on the stove, pours in a good dollop of oil, and gets out some eggs, bacon and bread. Without his wife at home, he's allowed to eat white bread, and he can use as much oil in his cooking as he wants. He's writing a list, in his head, of the pros and cons of not having his wife around, of having her *in the joint,* as they say.

Do they still say *in the joint* in the joint?

He makes a mental note to ask Bea when he goes in to visit. He hasn't endured that horror show yet, the thought like a gutful of wet cement.

This lining up the pros and cons is cold in the extreme. Red's aware of that: it's for this reason the list exists only in his head. The coffee machine lights green. He hits the button for a shot, dark juice spurts into the cup, and Red ladles three teaspoons of sugar into the mug.

In the frypan the bacon spits and pops and smells like a salt-meat heaven. He breaks three eggs into the oil and takes a sip of coffee, and it's then, as the coffee starts to go to work, that he feels the deeper activations of digestion commence. This is not the usual 8am post-coffee impulse. This is something far more urgent. Depth charges, with hydrostatic pressure fuses of varying offset timings, are erupting in muffled explosions along the full length of his intestines.

The better part of a bottle of Johnny Walker Black's down there; whatever remains of the oysters, calamari and wine, plus Christ knows how many beers. He'd started to think he'd got away with it – not exactly top of the Wazir, but not so foul he'd floored himself. But this elevation of mood, he realises, in the precise moment his digestive system announces its diligence, is due not to his iron constitution, the training getting piss-fit he's devoted himself to these last weeks and months, but to the persistent presence of alcohol bubbling in his blood. There will be a price to pay, that much is certain, and right now the price is the previous evening's repast, and maybe a few others to boot, or at least that's how it feels: the point being that all of it, *all of it*, needs to exit his body immediately.

Red rushes out of the kitchen, a painting shifting skew-whiff from his shoulder in the hall, and he makes the throne without a second to spare. There's an abundance of relief after the first wave, and he feels his body relax into the seat, basking in the commingled sense of revulsion and release.

God, that's better.

Should he have a shower right up? It might help. He casts a real estate agent's eye over the silver chrome of the taps, the huge freestanding bathtub that Bea loves so much. Not a bad bathroom, if he says so himself. Black marble right up the walls. Even if there *are* scratches on the marble tiles, he and Bea having renovated this bathroom together, their first significant project in the house. The old room had buckling walls and moisture problems. It was rotting at the timbers, a deep decay spreading throughout. Indeed, this was the reason he'd managed to convince the owner, an elderly woman recently bereaved, to let it go so cheap.

No one wants a house that's falling down, Red had told her.

She was gone not long after that. He'd seen it in the paper, some ten years ago now, how she'd come through the war and outlived her children. Bea planned the renovation meticulously, and he even helped with her decisions on taps and towel rails. They both wanted black marble floors. Marble stood for opulence. For old money, which he wasn't, but aspired to. And the black, well, that was because they were modern people, and as Lori had said when Bea brought it up, *Il faut être absolument moderne*, which even Red knew meant that you really should keep up with the times. The tiler did a magnificent job, and it looked like success, those first two days. But then the builders came back with the sinks and bath and cabinetry, and they put the boxes and woodwork straight down on those tiles, and they walked through with their steel-capped boots, and by the time he had his first shower, still dripping, he noticed the drag marks of boxes, cabinets, white smears etched in the soft black perfection. After a quick Google of how to get scratches out of marble he got down on his hands and knees to buff them out with fine sandpaper, close enough, or so it seemed, to what they were using on YouTube, and it looked pretty good in the low light, but his mistake was apparent when the sun came up, a mess which, as far as the builders were concerned, absolved them of all responsibility in the matter. So now the entire bathroom is a resplendent symbol of disappointment, of the fact that no matter how hard you try, it all turns to shit regardless.

It is this thought – the speedy and inevitable decay of all things – that he is turning over in his head when some goddamn awful noise squeals urgently from the kitchen.

Jesus! The cooking!

Red jumps up, makes for the door. It's the smoke alarm, obviously. Then, realising he hasn't completed the processes of ablution, he spins about to speed-reel a wad of loo-roll. He makes a quick swipe and exits the bathroom pulling up his undies, grimacing as he hobbles cowboy-legged down the hall.

Black smoke is curling against the ceiling, billowing into the lounge, swirling where the barred windows open to the front courtyard. In the kitchen, the entire stove is on fire. The plastic bread bag has melted and bubbled, and now the bread itself is burning, actually fucking on fire, where he's left it too close to the hob. There's a tea towel smoking where the plastic has melted onto it, and the eggs and bacon are an orange-black flaming mass.

Thinking fast – he congratulates himself even as he's going through the motion; this is why he's the best bloody agent in the Sydney market, this gut instinct is why he gets the big commissions – he grabs the vase of half-dead chrysanthemums that he purchased for Bea the previous week and upends it over the stove. A searing tongue of flame shoots from the pan to consume the rangehood in a ball of Armageddon. Burning grease splatters Red's face. For a moment he's sure that his eyeballs are on fire.

Headfirst, he runs into the lounge room and throws himself at the sofa, frantically patting his skull. It feels like half the skin is gone and it hurts like almighty buggery, but at least there are no flames. Through stinging eyes, he stares back towards the kitchen.

The black smoke's so thick he can scarcely make out the doorway, let alone the blaze within. There's a fire extinguisher in the garage. Down the stairs and out to the garage and he's got the extinguisher, and it's one of those ones with a funnel on the hose-end that means it's good for electrical, doesn't it? Back at the kitchen entrance he pushes down hard on the lever and there's nothing, so he pushes harder, the metal cutting into his hand. Still nothing.

The pin! Jesus, pull the fucking pin.

Red yanks hard and the pin comes loose and he points the funnel and forces down the lever with all he's got, taking a deep breath as the white cloud erupts, filling the room entirely. Red steps towards the hob, or where he imagines it to be, and waves the extinguisher about before backing away. He keeps on blasting out CO_2 until he needs another breath and collapses to the floor, leaving the extinguisher and crawling to the lounge room, coughing his lungs out, gas following him through the door and turning the air white.

The fire alarm screams from the ceiling above.

Red gets up. His head is ringing. He drags a chair over to the alarm and yanks the plastic disc from the ceiling. The alarm goes silent. He can't tell if the fire is still burning or if it's out. There's nothing around him but smoke and whiteness. He steps back to the kitchen, grabs the extinguisher, and from the safety of the doorway gives another spurt. It's like staring through a storm. A glimpse of the oven door, a tea towel smouldering over the handle. No flames, though.

Red treads carefully across the kitchen floor. He opens the windows wide, turns the range hood fan up to full, and goes to switch off the stove. The steel knob is scalding hot. There's a tea towel that hasn't caught fire, and he grabs it and switches off the gas, then uses the towel to fan away the smoke.

Scorched earth, all right.

Red stands in the ruins of the kitchen, gingerly touching his face with the tips of his fingers. His eyebrows and lashes feel crumpled, stubby, as though formed in grains of sand. There is scarcely a single hair left on his head, although admittedly there wasn't much there to begin with. Red opens the freezer, twists the contents of an ice tray into a plastic grocery bag and places it soothingly over the left side of his face. Then he drinks a glass of water, picks up his coffee, and walks back to the couch.

Out of the Dark

Chapter 3

Above her a girl and a boy in full-length wetsuits, the girl kneeling, rolling Lori sideways, even as she lurches to consciousness. Rising from the wet dark, into life, into pain and flesh, acid salt sick of throat, sand in her mouth. She pukes salt water, spits, pukes again. Her vision is spinning and the surf loud and close.

Lori closes her eyes until the blackness stops tilting, then lifts her head, squinting at her rescuers. They're on the hardpack, the shore break crashing close and running up cold to her ankles. Details flow in one by one, wobbling in and out: the surfboards tossed further up the beach safe from the tidal wash of water; her fingers gripping into the sand to make it still.

She retches and her stomach spasms, and she curls foetus-like, wrapping her arms around her naked torso, waiting for it to stop. A thin stream of salty bile trickles from her mouth onto her shoulder. Lori raises a hand to wipe it away. God she needs a drink.

'Water?' she asks.

'We'll get you some,' says the girl. 'Damo's gone for his phone, from the car, to get the ambos.'

'Water ...'

Lori points desperately up the beach, to where she left her things, but realising she left her water bottle in the cab, she lets her fingers fall back to the sand.

The two surfers exchange a look.

'Yeah, it's coming,' says the girl.

'How are you feeling?' the boy asks suddenly, scowling at her from under his long, surf-blond hair, then gazing back at the waves, remembering. 'That was a close one.'

She recognises him, the stare he had given her from atop his board, just before she went down the first time. Her head feels strange, still lost beneath the surface. She focuses on his face. About sixteen. So beautiful, so young. His hair dripping, tanned freckled skin.

'I just about mashed my board getting you out of there,' he says angrily, then pauses, adding in a hushed tone, as though embarrassed, 'You almost didn't make it.'

'Yeah.' Lori spits, trying to dislodge the last of the sand. 'That was the idea.'

The girl understands then; Lori can see as their eyes catch. 'Come on,' she says kindly. 'Let's get you cleaned up.'

The two kids lift Lori to her feet, their hands strong. The girl puts a protective arm around her shoulders, the three of them moving slowly into the soft sand. Lori stops, and turns back to look out at the headland. The sun has cleared the horizon. No clouds, but a burnished blue depthless infinity, and wave upon wave upon wave.

There are a couple more surfers paddling out, glancing back at her, as though she were some kind of show. She feels a desperate urge to get away. Get away from her rescuers, from the people on the beach staring, this bedraggled thing emerging from the sea; escape it all and get on with the rest, start her life anew. She hears a new refrain now, rising above the crash of the waves, a melody of the atmosphere, as though the air itself were music, an acoustic drawn from the caves and hollows. A world so full of suffering and joy it gives out a kind of singing.

It is time to get back to her life.

She has made a promise to her son, and this time she intends to keep it. To start living, right now. Not dying, but living. For that is the only way to make it through: to live, to really live, until you're dead.

Lori gazes from one to the other of the two beautiful surfers leading her up the beach towards the lifesavers' tower, and she grips the girl for an instant and kisses her passionately on the cheek. The girl jerks away, stunned, and the boy lets her go in shock. Lori would laugh if she had it in her, the surprise in their faces, and she offers a wave to them both, her arm giving a chaotic leap, and limps on with the two of them staring, the sun now growing so she can feel it on her skin, lighting the curved walls of the new surf club, reflecting from the upper floors of Campbell Parade.

'Thanks heaps,' she says, calling over her shoulder and staggering on. 'I've got it now.'

The two stand rooted as she stumbles up to where she's left her clothes and shoes.

'You sure?' asks the boy.

He's followed her up, but he's keeping his distance, as though trying to figure out precisely what it is he's pulled from the surf.

'We already called the ambos; I reckon you should wait,' calls the girl.

'No. I really can't. But thank you. Thank you both so much.'

Lori, steadfast, puts on her shirt and pulls her jeans up over her legs, oblivious to her wet skin, to the sand and salt catching in the denim. She wobbles and lets herself fall to the sand, coughing, waving back their hands as they rush to help. She gets her shoes on and picks up her purse, easing herself up, then climbing the grass embankment on all fours she manages to stand as it flattens out. Her rescuers follow at a distance, but she waves them off determinedly and totters on.

All about, Bondi is waking with the sun.

An old couple doing yoga on the grass. Joggers and walkers moving rhythmically along the pavement and up towards the headland. She is free, utterly free. Free and alive. The day is young, and she's going to meet with her boy, just like she promised. And they'll talk, and drink tea, and live what they have to live. The rest of it she'll just have to figure out, one step at a time.

Henrietta

Chapter 4

Red spends two days holding ice to his face. He can't see his GP. The mental image of Dr Cohen's quizzical gaze as Red recounts the event scorches him almost as much as the fire did. Besides, his skin doesn't look so bad after a day or so. Blotchy red patches, sure, but as long as he doesn't catch his own reflection, he can drink beer in front of the telly and – mostly – forget the whole affair. Of course the kitchen is a bomb crater, but the cleaner has taken care of the worst of it, and insurance will cover the rest. It's lucky really – they'll have a brand new kitchen when he puts the place on the market.

He cleared his schedule for the entire week post court case, so nobody is missing him at work. That said, even if he hadn't, the staff have followed the dramas for months anyway, so nobody is expecting him through those doors anytime soon. That's the advantage of being the boss, he thinks: regardless of what you do, people have to suck it up. Red smiles, but it turns into a grimace as the skin on his face crinkles drily. He reaches for the pump-pack moisturiser beside the remote.

The only thing he has to take care of, which he has promised Bea and can't renege on, is to go and check on Lori and make sure she's settled back into her apartment. He could make an excuse and cancel, but Mada, his nephew, is to meet him there, and word of his withdrawal would definitely make it back to Bea. Besides, despite all the crap they've ridden through, Red is feeling positive about Lori. Mostly it's the relief of having his sister-in-law out of his house for good: she's bounced between him and Bea and Mada these last few months, but now Bea has gone inside it's impossible for her to stay with Red. She needs to settle back into her own digs, otherwise he might strangle her. Maybe he'll call in at work as well, just for an hour or so, after seeing to Lori; got to keep them on their toes. He gets up and staggers to the shower, turning it on so that all the jets are blasting: there's none of that low-flow bullshit in Red's household, that's for sure.

It's on the way over to meet Mada and Lori in Rozelle, stopped on Broadway to pick her up some bread and milk, that Red finds the dog: sitting in the window at the pet store in the shopping complex. It looks so much like the other one that Red has flashbacks to the week before, to the sound of claws on cardboard. He pushes the thought out of his mind with a shudder and steps inside the shop. Henry, that's what Bea and Lori had baptised the floppy-eared little Kraut. This animal looks identical: the same disproportionate body and stumpy little legs, the same ears drooping down until the paws trip over them. It's ridiculously priced – almost a thousand dollars for a dog without legs. But it is, Red reasons, exactly what Lori needs.

A little responsibility, to teach her how to look after things.

She'll have to take it to the park each day. It will help her to get out and about and give her companionship to boot. Red is so taken with his own magnanimity that he forks out another hundred and fifty for a collar and a crate to carry it, and carts the animal down the travelator to shove it in the boot of his car. The freeway on-ramp is clogged, as always, but it's a nice enough day. He heads over the Anzac Bridge, taking it easy, just five kilometres over the limit, sun coming down through the factory tint and the Stones on the stereo and he's feeling pretty good about himself. Not so much like the last week, the last year, hasn't happened; more like it happened, but it's not the whole story.

Five minutes later, he pulls the Beamer to the curb in Rozelle, ignoring a No Standing sign, before opening the boot to get out the dog, crouched in the crate looking scared. It's a good quarter hour before he's due to meet them. He wants to get the dog inside before Mada arrives, to gain maximum kudos for his good deed. The animal gives a brief yap, but Red growls at it, and the thing falls silent.

'Smart dog,' he says. 'You'll do okay.'

Lori isn't in when he gets to the apartment, but that's all to the good. She must be with Mada. It's surprisingly neat and tidy – she hasn't had time to generate her usual mess, having just moved back two days before. Except for her work table. It's her only decent-sized table, really, and it's strewn with small sculptures and clay-smeared art books. He reads off a couple of titles. *The Encyclopaedia of Mosaic Techniques; The Art of Ceramics.*

Lori works to a theme, that's what Bea would say. In practice it means she makes a bunch of little figures that all look the same. After a bit, she'll find a new shape and work on that until the next idea arrives. The most recent series is of small anthropomorphic avocados with stubby little legs. She's been working on those for over a year now. They line the table edges and spill onto the floor, populating corners of the room in gnomic clusters, engaged in their own fixed and soundless conversations. Red puts the crate down under Lori's work bench, beside a troupe of these talking gnomes. The dog starts to whine, and he silences it with another growl and opens the balcony door. The sound of a car drifts up from the road that runs between the apartment block and the water. Red checks his watch – five to – and squints down between the bars, which run all the way to the roof, a special installation to 'keep Lori from having an accident'.

Down below, a familiar shitbox Corolla pulls up behind his Beamer. Mada gets out to squint up at Red. Lori is nowhere to be seen. If she's not with him, and she's not up here, where the hell is she? Red lifts his arms to indicate 'No bloody idea where the crazy bitch has run off to,' and sees Mada swear under his breath. But just then, as Red's starting to get his blood up, Mada's attention is drawn to the end of the street, and a taxi drives up slowly then pulls in behind Mada's wreck, and the passenger door opens.

Sure enough, Lori spills out, looking bedraggled, and seemingly half-covered in sand. Mada exchanges a wild look with Red and turns his attention back to his mother. For the love of all that's holy, what has she gone and done now? There's a long conversation between Lori and the taxi driver, and then the bloke gets out and starts jabbering at Mada. Red sees the boy's shoulders slump as he reaches into his back pocket and pulls out his wallet.

Typical.

Mada hands over a few notes, then takes Lori by the arm, and half leads, half carries her up the path to the apartment block. Well, even if she does forget her wallet, Red tells himself speciously, if she can travel around in a cab she's independent enough. Truth be told, Red wanted to move her back six months ago, right after the accident, but both Mada and Bea forbade it. She still wasn't okay, they said. Hell, she still isn't okay now, he thinks: it isn't physical, although that's starting to come; she's just out to lunch half the time. Her moods can fluctuate so wildly, with her temper so close to the surface, that she has taken a swing at him more than once. That, after he put a roof over her head?

She had been staying with Mada and his girlfriend, Zoe, for the last few weeks, through the trial, and even Mada said he wasn't sure she'd be able to manage on her own. But there's no question of her staying with him any longer; Mada's place is even smaller than this one, and they're all being driven mad by her. And as to going back to live with Red? Let her roam free through their designer furniture? No way. Not without Bea to manage her. Red said that it would be good for her, being by herself again, that she would have to cope, that necessity would make it happen.

'Yeah, right!' Mada retorted. 'Tell me the day Mum ever did something because she had to.' The kid had him there.

In the kitchen there's a fresh stash of bananas and five avocados. Obviously Mada has been stocking the place up too. He isn't such a bad son to Lori, considers Red. He opens the fridge and puts in the milk and bread and finds an unopened bag of coffee in the door. There's still a minute or two before Mada and Lori will come up in the lift; he can hear them outside below – Mada trying to hurry his mother along, Lori resisting, prattling on about something or other. Red puts on the kettle and pours some coffee into the plunger pot.

Mada is always on time to the minute. It's one of his better traits. Needs to get his life in order, though, start earning some real coin. All the same, he's pretty good at looking after his mum, and that counts for a bit. And he isn't one of those fucking useless Gen Ys, incapable of anything but playing games on their phones and wanking at the internet. No, thinks Red benevolently, not a bad kid at all. No doubt Red's position as uncle and role model is an important factor, impressing on the young man the importance of hard work, of respect for those who have made their way, got ahead. Mada's pretty good at looking after Bea too, truth be told. Red knows well enough that his wife can be a handful, and Mada has the knack of smoothing his aunt's rough edges.

Where's Bea now? Why isn't she here?

The thought comes to him from nowhere, and there's an unfocused second in which Red's mind drifts to where his wife might be, before he crashes headlong into the present, into the realisation that she is locked in prison, and will be for the next few years. How could he forget such a thing? It never seemed possible before now that life could take such a mangled turn, that things could go to crap with such vehemence. An event like that was always in the realm of other people's lives, like getting struck by lightning, or munched by a shark.

Not his life, not his family.

So much for that.

The faint *ding* of the elevator makes its way into his thoughts, muffled by the door, and Red shakes his head and walks over to the window, so that he can turn and look surprised when they come in, and they can find him looking pensive and benevolent. He gets into position as the door opens, and waits for two beats before turning to give his best welcoming smile. Mada comes in first, followed by his mother, but neither of them acknowledges him. Mada is explaining to Lori how she needs to look after herself or she'll have to move in with Red again.

Red stiffens, but he needn't worry.

'Over my dead body,' she says in response.

Mada's sigh is audible. 'Listen, Mum, I really need you to help me here.'

'Oh, I will.'

She talks airily about how nice it is to have her own space, to be back in her workshop. Mada is staring at her, nodding thoughtfully. Red hasn't seen Lori for a couple of weeks, and she appears thin and frail. Her T-shirt and jeans have wet patches darkening the fabric, and she's brought half the beach back with her. Well, reasons Red, the last few months have been hard on all of them, it's no wonder she's looking a bit spent and dishevelled.

Lori stops short as she registers his presence.

'Morning all,' he says.

'Hello Redmon,' says Lori. She often drops the second 'd', just to annoy him, as far as he can tell, but Red is in a mood to be generous.

'Good morning, dear sister-in-law. You're looking well.' He eyes her up and down, reflecting how markedly untrue this statement is.

'Piffle. Zoe says I look like a tree in autumn. All sticks and nubs.'

'Where have you been?' asks Red cheerily. 'Gone down the beach already?'

'None of your business,' Lori shoots back.

'Mum ...'

'Charming.' Red turns to Mada with the demeanour of one who has suffered much.

Mada looks unimpressed. 'Did you get to the shops?' he asks.

'Did I ever,' says Red.

Mada eyes him quizzically, but Red isn't ready for the big reveal. He steps in front of the bench so they can't make out the dog.

'Back at work, then?' Mada continues, appraising Red's suit.

'Yes. First day back today.' Red squares his shoulders and they exchange a grimaced smile, solidarity in the horror show that has been the past year of their lives. It's then that Mada sees, really *sees*, his uncle.

'Jesus, Red!' His eyes lock on the singed head. 'What happened to you?'

Lori turns and stares at him beadily. 'Yes, what *did* happen?'

'I might well ask you the same thing,' he responds irritably. 'You've got half of Bondi stuck to your jeans.'

'But your face!'

'I'm well aware of my appearance, thank you.'

'You've got no hair left,' says Lori.

'I didn't have much to begin with.'

'You had eyebrows,' she says, coming up close and peering at him intently.

'Yes, I know.'

'And lashes.'

'I know.'

'You're all … pink.' She pushes out an inquisitive finger, as though to palpate his face. Red slaps it away.

'*I know!*'

'Well,' says Mada, 'what happened?'

Red doesn't answer.

He goes over to the radio, switches it on, and steps into the kitchenette, drawing a glass of water and gulping at it. Mada follows him and sits on a bar stool expectantly. Road noise comes up from the bridge, a faint, persistent rhythm of rubber on steel, car tyres hitting the expansion joints. Red turns up the music, some old-time guitar hit he recognises but can't identify.

'What happened, Red?' Mada asks again.

'There was a fire,' Red says curtly. He walks out to Lori's work table, running his finger through a line of dust, through the mess of unfired offcuts, sculpting tools and art books.

'Where was the fire? How did it happen?'

'In the kitchen,' he says, then adds somewhat proudly: 'I put it out, though.'

'Where was this? Your place? In Glebe?'

'Yeah.'

'Was anyone hurt—'

'Besides me?'

'Sorry. Yes.'

'No. It's fine. Let's focus on the job at hand.'

'I'm going to change,' says Lori, as though determined to show maximum disdain for the subject of Red's health.

'Okay Mum.' Mada turns his attention back to Red, not to be thrown off. 'But what about the house?'

'Still standing. Kitchen needs a coat of paint, though.' Red clasps his hands behind his back and runs a critical eye over the walls. 'Not unlike this place.' He surveys the room with meaningful attention, offering the kind of expression he uses when he wants a seller to drop their price. Lori emerges in a fresh T-shirt and underpants, and, deciding that now is the moment, Red strides over to the crate.

It's time to get the morning back on track.

'At any rate,' he says, 'I found a welcome home gift for you, Lori, and picked it up on the way over here this morning.'

She squints at him suspiciously. 'Oh?'

'Yes,' says Red. He offers a sweeping gesture in the direction of the dog.

Lori walks over to stand nonplussed before the crate.

Red is expecting a better reaction than that. He bends down for a closer examination. The stupid thing is sleeping through its big moment, curled up at the back like a small sack of fur. He gives the bars a shake, slides the crate about on the floor until the dog lifts its head. The animal gives a whine and wobbles unsteadily into the room. Red goes to scratch it under the chin, but it backs away in alarm and goes to hide behind Mada's legs.

'Oh,' says Lori again, a small sound, more an exhalation than a word. 'I thought you said Henry died at the vet.'

'He did, love.' Red clears his throat. 'This little fellow is going to make up for it.'

'I see.' Lori meanders into the kitchen.

Mada gawks at the animal, confused, as if he's never laid eyes on anything of the type. 'You got her a dog.'

It's a statement, not a question.

'Yes,' says Red, beaming.

'How's Mum going to look after a dog, Red?' hisses Mada.

'She could do it before.'

'No. She couldn't. Bea did it. All of it.'

'Well, yes, but ...' Red feels the breath suck out of his chest. 'Don't look at me like that. It was the right thing to do.'

'What are you talking about? What's right about it?'

'Well—'

'Red, how is a dog going to help?'

'It'll be good for her,' says Red. He begins to recite the list of pros he has generated in the 'positive attributes' portion of his brain. Companionship. Exercise. Teaching her responsibility.

'Zoe and I can't look after it. We're in a rental, and it's no pets.'

'Of course Zoe's not bloody looking after it. The whole point is that it's for *her*.'

'Terrific,' says Mada flatly.

Lori comes back in, nursing a cup of tea, and gets down on her haunches in front of the dog. Clearly deciding that she cannot blame the animal for her brother-in-law's shortcomings, she bends right down to kiss it on the nose. Immediately the animal sets to licking her face, a task it embraces with great enthusiasm.

Lori giggles.

'See?' says Red, vindicated.

'Oh yes. Terrific. She'll be walking on a carpet of turds, Red,' says Mada under his breath.

'A bit of toilet training and it'll all be apples.'

'Right. And you're going to do that?'

'I thought we could call him Hank, after Henry,' Red ploughs on, valiantly ignoring him.

'Henrietta might be more appropriate,' says Mada.

'Hmmm?'

'It's a bitch, Red.'

'What?'

'A girl doggy,' says Mada.

'But it's got—'

'That?' Mada points to the dog's nether regions and gives a snort of laughter. 'No. *That* is a sprig of hair.'

'Oh, well, yes, it would be ...'

'I have to go.' Mada offers Red a stony glance and crosses the room to give Lori a kiss on the cheek. 'I've got two tutorials to teach this morning, and I need to get to the uni. I'll drop by tomorrow to see how you're doing, Mum.'

'Okay darling.' She has the dog in her arms now, its tongue darting about her face.

Red walks Mada to the door, taking him by the elbow. 'Actually, mate,' he says conspiratorially, 'there's something else I wanted to chat with you about.' He shoots a look at Lori and steps into the corridor with Mada, closing the door behind them. 'No doubt you heard about the endowment,' he says.

'From the widow? Four acres of bushland on the campus boundary? The largest undeveloped pocket of private land east of Parramatta. Yes, Red, I heard all right.'

'Well, it turns out the dean and I went to school together. In fact, there are a few old Elderstone College fellows on the university council. More than I'd realised. I golf with a couple of them, and' – he gives a wry chuckle – 'the old-boys network is alive and well. I'll tell you that right now, but, you know, it wouldn't hurt for you to put in a word for me. Just let them know I'm your *uncle*.' The word comes out awkwardly. Mada flinches. Red, ignoring this, goes all in. 'I've got a very good chance, that's all, and you know it would help us all … me, your aunt, your mum … if I got this contract. The commission could help us open a new office. If they know I'm connected to the university through more than just the Elderstone boys, you know. I'm not looking for any guarantees, mind you, it's just about improving my chances—'

'Chances of what?'

'Of handling the sale!'

'What sale?' asks Mada, nonplussed.

'The sale of the land, of course.' Red stares at him, exasperated. This is what his taxes have to show for five bloody years of university?

'It's not being sold,' says Mada, with the slow patience of someone explaining that clouds bring rain. 'That's where the new labs are going to be. Not to mention a whole new arts faculty.'

'Well, on some of it, yes. But someone's got to pay for them, the labs that is, and, you know, I'm hoping to do my bit, helping make the uni a bit of coin. So if you could talk with the dean, you know, drop my name in—'

'Drop your name in? When I'm talking to the dean?'

'Um, yeah ...'

'Maybe over lunch?'

'Well ...'

Mada blinks, slowly, then, without speaking, he hits the button to summon the elevator. There's a good ten seconds in which he stares at Red, who feels abruptly emptied of things to say. Down the hall, the Eagles are playing on Lori's radio. Finally the doors slide open. Mada steps into the elevator, shoots one more stony glance at Red, and knuckles the button for descent.

Well, it could have gone worse, thinks Red.

He could have said no.

He walks back to Lori's apartment, humming along to 'Hotel California'. He turns the handle and pushes at the door, but it's locked. Just below the blaring music, he can discern the sound of Lori singing.

Red raps smartly on the door. His keys are in his jacket, inside, with his wallet. There is no response, so he hammers on the door with his fist. 'Hey!'

From within, Lori's singing grows louder.

Her First Mistake
Chapter 5

Her possessions are removed and recorded by a cop using a biro that looks older than he is. He says the name of each item in a drawl, before writing it all down one thing at a time, slow, uninterested, as if the universe doesn't care and you can be damn sure he doesn't either. Who she is. What she's doing there. What she might, or might not, have done.

'Two earrings.'

'One T-shirt.'

'One white bra.'

They take the drawstring from her tracksuit, and the pants crumple to the floor to bunch at her feet. She pulls them off over her heels, thinking how they'd seemed the most practical thing she had to wear in the terrified haze of the previous night.

Next come her undies.

The cop examines them closely, holding them up on the tip of his pen. 'One pair of underpants. Black. White band.'

Bea makes herself think about anything but this. Even remembering the court case is preferable: how it might have gone, ways it might have been different. If she'd chosen another lawyer, what she might have said. She'd surrendered her passport, but what if she'd taken flight, starting up a new life in Mexico or Rio? But it's only two years, that's what Redmond said, and anyway there's the feeling, deep-seated, terrible, that she deserves what she gets. This is what she's decided, or at least what some part of her has come to believe.

Nothing that is happening now belongs to her. Someone else has stepped inside her brain and body, seized the levers, so that Bea is looking out at the world through foreign eyes. Or rather, at the room. Three chairs, two men. Blue uniforms. Black boots. One has a face of palest white, the other one, on his left, is ruddy and fat. He looks overheated, his pants forced beyond any endurance that should be required of them.

This is the first time Bea has been made to undress in front of guards, and the humiliation is beyond all proportion to the act. It feels like a part of her is being taken away. She stands naked on the cold sheen of concrete, reduced to goose-flesh skin.

The guards look her over.

She shifts her weight, one foot to the next, awkward.

It is at this point she realises that all her rights have gone. Before, it had seemed abstract: you are incarcerated, you have your freedom 'taken away'. But it is far more absolute than that. This body is no longer *her* body. It belongs to the state. It belongs to the government and the guards. It is weak, pliable. They will treat it as they will and there's nothing she can do.

They get her into prison greens, the colour vibrant, unnatural, and import her fingerprints to a scanner. Her height and eye colour are recorded, a general physical description. Blonde hair. Grey eyes. One hundred and sixty-six centimetres. She is given a toiletries kit – soap, toothbrush, shampoo – and the memory that comes to her is of flying long haul, to see her cousins, small kits perched atop folded blankets on every business class seat. This could not be further from that experience. This is more like anti-flight.

A leaden descent.

She stares down at her hand protruding from the green cuff, and knows for a fact that it is no longer her hand. The lines are different, the way they break off. Older. And the skin has a sickly, alien hue. It's not her skin. The thought stays with her as she's taken to the holding cell. That it's not her hand, her skin. She says this out loud, she's not sure how many times, before she realises she's actually voicing the words, that there is an echo coming back from the walls and that it originates with her. She looks about, but the guards have gone and there is no one to hear.

Later in the afternoon, a woman with a clipboard sits her down for an interview. She questions Bea about her emotions. Tells her what to expect at Silverwater.

'Can you guarantee your safety?' the woman asks.

'No,' she says, thinking: Safety? Here? You've got to be kidding me.

But she's misunderstood the question, and the woman shakes her head in slow dismissal.

'Jesus,' she says. 'Another one.' But it takes a few hours before Bea realises what this means.

When the interview is over, Bea is taken to a smaller cell than before. The door is locked behind her. Concrete floor, no mattress. It has a steel toilet in the corner. Three small cardboard blocks are stacked neatly beside it. The entire room is otherwise empty. Just concrete and steel. The place has a weird smell, somewhere between a public toilet and a mechanic's workshop. She tries to distract herself by figuring out what the smell is. There is an oily hardness to it. Like an engine. Or a gun. Then she realises that, if steel has a smell, this is it. She sits on the floor and looks at her hands. Her skin definitely looks strange. And what's with her breathing? She can't get enough air in. Even when she thinks hard about it. She's not sure how fast to breathe, that's the thing. Her pacing is gone. Does she leave too long between breaths? Or is it too short? Normally she just breathes, but some part of her has forgotten how. She puts her back to the wall and slides to the floor.

When they bring her dinner, it seems a day has passed, and they push it into the room via a small metal hatch. There is a paper plate, with another paper plate coming loose underneath.

'You forgot cutlery. I need a fork or something.'

'Not on suicide watch. You got to fold up the plate on the bottom, use it as a scoop.'

'But I'm not a suicide risk,' she says, thinking it mostly true.

'If you weren't, you wouldn't be here.'

She shoves her face into the door-slot. 'I'm not. The woman asked if I could guarantee my safety. It was a misunderstanding. I thought she meant safety from everyone else, not from myself.'

There's a grunt, then the sound of boots moving off, a squeaky wheel from the trolley. The steel slam of the far door. Bea picks up the food and looks at it. Uncertain meat granules. Kidney beans. A reddish sauce on rice. She rips the extra plate in half and scoops up a mouthful. Watery sauce runs down the plate onto her arm.

Bea eats what she can then curls up on the concrete with her hand pressed to her forehead. She tells herself over and over: 'Sleep. Sleep. Sleep.'

Eventually, she does.

She makes her first mistake while she's still in Silverwater. Maximum security. Bad place for mistakes. Awaiting classification: they have yet to figure out where to send her. Most likely it'll be Emu Plains, so speaks the lawyer. Classo-ed, that's what the regulars call it – and there are plenty. Women lining up the next job while they're still inside. Out in the open, proud. Bragging about the pigs they've hit. Sitting and smoking and sketching out plans as if they're chatting through Christmas vacation ideas with the family. Stealing. Smuggling. Selling a kilo of ice. What ya gonna do when some cunt wants to take ya on. How easy it is to hold up a servo, how all ya need is guts and a knife.

The correctional service overlords put everyone to work in a hangar, putting foam on headphones for Qantas. Fixin cans, so it runs in the lingo. Your sound on the national carrier, brought to you today by the unlucky fuckups in Silverwater Correctional. On Bea's fifth day inside, she puts a note on the payphone, reserving it for 4pm. She needs to call Mada when he gets home from uni, when she's done with the fixing of the cans.

It's a yellow Post-It Note, saying *Bea @ 4*. She's seen it done by some of the others, but she doesn't know the score, who's got the right, and word gets around.

Bea @ 4.

Her small yellow beacon on the plastic receiver, a signal to the compound, and Bea doesn't know the code. When she picks up the phone that afternoon, she can feel the eyes on her, feel a change in the air of the place. A week or two later, she might have reacted differently. Might have put the phone back on the cradle, searched out a place near the guards. But she's a newbie. Dumb fresh meat. She hasn't developed that internal barometer, a way to gauge the atmospheres and pressures by which violence in the place gives its early warning. Doesn't understand the lines of power her yellow beacon has ignored.

Bea punches in the digits.

The meltdown starts as soon as the phone hits her ear, the woman making for her, swelling at the edges like a shaken can of drink. Bea is listening to the ringing down the line, trying to ignore it, trying to believe it has nothing to do with her. Then the woman explodes, frothing, yelling about how Bea's gonna get stomped, eyes popping out of her head. Bea spins away, huddles into the wall with her arm over her head, holding the phone to her ear as her nephew, Mada, picks up.

Immediately, Bea starts blabbering.

A lot of screaming behind her, but still no blows.

She babbles to Mada as if the talk might hold it back. Not even sure of what she's saying. The food. The smell. What her lawyer did. How they did a urine test after she was remanded, before they even got her to the prison. Faster and faster. Not a word on what's happening behind her. Her teeth, her life, hanging in the balance. She can hear it in her own voice, the pitched whine of mania, but she's unable to change it, unable to make it stop. Mada is more of a surrogate son than a nephew, and she hears the fear in his voice when he asks about the yelling. Bea responds by talking even faster. She does not turn. She does not look back. As though if she just keeps talking nothing in this place will be real: the umbilical copper of the telephone, running through the walls and chainlink and out into the world. A solid wire connecting her to the free and the real. That place where people do the things they want to do, walk into shops and pick up telephones, where violence is not as constant as talk.

When Bea eventually turns around, she sees a tall, muscular woman with her would-be assailant in a chokehold. She knows her saviour, at least by reputation. One of the inmates had pointed her out. Serving twenty years for the murder of a tourist, she had come in as a man, and sued the government, successfully, for the cost of the sex change. Unlike most stories in the place, this one is true, Bea was assured. The attacker has stopped screeching, and hangs limply in the larger woman's grasp. Not unconscious, but not far off it. Everyone meanders off as the screws turn up, and Bea says something to Mada, that she'll see him later, she loves him, she's not sure what, and as she hangs up her mind is blank of everything she said, blank of her entire life before she came within these walls.

A short, wiry Koori girl gives her something like a nod. Looking without focusing. Her attention sliding along the wall and settling on the phone.

'Lucky one, sissie. That chick woulda jumped on ya head.'

'Why?' Bea stammers.

A shrug. 'Ain't your phone.'

She spots the tall, muscular woman who saved her as she's lining up for dinner, goes up to thank her, but the words are shrugged away. Not as if she doesn't give a shit, more like she's annoyed by the idea: thanks, compassion. That they'll only get in the way.

'No big deal,' she says. 'Just didn't want to see blood today.' Her voice comes out deep and cigarette rough, Adams apple bobbing up and down as she talks.

The day of the transfer, two screws come to collect Bea from the cell. It is Monday, close as she can figure. Mid-morning. She hasn't been able to keep food down since the incident, and she isn't feeling steady on her feet.

'Come with us.'

'Where are we going?'

'Emu Plains.'

And that's that.

They cuff her and take her to a holding cell and tell her to wait. The door shuts and she sits, obedient, pushing down the unhelpful feeling of hope. Then one of the screws returns and now there's a woman with him.

'You need to take your clothes off,' the woman says, undoing the cuffs.

Bea complies. Numb. She lets the trackpants drop to the floor. The prison undies.

'Turn around.'

She's given a plastic sample cup and told to urinate into it. The male guard watches, unblinking. She turns around and squats over the cup, but her bladder won't obey.

'I can't do it,' she says.

The screw keeps staring, his expression bored.

'Can't piss, it's a positive. You stay here.'

'But I can't,' she says, trying, really trying.

He shrugs. Bea tries harder, desperate now.

She thinks about waterfalls and rivers. The ocean with Red in Bali. She thinks about taps being released, a garden hose, a steady flow. Finally she feels a thin trickle. Not much, but it'll do. She screws on the lid and hands over the container, a millimetre or two of yellow-brown liquid pooled at the bottom. 'This way,' says the woman, not unkindly, indicating the door. 'I'll bring you some water.'

Bea is marched outside, where a white van is parked on the baking asphalt. She passes grey metal gates. Cameras. Razor wire. Behind the van, a mirrored window. The sun beating down. Above her the sky is a hard cloudless blue. The male screw opens the door of the van and points inside.

'Mind your head.'

Bea climbs the steps.

Inside, it's as airless as an oven. The door shuts behind her and she sits on a bench towards the back. Tiny windows up high. It is very hot. Her mouth has a metallic tinge, as though she's touched her tongue to the railing of a carpark. The thought of the promised water sits in her mind like salvation, but it doesn't arrive, and she can feel her gums rubbing on her teeth. When she's been onboard for about twenty minutes, sitting in the sweat and heat, the Koori girl, the one who was there when she nearly got bashed, gets loaded on. She gives the screw a big grin and comes over and sits close to Bea. Not aggressive, but not exactly friendly either.

'It's been fun and all, but I'll take the bus outta this shit'ole any day,' she says.

Bea nods. 'Too right.'

They sit there for another hour. No air-con. Not moving. The sun well up and coming through the slit widows and beating on the roof and Bea has no idea what the wait's for and no idea how much longer: just sitting, too uncomfortable, too nervous, to even be bored. Her head is swimming. It occurs to her that this is part of the punishment. *Put em in the oven.*

'Emu Plains is a whole lot better than this place, sissie,' says her new friend, breaking the silence. 'Minimum security. You'll see.'

'You've been there before?'

'Oh, yeah.'

The way she says it, it's as if the prison, the system, is home. But she only looks to be seventeen. Her face carries the small, youthful features of a girl. All except the eyes. Those eyes are sunken black mirrors that give nothing back, nothing but a dark reflection of what you put in, and a grim kind of merriment. As though the whole parade isn't her concern. At most, a sad joke.

The girl asks Bea if she wants a ciggie.

'Where are you going to get that from?' Bea asks. Her tobacco ration was taken from her before they put her on the bus. But there seems a kind of promise in the girl's question. Bea is eager to know the secrets, the gaps in the system, the ways to evade the search. She has an urgent need to figure out the shape of the cage, learn the exceptions where a spark of life might remain.

The girl puts her hand down the front of her pants, squirms a few seconds, then flourishes a ziplock plastic bag containing tobacco, rolling papers and a lighter. She gives a wicked grin in the fleshy waft, pulling out the papers and starting to roll as she looks questioningly at Bea.

'Um, no thanks.'

The girl shrugs. 'Box it or lose it, sissie.'

She lights up her smoke, inhales, blows into the stifling air, leaving the tobacco and fixings in her lap. 'So … what's ya name?'

'Bea.'

'Bee? Like them yellow and black honey makers?'

'Yeah,' says Bea, smiling. 'Just like them.'

'Stacey,' says the girl, slouching back against the seat.

Bea sees it, then: the gaps. That they aren't in the system at all. They're in the body. In the self. If there's a space that remains yours, remains free, it's only the space that you can make within yourself. Maybe your body is no longer yours, but they can't police the inside, not if you go deep enough: head, mind, vagina. The deeper you go, the less chance they can crack you open, scoop out what remains. The only thing to do is find that part of yourself that's still your own. Seek it out. Crawl inside. Come out when it's safe and clear.

The door swings open with a rush of slightly less stinking hot air. Two women climb in and sit on the seats on the opposite side of the van. The door slams shut again.

'How youse doin?' asks one.

'All right.'

The second woman says nothing. She stares rigidly ahead, chewing on something, or maybe nothing, with her front teeth. She looks about ready to pop. To do herself in, or someone else. When the bus finally shakes itself to life, Bea watches as she nods slowly and eases back on the bench. The metal links in Bea's cuffs swing back and forth as they exit the driveway. An imagined city, with its people free, its silent, invisible suburbs, slides past beyond the van's metal walls.

The Meeting

Chapter 6

Zoe is already sitting up, reading in bed beside him, when Mada wakes on Monday morning. The day of the dreaded meeting, already looming large. He blinks out a small splinter of sleep, reaches over and pulls back the curtains. The sun is on the way up, but still below the skyline. Early morning Redfern, backlit trees and terraces, glimpses of a train moving away behind a line of cars.

Mada lies back and pillows his head on Zoe's breast, nuzzling the smoothness of her skin as he slides his cheek to the edge of her nipple. A small firm strawberry, dark on her tan flesh; that smooth runner's body, with its perfect perfume. He leans back and takes her in, her brown eyes sharp, focused, the strong line of her neck. She tilts her head, crinkles her nose and gives a goofy grin to acknowledge his attention, all the while not taking her eyes from the book.

'How long have you been awake?' he asks eventually.

'Since four.'

'Thesis brain?'

'Mmmm.'

'Whatcha reading?'

She frowns. Doesn't answer.

He can see her eyes skipping back, reloading a sentence. Trying to unpack it. Mada fumbles for his glasses and finds them on the floor by his laptop.

'Saussure? That's a hell of a way to wake up,' he says. Not too loud, though. She's been touchy lately.

'It's something one of my supervisors said on Friday. Gender as commonality and divergence. Made me think of him.'

She gazes at Mada, touches his cheek. He can see the effort it takes her to lift out of her brain. 'Did you sleep okay? How are you feeling?'

'Better.'

'You look better. No more dreams about your mum?'

'I guess not.'

'And not freaking out about today's meeting?'

'Nope. Just regular mid-range PhD neurosis.'

She glances back at the text, a new thought visibly entering that portion of her brain still processing what she's reading, then works hard to return her attention to Mada.

'It's all right,' he says, giving the book an ironic pat. 'Keep at it, I've got to get moving.'

She points at her lips and Mada plants a kiss.

Zoe has been more or less subsumed by her dissertation for over a year. She came up for air at the trial, but only briefly, and

Mada knows that if he hadn't needed her as badly as he did, she would have stayed lost inside her work. He understands this well enough: besides being obsessed by his own research project, he's seen plenty of others go through the PhD grinder. Some lose it completely, bomb out from the pressure; others are all but paralysed by anxiety. More often than not, their relationships get ground up as well.

He's not going to let that happen, even though there's *nothing* in his life he cares about more than his research into Huntington's disease. It's more than study to him; it's a kind of haunting. Something he can't escape. Not only because it affects his mother, and, perhaps, himself – he's been putting off going for testing for years now, ever since he became eligible at eighteen – but because he's devoted himself to it, dug a kind of mental cave inside it, and he feels happiest, freest, most himself, when he's deep in study. Which means that between his research and her own, some days Zoe feels as far away as a cure itself.

He watches her eyes darting over the page, her brow furrowed in what he calls her 'thinking crease'.

'Is he offering to make her tea?' she asks without looking up.

'Yes, he is offering The Majesty tea.'

Mada deposits a kiss on that point of intellectual strain, pushes himself from the bed and heads to the kitchen. There's no pressure quite like a PhD, he thinks. It isn't the quantity of work, so much as its nature. As though the process is testing not only knowledge and technique, but essence. What do you have in you? Are *you* good enough? Being riddled with self-doubt is, so far as he can figure, part of the normal running of the postgrad's brain. Perhaps if you're a genius you never know doubt. But

Mada has never had any illusion that he is the smartest person in the room: no, he has always known he will get by on sweat alone. Hours and hours of reading and thinking, hours and hours in the lab. That, and maybe a bit of luck.

And weirdly enough, today he feels kind of lucky.

This is inexplicable, as he's sure the outcome for the meeting he's soon to attend, on the question of whether he can refocus his research at the university, has already been decided in the negative by his head of department. He hasn't yet thought through what the consequences of that 'no' might be: he loves his supervisor, yet the department is a mess; he likes the facilities, yet hates the politics.

And still, he's feeling lucky. He ponders this as he hands Zoe her tea and goes through to the shower.

Getting dressed is difficult. Mada doesn't own a suit, not that he thinks they'll be expecting one, but he wants to be as impressive as possible. He's starting to look skinny – he needs to get back to the pool. His legs protrude from under the towel like thin tan sticks. After several failed experiments, he settles on a collared long-sleeved shirt with broad grey stripes. Zoe's least favourite: she's tried to give it to the Salvos more than once. Yet there is an association in the common mind between dullness and dependability, and today is not the day to buck it.

'I should be home by six or so. I want me pipe packed with baccy and me dinner on the table when I get in.'

'You'd be lucky.'

'You'll feel the back of my hand if you're not careful.'

She leans forward and rubs her face, catlike, against his fingers.

'You know,' says Mada, 'I do feel lucky today.'

'That's good. You'll kick arse.'

He kisses her again.

'Give them hell, my love,' she says. 'They should say yes.'

'I doubt it. Brandis is a bureaucratic fucktard.'

She raises a finger. 'The "tard" word is not okay.'

'Blah blah. You and your politically correct leftists are destroying the world.'

'Besides, it's a category mistake. His failure is ethical, not temporal.'

'Okay, thrill me with your etymology.'

'He's not running late. He's an arsehole. But it's Latin. From *tardus*. In French it's not an awkward word. It just means late. *Tu, mon amour, n'es jamais en retard.*'

'Ha! When the nerds rise to take over the world, you'll be last against the wall.'

'What are you talking about? I'll be leading the revolution.'

'Yes, at first,' he says. 'But these things always end in purges.'

'I love you, too.'

He bends down and kisses her again, longer this time. She smells so good he wants to crawl back into the sheets, into her. Mada pulls slowly, unwillingly, away.

He walks up the block, to where he managed to park yesterday afternoon, and gets into the car. Three hundred thousand on the clock and still going strong. Mada turns off the radio for the drive to the university. Focusing. Getting it all straight in his head. There are good reasons for them to support his proposal, but no matter how he thinks it out, he's sure they'll say no. The feeling of an exercise doomed from the outset returns, his sense of good fortune draining away every kilometre he drives from Zoe. By the time he reaches the university, his impending failure is there as an unshakable fact, a weight that grows as he walks up the hill to the pharmacology department.

Paula, his doctoral supervisor, is in her office. Head down, frowning at some papers on her desk. There's a poster of Madame Curie on the wall behind her, books stacked on every surface.

'We need to get this locked away,' she says, the moment he comes through the door. As though they're halfway through a conversation. Not even looking up at him.

'Good morning to you, too. What needs to be locked away?'

'All the adverse reaction stats.'

'Do you think it'll make a difference? They won't have time to look at that level of detail and, besides, they're not going to let me.'

She glares at him briefly and goes back to her papers. 'Not with that attitude, they won't. Just wait. We will see. I have to go over early. You should come a little later. What time did they tell you?'

'Ten thirty.'

'Okay. Come into the room and sit down. Don't talk too much. Be polite.'

'Aren't I always?'

She smiles. 'Brandis will be unpleasant. *As always.* You mustn't let him get under your skin. If he acts the *cabron*, don't make it your problem. It isn't. I will deal with him.'

'It's not me I'm worried about.'

It's true, too. Last time they'd been forced to share the same room with the departmental head, it was Paula whose temper had ignited. She pointedly ignores his comment, eyeing him up and down, examining him properly for the first time. 'You look … smart. Horrid shirt. Perfect for the occasion.'

'I was thinking much the same. You think I need a tie?'

'In this place? Half of those here wouldn't wear shoes but for the laboratory rules. Would you mind going to the printer and collecting the materials? That new paper from the *Lancet*. There should be four copies.'

He walks down the corridor into the copy room. The smell of toner is especially strong today. One of the fluorescents is on the fritz, flickering intermittent bursts. He checks the pages, then waits for the thing to stop spitting out paper. For Mada's whole life, he reflects, his timing has been crap, and his arrival at the University of Eastern Sydney is a case in point. For a small, newly established university, it's had more than its share of big political trouble. The year he started his candidature, the previous department head, Professor Smithe, was ousted, her funding withdrawn and her research attacked, an accusation of inappropriate conduct levelled. It had all been stage-managed, that was obvious enough to anyone who knew how to read the politico-academic weather patterns, but it's left Paula, Professor Smithe's star recruit, on extremely shaky ground. Nothing is ever made explicit, of course. Perish the thought – this is a university, not some realtor's office! But the atmosphere is poisonous, departmental gossip circulating like Legionnaires' disease in the air-conditioning ducts, so that now, a little over a year into his candidature, Mada wonders if he's ever going to finish.

Motivating these academic manoeuvrings was a mistrust of Smithe's 'newfangled' emphasis on systems biology research, fostering as it did an attitude to scholarship that the department's principal sponsor, Allegra Pharmaceuticals, found ideologically unsavoury and commercially impractical. This alone had been sufficient recipe for animosity, but when the professor published a paper in which she openly criticised Allegra, not only for bio-piracy in the Amazon, but for wilfully warping data on one of its greatest money-makers, a pill for erectile dysfunction, spirited departmental disagreement transformed into all-out internal war.

Now it seems to Mada that half the staff are afraid for their jobs, and the other half are making damn sure those fears are well founded. Allegra Corp is busy stacking the board with their own appointments: men – and the new appointments are *all* men, as Paula repeatedly points out – more open to integrating a corporate pharmaceutical model into departmental research aims. Despite the apparent problems with RF9, the drug that Mada is meant to be assessing, he knows in his gut that his application to shift his research focus away from established Allegra agents will be refused. And yet he's determined to go to the meeting with optimism and a sense of purpose. He is, after all, *right*.

RF9 is an anticonvulsant, one of the hundreds of potential medicines patented by Allegra Pharmaceuticals. It hasn't proven much use on its own, but a few years back a paper claimed that it could be combined with sodium valproate to limit seizures in neuro-degenerative conditions like Huntington's. Mada, who'd been obsessively reading every Huntington's-focused research paper he could get hold of, saw an answer, or the start of one. A way to save his mother, or at least limit her symptoms. As the disease progresses in Lori, the jerking movements – the chorea caused by a breakdown of nerve cells in the brain, the fatal dance by which Huntington's is most frequently identified – will make her life increasingly unmanageable. Not to mention the mental and behavioural declines that go hand in hand with the physical ones. If only Mada can find a way to limit the chorea, save what remains of her brain, his mother's life will be far more enjoyable.

'Your mother is still young,' one doctor said some five years before, 'and the science is moving fast.' Mada is desperate to be a part of that movement. At least Lori is only in the very early stages of the chorea – it's largely invisible unless she's angry or stressed – and he wants to find a solution before it's too late.

As to his own status, most of the time Mada tries not to think about it, but truth be told it's never far from his mind, the shuddering genetic death sentence powering the urgency of his search. His failure to be tested before now is something that he doesn't fully understand, but he suspects it largely comes down to the echoes of testimonies he's read: that you cannot un-know once knowledge has been granted. Who would choose, willingly, to know the time and manner of their passing? And what is the use of knowing if there's no treatment, nothing to be done? All the same, the question eats away at him, as does the feeling that, sooner or later, he will simply have to find out.

When he approached Paula almost two years ago about a doctoral grant, designing and implementing RF9 trials, she agreed to supervise him. The drug would generate a funded place at the university, and that meant that they could work together, and explore other potential therapeutic compounds at the same time. The thing is, when he dug into the RF9 research, the data didn't stack up. The anti-convulsant properties had been overstated, the adverse reactions more severe than indicated. The list of side effects is growing by the day. This is a depressing enough prospect, but with Paula's position teetering on the edge, and the bureaucracy at the university seeking an ever-tighter grip on every ounce of his time, it's hard to see his candidature at Eastern Sydney as anything other than two years down the gurgler. And the politics of the place is abysmal. As Paula puts it: *En este lugar me siento como un pulpo en un garaje.* This place makes me feel like an octopus in a garage.

A shiver runs through Mada as the printer powers down and he gathers up the last of the pages and drops them on Paula's desk. She's on the phone and doesn't look up, so Mada goes to the departmental kitchen to get good and caffeinated for his oncoming grilling.

Even before he gets to the meeting room, Mada regrets the third coffee. His chest is tight and breathless. As he walks in and sits down, he is sure they can hear the blood straining at his aortic walls. At the head of the table is the departmental powerbroker, Professor Mike Brandis. Mada sits in the chair that Brandis indicates, opposite Paula, with Professor Tom Evans at his side. At least the panel seems mostly balanced, his affection for Professor Evans a kind of counterpoint for his dislike of Brandis. There are several other academics sitting around the table, some of whom he likes, and hopes are sympathetic to him, but Mada feels incapable of holding a thought in his head.

'Mr Vaughn?'

'Huh?' His heart thuds.

Jesus. What did they ask? Get with it.

'I'm sorry, can you repeat the question?'

Paula gives him an almost imperceptible 'get your shit together' glance.

'We were hoping,' says Brandis, 'that you might take us through your research to date, then run through the proposed project alteration in detail. That is, if you're not otherwise occupied.'

'Yes professor. Of course.'

Mada breathes deeply and launches into a justification of his existence at the faculty. He feels as if his mouth and head are full of rocks. He's almost glad that his presentation is overshadowed by the grudge match between Paula and Brandis – parachuted into his professorial chair from his previous corporate position, with Allegra no less, some two years earlier – which flares up constantly. Soon he's swinging his gaze from one to the other, as if his career is being batted back and forth.

'You understand that it is a difficult thing to justify. This is simply not the project that was originally funded.' Mada sometimes thinks there's little Brandis enjoys more than setting an uppity academic on the righteous path of accountability.

'The funding was to test a compound that could limit symptoms or delay onset, and to design a study using transgenic rats. It now emerges there were significant problems with that data set, and, as such, the research aims cannot be met—'

'That is for this panel to decide,' Brandis interrupts her.

'His scholarship is governmental, Professor.'

'And requires our approval.'

'Yes. But it's not you, or Allegra Corp, who pays him, is it?' Paula shows Brandis none of the deference that the rest of the staff offer him. As she has it, the entire Australian university system is slowly strangling itself with Brandis's kind. Idiots! Vampires! Their contact with the research and teaching end of the university remains at virtually zero, but this doesn't stop them presenting financial ultimatums with such deadpan chutzpah they would be comedic if they weren't destroying so many careers.

'The government is also interested in seeing this research funded.'

'Perhaps. I'm sure, with your keen interest in the issue, you would have read last month's piece in the *Journal of Neuropharmacology*. There is some anecdotal evidence among the patient body of far worse side effects than reported.'

'Anecdotal evidence is a misnomer.'

'Indeed. It is for this reason that the Dalhousie analysis is so valuable.'

'Dalhousie … that was it. Not exactly Oxford. Where is that? Nigeria?'

'Halifax, Canada. A small country, you're probably not familiar with it. Shares two borders with your American boss. Where did you complete your postgraduate study, Professor? I don't seem to remember...'

'What does that have to do with Huntington's research?'

'Very little, from all reports.'

Professor Evans coughs. It's not clear if he's trying to intervene or stifling a laugh.

'The government's position on these trials is a simple one. Organisations like Allegra pay campaign finances. But yours is simpler still—'

'Listen to me, *Doctor*,' Brandis gives the relative inconsequence of Paula's title special emphasis, 'you are one step away from a security escort from the premises. I'm sorry that your position here has become difficult—'

'So terribly sorry.'

Professor Evans coughs again, louder this time. 'Please, both of you. Let's not flog this old nag skinless. I'm exhausted by it, as I'm sure is everyone else here.' He gestures about the group. Dr Johnstone, at the end of the table, is staring out the window. Across from him, Associate Professor Stephens is rearranging a stack of application papers, intent on the precision with which she straightens them, as though the stack were a slide beneath her microscope. She's no fan of Brandis, but she's far too fond of her job to say it out loud.

Paula offers Brandis a curt nod. 'I apologise. This argument has indeed turned dull.'

Professor Evans shoots a glance at Brandis, whose turn it is now to leaf through the papers in front of him.

'At any rate,' offers Stephens, 'we need to be assured that Mr Vaughn will complete what he has committed to, and do so before being distracted by other research objectives. The university has invested a great deal in his training. It would seem only appropriate that such an investment is repaid.'

Brandis purses his lips and nods sagely. The central prong of the research funding oversight committee, so he likes to describe himself, without apparent irony. He looks like a prong, all right, thinks Mada. So utterly devoid of fat, he seems almost to be constructed of wire. Apparently he does triathlons: photographs of him decked out in lycra appear randomly on departmental bulletin boards, with even more randomly positioned genitalia drawn on in black marker, whether by staff or students is unclear.

Paula once described Brandis as 'smart, boorish, and utterly tone deaf, just like all North Americans,' a diagnosis that was far too broad and extreme for Mada, who's largely liked the Americans he's met. It was one of the very few times when he felt her judgment was skewed, though he forgave her, on the grounds that the CIA had attempted to overthrow the government of her homeland, which she both believed in and had voted for. As far as Paula was concerned, Chávez had overseen a vast increase in medical services in Venezuela, a policy that affected her directly. But for Mada, the CIA isn't America any more than ASIO is Australia.

The strain in Brandis's voice brings Mada back to the present. 'There are significant questions as to the value of this work. The university is quite justified in guiding its investment.'

'Guiding its investment? Is this the phrase for it?'

Professor Evans clears his throat again.

Paula nods her assent. 'Yes, the old nag. The fact is, this absolutely falls within the criteria of Mr Vaughn's original research proposal. What is more, it is important work. All the data from ULA is promising. Previous stages of testing have demonstrated positive outcomes.'

'That is not the point,' cuts in Brandis.

Professor Evans raises a hand to forestall further objections. 'All the same, we will consider the request.' He stands, collecting his various documents into a folder. Paula gives Mada a reassuring smile and tilts her head at the door.

They walk out in silence, navigating the sea of backpacks outside the upper lecture hall.

'I'm going to the labs,' says Mada.

'Good idea. Carlos is there. Get lost in work for a while. But Mada, listen, I want you to do something for me. He's got his refugee status review coming up. I'm planning a little "barbie",' she says this in her version of an Aussie accent, and puts quotes in the air with her fingers, 'and I thought you could ask that formidable girlfriend of yours along, and your mother. It is important we meet your mother, professionally and personally. I know Carlos is eager to talk with her.'

'Mum will come in a heartbeat,' says Mada with a smile. 'She loves an outing.'

'Good,' says Paula, grinning.

He turns to peel off towards the labs, but Paula stops him. 'Don't worry too much about all this, Mada. You're a good scholar. You will do great things. An idiot like Brandis won't stand in your way too long.'

Emu Plains Correctional Centre
Chapter 7

As they come up the drive to Emu Plains, Stacey stands and presses her cuffed hands onto the window glass. She gestures at Bea, indicating the adjacent high, narrow window.

'Check out them girls, sissie.'

Bea joins her, gazing into the glare, the smeared glass opaque with midday sun. Outside, on the far side of the fence, girls are hanging off the wire. One of them sticks her tongue between the links. They're not girls, Bea thinks, they're women. And if Stacey is anything to go by, they were never girls at all. Although women doesn't quite fit either; there is something animal about them, not as individuals, but the way they bunch together, the way they move, responding to each other, the way they open their mouths to yell at the van. There'd be no reasoning with a pack like that, no pretence of control.

This must be what a pig feels like, Bea thinks, on first getting the stink of death, arriving at the abattoir. She sits down and fixes her eyes straight ahead, and does her best to look as though she's not afraid, as though she doesn't care. But her hands are shaking, and she can't make them still.

The door opens and the four of them are told to get out. Bea is the last one to step down, and she stands slouched on the asphalt, staring at her cuffs while she waits for instructions. Two women are hissing through the wire. Another gives a wolf whistle behind them. 'Stace! Ya come back, sis!'

Stacey offers a wicked grin. 'Couldn't stay away, mate!'

Bea is assigned to 'the huts'. Small houses at the end of the compound. There she will stay, an officer tells her, until they figure out what to do with her. Stacey is in the hut next door, and this makes Bea feel as if she might survive the place – an ally, a survivor, one who has lived inside the system and has managed to get out, will be close by to guide her.

First morning, the siren sounds at six thirty precisely. Wailing in the early light, it sounds like something from a movie, a bad one, the announcement of an air raid. Bea rolls over and wishes for the small escape of sleep, and if not that, hopes, only partly ironically, that sweet death will embrace her. Only do it quietly and gently, in her sleep. The threat of being bashed to crippledom, left in some compassionless corner, is more frightening than oblivion.

The worst part, she thinks, isn't even the constant threat of violence. It's the bloody compulsion to be quiet in the face of it all, knowing that if you break the code of silence and 'paper' someone, even if they're trying to kill you, your life is not worth spit. The siren goes off again, and Bea drags herself from bed to stand limply in the centre of the room. She pulls on the green tracksuit pants, then the top, and sits down again, resting there with her head in her hands.

Not crying, only resting.

She says that out loud.

When the front door swings open, Stacey is there, yelling at her with cheerful belligerence. 'Come on, sissie, if ya not there for roll call, they charge ya. That's time on ya stay. This place is nice n all, but it's borin as batshit. Ya don't wanna stick about any longer than ya have to.'

Guts churning, mind racing, she walks into the day.

There are a few hundred women in matching tracksuits assembled in a field at the centre of the compound. Milling about, eyeing each other with the same show of nonchalant threat, then slowly spreading out in crooked lines. Bea keeps her gaze on the dirt at her feet while Stacey natters on, only shutting up when the security director starts patrolling the lines. The way she moves, wide-armed and muscular, she seems part of the place, built of the same stuff; half woman, half machine.

She stands in front of Bea and spits out a torrent of hard, foul-mouthed abuse, so that Bea is cowering even as she tries to hold herself tall. She isn't even talking to Bea, but to all of them, especially the newbies. She moves down the line, telling them what a bunch of useless cunts they are. She yells about what will happen if they get caught using drugs. How they'll get tipped. This is for the benefit of the new girls, she says; for the rest, they shouldn't need a reminder. All the same, because they're useless cunts, because they're dumb as dogshit, because they can hardly remember how to tie their fucking shoelaces, she'll give them a reminder anyway. Urine tests are random: you can't piss, you're guilty. Caught doing standover, you get tipped. As she says this, she stops in front of a solidly muscled woman with a square head, a few down from Bea, loudly detailing these facts into her face. The woman's posture doesn't shift, she stands there mutely deflecting the words, and raises her hand to wipe the spit from her face when the uniformed officer moves on. Two years get added to your sentence if you're caught with any part of a mobile phone. Even if it's just the antenna. Even if it's just the battery.

Two years. So don't fucking try it.

And in case you forgot it, you're a bunch of useless cunts.

'The next one I catch with contraband,' she frowns up the line, 'I'll tip straight to Broken Hill.'

This is the threat to offer those already stuck in a nightmare: somewhere in the red dust heat of the state's outer lands, a place worse than this, worse even than Silverwater. The threat hangs toxic in the air, like a day of judgment, fire and brimstone, a ninth circle of hell built of concrete and heat. Once that vortex sucks you in, you'll never see another spot of rain. The thought of a place worse than Silverwater makes Bea feel as if she might puke. It's like standing with the phone to her ear, anticipating the blow.

When it's over, Stacey slaps her arm and tells her not to worry. 'She's a fucken piece a work, eh sis. Don't sweat it, but. Just stay outta her way. She's the least of ya worries in this shit-ole.' She fires another wicked grin and gives a cackle. 'And don't look so freaked, or someone'll swat ya just for the fuck of it.'

* * *

Bea is assigned a house with nine other women. She makes herself a promise that she will get out of this place when her time is done, this one and no other. That she will keep her head down, keep her nose clean, will do her time, and walk out free and whole the second they grant parole. What such a promise is worth in the face of the guards, the inmates, the rust and steel of the place, is beyond her capacity to fathom. She has been given over to the system, has forfeited her right to choose.

Everyone has to pitch in cleaning the house. Sweep the floor, mop it out, keep the dump tidy. There are inspections, a roster. A washing line stands between their house and the wire. You've got to do your own washing and cook your own tea. If your house has been tipped off for contraband, the screws come in to ramp it. That's when they turn everything upside down. Everyone gets marched out, strip-searched and interrogated. Then they put you into management cells, and you have to stay there until the whole house has pissed. A screw watches the entire process, to prevent urine getting swapped.

Some of the screws are septic, others try to help where they can. Just like everything else inside, there is a strict code for the guards as well. For those who choose to follow it. No favouritism. Toe the line. Bea doesn't see corruption, no fucks for favours, but the place is so thick with every kind of substance, there must be graft in the nooks and crannies or half of the inmates would have the shakes.

Every morning that alarm goes off, a long wail of horror in the barren dawn. Six thirty, on the dot. It sounds again at six forty-five, in case you've missed the first one: utterly impossible, of course, unless you've been mashed to a pulp in the night. Even the deaf, probably even the dead, thinks Bea, could feel that obnoxious wail penetrate their skulls. There's no way to block it out, no matter how hard she holds the pillow over her head. After the alarm, the houses are unlocked and the screws come in for the roll call. Everyone has to be up and dressed: prison greens only, no pyjamas; you wouldn't want to let yourself go.

She survives the first week. Then the second, the third. Monday on the fourth week, the woman from Silverwater who tried to bash her by the phone steps down with the morning arrivals. She picks out Bea in the afternoon line-up, venom in her eyes so there's no question she's forgotten.

'How the fuck did she make minimum security?' Bea hisses.

Stacey gives a shrug. 'Nothin matters but what they caught ya for. Don't matter what you've done inside.'

Two days later she's on her way to the house, walking under the awnings, when there's a blow to her face so sharp and sudden, Bea is on her back before she knows what's happened. She lies on the concrete, light flashing in her vision, holding her hand to her eye and feeling blood seep through her fingers. She rests there, dazed, until one of the screws walks past, clocks her and stops.

'You all right?'

She can't even imagine how to respond to that one. She's not all right, not one iota, but knows there's no help for the asking.

'Come on,' he says, 'let's get you up. You might need a couple of stitches there.' He leads her to the hospital wing, a hand under her arm, and sits her down to wait for the nurse.

'So,' he asks, 'what happened?'

Bea shoots him a scared glance. 'Guess I must have slipped.'

He gives her a look that might almost hold sympathy, and leaves her to wait for medical attention.

On the weekends they get two visits per day. One in the morning, one in the afternoon, with each visitor announced over the loudspeaker – 'Campbell, four-oh-seven-one-six-eight. Visiting area.' And often that's the first you'll know of it.

When Lori comes to see her, Bea makes her way over with a sense of foreboding. The visits are in a prefab, on the edge of the compound, close to the gates. Mada came the week earlier, and let her know he'd be driving Lori out to Emu Plains the following Saturday.

'Doesn't seem like a good plan,' Bea said. 'Not that I don't want to see her. But having her in here will stress me out. God, it'll stress *her* out too.'

'I know,' he said. 'But she won't let it go. You know how she is when she's got something in her head.'

Yeah, Bea knows all too well. Now, with Lori about to arrive, she can feel her chest tighten with anticipation. Her sister won't go well in this place; she'll find the screws overbearing, the atmosphere strained. And that's not even counting the fact that Bea still has a shiner and three rough stitches over her eye.

In the prefab there's a strong stink of bleach. Not enough to kill the mustiness, more that the two scents form separate notes in a putrid perfume. There are vending machines, plastic tables and chairs, a whiteboard against one wall with an old piano against the other. Between them is a worn, frayed carpet. Its indeterminate colour, should it need to be described in a catalogue, might be pegged as sallow desperation. Near the entrance is a reception desk where three screws sit and keep an eye on everyone, and it is there that Bea spots her sister. Lori is swaying a little unsteadily, as if drunk, though Bea knows it's the stress and the chorea, and it's clear from the looks she's getting that the screws have no idea what to make of this woman. She always seems to feel cold, and is dressed, despite the heat, in an army surplus great coat and stout black boots, a floral dress underneath. Her hair, indeed her entire corporeal form, is a study in disarray.

'Mada said I could bring in change. For cigarettes and whatnot.' She gropes about in her pockets, pulling out a plastic bag filled with coins. 'This is what he gave me. To bring in.'

'Well, thanks. It's good of you to come.'

'Wanted to see my sister.'

Bea kisses her on the cheek before steering them through the door, out to a fenced area of grass, where they can get some sunshine and a little space. There's another screw outside, one Bea recognises, a thin, vicious man who strip-searched her after Mada's visit, getting her to take everything off, socks, shoes, arms up and out, making her squat and cough, in case she'd boxed any contraband. He seems to have taken a particular dislike to her. Either that, or he's just another unhappy arsehole, keen to exercise what power he has in any way he can.

The sisters move in silence to a far bench, where they sit down. Lori pulls Bea close to examine her in detail.

'What happened with your face?'

Bea lifts her hand to the swelling, running her fingers over the stitches. 'I had a ... fall.'

Lori stares at her, first scared, then angry. 'Did someone hit you?'

'Yes, but it's okay.'

'How can it be okay? Do they know about it? Do the men know?' She points over to the guard, who's eyeing them with suspicion.

'Yeah. They know, all right. You've got to understand how it works in here, Lori.'

Her sister says nothing to this, but she settles down all the same. Soon she's telling Bea all about her latest sculptures, about how nice it is to be back in her apartment. She's coping all right, better than Bea had hoped.

It's when she's headed out that the trouble starts. They hug tightly, in a way they haven't for years, and Bea turns towards the exit, walking back over the grass, thinking Lori is behind her.

But her sister has not followed.

It is at this moment that Lori's voice travels across the compound. Bea can't understand all her sister's words, something about her, about her face, but the tone is clear enough. Accusatory, angry.

Bea backtracks across the grass, to where Lori is raving at the guard. She reaches out to take Lori by the shoulder, but at that precise moment her sister's arm shoots out, the speed of it remarkable. It's only a shove, but the guard is not expecting it. He trips and lands heavily on his arse, and Lori stands over him, shouting and shuddering and swaying in her fury, and then another guard turns up, and Bea is face down with earth in her mouth, and Lori is wailing death at the fascist bastards who are killing her sister.

The following morning, Bea is transferred to Silverwater, to the mental health unit, where she spends five days in an isolation cell. The authorities are conducting a psychiatric evaluation on account of her 'depression'. This is where the real nutcases are, girls banging on cell doors, yelling, screaming, losing their minds at maximum volume in maximum security. Her cell has a thin mattress and a toilet, supplied with the familiar squares of tissue, and for twenty-three hours of the day she is locked in this room, by herself, while they wait for the duty psychologist to return from vacation. There is non-stop surveillance, and food of such repulsiveness she cannot eat it. For one hour of the day she is let into the exercise yard to smoke.

Her talks with the psychologist do not begin well.

'It says here you were on suicide watch when you were first admitted,' he says after some preliminaries.

'That was a mistake.' Bea explains the misunderstanding.

'Okay. So do you know why you are here now? Is this a mistake too?'

'I got angry with a guard who was abusing my sister.'

He stares down his glasses at her. 'Do you think getting angry with the guards will help?'

'No,' she responds sullenly.

'I can see from the incident report why you were angry … but there is concern over your wellbeing.'

'My wellbeing is fine.'

'Is it?' He eyes her pointedly.

'Yes.'

'Okay. So have you been experiencing feelings of hopelessness?'

'During this interview?'

'Let's focus on this past week.'

'Then, no. Not until now.'

The psychologist puts down the pen, folds his hands on the notes in front of him, and fixes her with a look. 'Mrs Campbell, my job is to determine whether you are able to return to Emu Plains to complete your sentence. You have said that you find the conditions here at Silverwater difficult. Why don't you try to make my job easier, rather than harder?'

After that, Bea puts on such a show of enthusiastic sanity that she almost fools herself. Almost, but not quite. In truth, she feels as low as when she was first locked away, and despite what she said to the shrink, it seems to her that she might just crack. The time of her incarceration unfurls before her, an unrelenting stretch, and for Bea to survive it, surrounded by the stink of sadness and metal, appears beyond hope.

Red comes for a visit the Saturday after she returns to Emu Plains. The prefab is almost full, but she manages to snag a couple of plastic chairs over by the vending machines. He's dressed for the office, as if he's on the way to a showing. Blue suit and tie, pale blue shirt. His face is so drawn and empty looking, Bea's heart sinks into her shoes. She feels guilty bringing him there. He hates it, she knows that. Not just the prison, but the people around them, even the suburb itself. Full of bogans and junky dipshits, that's what he would say. How far they've both fallen.

But once they sit down, he doesn't seem capable of saying anything that relates to the place at all, or anything, for that matter, that relates to her. He talks about work. Tells her about Mada and the potential university deal. How he's been asked to handle a deceased estate in Glebe, only a few blocks from their own house but right on the harbour, how he's going to buy it for the two of them so when Bea gets out they'll have water views right up the wazoo. She lets him go on. It helps, at least a bit. Makes things seem about as normal as they can be. Reminds her she will get out of here one day.

One of the inmates is clutching at a man with a shaved head. Their faces locked together, fumbling inside each other's clothes. He has an anarchy symbol tattooed on the back of his skull, under a thin fuzz of hair. It's been so long since Bea saw a real skinhead that she's weirdly nostalgic, not for skinheads but for the eighties, when skins were everywhere. Back when she was at uni, when time in a place like this was inconceivable. She realises she's staring, that the woman pashing the skinhead is glaring at her as she goes at it, her eyes open and locked on Bea's.

Without warning, the enormity of the years before her land like a weight. Solid. Real. Suffocating. So impossibly long. Too long to survive. It's like finding out that the world itself will end, that the future has died. She is not even aware that she is crying until Red breaks off, stopping mid-sentence in his walk-through of a Point Piper eight bedroom, staring at her.

'Dar-ling?' he says slowly, so it comes out as two uncertain words. 'Dar-ling? Are you okay?'

Bea doesn't know. She *was* doing okay. She was holding herself tight. Now she can't talk. Now she can only shake her head. Apparently he thinks she's having some kind of fit. He rises from the chair, as though ready to ask the guards for help. Bea grips his arm and pulls him down.

'Stay with me,' she hisses.

'Yeah, it's just ...'

She drives her fingernails into the fabric of his suit.

'Yeah, yeah, course.'

'Don't leave me. Don't leave me here. You've got to. Get me out.'

He starts, then leans back, staring at her with narrowed eyes, as if she's flipped her lid. She can feel him slide away from her, so he's there but not there. Surely he understands, surely he can tell. It's just not possible. Seven hundred days like this one? Seven hundred days waiting to get bashed. Waiting for someone to jump on your head.

'I can't do it, Red. I can't. Not two years. It's just—'

'But the lawyers. There's nothing to be done. They said—'

'Fuck the lawyers.' It comes out as a sob.

He pats her knee and puts his hand in his pocket, as though going to check his phone to wait her out and then remembering it's not there. 'Okay, sure, sure,' he says. 'We'll talk to them, honey. We'll see what they can do.' But she knows he's mouthing platitudes, that he doesn't believe a word.

For a real estate agent, he's a really shit liar.

She can't bring herself to kiss him as he's walking out. He tells her, without conviction, not to worry, they'll find a way.

When she's through security and back inside, the woman who was grappling with the skinhead pulls her over to the wall by the collar. Purposeful, forced, but not painful, not yet. She hasn't spoken to Bea before. She's one of the rough nuts. Bea still isn't back in prison mode, though. She hasn't managed to pull on the hardened skin that gets her through the place, and she flinches at the woman's touch. A mistake and she knows it.

'Take a chill pill, sissie, I ain't gonna hurt ya.'

'Okay.' It's all she can manage.

'Is that your lawyer?' the woman asks.

Bea gives a snort. Despite everything, the idea is funny. Red would love it, too, being confused for a lawyer. 'No. That's my husband.'

'Looks rich.'

'He's a real estate agent.' As if this should explain it.

'Is he? Shit eh. Ya didn't see anything back there, did ya?'

'No,' says Bea honestly. If she thought she was supposed to be not seeing something, she would have faced the other way. The woman glares at her a moment before giving a curt nod.

'Good. Cos if I get papered, I'll know who it is. And ya know I'll fucken smash ya.'

'Uh—'

'Cool,' says the woman, suddenly breezy. 'See ya then.' She spins about and walks off towards the huts. Bea leans back against the wall, shaking. Panic is living in her body, tightening her lungs, not leaving space for breath. It's everywhere. Waiting behind doorways, in the shade of passageways, the dark places that the cameras don't catch. Bea starts to walk back towards her room, eyes darting, hugging the undarkened sides of buildings and awnings, searching out the light.

The woman who shares her bedroom tallies each day on a calendar, putting a cross on each one as she counts backwards towards release: 'A hundred and forty sleeps to go; a hundred and thirty-nine sleeps.' Bea isn't sure where the count began. Four hundred. Six hundred. Two thousand. To her it is a madness that only extends the pain: every day a fragile thing, hung to the air, exposed. If she screws up, if her stay gets extended, she will have to start the count again.

Bea keeps telling herself that it has to be a moment at a time. That is the only way to do it. The past is made of regret, sinister and unthinkable; the future an impossible dream. Fate is never to be tempted, not even with stray thought.

Yet at the end of her second month, staring into that ceiling while her roommate snores in the adjacent bed, the thought comes to her like this: another day gone. I'm alive, and another day gone. This is the meaning of the prisoner's daily tally, the cliché of hash marks on a dungeon wall. Not time passed, but time survived. And inside her mind is a knotted thread of hope. A thought, minute, fragile, which says she is going to make it out, that her life might be fucked but that it's not completely broken.

This place will not destroy me, she thinks. All I have to do is stay alive. All I have to do is get through. If I can last two months I can last a year. A few black eyes, a dozen stitches: she'll survive it all. Head down. Do the time. Keep yourself alive. And so one moment gives way to another, a navigable horror. Adrift in the deadly stretch of days.

The Origin of Love
Chapter 8

Zoe stares out the library window at the neo-Gothic sandstone of Sydney University. Above the tower, the sky is an imprint of blue so deep, so perfect, that its very colour offers an autograph of universal possibility. Not God, not for her, not in any simple way at least. Given that she has an apostate Anglican minister for a dad and a Darumbal activist mum, Zoe's sense of the spiritual is complicated, quite beyond any act of naming. But isn't that what universal possibility stands for: a future, a potential, that is yet to be known?

Zoe had been in the library, working on an essay a few tables down from where she now sits, the day she first talked to Mada. She was in her second year of a philosophy degree, and he was doing his undergraduate study there too. She'd seen him around campus a few times and thought him handsome enough, with his kinky hair and dark skin, if a bit odd looking: there was something about the dimensions of his nose, a certain Greco-Roman quality, Zoe decided. He was a little skinny perhaps, kind of underfed, although he had filled out nicely in the subsequent years … She discovered early on that if she got him to the pool a few times a week, to swim some laps and focus on something besides a helix of DNA, he was much easier to live with. The eyes above that nose were eerie, their colour slightly mismatched and constantly changing, so from one minute to the next they might go from brown to eucalyptus green, but always with an intense sharpness about them. And he had the most enormous lashes she had seen on any male. Ever.

Not that he was particularly cool or stylish. He didn't wear black skinny jeans. There was no waistcoat or goatee, no tats on sculpted biceps. There was nothing at all, in fact, that marked him as part of any particular student 'tribe'. Perhaps it was the absence of any obvious label she could hang on him that piqued her interest. More than anything, he had a seriousness about him, about the way he was sitting, by himself, but not looking at all lonely, more as if solitude was a choice. He seemed purposeful in a way she was not accustomed to. She had the impression that roughly half of the university was only there to get laid, with graduation an unintended by-product of the important work each was doing on their sex lives.

Not Mada. This was a boy, she decided, that she had to know. So when she chanced upon him in Fisher Library, frowning into a book on ethics, she dumped her bag on the next table, straddled the closest chair Christine Keeler style and watched him. He glanced up at her, a crinkle of puzzlement crossing his brow, then he looked back into his book, and for what seemed like a full five minutes ignored her. Eventually he sighed, fixed his eyes on her irritably, and said, 'What?'

Zoe knew she was an attractive girl. This wasn't bragging, but a statement of fact. Boys liked her. When they were being polite, they made bumbling attempts to pick her up outside lecture halls. When they weren't, when they were players or when they were drunk, they told her flat out that they wanted to get her naked. Occasionally, she would let them. But this boy looked at her as if she was an impediment to his reading, and that was a look she was accustomed to giving rather than receiving. She batted her lashes – ironically, a moment of theatre – but a part of her was nervous it might not work.

It turned out that his name was Mada, a curiosity of which she approved, and that he had picked up an elective unit in philosophy, the fuzziness of which had him tearing out his hair. It wasn't the ideas themselves that had him in a lather, but the absence of concrete goals. What was the point of philosophy? he asked, after she got him talking. At what point would he have learned what he was required to learn, and what was the point of learning it?

'Even if I memorise the entire book,' he said, 'it's not really going to help one iota in deciding if an action is truly ethical or not. And the book is called *Ethics*! Jesus, what hope is there with metaphysics? I don't even know what that word means. All it will do, so far as I can figure, is help me formulate more precise questions. Philosophy is bunk.'

Zoe raised a combative eyebrow. 'What are you majoring in?' she asked.

'Biochemistry.'

She laughed.

He frowned.

She stopped.

He looked despairingly back at the book. 'It's too late in the semester to drop the course, and I need a distinction.'

'Why?'

'I'm thinking maybe postgrad.'

'You can still get a D,' she said, 'even an HD if you put your mind to it.'

'How? None of this makes any sense.'

He was genuinely exasperated, and Zoe was genuinely charmed. It was easy, then, as a philosophy major, to suggest she help him with his essays, get him reading the right secondary literature, guide him through the cracks in Kant's impenetrable language. A few weeks later, after a cheap Thai dinner and a shared longneck of beer, they had sex on a rug on the lounge-room floor of his rental apartment, surrounded by philosophy books. Afterwards, they wrapped themselves in a flannelette sheet and read some favourite passages to each other, side by side, gently touching as they talked.

For Zoe, it was heaven.

It wasn't the sex itself. By the time they met, she'd had her share of boys … and men, for that matter. What got her about Mada was his tenderness. The intimacy they fell into, all her senses swelling. The touch of him, the taste of him, the scent of them both mingling and so natural and unaffected, and the attention, the joyful appreciation – hell, the carnal worship he gave her body – spoke of spirit, and chemistry, and alchemy in equal parts. She could tell how present he was, how deep his will to connect. He was trying to penetrate the core of her, trying, by this weird miracle of flesh, to turn two bodies into one, drive himself so deep inside her that he tickled her brain.

What's more, he succeeded.

They ate Vegemite toast dripping with butter, then made love again, had more toast and made more love, and talked until the sky lightened.

'Where are you from, Mada?' she asked, stroking his jaw tenderly.

'Sydney.'

'That's it? I mean, I'm trying to place you, but you're kind of an enigma. You got people somewhere?'

'Well, my mum's family came out from Europe before the war. I don't know about my dad.'

'You don't know where he's from?'

'I don't even know who he is. Never met him. A surfer from Byron named John, that's all Mum tells me.'

Zoe grinned at him. 'You just get more and more interesting, don't you!'

'I'm glad you approve.'

'Oh yes.' She licked her lips, running her fingers over the fine muscles of his chest, tracing their outline until she felt him shiver. 'What do you do for exercise?'

'I swim.'

'Thought so,' she said. 'Want to head to the beach? Tamarama?'

'Now?'

'Why not?'

His face cracked into a huge grin. 'Let's go!'

She took over the stereo on the drive out, playing Kate Bush at full volume, keeping it at the edge of distortion as they blared through the awakening day. Along Syd Einfeld Drive with the windows open, Bush calling down immaculate ecstasies, sky lifting over the dash. Zoe's hand was cupped over his on the stick, their fingers looped together.

The sun was pushing just above the water as they parked. All gold. One solitary jogger. Mada had his boardies on, and Zoe stripped to her undies, enjoying the pleasure in his eyes as he took her in. And the way he looked! Smooth, as if carved from dark stone, skin perfect in the early light. She leaned forward and planted a kiss smack on his lips, then bolted for the water, pounding over the soft sand towards the ocean.

He caught her at the hardpack of the water's edge and raced in front, charging into the first wave of the shore break, throwing himself bodily into the wave with a wild kind of happiness, and then they were both under it and through the other side. Still in the shallows, she leaped onto his back in the trough of the next wave, so he had no choice but to charge through it front on, crouching, blasting headfirst into its wall, the two of them breaking out the other side and diving together, swimming out to where it was deeper, calmer. Taking her arm he spun her about, the lush music of their tongues a game of salt. He tasted better than anything she had ever known, a kiss drawn from beyond even the ocean depths, inside his body, inside her own, a well deep within the world.

That afternoon she returned to her flat, her roommate Ange offering a long wink as she came into the kitchen, to indicate an awareness that Zoe had not changed clothes in over twenty-four hours.

'Coming along well with your biochemist, I see. Want a cup of tea?' She flicked on the switch for the kettle.

Zoe collapsed into a chair by the kitchen table. She could feel her body vibrating softly, as though a current was running from her toes up through her legs and spine and tickling her hippocampus.

'Yes, and yes,' she said.

'So – dish it on the dish.'

'Yes, he is.'

'And ...'

'Where's my tea?'

'Don't stall.'

'There's something different about him. Almost alien. Maybe he's on the spectrum or something, but fuck it's a good spectrum. Totally obsessed with planning his masters, although he's only halfway through undergrad. But he's gorgeous. Swims like a dolphin.'

They drank their tea. Ange gave her a grin. 'He sounds really good, Zo. I'm super happy for you.'

'He is. He's the first boy I've talked to, really talked to, since ... forever.' Zoe leaned back in her chair. Cobwebs and dust had colonised the light fitting hanging above the table. Later today, after a sleep, she would clean the house.

'Ange,' she said, staring at the ceiling, aware, as she spoke, of her tingling body, of the endorphin buzz running through her bloodstream, aware that she could still smell him on her, or thought she could, even after the swim. The remnant scent of his sweat ingrained in the pores of her hands. The faint musky sweetness of him wafting through her nostrils. She had forgotten what it was like. How full it could be. How every sense can sing to the other, the joining of two bodies pulling all her separate parts together, as though Aristophanes' myth were true, as though she had at last found the other half of herself, the half sliced away by Zeus, for which she had ever since been yearning.

'Ange,' she said, 'I've found the man for me.'

The memory of that first morning is one she holds inside her body, and it is this, its depth and penetration, and then the question of what an embodied memory might be at all, that she puts her mind to a moment, before she decides to give up on work for the day. Her head is not in it, and at any rate she's promised Mada she'll go to Paula's for lunch. Zoe packs up her books and heads for the exit.

A dry blast of summer bleaches the air as she skips down the steps. Bushfire season is getting longer. Even here in the city, the air has that tinder-dryness that speaks of its readiness to burn.

Two hours later, Zoe is playfully stroking the nape of Mada's neck as he drives the four of them through the backstreets of Newtown, navigating weekend traffic. Red is opening and closing the window, trying to figure out which way's cooler, Lori staring hard-eyed the other direction, pretending he's not there. Mada makes eyes at Zoe. Her response is to play with her window too: 'Window goes up, window goes down, window goes up, window goes down ...'

'You'll be surprised to hear that isn't helping.'

It's just gone midday. The air is sticky, filled with heat and hovering dust.

'Is the air-con up?'

'Yes Red, it's "up". That's the fan you can hear, because Zoe's music was, and I quote: "troubling the ulcer".'

'I can hear the fan all right, I just can't feel it. Point some of it back here, will you? Does it even blow air? Maybe it just makes noise. And I didn't know it was your music, Zoe.'

Zoe offers a noncommittal shrug. 'You could take your jacket off,' she adds helpfully.

'I haven't got room to pick my nose, let alone get my jacket off.'

Red leans forward from the back seat, straining to reach the dials around the lit-up green A/C on the dash.

'Stop it.' Mada slaps back his hand. 'It's up as high as it goes.'

Red slumps back in his seat, exhaling so everyone feels it. 'You should get rid of this shitbox.'

'So you said.'

'I mean it.'

'You said that too.'

'You could get out and walk.' Lori suggests. They're the first words she's said to him since they picked him up.

'You'd like that, wouldn't you?'

'Oh, yes!' Lori gazes through the glass, smiling wistfully, as though picturing him hotfooting it over the baking pavement, direction King Street. She exchanges a glance with Zoe and they both start to giggle.

Mada is counting the numbers down. 'Sixty-two, sixty, fifty-eight. This is it.'

'Thank Christ,' says Red. 'I've just gone medium-well.'

'Don't blaspheme,' says Lori.

Zoe turns to stare at her. 'When did you get religion, Lori?'

'I haven't *got* anything. Christ was into love, that's all. So am I.'

'I know it,' says Mada. He glances in the rearview and blows a kiss at his mum's reflection.

'If you're on such good terms with him, how about getting us a parking spot,' Red growls.

'He's not a valet,' Lori responds crisply.

Zoe snorts in laughter.

'Besides, apparently he's dead,' says Red, giving a nod to Zoe as if he wants her to know he's heard of Nietzsche, he's hip with the young cats.

'Maybe he lives!' Mada slows the car. 'There's a spot!'

It's tight, but he manages to wedge the car between a rusted white van and a fancy-looking Audi. Red untangles himself from the seat and stretches his back theatrically, ogling the Audi and taking off his jacket.

'You want to leave your jacket in the car?' asks Mada.

'Around here? This is Hugo Boss.'

'Suit yourself.'

There's no shade as they walk up the street to Paula's townhouse, heading into a stream of cars and exhaust. Red strides ahead, leaving Mada and Zoe with Lori, who only ever moves at her own pace and will not be hurried for love nor money.

'What number is it?' Red calls back.

'One fifty-eight.'

Red turns in at the house without a backward glance.

A bougainvillea vine flows purple over the wall, and Lori stops at the entrance to pick up a fallen blossom. She brings it close to her face, examining it minutely, then turns to beam at Zoe.

'Isn't it beautiful!' she says ecstatically, holding it forth.

Mada is peering uncertainly through Paula's door. It's wide open, flamenco guitar rhythms spilling into the street. It's not common for students to socialise at the homes of academic staff, and more or less unheard of to turn up with your family, but Mada's relationship with Paula has always been different. Zoe can see her talking with Red at the end of a long entry corridor. As Red meanders off, she turns to grin, as though detecting their gaze, beckoning them in with typical enthusiasm.

Mada walks through, submitting to Paula's effusive hug.

'I'm sorry to say my uncle invited himself along,' he tells her under his breath. 'He made a speech the other day about wanting to participate more actively in my development. I think that's how he put it. But I'm pretty sure the development that really interests him is the real estate deal going on at the uni. I take no responsibility for him.'

Paula stiffens, then shrugs. 'As I said, your family is my family. Don't worry so much. We'll have some drinks, listen to music, enjoy the sun. All will be well.'

She turns to Zoe. '*Guapa*, firecracker! It's good to see you.'

She walks them through to the back patio, where Red is chatting with Carlos, and plunges her hands into a tub of ice, pulling out two beers. She has a way, as Zoe said on the way over, of making you feel like an old friend the very first moment you meet her.

She takes Mada and Zoe by the arm. 'Come through. Carlos has had some news. We must lighten the mood.'

Carlos, the Venezuelan pharmacist Mada has been working with at the university, sits at a white plastic table, leaning back in his chair so it teeters on the edge of the garden, his long, wiry frame all sinew and bone. He's about Mada's age, perhaps a few years older, with tan skin, dark, deep-set eyes and jet-black hair. He flew to Australia, not long after Mada began at the university, and claimed status as a refugee, but the immigration department is not, as Paula puts it, inclined to be sympathetic. Zoe assumes that he is Paula's lover, although Mada hasn't said so. She must be close to twice his age, but Zoe has the feeling that this wouldn't much matter to either of them.

'Nice to see you, kangaroo,' Carlos says with a smile. He gives Mada a hug and extends a hand to Zoe, drawing her in and kissing her on both cheeks. His skin is firm, calloused. It reminds her of her father's hands, after a summer outside in the garden.

'Paula says you have some news on the application?'

'It went ... not so good. The Federal Court says the Australian government is right and that my claim isn't valid, for the little reasons of this and the little reasons of that. Despite the fact that a powerful idiot in my homeland seeks to kill me. I'm going to appeal, and if that fails, I'll be sent back to Venezuela.'

He grabs a handful of ice from within a mound of beer and tosses it into a glass, before half filling it with whisky and sliding it over to Red. 'Yes, they will be very interested in my return. Of course, it changes nothing for Paula. The dead old red is still her greatest love.'

'You are my greatest love, Carlos. And you know this.'

'Your other greatest love is who?' asks Zoe incredulous. 'You mean Chávez?'

'Perhaps he was, when he was alive.' Paula shrugs and sits at the table. 'Our destinies have always been linked. I was born in 1964 in Barinas, ten years to the day after Chávez, and just fifty kilometres from Sabaneta, Chávez's own birthplace. It's strange, but yes, there is some love. When his attempt at the coup failed in 1992, and he appeared on television, my father called out to me: '¡Ven! ¡Mira! Mira a este hombre, come and look at this man.' Like him, I was transfixed. And then, watching him on television in 2006, at the United Nations podium, waving away the stench of Bush's brimstone, I cannot deny he captivated me. "*Ayer estuvo el diablo aquí, en este mismo lugar, huele a azufre todavía, en esta mesa, donde me ha tocado hablar.* The devil was here ..."' She laughs loudly. 'The utter perfection of it. Not that I hated Bush so much, not so it got my blood up. It was more that, well, he was a man convinced that he was John Wayne in a slow-motion replay, that he ruled a world of goodies and baddies, and there was no question which side Venezuela was on. Yet within the corridors of power there was no choice but to shake his hand, to genuflect, to bow. But not Hugo Chávez. Not our commandant, nor my beloved Venezuela. He said what everyone was thinking: Bush is an idiot, he acts like he owns the world, enough is enough. What's more, he said it so elegantly, with such beautiful showmanship, quoting Chomsky right back at the American president. It was impossible not to fall in love.'

Carlos is shaking his head gravely. 'I've told her many times that her love of Chávez clouds her thinking, that it makes her incapable of seeing the signs of dictatorship, recognising that his economic policies have led to our country's collapse. But what is one to do,' he throws his arms out in mock angst, 'with a madwoman when she is in love?'

'Perhaps this is true. *Todo amor es la ceguera*,' says Paula. 'Love may sometimes be blindness, and our homeland is certainly a mess. *Los malandros* rule the streets after dark, the murder rate has climbed to a point of impossibility, and even Chávez's old supporters describe him as a kind of high diver, who climbed so far up the ideological tower he could no longer see the pool below. But politics and love aside, what's to be said when one can't buy bread, or toilet paper.'

'And yet the love remains,' laments Carlos.

'If you'd met him, you would understand.'

'You met Chávez?' asks Red.

'*Sí*. On three occasions.'

'What was he like?' Zoe wants to know.

'Ah, be careful, this is how it starts,' Carlos warns. 'So far, she's just been warming up.'

'I'll take my chances.'

'Like no man I ever met, before or since,' says Paula. 'My father introduced us. He was working at the university. He had lived among the Yanomami, you see, one of the larger indigenous tribes, and argued strongly for their autonomy, for a right to share in the wealth their land was creating, their right to protect the forest. He published widely, and Chávez was sympathetic. Venezuela's oil reserves are enormous, yet when Chávez came to power, the poverty rate was over fifty percent. I lived this madness every day: one of my father's colleagues lived in a tiny apartment with his wife and three children. Two of the children slept with their feet in a wardrobe; the doors were opened to let them stretch out, then closed when they had awoken and packed away their bedding for the day. This is not a joke. Meanwhile one of my father's old school friends lived with his family in eastern Caracas, in a palace. It had a billiards room and its own bowling alley; there were more bathrooms than you could count, and all the houses in his suburb were equally enormous. One drove towards them past machine-gun nests and a twenty-four-hour armed guard. Chávez attempted to change this.'

'And now his mob wants to kill Carlos?' says Red. 'What's he done to them?'

'Not his mob, no. Those who took over after his passing. Carlos can be decidedly lacking in diplomacy, and he offended the wrong people. In my homeland there are certain officials it is wise not to annoy.'

'I scarcely think you're the poster child for diplomacy,' comments Mada, 'after seeing you and Brandis the other day.'

'That fool? He has no real power, only the ability to make things tricky. I speak of the power over life and death.'

Zoe reaches for another beer, watching as Carlos tops up Red's whisky glass again.

Lori has been silent so far, contemplating her bougainvillea flower. She gives an abrupt jerk, glaring at Carlos. 'Tell me about it then. Venezuela. Your work on Huntington's.'

'Huntington's,' Carlos repeats gravely. '*El mal de San Vito*. The genetic marker you possess has an interesting history in my country.'

Paula picks up the story, taking over as she so often does. 'According to legend, it was a European sailor who visited our shores in the 1800s who first imparted the disease, leaving behind several children, and with them, the dubious gift of his genetic code. His apparent legacy was carried by a woman, probably his daughter, called Maria Concepción Soto, an appropriate name if ever there was one, who lived in one of the stilt villages on the shores of Lake Maracaibo. Maria Concepción founded a dynasty in excess of ten thousand people, many of whom carry the gene for San Vito, the largest single population of Huntington's in the world.

'Venezuela in the nineties was different. *Tal cual*, everything in our homeland was different then. To look back, we felt hopeful, rich in possibility. But this is another story. The villagers of Maracaibo gave a sample and returned to their lives on the lake. With the data, scientists were able to narrow down the location of the Huntington's gene. This discovery was a huge scientific breakthrough, not only in the search for a cure, but also for understanding genetic inheritance. After this, we could identify genes for Alzheimer's, dwarfism, cancer. Of course, the majority of research was carried on in better resourced locations around the world, and to this day those little fishing villages on the shores of Maracaibo, their populations mined for their DNA, carry on in poverty. When I have time to finish it, this will all be in my book. The definitive story. *El mal de San Vito*. It's living history. For ten years I've worked on it.'

'Are you going to give Mada the lead role?' asks Red.

Zoe glances at him, detecting the faintest slur. They haven't been there that long, but he's put away an impressive quantity of whisky.

Paula gives a light laugh. 'That's the big question, isn't it? What to put in; what to leave out. In the beginning, I thought that it might contain everything: those who fight, those who suffer, the medicine and the science. The research moves very fast, of course. We feel on the brink of a great discovery: a cure, perhaps, or a way to cheat the disease of death. But the more I write, the greater the gaps between the words. Just like the disease itself. It's there in the language of things. Huntington's is but a stutter at the top of chromosome four. But if the universe stutters, if the language of existence is misspoken, the consequences are very large. It may bring hope, it may bring death.'

'A stutter,' says Lori slowly. 'That's what they called it when I was last at the clinic. Chromosomes, you know, taking a bit of extra time to find their words. The order gets confused. Oh, how science loves to reduce things to letters.'

'Language is what we have,' says Paula.

'But it pretends we have an idea,' says Lori angrily. 'That we know this language of things. Pretends that we know what we're doing. Oh yes, we've a fine sense of how all those parts move about, don't you worry about a thing! We've made some blueprints, see? Like you've planned it yourselves. All you scientists. This is how you talk. Like you have all the answers. But you don't have *any* answers; you don't even have any good advice on how to get by, how not to go crazy when you see death coming towards you.'

'That's why it's so important to search,' says Mada, grabbing his mother's hands. 'And what do you expect us to do? You can't blame us for wanting to know.'

'I don't blame anyone,' says Lori huffily. 'Certainly not you. And not you either.' She glares at Paula, as though willing her to contradict. 'It makes me mad, that's all. The way they treat you. Like you're a problem that needs to be solved. Let's just get these letters arranged, get the order right. But I'm *not* a problem.' She turns to Mada. 'And neither are you. You're my boy and you're perfect.'

Mada flushes. 'Thanks, Mum.'

'I'm sorry if I offended you, Lori. That was not my intention.'

'Oh, it's not you, it's just … who was Huntington, anyway? Some American who put his name on something. Bloody rich Americans. They get my goat. All that privilege, huge cars.'

'It was the nineteenth century, Mum. Huntington was twenty when he published his observations on chorea. He outlined a pedigree, helped dispel myths that were practically medieval. And his car would have been pulled by a horse.'

'Oh, ha ha. But why do all these men have to put their names on things? I hate that name. It's got nothing to do with me. The disease was about long before him. *He's* got nothing to do with me. *Nothing!*' She juts out her jaw, her characteristic face of defiance.

Zoe can feel the corners of her mouth pulling into a grin, despite herself.

'Then what should we call it?' Mada asks lightly, stroking his mother's hand.

'I like the name Carlos gave; what was it again?'

'*El mal de San Vito*,' he responds sombrely. 'Saint Vitus's dance, as you say in English.'

'Saint Vitus is one of the Holy Helpers,' Lori says with slow determination. 'He protects against conditions of the nerves.'

'Just when I think you've been cured of your Catholicism,' Mada sighs.

'So how do you get from the saint to a disease?' asks Red, apparently following the discussion despite all the booze.

Paula lifts her head, as though smelling a scent on the air, the breeze of an old memory stirring. 'Poor Saint Vitus. I've no idea how that poor kid could have cured anything. According to Catholic myth the Romans killed him when he was just a boy. He was reputed to have healing powers and was taken to Rome to drive a demon from the emperor's son. He dutifully drives out the demon but won't renounce his Christian faith. So they boil off his skin.'

'Can't you just see it?' says Carlos. 'All the men gathered about the pot, calling: Dance, Vitus, dance. Humans can be the most revolting beasts.'

'And so he turned martyr and saint,' continues Paula. 'There's another explanation, though, for the dancing reference. In the Middle Ages, religious fanatics who survived the plague, or wanted to, would journey to St Vitus's shrine and dance about his statue. You can imagine how happy everyone was, can't you? Not being dead! Or not yet! They danced very enthusiastically, their movements jerky and uncoordinated, a little like the chorea.' She blinks, gives Lori an uncertain smile. 'It was not a very nice time to be alive, so this would have been a mixed blessing. Half of Europe lost to the fleas found on rats. There must have been great merriment, dodging the fleas' bullet. And so dance becomes malady and celebration. People dancing about a statue until they are cured, or until everyone dances beyond the realm where there is a difference.'

Lori sighs, leans back in her chair, swirling the remnants of beer about in her bottle and tilting back her head to drain it off.

'It was so long ago, but it makes me sad,' she says. 'Names matter. It matters what is true. That old name has more history in it. It's not about graphs and numbers.'

'Yes,' says Zoe, smiling at her.

She finds Paula's account weirdly comforting. Not that she hasn't heard some of it before, but it makes her feel closer to Mada somehow, as if their research braids them into a long tradition, strengthening the tendrils between a universe of truth and that fragile thing called knowledge.

Two hours in, and Mada is starting to think that his paranoia about Uncle Red sending the day pear-shaped is misfounded, though he's watched Carlos and Paula pour near on a bottle of Scotch over ice into Red's glass. Zoe, Lori and Paula, mostly Paula, are the ones who haven't stopped raving. For his part, Red appears deeply appreciative, offering Carlos an increasingly derailed detailing of Sydney's real estate market: a transaction that Carlos absorbs with unreadable silence. The food is finished – steak with patatas bravas and salad, then *quesillo*, a kind of Venezuelan flan – and Mada is contemplating the best way to navigate Red and Lori back out the door, when it all starts.

Mada has gone off to use the bathroom, and he's slowly making his way back through Paula's lounge room, via a wall of photos she has Blu-Tacked to the paint, when a note of panic in Red's voice alarms in his ears.

'Jesus, mate, don't give her any of that. She'll be a loon the whole drive home.'

'You've no say in what I do, Redmond. Not now, not ever,' comes Lori's retort.

Mada stares through the door. Lori is defiantly lifting her chin at Red, who's half out of his seat. Carlos holds an enormous smouldering joint in Lori's direction, and Red, more than two-thirds sideways, is attempting to intercept it. Even from the screen door, the pungent funk is overpowering. Carlos, holding out the smouldering stick respectfully yet forcefully beyond Red's reach, is gazing at him impassively. Lori has no interest in being thwarted. She lumbers around Red, pushing him hard so he falls heavily into his chair, and sits on Carlos's far side where she's half-hidden in the ferns, deep in the corner of the garden. She takes the joint from his fingers, nodding appreciatively, then, placing it between her lips, she inhales deeply, beaming an enormous smile at Carlos. She inhales again, a waft of smoke flowing from her nostrils and drifting into the foliage.

'Two is enough to start,' Carlos says sombrely, gesturing for her to pass it on. 'It's quite strong, I never mix tobacco and herb, and if you're not used to it, after the beer …'

Lori holds the joint out to Mada, who waves it away with a grimace. 'No thank you, Mother,' he says, irony restrained.

Her smile reverses incrementally. 'Sometimes I wonder if you really are my son.'

'I'm only taking your word for it, but I figure you'd remember.'

'Very sensible.' Red folds his arms, nodding sagely.

Mada has a near irrepressible urge to take the stinking baton from Carlos, blast out into another headspace, but weed doesn't transport him anywhere but to some paranoid interiority, plus there's the drive home. He could almost do it though, if only to get up Red's nose, no matter how much he hates the stuff. But his one and a half beers already have his head spinning.

'I'll bite,' says Zoe. She squeezes his shoulder and reaches out.

Lori passes her the joint, and she takes it and draws in the smoke. After each inhalation, she lays back her head and exhales a rich cloud – once, twice, three times – then raises her brows wickedly to Carlos before holding it out vaguely.

'Where did this come from?' asks Paula. She takes the joint and inhales a perfunctory gasp, an apparent act of solidarity more than anything else, just to clarify that she sides with the libertines.

'Ronny and George,' Carlos says. Then, calmly to Red, by way of explanation: 'The two homosexual gentlemen who recently moved in next door. I was out here, cleaning things up for this afternoon, and they asked me in for a drink, said a friend of theirs in Wollongong has a green thumb. I told them about my research, and they promised to make introductions. Their friend is apparently quite the aficionado, and those two were most generous.'

'I bet they were. I'm sure they would have quite enjoyed your company. They don't waste any time, do they?'

'I like them. Time is life. To waste it is a crime.'

'And this from a stoner,' shoots out Red irritably. He's still sitting with his arms firmly folded, as though cementing himself as the only sensible person at the table. Mada is pretty sure that it's less the weed that has him annoyed than Lori's flouting of his will. That, and the fact that he has tried to turn the conversation around to the property endowment several times, but Paula refuses to be drawn.

'Time spent in contemplation of the universal mysteries is never wasted,' offers Carlos gravely.

Zoe is standing behind Mada and running her hands through his hair, clearly high; he can tell by how deep she is in her task. It feels divine. The perfect smooth-sharpness of her fingernails dragging over his scalp. He reaches a hand behind him and grips her calf.

'My favourite president of the United States was a stoner,' Zoe says airily. 'Scarcely a wasted life.'

'Contemplation of your navel, more like,' growls Red, jolting Mada out. 'I mean, how much did he get done?'

'I think we can blame the Republicans for that,' Carlos says irritably. 'He is a day in office and they don their sheets and light their crosses and pull tall their hoods, chanting that this nigger won't—'

'Carlos, please,' says Paula.

'Healthcare reform isn't *nuthin*',' says Zoe seriously. 'Not in America.'

'Please, let us not talk politics,' insists Paula. 'I am so very tired of it since that orange buffoon.'

'Aren't we all. Enough!' Carlos turns to each of them, grinning. 'Let us talk of this meeting across continents. Two hours ago, Zoe was but a name. One year ago, Mada and I had never met. And now we are friends. Good friends. This feels like the beginning of something, yes? A grand adventure! You should come to Venezuela, Mada, once we have resolved my *little problem* and the country is back on its feet. We do good work there, we could benefit from your knowledge, and you from ours.'

'No he bloody shouldn't,' says Zoe.

Her fingernails dig into Mada's scalp.

'Ouch.'

'Sorry, babe.'

'But the times we could have,' says Carlos. 'Oh the times!' He rhapsodises over his homeland: the sunshine, the people, the mountains, the jungle. As Carlos talks, Lori pushes back her chair, so she's right in the garden, taking the last of the sun. She peels off her white T-shirt and lays it over the back of the chair, lazing in her seat and fanning herself with a beer coaster. She's not wearing a bra, having abandoned them years ago, as she's fond of saying, and her breasts hang, wrinkly and small-nippled, pale blue veins translucent in the sun. She takes a long draft of beer. 'That's better,' she says.

'For god's sake, Mum, put your top back on,' says Mada.

'No.' She sulks at him. 'It's too hot.'

Carlos gives a generous laugh. 'There. You see! Now we are closer still!'

Red is so flushed his face is glowing. He stands, pushes his chair back so it tips into the garden, and throws down the last of his drink. 'Okay, now we're going. Get your clothes on, Lori, or you can bloody walk home.'

'Oh, piss off Redmon,' she says. 'You've got no say in what I do. I told you that.'

'It's only flesh,' says Paula gently. 'We're all made of the same stuff.'

'Yeah, Red, take a seat,' says Zoe. 'It's all good.'

'No, it is not *all good*,' Red retorts. 'It is most certainly not all good. None of it is good, let alone *all*.' He glares at each of them in turn. 'I'll take a cab.' He spins on his heel and strides through the house, slamming the front door behind him.

'*Qué lástima*,' says Carlos, his face inscrutable. 'Such a pity. Now, who needs a drink?'

Min Fang

Chapter 9

The first time Red meets Min Fang Boucher, she is dressed in flowing red silk, and looks every aspect of Angelo's description of her; Angelo, who insists on calling her the Sorceress Min Fang. She really could be a sorceress, thinks Red, watching as she unfolds herself from the seat of the Jaguar. If Angelo's mythologising is correct, Min Fang is the love child of a French diplomat and the heir of one of Hong Kong's big four families, but whatever the truth of the rumours, Red can't take his eyes off her. Her hair is straight and black and long, her eyes piercing bright green – Angelo had told him about that part. What's more, at this very moment, those eyes lock on Red's across the carpark, and will not let him go.

This, and they are yet to meet, yet to exchange a word.

Min Fang Boucher lifts her golf clubs from the boot, lightly hefting a black bag of crocodile hide that looks like it would cost a Sydney mortgage. She gives a mischievous grin and steps in his direction. As she strides his way, she doesn't deign to glance at the white SUV bearing down on her, driving too fast into the carpark, and it comes sharp around the bend to jump on the brakes. There's the rip of gravel and rubber, but Min Fang keeps walking, eyes front. At some indeterminate point since she stepped from the Jag, Red lost the power to breathe. Min Fang is like destiny come calling, and Red can't look away.

The Sorceress Min Fang.

Angelo had bestowed her title as though it were official. His Holiness the Dalai Lama; Her Majesty the Queen; the Sorceress Min Fang. The two of them were on the far side of the seventh green last Friday when Angelo brought her up, convincing Red that he had to meet her, no question at all. And, even stranger, that this was the place to do it.

It was their regular Friday-afternoon round, and Red was crowing over two plum properties, the sale of which had just fallen into his lap through an old school mate, complaining that he was unlikely to clear more than four point five mill for each, and how there was no word on what was going to happen with the university land. The wet blanket greenies were fighting the sale, and now it looked like it'd be dragged through the courts.

'The two new places are perfect for the foreign market, but I'm not getting any traction with the big end of Asia-town,' moaned Red. 'They're about, but they won't cough up. I've been putting ads in the Chinese papers. Even got a new Chinese secretary.'

'That receptionist of yours?' Angelo asked.

'Yeah.'

'Think she's Thai.'

'Close enough.'

Angelo snorted, shaking his head. 'And you wonder why you're not getting traction?'

Red shrugged. Truth be told, he resented having to know one Asian country from another. It wasn't geography exactly. More that the whole idea of 'Australasia' had him baffled, and as far as Red was concerned, anything he couldn't understand wasn't worth knowing. Red liked everything to be tucked in its box, impossible for him to confuse.

'The high-net-worth Chinese can be tricky,' Angelo went on. 'You need to get the right introductions. Actually, what you need,' he paused for effect here, 'is the Sorceress Min Fang.'

Red looked at him blankly.

'She's in town at the moment. I'll see if she can come for a round next week. I can bring my office manager too. She's a pretty keen golfer, though not in the same league as Min Fang Boucher.'

'Why ruin a good day? Golfing with women is annoying. You know how it goes when Rodger brings his wife. Sophie? Cindy?'

'Susan,' Angelo said, wagging a finger. 'Golfing with Susan is a pain in the arse because Susan is a pain in the arse. Golfing with you is a pain in the arse,' he paused again, poking Red in the chest, 'when you are being a pain in the arse. Like now.' He sighed, before conspiratorially taking Red by the arm. 'Look, it won't be the same with Min. I tell you: I had a round with her on Tuesday. She was three under me. And I was having a good day. A very good day. She drove the fifth clear onto the green.

No shit. On *that* fairway. We've never played a round that she didn't break eighty-five, and she's only about five foot tall. Jesus, I don't even remember her playing much over eighty.'

'That's even worse,' Red protested. 'She kicks my butt, it'll send my ulcer septic.'

'The hell with your ulcer. You want to get maximum payload on those big sales or not? She knows the Chinese end of the market like Sydney Harbour runs into Kowloon Bay. Seriously. I took her out after golf one night. Don't get me wrong, I was the perfect gentleman. Just business. I play with a straight club these days, and I dropped her home and on I went. A week later I had half a dozen orders fall into my lap.'

'From her?'

'No. Just … people she sent my way. A politician I'd seen on TV. Rich Asians. Some bloke from the US consulate. Well-dressed types. And that's just the cars. She's a property lawyer and registered accountant. Looks through national borders like they don't exist. All the leftie wankers complaining how Sydney's unaffordable? How another big correction's coming? What about the young people, what about the homeless, boo-fucking-hoo? Well, she thinks Sydney is *undervalued*. I've got a buddy who helped her with some stuff in Queensland, says her mediation on the upper-end stuff is magic.'

'That *is* what I need,' Red allowed hesitantly.

'You bet your arse it is.' Angelo grinned at him. 'It's her client base that matters. Her fees are astronomical, but she'll earn them. Oh yeah. Just meet her and you'll see.'

Red hesitated at the mention of fees: 'Angelo …'

But his mate wasn't going to let it go.

'Trust me,' he said, 'she's worth it. There's just one thing: don't take her for a ride. She's connected. Big end of town. Maybe triads. Who knows?' He shrugged. 'Party officials for sure. She knows everyone, and I mean everyone. Both sides of the table. She's on the level, though; you'll see. Now fucken listen to me, Redmond, be *polite*. Not only is she connected, she's a friend.'

'Aren't I always?'

Angelo didn't answer.

In the end, Red consented. He trusted Angelo's judgment in just about everything. Trusted it better than he trusted his own these days, which, truth be told, wasn't saying all that much. So he let Angelo line up a meeting – a foursome on the course; casual, a good chance to talk.

Only now, after a decade of golfing together, it's the first day Angelo has ever stood him up. There is a text message: *can't make it. enjoy the Sorceress* ;), and when Red calls him, Angelo won't answer. Angelo's text has only just come in, and Red is considering pulling the pin himself, but then he catches her eyes across the carpark.

And that's that. Red is bolted to the spot. There's no way he can run now: no way he would want to.

It's as she crosses in front of the white SUV, her red garment billowing in the wind, that Red realises she isn't wearing robes but a jumpsuit, the westerly breeze on silk highlighting her body's perfect topography, the fabric's sheen gifting valleys and hollows in the dry summer wind. The sun is out and full and blinding, and Red blinks in astonishment at the smile she gives him as she strides across the asphalt.

'Hello,' she says, taking his hand in her firm grip. 'You must be Redmond. My name is Min Fang.'

Sure enough, it's a terrific round. Red breaks eighty-five, and Min Fang finishes up four over par. He's not sure how much of it is her smooth client relations act, but she's laughing at his jokes, and telling some of her own, and revealing a sense of humour that's as crude and more fearless than Red's. She doesn't seem to possess any cultural loyalties, so she's mouthing off about conservative local Chinese matriarchs and in the same breath eviscerating Pauline Hanson and her moronic deep-north bogan horde. At Angelo's suggestion, Red lets Min Fang steer the conversation, and they talk about everything but work until the golf is done and they're back at the carpark. Then she fixes him with a steely gaze, as though weighing him up and deciding that she can trust him.

'Okay, Redmond, let's introduce you to some of my associates. I'll call you mid next week and we'll go from there.'

And with that she shakes his hand, her grip sure and firm, and walks to her car, leaving Red with a sensation between arousal and awe. It's easily the best day he's had since Bea went inside, and there's a chance it will help him get rich enough to finally make him happy. He's desperate for more capital for the new place he's bought in Glebe. It was too good to pass up, but the repayments are killing him. She turns to give him another wave as she slips into the Jag, clearly relishing the impact she's made, and Red realises he hasn't moved an inch since she shook his hand in farewell.

True to her word, Min Fang calls him Wednesday morning, at nine o'clock precisely. They play a few rounds over the subsequent weeks, the conversation slowly moving into property sales, until she feels like a long-lost sister. Not that she hasn't got him hard as a club, but it's all strictly professional. Red enjoys her company more than he has any soul these past months. She's smart and sassy and sexy as hell, and Red is smitten. And if that isn't enough, he golfs better whenever she plays the round.

To Glimpse the Future

Chapter 10

Mada asks to meet Lori at the corner café, the one near her apartment, 'good coffee' the excuse, but really he wants to make sure she's getting out, that she is still capable of navigating the streets. When he comes by with groceries, she always seems to be in the same place, moulding clay at her dining table, as though she doesn't move, even to sleep.

It's funny how he still considers his mother more of a sibling; it's his aunt who's played parent most of his life. Mada remembers clearly being a teenager out on the town one night, arrested for using false ID. He'd been trying to get into a Manly pub, where his friends, all over the legal age of eighteen by a minimum of two and a half weeks, were getting drunk with the clumsy enthusiasm that being newly legal engenders. As Mada was only a few months shy of his birthday, and in a new high school where there was pressure to find a place, he was keen to join them. But his status as 'almost legal' mattered not one iota so far as the law was concerned, and after the bouncer clocked him he was dragged to the cop shop at three in the morning, where he was asked to supply a phone number for his parent or guardian, and required to wait until they came to collect him.

It was Bea's phone number he had given the cops that night, Bea who had taken the call then picked him up in her tracksuit, Bea who had listened in silence as the cops lectured her on parental responsibility. Then she drove Mada home in equal silence, apparently annoyed she'd been dragged from her bed, but otherwise approaching it as though he'd been picked up for nothing more serious than his ill-fitting pants. She made no comment regarding Mada's desire to call her, rather than his mother, just as she made none about the myriad other ways in which she had played parent.

Bea took on this responsibility with the same stoicism that characterised so many of her actions: because *of course* it was Bea whom Mada had called. What choice had there been? The image of his mother turning up to collect him had reduced him to stammering when the officer demanded the phone number of a parent. What endless possibilities might arrive with Lori passing through the station doors? She might stroll in shoeless, oblivious and obviously naked under her silk coat, having walked from bed to a taxi without a moment's thought. She would be just as likely to end up getting stuck into the cops herself, calling them a bunch of fascist storm-troopers, and none of it ending well.

Even in the best circumstances, it was impossible to so much as leave the house with his mother and not have some unexpected encounter. He never knew when it would come:

on the street, in the supermarket, stopped at traffic lights. Abruptly she would be off, pontificating with a staff member at the checkout while the woman's eyes shifted awkwardly to the growing line behind her, or taking umbrage at a policeman whose manners she found boorish.

There was a period, before Mada started high school, not long after his grandpa died, when the two of them moved out of Bea's place in Glebe for a second-floor walk-up rental in a huge old Stanmore terrace, right by the train station. They all needed to escape each other for a while – even at age ten Mada could tell as much. She wasn't up to looking after him, and he certainly wasn't up to looking after her, but nothing Bea could say would dissuade her. Their apartment was directly overlooking the tracks, and Mada would lie on his bed and stare out over the tall brick wall that separated the road from the rails, watching the trains hammer past. Lori was insistent she could manage on her own, that she was going to home-school Mada, complete his education 'in the world'. Bea had forbidden it of course, but since when had that made a difference? What followed were months of boarding trains and buses, hitchhiking, meandering up the coast, going to museums – anywhere Lori's whim might direct them. Of course she would rarely purchase a ticket, so inevitably there would be an altercation at some point. His mother felt entitled to go anywhere, talk to anyone, do what she wanted. After all, it was their world too. That was the thing, what Huntington's did – there was no filter, no sense of impropriety, nothing, so far as Mada could see, that resembled regret. Or at least part of it was the Huntington's. The other part was pure Lori.

So of course he proffered Bea's mobile phone number in the police station that night. Not the home number for his aunt and uncle. Certainly not Lori's phone. Should his mother have turned up, the best-case scenario – itself nothing to wish for – would be that she was just her usual self, and would be so vague before the law they could easily take it for disrespect, which, in many ways, it was.

This is the way his family has always been. Nothing quite fits.

He's waiting at the café table some twenty-five minutes before Lori arrives. Finally he sees her ambling along, Henrietta trotting beside her on the thin pink leash that Mada purchased, once he'd resigned himself to the dog's continued presence.

'Darling.'

'Hi, Mum. How's it going?'

'Oh, well …'

He gives her a tight hug. There's not much fat on her ribs. Lori ties the dog to a chair and sits down beside him. Still, she looks pretty good. Better than she has for much of the year. Mada orders coffee; Lori goes for tea. The dachshund offers an uncertain bark at a Great Dane across the street. 'Now, now, Pepita, what are you even trying to say there, you'd be swallowed in a gallop,' Lori murmurs.

Henrietta glances up at her, chagrined, much to Mada's surprise. Lori picks her up, scratching behind an ear while the dog stares off with a zoned-out, satisfied air. The waitress places their order on the table.

'What's so important that you bring me down from my tower?' Lori sips her tea, a crease touching her brow, her attention on the dog.

'Just wanted to see you, Mum.'

'Yes? What's wrong with coming up?'

'Well, it's nice to get out. You know how it is. We've all got a bit cooped up lately.'

'I haven't,' Lori says defiantly. She tilts her head back, takes a swaying perusal of him. 'How's everything at work? You okay?' She removes a set of circular reading glasses from her pocket and fits them on her face, eyeing Mada beadily.

'Are you eating enough?' She leans in to poke at his ribs.

'I'm fine, Mum, give it a break.'

'Are you sure? You look … pale.'

'I'm fine.'

'And work?'

Mada sighs. He can give her this one. 'I've been teaching a lot. There's a lot of admin, and it pays twice as well to wait tables. I'm tired, that's all. Isn't everyone these days?'

'What are you going to do when you finally finish all this? The fabled thesis?'

'I don't know. Look for a job. Maybe aim for a postdoc.'

'Post. Doc.' She separates out the syllables. 'What does that mean?'

'A few more years of study, I guess.'

'More study? Is that wise? You should spend more time living, less time staring at books. Life has its own lessons. You don't need to be reading all the time.'

'Thanks, Mum. Your advice is always helpful.'

She straightens in her chair, visibly miffed. 'Don't be like that.'

'Well, you put the first book in my hand. Do you want to take that back?'

'Don't be silly. It's just … are you sure it won't be too much work? That's all I mean.'

Mada feels the corners of his mouth twitch, and he gives her elbow a squeeze. 'I don't think so.'

'You must know an awful lot by now.'

'Well, the thing is, there's always more to know.'

'That's the problem. Nothing ever *is* enough. You've always been like that – just like Bea – always focused on the moment to come. Ever since you were a little boy.'

This insight annoys him all the more because it's true. Every time he sees his mother, regardless of how protective or paternal it makes him, some other part turns back into a kid. It wouldn't matter so much, but right now things feel fragile. The PhD is inside his nerves, from his torso down to his toes, taut and stretching and pulling uncomfortably every time he moves or thinks. The more he discovers of the body, its states and the agents acting upon it, the less certain he feels in his knowledge. Even the victories feel like this – last month, for instance, with his name as co-author on a paper he'd helped massage towards publication with Paula, he couldn't help, on re-reading, but be drawn to the places where it could have been sharper, where he might have pulled a little extra from the data if he had taken more time. No matter how much he devotes himself to cold hard fact, there remains a place where the pharmacological maths does not add up, where, for example, the substance might work, but not in the way expected. In so much of the terrain he navigates, there are functional mechanisms that are not understood, places where a splinter of the indivisible prevails.

Mada swallows his retort and lets her talk. The sun catches her hair, shining in the grey threads. She really does seem better. Not just her mood, but her focus. As if a cloud has lifted. Yet even as the thought comes to him, he has to remind himself that he can't rely on it, that his mum's capacities are always sporadic, gifts she might bestow or be bestowed with, rather than an attitude he can depend on.

One part savant and one part child. She seems to sense his mood and stops talking to gaze at him, then, holding her arms wide for a seated hug, she smiles. 'You're enough,' she says. 'When will it be enough for you?'

Mada succumbs, and she nuzzles her face into his chest.

'When I find a cure,' says Mada eventually. 'Then it will be enough.'

'How did I get so lucky? How come you grew up so beautiful and clever?'

'Good karma I'd say, Mum.'

'That must be it. I bet you're great at teaching.'

'I have my moments.'

'I bet the girls like you.'

'Maybe,' Mada squirms.

'Be careful, they'll fall in love with you,' she offers knowingly. 'I used to adore school, Tuesdays and Fridays, with Mr Linn. He was my art teacher.'

'Yes. I think you mentioned him.'

'He had the most wonderful brown eyes. All the girls were in love with him. Boys too, some of them. His hair was very long and very black. It came halfway down to his waist, and at the start of each class he would secure it in a ponytail to keep it from getting full of paint. He was an actor, too. He took drama classes.'

'Were you in love with him as well?'

'Oh, certainly, everyone was, but he would always give me top marks ...'

Her face turns cagey a moment, then impish, like a naughty child caught in the act. Very softly, she starts to hum.

Mada pushes back his chair and goes to stand, not to leave but out of restlessness, before stopping himself and leaning closer towards her. 'There's something else, Mum. I'm going to the clinic to get the test tomorrow. For Huntington's.'

Lori's face goes bright red. 'Why? What for? It's not you, you're not—' Her words tumble out all at once. 'You don't have it. You're my boy. My boy. You don't have it. I've always known you don't.'

'It's okay, calm down, Mum. I'm going to talk with them, that's all.'

'If they think you've got it, they take things away.'

'I only need to talk with them.'

'They do!' She scowls at him angrily. A bus squeals to a stop on the street beside them. Lori starts, then brings her attention back to Mada, a crestfallen look on her face. 'It seems such a small thing, doesn't it? The little parts inside you, the letters that spell out the self, how they could be all messed up.' She takes his hand, running her finger along a line in his palm, gazing at it.

Mada stares down at her blue veins and fine, thin tendons, her pale fingers over his tanned flesh. Those hands he knows so well.

'Are you sure about this?' she asks eventually. 'The testing. What's the point? Once you know, you can't take it back. It changes things ...' She trails off.

'I've put it off forever, Mum, and not knowing is killing me,' Mada says.

'You think it is. You think not knowing must be the worst. But it's not. Knowing is worse. Knowing, and watching it seep away. As if it's not even you that's changing. But it is, and you can feel it, but you don't. Because it's you, it's always you. Do you really want to glimpse the future? What's the point of testing if there isn't any cure?'

'Because I feel it hanging over my head. Every day. I wake up and it's what I think about. It's eating me away.'

'Well it shouldn't!' Lori says indignantly. 'I'm sure you don't have it. I just know it. And anyway, you were telling me just the other day about how close we are, all that research you're so proud of.'

'I thought you were suspicious of all that science.' Mada grins at her, putting air quotes around 'science'.

'I think it has its models wrong,' Lori retorts. 'That it gives up the living world, puts everything in compartments. Categorised, organised. But only dead things can be slotted away.'

'Well, I may not be dead, but I do want my genetic status slotted away,' says Mada with determination. He wipes his hands, as though to wipe away the stain of disease.

The river is visible from where they sit, glinting between two apartment blocks down the end of the road. They watch as a bus stops at the kerb on the far side of the street. An old man in a suit makes his way slowly down the aisle, disappearing from view as he descends the steps, and reappearing as the bus roars off. He moves with deliberate steps along the footpath, one foot, the next, an umbrella under his arm although the day is clear and deeply blue.

Lori turns back to Mada. 'I've seen him before,' she says. 'Lots of times. He seems so sad. I tried talking to him, asking him about himself, but he stepped around me and kept on walking. You know, I've always loved how busy it is here. The activity on the streets. Every day something new. Now it seems I watch the same thing over and over. The same people going up and down. The same buses. Cars. The sound of the buses used to put me to sleep. Can you believe it? Now I spend the night with my eyes glued to the ceiling, watching the headlights. They run half the night, you know. All the way across the bridge, coming back up, all the time. I've no idea who catches a bus at two in the morning, but the world is full of so many people, and they're all so busy, it must be someone.'

She sighs. 'You do what you must, my darling. All I'm saying is, once you know, once you find out … you can't take it back.'

The next day, Mada makes his way west down the motorway, his heart wrapped tight. Parking is a mess. It always is at Westmead Hospital. The traffic into the parking station is banked across the road, and no one is going anywhere. He does a U-turn before he gets jammed in, and drives on down the street. There are cars hanging off kerbs, wedged between trees up the roadside. Even the spots that aren't real spots are taken. Mada does another U-turn and drives a kilometre down the road from the hospital, pulling over outside a block of apartments. The sign reads 'No Standing', but it will have to do.

By the time he has made his way to the Huntington's disease unit, Mada is irritable and sweating, cursing the government, cursing himself, cursing the gods of resource allocation. What is he even doing here? His mother is right. What is the use of a diagnosis for a disease that has no cure? Just to know? Is that worth it? It's genetic, it's not as if he can give it to anyone casually. And what if it's positive: it's better *not* to know than to sit around waiting for death to arrive, no fraction of a doubt. Mada takes a series of deep breaths, then walks through the glass doors and into the antiseptic cool.

The waiting room is horrifyingly similar to every other medical office he's been in: stacks of ratty magazines, the place lit with the overbright whiteness of banked ceiling fluorescents. The plastic chairs are mostly empty. In one corner of the room, a man and a woman sit either side of a young boy. He's shifting about in his chair, not in a way that is obviously symptomatic, but fidgety, restless. The resigned sorrow on the face of the woman makes Mada look away, and he goes over to the admissions area and gives his name and details through a window to a man in a blue uniform. Down the corridor to his left, a woman is moving jerkily through the door to the toilet. Saint Vitus's dance, thinks Mada: a dance so exhausting it will carry on and on … until it stops.

An answer, he thinks. If only I can find an answer.

A woman comes out and introduces herself. Carol, she says. She's wearing a lab coat over a homespun jumper, something her gran might have knitted, though she's a good way towards gran vintage herself. Maybe she's the knitter, thinks Mada. The colours are a terrible knot of pinks and oranges, not seventies cool, more like the seventies threw up a ball of yarn, and Mada is staring at the jumper, feeling nervous and annoyed, until he realises he's staring at the rounded curves of her boobs beneath the wool, and, embarrassed, he lifts his gaze to her eyes and says hello again, although he's already greeted her, trying not to stare at her chest, even though the jumper is pulling at his eyes.

He follows her down a corridor and into a room with more plastic furniture, with posters on the wall depicting couples and groups of people, mostly smiling, some in wheelchairs and, according to the advertising copy, they are all 'living with their disease', and although he knows this is intended to be optimistic, intended to make him feel he has a future, that he too can live, regardless of the result, he feels a jagged shard of anger working its way from his chest to his throat, and he thinks: I don't want to live with a disease.

Mada feels as if he's waited his whole life for the numbness to start. Every time he drops something, performs an act of clumsiness – is this the mark of neurones dying, is this the disease making itself known? He remembers clearly the day Bea was sentenced and how he was sure he could feel it coming: numbness moving over his body. Bea, his surrogate mother, on her way to prison. Her face had been drained of blood, drained of its usual cynicism, its dark humour, drained of everything he knew so there was only her mouth half-open, moving feebly, and some sudden slackness came over him, a numbness moving up from his feet. He only had to sit there and not move and eventually he would cease to be and it wouldn't hurt anymore, sit there until the past changed, until it was no longer true or else it ceased to matter. She got one last look at him as they led her out. Her lips mouthing words but he couldn't make them out and no sound carried to where he sat. Then she was gone. The numbness moving out from his spine and down into his arms, cold, terrifying.

Carol sits across from him, a smile on her face of practised neutrality, as if there is nowhere she would rather be, and in looking at that smile Mada has to stop himself from standing up and walking out to where his car is parked, illegally, a kilometre away, driving home and forgetting the whole thing. But inside his head a cascade of questions turns over and over in a continual wash. If the gene is present, how long will he have before things fall apart? Onset can vary wildly in Huntington's. And how will Zoe cope? He would have to break up with her immediately: there's no way he'd expect her to endure his shuddering deterioration.

A morbid slide show plays through Mada's head: he's standing at the Gap, looking over the cliff edge to the water churning white, trying to muster the courage to leap; or maybe pills, booze, and massive organ failure: a slower but less terrifying choice; or sitting in the car, listening to music, while a hose connected to the exhaust pumps carbon monoxide through the window. And this prompts a new line of thought, for what *would* be the ideal music to do yourself in? Arcade Fire? The Strokes? And then, like a shard of genius, the idea of Philip Glass comes to him, and the morbidly romantic image digs into his mind: sitting in the car with *Koyaanisqatsi* blasting from the stereo, engine purring gently. He could turn it up as loud as he wanted. No need to worry about hearing loss. No need to save the battery with the engine going the whole time, purring away until the fuel runs out. But as to that, why look so far from home? Nick Cave is the man: who runs the edge of beauty and death more than the Prince of Darkness?

Carol watches him, silent in the face of his unspoken litany of anxiety and potential endings, and when she judges he is ready to begin, she talks through the process ahead. She explains to him the stages of testing, discusses the implications of the results.

Mada nods.

She looks at her notes and talks about what he's studying, acknowledges that he must know a great deal about the disease already, and he nods again. She deploys terminology very precisely, as though within it there is a kind of safety: a clinical fact, distant from muscle spasms and premature mortality. Test results offer no indication of when symptoms can first appear, she reminds him, even though research is advancing in this area, and there have been some promising developments of late. She reiterates that Mada probably knows all this as well as she does, but all the same she must tell him. If he wishes to continue with the process, they can fit him in for a blood test the following month and begin the task of finding out.

Yes, he says eventually. He agrees to the blood test. He recognises that he can choose *not* to be given the results, that he has this opportunity right up until the moment they are given to him, but that once he has them, once he has read them, he cannot un-know what he has learned. As he watches her talk, her title plays itself out in his head: *genetic counsellor*. He imagines her, in her woollen jumper, talking with the same calm compassion to a circled group of genes. Inviting them to share their feelings.

Explaining the difficulties and risks. In his mind, the genes have the amorphous shapes of single-celled organisms, and chatter in small, munchkin voices. They babble an endless flow of letters *a c t g a c t g a c t g a c t g a c t g* tickertape repetitions, chattering out long spools through blobbish, shapeless mouths.

Back on the motorway, he briefly considers not going in to the uni, giving himself the chance to go home and defrag, but there are still a few hours left in the day and the guilt would be too much. Brandis has been poking around all week, he and Paula discarding all pretence of civility and openly insulting one another. To make matters worse, rather than giving the university more options, the widow's endowment has become a source of conflict, with open disagreement about how the land should be used. As far as Brandis is concerned, the university needs money more than space: buildings can always be made taller, so if it's merely a question of floor space, just build up. The fact that selling off the land conflicts with the widow's bequest is of little interest to him: the university has its own charter, its own necessities, and it 'will not be dictated to by a dead old woman'.

'Charming,' Paula had responded.

Obviously Mada hasn't said a word to the dean about Red's request to be involved in any sale.

He heads past the airport, taking the eastern suburbs exit. He can't stay away, and right now the only thing for it is to lose himself in work. He steers the Toyota into the parking area, grabs his pack, and heads for the library, but he's on his way across the courtyard when he sees Carlos ahead of him, sauntering in the direction of the science faculty.

'Carlos!'

The tall Venezuelan stops and turns, surveying Mada with an air of expectation. 'Paula told you?'

'Told me what?'

'I went down to Wollongong: the first crop is ready. And the vine arrived from my friend in Peru. We've booked one of the labs.'

An ominous feeling moves up Mada's spine.

'The vine isn't *Banisteriopsis caapi*?' he asks tentatively. But he knows it is. Carlos has talked of little else but this essential component of ayahuasca for weeks.

'Yes.'

'If customs intercepted that—' begins Mada.

'But they didn't, and now we will learn,' Carlos responds shortly, setting off again in the direction of the labs.

Mada groans, staring at the Venezuelan's departing back. Eventually, he follows. Carlos's determination to find a plant-based anti-spasmodic, 'something simple, a tincture, that villagers can produce themselves', has already been the cause of several clashes with the administration. Mada's not sure if he has the strength for another dust-up should Brandis or one of the other less sympathetic professors stumble across them: he doesn't even want to imagine what would happen should the bad-tempered bureaucrat get wind of them assaying cannabis, let alone ayahuasca. He was bad enough when he heard they had a set of calendula studies lined up.

With Mada slugging his way down a long dead end with his own research, he's decided to invest some time in these experiments with Carlos, not because he believes in them, at least that's what he tells himself; more because he likes his company. The loud and endless running-down of the value of Paula's and Carlos's research, which Brandis broadcasts at every opportunity, is finding its mark: whole plant remedies simply have too many compounds and variables affecting potency, altering biochemical processes and results, thinks Mada. Yet that doesn't prevent Carlos being obsessed by the idea.

'Carlos,' says Mada gently, once they're in the lab. 'Do you really think it's possible to generate something real out of what you're doing?'

Carlos ignites a Bunsen burner. 'Real? What does that mean? Real, as in *it works?* Real as in medicine that people might be able to access? Nobody living in the stilt villages on the shores of Lake Maracaibo can afford Tetrabenazine, or pay for gene silencing when it becomes reality. Besides, not all healing fits inside the constipated bowels of Western medicine.'

Mada points about the room, as if the white enamel and stainless steel of the equipment express the paradigms of medical science. 'If we're going to develop treatment protocols that are of use to Western medicine, we're going to have to deal with its systems, constipation aside.'

'Systems! I'm interested in discovering what might grow in your garden, yet make life easier for those who suffer.' Carlos gives a hollow laugh. 'What use is an anti-spasmodic that costs five hundred dollars a month when you're earning two dollars a day?'

'It still needs to be effective.'

Mada picks up Carlos's notebook, reading off the ingredients of his latest concoction. 'Caapi vine, calendula, viburnum, cannabis. It might be illegal, but not to worry: when the trials demonstrate nothing and we all get fired, we can go into business selling weed in the dorms and making hand lotion.'

'These ingredients have shown significant promise. Cannabinoids increase ATP in transgenic rats carrying the mutant Huntington's protein; mRNA levels increase tenfold. There's anecdotal evidence—'

'I hate to echo Brandis, but anecdotal evidence is a misnomer.'

'Indeed. That's why research is needed. What they demonstrated on HD affected cells—'

'Properly motivated, you can induce anything in a slice of striatal neurons. Swell the data here, tap it there. Jesus, I've wasted the last few years because Allegra were more interested in money than science and skewed the data.'

'Your faith in research is touching, considering your chosen field,' Carlos responds, eyebrows raised. 'Look, I'm sorry if you find it unpalatable, but from all appearances these plants, even in their raw form, show more promise, both in the alleviation of symptoms and onset delay, than the compounds developed by Allegra. We know that they're neuroprotective, and we know that with their use we can reduce the severity of molecular pathologies.'

'Says who? Everything I've read on cannabis points to a reduced threshold to seizure and no capacity to reduce disease pathogenesis; besides which' – Mada picks up a nugget of bud and holds it up before them – 'I'm not sure if anyone has broken it to you, but this stuff is actually illegal. If Brandis walked in now, he'd be in his rights to pull my grant.'

Carlos gives a dismissive wave of the hand. 'That's why I locked the door. Just worry about the protocols.'

He pulls on blue rubber gloves and stuffs the green, crystalline flowers into a paper thimble, then slots it into an extractor jar and sets it in place over a bulbous boiling flask. 'Same as for calendula: we dissolve the oils in ethanol, then filter and assay the result. Push it until you get a colourless exudate. CBG has shown promise as an anti-spasmodic, has demonstrated success in limiting seizures, as have several other cannabinoids.'

Mada inwardly steams while they stare at the solvent rising through the pipes. It fills the thimble, and all the while Carlos rhapsodises over the magic of the plant with an evangelical fervour that, in itself, makes Mada uncomfortable. He describes the various stages of growth, the varieties and aromas and colours of the flowers. The diversity of terpenes. 'When you smell them in the early morning, the aromas are sweeter, more powerful and more subtle than any rose. You know, there are conspiracy theorists – the tin-hat community that lives in cyberspace – who believe the plant was seeded here by aliens, so different is its makeup from the rest of the eukaryotes in the plant kingdom. The sexual differentiation is unique.'

Mada fidgets, but Carlos is only warming up. It is when he gets onto the therapeutic benefits of the plant that he really opens the throttle. The buds they are using are the result of Carlos's own breeding program, progeny of seeds he brought with him from Venezuela and is growing on the outskirts of Wollongong. He's been working for years to develop a plant with high CBG. 'Normally this compound appears only in the early flowering stage. I'm working to stabilise it, to increase the content in mature flowers.'

Mada gives an audible sigh, and Carlos rounds on him, his

irritation clear. 'This is among the oldest medicinal plants known to humankind. It's been used in the treatment of everything from Alzheimer's to cancer. This plant, which is medicine, which you can grow yourself, which is harmless—'

But Mada has heard it all before. 'A million bong-head teenagers would probably argue with your definition of harmlessness. Or rather, they wouldn't, because, you know, *peace man.*' He holds up two fingers and offers his best daffy grin. 'It's illegal because it's dangerous, Carlos.'

'Don't make me laugh. You know one of the leading causes of global overdose death? Headache tablets. You buy them from the corner shop, and those little *putas* kill more people than airline disasters. But you find them in every bathroom in the Western world. Just sitting there, bottom drawer, enough to make your liver die. Cannabinoids don't accumulate in the brainstem, not in areas that control breath, so it is impossible to overdose. Still there are more people in American prisons for cannabis than violent crime. And that's despite the spread of legalisation. Naturally it's mostly black and brown people, people like me,' he adds hotly, 'who get put away. Funny, isn't it, with usage rates largely equivalent across race lines? The damage done by prohibition is enormous, and that, my friend, is data-rich science. There are methodological challenges. There are ethical challenges. There are financial challenges. But does that mean we shouldn't continue? We can help people. Isn't that the point? You need to have some trust,' concludes Carlos.

'Trust?' says Mada. 'In who? You?'

'No. In this world. In the plants themselves.'

'Oh Jesus.'

'These plants are nature's way of talking to us. You must learn to listen.'

'Talking plants?'

'If you'd seen what I've seen, you'd be a fool to think otherwise. The accounts of the shamans all say the same: the plants communicate; the plants tell them of their function, their purpose. We must try to adjust our consciousness to that of the plants.'

Mada gives a snort. 'A frontal lobotomy should do it.'

'Perhaps it sounds strange to those who haven't *seen*. Crazy hippy shit. But it's no less true. You are made of energy, my friend. That same energy the plant contains. All things communicate, plants included.' He grasps Mada's shoulders in his firm hands. 'Together we will suck the secrets out of nature. Nature is our source, the source of all magic.'

'I believe in chemicals,' says Mada flatly. 'The world isn't magical.'

'Of course it is.' He seems almost surprised by Mada's assertion. 'Perhaps not *abracadabra* magical, but the energies that connect you to this cosmos are a magic all the same. Physicists argue over the theory of gravity, of how to bring sense to the mathematics of the universe. We know so little, yet you are sure of so much? This is an opportunity. We need to stay open to the challenge of wonder.'

'You don't spout this crap in your academic essays, do you?'

'You must stay true to the grammar you are using. But these aren't opposing systems, only different ways of understanding. The caapi vine has a long history. So does cannabis. At least as long as that of Western medicine, although even that distinction is false. When the shamans claim it is both medicine and knowledge, they mean that the vine communicates with them; if they ask questions, it will respond. I myself have undertaken many rituals. There is much to learn.'

At that moment, Paula comes up behind Carlos, reaching out her hands and massaging his shoulders. She's unlocked the door and come in without them noticing. 'Don't over-exert yourself, *mi nigro*, my profane prophet,' she says. 'You can't convert the entire world to your cause.'

'No, much to my sorrow,' says Carlos, noticeably calming down. 'You're right, let's keep to the science.' He turns his attention back to his work, leaving Mada to stew.

The previous month the Venezuelan had been singing the praises of calendula, which he'd been cultivating out the back of Paula's townhouse – almost the entire yard had been filled with it, hundreds of pots on every free surface of the patio's brickwork and table. The bright yellow flowers were dried in the shade before he brought them to the lab. This 'unscientific' approach, so typical of Carlos, contradicted Mada's experience of what medical research should look like, the way it should be practised. He's accustomed to dealing with synthesised chemicals, contained as they are in predetermined quantities and stored in chemically inert containers in stainless steel refrigeration units. Collecting flowers from the yard and soaking them in ethanol for weeks is just not science, not as he is used to practising it.

Mada pulls out his laptop and goes to sit at one of the desks. On the wall above him is a poster of a lake: *Maracaibo, la tierra del sol amada.* The land of the beloved sun. One of Paula's additions. He takes off his glasses and presses his palms into his eye sockets.

Patterns of black and red erupt in his skull. His sleep patterns are a mess. He'd woken in the early hours of the morning, adrenalised and unable to rest, and spent hours composing essays in his head, lying on his back with his hand on his chest, like some novice priory monk debating the existence of God. He could hear Zoe tapping away on her laptop in the lounge room, then stopping, flipping the pages of a book.

Mada gets up and puts his laptop in his pack, glancing about. 'Where did Paula go?'

'Back to the office.'

'Okay. If she wants me, I'll be in the library.'

'Suit yourself,' says Carlos, returning his attention to the vaporous tube in front of him, scribbling notes in his neat, precise hand.

Mada heads towards the library, feeling impatient, complaining in a text to Zoe about how he's wasting his time with Carlos. Hippie crap and herbal remedies. Then he registers someone stepping across his path and stopping right in his way. Mada doesn't look up, and when the person refuses to shift as expected, he tries to stop short but wobbles forward, unbalanced, so that he ends up almost touching noses with the one person he is least anxious to see.

'The student marches forward into knowledge, deep in cogitations of a world-changing nature. Thus are the pathways of science progressing. Is your generation incapable of taking so much as two steps without being lost inside one of those infernal devices?' asks Brandis.

'Sorry,' says Mada. He readjusts his pack and slides the phone into the pocket of his jeans.

'It's no wonder we live in a time of ecological crisis: there's an entire generation incapable of lifting their eyes.'

'I'm not much of a representative for my generation. And anyway, blaming those under thirty for climate change is a tough argument.'

'Fair point. But I walk about this campus each day, and do you know what I see?'

'Bad modernist architecture?' says Mada.

'Ha ha,' Brandis responds sourly. 'Talk to the architects. But do you know how I see it?'

Mada ponders a moment. 'Corneal focus of light rays through a crystalline lens and vitreous humour falling on your retina. At some point the optic nerve transmits this signal to the visual cortex. I think that's about it.'

'You are a clever one, aren't you? It's worth remembering that all these wonders are possible because those nerves are permitted to see the world in the first place.'

'There's a real-world person at the other end of this device.'

'That may be true. All the same, once in a while you should try having a live conversation. My students spend most of my lectures on their laptops, looking at Facebook. They think I don't know, but I do. I can tell.'

Mada refrains from noting that this could be something to do with the department head's lecture style.

'It's impossible to talk to anyone under thirty in this place,' continues Brandis. 'The entire student body stumbles about campus in a trance.'

'You don't have a phone?' asks Mada.

'Of course I have one,' Brandis huffs impatiently. 'When I need to talk to someone, I call them. But I don't exist in a state of perpetual connection that makes me incapable of departing the house without checking in on Twitter. Anyway, all this is beside the point.' He plants his briefcase on the ground, looking Mada over. 'How is your work progressing?'

'Slowly,' says Mada, struggling to hide his irritation.

'Look. You're a bright student. You could do a lot. But you need to realise that departmental resources are finite. Projects need to be completed. Our jobs depend on it. Your job, mine. I'm more sympathetic to these research fads than many of my colleagues, but we need to be sensible.'

'Fads, Professor?'

'Viewing every cooking ingredient as a potential cure for cancer. Someone proposed a PhD on *basil* in the last round of applications. Claimed it was an ancient remedy for everything from diabetes to impotence.'

Mada shrugs. 'I like basil,' he says almost insolently.

'Who doesn't? It's basil. It's delicious. Look, we'd all like to see an efficacious and low-cost treatment for Huntington's. Or cancer. Or any of the dastardly armada. But basil isn't it. These trials cost money, and that money must come from somewhere. That somewhere is Allegra. More importantly, though, this "systems approach" is bad science. Compounds need to be isolated, treated individually, for maximum efficacy. You know how hard it is to maintain patient interest in long-term trials. Two years is hard work. But five? Ten? Even if these ingredients are effective, and that's a big if, it's not going to happen. It doesn't add up. I appreciate Paula's crusade for a healing garden, but there are reasons for our extraction of active compounds, their isolation and concentration. It's not the ravages of capitalism and the death of pure research, as she likes to say. It's about controlled, therapeutic dosage. It's about achieving predictable outcomes from standardised medicines that patients can rely on. Paula is nostalgic for some shamanic Amazonian past, but it doesn't exist and it never did, not as she imagines it. And it won't be part of our future. Not at this faculty.' His voice has hardened, and he pauses, changing tone, surveying Mada with a concerned, paternal gaze. 'We can't always do the good we would like, but we must not harm our patients.'

'Huntington's is a terminal disease,' Mada says, more aggressively than he intends. The scary thing is that Brandis is making sense, echoing Mada's own doubts.

'Life is terminal,' retorts Brandis. 'That doesn't mean that the lives of patients are ours to play with. The road to hell is paved with good intentions.'

'You believe in hell?'

'Don't be absurd. What I'm saying is that there are consequences for our actions. If your research outcomes can't be implemented, what good are they? You're an important part of this organisation. We have invested in you. It's not because I don't respect Paula's research. Even when her work veers towards the beatnik bio-spiritualist pseudo-science so popular in some quarters, she is, in her way, a rigorous scholar. But you, Mada, need to understand: there's no future in it. Professor Evans has overstepped the mark on this one, and in the end it will not help you, or him, one bit.'

'Thank you, Professor. I'll keep it in mind.'

The Pacific Course
Chapter 11

'Get a seat on QF 421 to Melbourne, Redmond. Tuesday the fourteenth.'

Red was crossing the Harbour Bridge, on his way to look at a house in McMahons Point – four million easy if the shots were anything to judge by – and the traffic jammed up as her call came over Bluetooth.

'I've got to work,' protested Red.

Min wouldn't have a bar of it. 'I've seen how you work, Redmond. Get one of the girls to handle things. I insist on an early flight. You must have time to relax. You know how you get when you're not relaxed. The first meeting is important.'

She was introducing him to some of her international connections, and Red could tell the idea had her hopped up.

'We'll go for a round,' she told him. 'I have a membership at Kingston Heath – we can loosen up before the meeting.'

'I don't want to travel with clubs,' Red protested, realising how lame it sounded as soon as he'd said it. Truth was, the idea of the meeting – so long desired – spooked him.

'What are you talking about?' she asked. 'They'll have clubs for you. Why are you making excuses?'

'It's only, you know, I'm not sure if I can play just before the meeting, I haven't been feeling that flash.'

'You can, Redmond, and you will. You'll play if I have to tie a rope around your neck and drag you to the tee. We'll relax on the course, and then, in the meeting, when we talk business, you'll be relaxed too. I've seen you find focus. I want you to think about being out on the course, those moments when you hold the club so lightly it's scarcely in your hands, yet your grip is iron, your shoulders loose and free. This is what you must do, Redmond. Swing loose and free. Be polite, but let go of your worries, and swing loose and free. If you feel you're clamming up, imagine you're on the course, imagine you are the ball, flying out into God's great universe. Be the ball, Redmond. I want you to imagine yourself, utterly poised, your body only waiting for the signal – *smack!* – to ping through the sky. Golf is what you need, Redmond. You need to find the art of focus and release. And you will!'

Clearly she thought she needed to psych him up. And it wasn't that he didn't appreciate the effort. The previous week she'd yelled at him excitedly on the seventh fairway, shaking him to adjust his posture, slapping his shoulders, announcing all the ways that his body must be released to the swing.

In almost all other ball sports, keeping your eyes up is how you stay in the game. But not golf! She'd proclaimed this with a maniacal glee. With golf you've got to stare down into yourself, into your soul, see what you've got down there. What quietness can you muster against the savagery of the world? 'The ball does not move, Redmond. The wind does, and there'll be times the surface isn't as you imagined – steeper or fast as marble or like wet cement. There are bunkers, trees, lakes. But these are only obstacles in as much as you allow them to be. Focus, Redmond! When it comes down to it, there's only you, how smoothly you can swing that club in anticipation of the world, and the ball, sitting, with its small white eye. This is why golf is the perfect game, the most pure. It's about you, face to face with the white eye of the self. You must face that self and win, Redmond.'

Ah, that woman.

All the same, Red's now feeling upside down. For one, he doesn't know exactly whom he'll be meeting with: Min hasn't given him even a business name, much less a number or address. 'An Australian company' is all she'll say, 'with significant international funding.'

She's flown in the previous evening, having organised his reservation at the South Wharf Hilton. They'll meet her consortium at Vue de Monde, seven sharp. The Dom Pérignon Room has been booked under the name of Campbell. Red doesn't know Melbourne well, but even he has heard of it, and Min had insisted that this was the place. They would be impressed. They would know that he was serious.

'Won't your presence make that known?' he asked.

'Yes.' She smiled, inclined her head in appreciation of his flattery. 'But we must obey the protocols. Also, you must pay the bill. It will be expensive. It *should* be expensive. You'll order the best Australian item on the wine list. Not champagne. Not until after the business is concluded, if all goes well. Start with a chablis, or a Margaret River chardonnay – the Pierro perhaps, or an Art Series. Then a bottle of Grange. The '90 or the '98 if they have them. Order casually. Drink with appreciation, but don't go on about tannins or fruit or other silliness. I'll let you know if champagne is appropriate.'

Her description of the ritual had him projecting awkward visions of social embarrassment, and Red could feel a knot of panic forming in his chest.

'How will I know? What will your signal be?'

'I will say: "Let's drink champagne."'

And now it's the day of the meeting, and he's in a cab on the way to the airport and everything is making him nervous. It's been relentless since the second he woke up: his morning coffee was like acid in his guts. He's about to get out of the cab when a phone call comes through from Mada. Red is so lost in his own thoughts that he almost jumps out of his skin. He glances fearfully at the phone and lets it go through to voicemail. His stomach is churning and he's farting with such frequency and pungency it's like death seeping out. The cabbie keeps glancing at him in the rearview mirror, but if he doesn't let it out now he's doomed.

Red winds down the window, and it's the manual kind; the cab's an antique. Winds it down casually. As if it doesn't mean anything, as if it's the ancient cab that has this smell to it. Death and old cabbage. He imagines the meeting, imagines not being able to hold his gut, and a stench wafting forth that clears the restaurant floor, rising about the entire table like a stale, toxic funk. It's a certainty that it will go badly, that he'll do something stupid, say the wrong thing, use the wrong fork, fart to clear the room.

At the airport his plane is full, and somebody is sitting in his seat. Red checks his boarding pass and then the pass of the woman in the seat, and both of them have the same numbers and letters and date, identical in every respect but the name – the moment surreal, as though he might be dreaming, as though he does not in fact exist and this is the first proof. He and the woman stare at each other, then back at the boarding passes and she hits the button to summon the steward. While they wait, they gaze purposefully in opposite directions while Red is pummelled by the passing traffic.

Eventually another seat is found for Red, at the back of the plane, the *very* back. Not in Business, scarcely in the plane at all. He can smell the toilet chemicals from where he sits, their residue in his throat, his mouth filled with disinfectant. The hour-long flight stretches interminably.

Once they land and taxi to the gate Red is the first to his feet, but having brought down his carry-on he's forced to stand for twenty minutes while the entire aircraft fumbles with bags and plods towards the airbridge, and he exits the terminal into Melbourne weather with a growing sense of dread. It's just as dreary and wet as he remembers, the wind cutting through his suit jacket the moment he passes through the sliding glass doors. He really does not feel good. Standing in line for a taxi, he lets out a fart of such silent magnitude that the woman behind him drops her phone. It clatters on the pavement, and she hesitates, frozen, eyeing him with horror before stooping very fast and grabbing it and pretending to take a call. She wheels her bag away from the queue with another surreptitious glare and rejoins it, six people back, at the rear. Red stares fixedly at his own device, trying to open the email app, but he can't read to save himself. He's too filled with bodily loathing, a nausea not so much of the stomach but the humours: blood, black bile, phlegm.

His mood hasn't improved by the time he meets Min Fang. She's waiting for him in a café not far from the hotel. It's one of those wanky Melbourne places where even the pigeons wear black, run by some Italian bloke, of course, the kind who thinks he invented coffee, and Red knows the bastard would frown at him if he ordered a cappuccino this late in the a.m.

Fucking Melbourne.

But he can't let her know what state he's in, or she'll bust his nuts to paste. Red puts on his best real estate agent smile and crosses to where Min Fang is sitting, sipping an espresso and talking animatedly with a waiter in Italian. Red glowers at the bloke, behind her back, and the greaseball goes off to molest another patron.

'How many languages do you speak?' Red asks her, pulling out a chair.

'Six,' she says. 'Plus enough Russian and Arabic to get through customs. I was fortunate enough to have a diplomat for a father.' She leans back in her chair to look him over appraisingly. 'Is something the matter?'

'No,' he responds, trying to look surprised, 'of course not.'

Red sits back and folds his arms, before it occurs to him that this is a posture of defensiveness. He straightens up and unfolds them. Suddenly, though, he's not sure what to do with his hands, and he's stuck in a gesture that makes him look like he's praying, which he isn't, and doesn't. He pulls his arms off the table and hides his hands in his lap.

Min Fang observes this with narrowing eyes. 'Redmond! What is going on?'

'I've had a morning, that's all,' he responds weakly. He looks at her pleadingly.

Her eyes narrow further. 'Get your shit in a line, Redmond. Don't flap about like this tonight or they'll eat you up, bones and all, like an ortolan.'

'Eat me … what? Like an ottoman?'

'An or-to-lan,' she sounds it out, as though speaking to a child, 'is a tiny songbird they eat in France.'

'Like a spatchcock?'

'Spatchcock is not a bird, it is a way to flay a chicken. An ortolan is more like a robin.'

'Does it taste any good?'

'Yes. It tastes like fig and hazelnut have fornicated in your mouth.'

'So that's good, right?'

Min grabs hold of his tie and pulls him towards her. 'To prepare the bird they drown it, literally *drown it*, in Armagnac; it becomes half liquor. Then the feet and feathers are removed and it is roasted until its pale yellow body fat is sizzling. When you eat it, you eat all the bird, even the skull, covering your head with your serviette to hide your shame. You crush the skull in your back teeth and the sweet, nutty brain juice fills your mouth.'

'Jesus Christ.'

Min sits back in her seat. 'A little like him, but more carnal.'

'You scare me sometimes, you know that?'

'Of course I do,' she says dismissively. 'But less than I should. Now, are you ready for tonight? I've worked hard to bring these people here. They're wary about dealing with new people, but I've told them that you're okay.' She fixes him with a stern eye. 'We've known each other two months now. I think I trust you. But know this: if you embarrass me, I will kill you.'

Red swallows awkwardly. 'Metaphorically?'

She examines his hairline, scowling, as though phrenology might unlock the clue to his resolve – or lack thereof. 'Yes, Redmond. I'll kill you, as a metaphor.'

'Well. Good then.'

'But I'll use a Ming knife.'

It abruptly comes into his head that Min is nervous about this meeting as well. He's not sure if this makes him feel better or worse, but he is definitely curious. 'Why do they matter so much?' he asks.

'They're important colleagues. They've taken an interest in Australia, they're significant individuals, and their friends are very, very significant individuals. If they think you're not up to the task, well ...' She gives a shrug.

'What kind of *significant individuals* are they, exactly?'

'International clients. Clients who live in world cities and want the best in those cities.'

'The best real estate?'

'The best of what there is: land, property, companies, connections.'

'And this is what you give them?'

'After a fashion. I introduce people. Those with mutual interests. Those with things to sell. Those with money to buy. Like tonight.'

'So who will be there tonight?'

'I've told you already.'

'No, you haven't. You told me they're from an internationally funded Australian firm. But that's not what it sounds like.'

'That's what it is,' she says flatly. 'On paper, anyway. And paper is the reality that matters.'

'So this isn't strictly legal?'

She doesn't blink. 'Naturally it is. We use the laws of the countries in which we operate.'

'Use them?'

'Yes.' Her green eyes bore into his. 'The international community has money to invest in real estate. They like it here. People from Hong Kong, from California, from Belgium, like to own summer homes in Australia. The government and market are largely reliable. It is good for Australia, as money flows in and the food gets better. The country is less isolated. It's good for you, Redmond, as some of this money flows to you. You're dealing with a big Australian company. But if you want to play, you have to get into the right room, be in the right frame of mind.

'And you have to be polite. Beyond all else, don't bother them with questions about the law. If they think that you're stupid, that you're not serious, or worse, that you're not polite ... Well, you don't, you *really* don't, wish them to think that you're not polite.'

* * *

In the end, it goes far better than he had dared hope. There are nine of them eating and drinking like kings, laughing at Min's ribald jokes, and even the bill isn't *quite* as bad as he had feared.

Red returns to Sydney with a new spring in his step. He plays the Lakes with Min on Tuesday and only loses one ball, then goes home afterwards, heats up a frozen lasagne, and manages to limit himself to three glasses of pinot. Next morning he's up at seven thirty for his regular round with Angelo, feeling about as good as he's felt in years.

He's screening his calls with even more gusto than usual, sending almost everything through to the office, so he doesn't take a lot of notice at first when his sister-in-law's neighbour calls to complain about the dog. Even when she calls three times in as many hours, Red merely glances at her number, having listened vaguely to her first message, and wonders why she's so insistent. As far as he's concerned, it's simply not his problem.

So when his phone starts playing the theme from *Rocky* yet again, his new ringtone as of Sunday, Red assumes it's the neighbour. He checks the screen and is surprised to find an image of Emma from Wealth Trust smiling up at him – his private banker. What could she want?

'Hello, Emma.'

'Good morning, Mr Campbell.'

'What's happening?'

'I'm just following up on some unusual activity in your account.'

'Oh yeah, what's that?'

'A withdrawal, sir. Twenty thousand dollars. It's unusual because it's in cash.'

Red feels a sliver of ice move down his spine. 'Which account?'

'The cheque account ending in 712, sir.'

There are only three people with access to that account. Red is one and Bea is in prison. So what the hell is Lori doing with 20K? 'When did *she* withdraw twenty thousand dollars?' he asks.

'Ten minutes ago. Ms Vaughn performed the transaction at the Bondi Junction branch.'

'And they gave her the money?'

'Of course, sir. It was a valid transaction. Ms Vaughn's identity was confirmed. She said she was going to buy a car.'

'She doesn't have a licence.'

'Regardless, she's within her rights—'

'Then why are you calling me?'

'Because it's unusual, sir, and because when you came into the office earlier in the year we spoke of Ms Vaughn's condition … would you like me to put a hold on further transactions?'

'Yes. Grand idea. And make it active say fifteen minutes ago.'

Red hangs up without another word.

What the hell would Lori be doing with twenty thousand dollars? It doesn't make sense. Even so, Red isn't freaking out, not at first. If she's pulled out cash, she'll still have the bulk of it; it's not like she's going to flee the country. It's the kind of thing she might do on a whim. He'll head over to her place after his round with Angelo, on his way to the office. Then he can give her what for about the money, not to mention keeping the dog quiet. There's no point ruining his morning.

Head down. Be the ball.

After the round, Red is feeling buoyant. Not just because of Angelo's company, which always peps him up, but because he hit a very respectable six over par. Even Angelo is impressed, and asks what he's doing that's new. His drives are improving with every swing of the club, and his putting game is on point. Red doesn't want to tell him how often he and Min have been at the course together – not because he's trying to keep the reason for his improved game secret, more because he wants to avoid a lecture on 'treating her right'. What matters, Min says, is golf. All else – cars, real estate, even money itself – only matter in so much as they permit more time for better golf. Even going over to deal with the 'Lori situation', as Angelo has been calling it in response to Red's complaining, doesn't faze him overmuch.

He and Bea had argued about Lori's access to their business accounts, but, technically speaking at least, Lori owned one-third of the company, as it was Bea and Lori's shared inheritance that had provided much of the start-up capital, and for a time Bea was entertaining a fantasy in which Lori would help with the banking. 'You don't need to give her the internet codes, Red. She can have a card and a passbook. It will make her feel independent.' In the end he had conceded the point – yes, yes, it was her money, and at any rate when had he ever won an argument with his wife? As for the dog, he's sure she just needs to feed the animal, or take it out for a walk. He tries ringing her as he's leaving the course, just to make sure she'll have some clothes on when he arrives, but no luck. He dials Mada, and this time the phone is answered.

'G'day Red. What's the story?'

'Do you know if your mum was planning to buy a car or something?'

'No chance. I'm not even sure she's still got a licence. Why?'

'No. She doesn't. It lapsed when she was living with us; I saw the paperwork. It's only that I had a call … and the neighbours are complaining about the dog.'

'The dog? I told you, Red.'

'They haven't had a problem with it before,' he says defensively. 'But apparently it was barking all night.'

'Where's Lori?'

'I don't know. I tried calling, but her phone is off. I'm on the way over there now.'

'I hope she's okay. I haven't seen her for over a week.' Mada goes quiet for a moment. 'She seemed distracted when we spoke the other day.'

'More than usual, you mean?'

Silence. Then, 'You say you're going right over?'

'Yeah.'

'Okay, let me know. I've got a small window in half an hour. I can meet you there.'

'Oh, I wouldn't worry, I'm sure it's okay,' says Red magnanimously.

'I am worried, Red. If the dog's barking, it means she's either not there, or she's there and she's had a fall or something. If she's gone walkabout again, then she could be anywhere. I'll head over as soon as I'm done here, but call me when you know.'

Red hangs up. Mada always over-dramatises things, especially as far as his mother is concerned. Lori isn't one to have falls in the shower. She's in her forties, for god's sake. She's got a few wobbles, but she's steady enough. She's probably been out with some bloke, a derro she met at the pub, and has spent the night rolling about in his bed. All the same, the idea she's gone walkabout with Red's twenty thousand does see him run a few lights on the way.

It's deathly quiet when Red gets out of the elevator, and there's a bit of a stink in the hallway as he approaches Lori's flat. He stands there listening a moment. No radio, no TV. Not a soul in the entire complex seems to be at home. He cracks the front door and a rank, fetid waft blows into his face. Christ, the place smells awful. He steps over the threshold. There are dogshit landmines scattered about the entry hall. No sign of the dog, though. Maybe she's finally taken it for a walk.

Red closes the door behind him, and, stepping carefully, goes through into the lounge room. He hasn't been there in months, and besides all the dog crap, the place is pretty neat. Even the sculptures have been put away. Mada has obviously been squaring things up, as Lori, left to her own devices, would sooner step over something a hundred times than put it in her wardrobe. A lump of clay sits on her work bench, looking a lot like the decorations the dog has gifted to the flooring. It's there, curled under the bench, that he finds the animal, asleep. It scarcely even stirs when he gives it a prod. So much for relentless yapping.

Red gives it another poke.

'Wake up, you useless lump.'

The animal lifts its head weakly, gazing at him through half-lidded eyes, then gives a small whine before lowering its muzzle. Its nose feels remarkably dry, thinks Red.

He goes and pokes about in the kitchen. There's a dried-out half lemon, a few days old at least, and a brown, shrunken wedge of avocado with the stone still attached on the bench. The dog's water dish is bone dry, and there's a salad bowl half-filled with kibble beside the fridge with a small pile of puke beside it. Red fills the water dish and sets it down near the dog, which wobbles up immediately, standing there on its stumpy little legs, drinking until its belly is brushing the ground. It then stumbles over to him, collapses, and rests its head on his shoe.

Poor little bastard. It stares at him through half-closed eyes. It really is cute — the shape of its face, the fine brown hair, the ridiculous dangling ears. The animal heaves a great sigh, impressively full of pathos for a funny, furry sock puppet. Red bends down and gathers the long, apparently boneless, creature in his two hands, bringing it up to clasp it to his chest. It lifts its small head and gives his fingers a feeble lick.

'Well played, dog,' he says.

He places the dog gently on the sofa, and opens the balcony door as wide as it will go. A wash of noise and wholesome air pushes in off the road and river.

By the time Mada arrives, Red and the dog are on first-name terms, and the animal seems to be feeling a whole lot better, trotting about happily. Red has cleaned up the landmines from the floor, dropped the plastic bag down the garbage chute, and sprayed an assortment of random aerosols around the flat in the hope of disguising the smell. Mada will, Red is sure, let him know with ringing clarity that he, Mada, was right, and that Lori was incapable of looking after the animal, and frankly Red has no interest in listening to him bleat, 'I told you so.' Not again. Even with the glass balcony doors and all the windows wide open, however, the stench is slow to dissipate, and Mada enters with a wrinkled nose and deep frown.

'Bloody hell. It stinks in here. You can smell it as soon as you get out of the lift.'

'Looks like she hasn't been here for two or three days,' says Red quickly. 'I've cleaned up the kitchen a bit.'

'Any idea where she's gone? Did you look about? Last time she left a note on her desk.' Mada starts searching the work bench, picking up stray pieces of paper and discarding them.

'Yeah,' says Red, 'I couldn't find anything. I called that friend of hers, the one she was staying with for a bit.'

'Right. What did Linda say?'

'She's got no idea. Said they had a falling-out.'

'Terrific. Looks like you bought yourself a dog after all.'

'Me? She's your mother, not mine.'

'I told you, Red. If I take the animal home with me, I'll lose my lease. You know what cut-throat bastards the real estate agents are in this town.'

'Very funny.'

'Don't make me state the obvious, Redmond. Who was it—'

'Okay, okay!' Red waves the words away.

Mada hunts about in the bedroom, looking for some sign of Lori's whereabouts, then sits on the lounge scratching the dog while he calls everyone he can think of who knows his mother. But no luck.

'I have to get back to the uni,' he says after a while. 'I've got a full teaching load at the moment.'

'You just walked in the door.'

'And I shouldn't have. I just wanted to make sure she wasn't ...'

'Yeah, well.' Red adjusts his cuff. 'Why are you teaching so much anyway?'

'I need the money. For a research trip. Sorry, Red, but I shouldn't be here at all. The traffic is terrible, and I've got about twenty minutes to get back to the campus.'

'All right, all right. I'll clean things up a bit more and let you know if I discover anything.'

'Thanks. Oh, and Red, why did you ask about a car?'

'She made a withdrawal from the bank.'

'How much?'

'Twenty thousand.'

Mada sits back heavily onto the sofa. 'Jesus. She's gone off again, Red, she must have.'

'Maybe.'

'You'd better call the cops.'

'It's a little early for that, don't you think? She's probably just ... you know, found a new friend.'

'Then what's the money for?'

'I don't know. Anything. You know how ditsy she can be.'

'Just call them, Red. I'll come back when I've done this next tutorial.'

Once Mada has gone, Red lets himself fall into the couch, releasing a long sigh. Now *he's* starting to worry. Bugger the office, they can do without him. The dog is making a valiant attempt to jump up and join him. Its crate is still in the corner by the door, and Red shoves the animal inside and closes the latch. It sits there staring at him, sad-eyed and silent.

Back in the kitchen, he examines the endless sheets of paper on the fridge: menus for food delivery, random pamphlets and notes. It looks the same as it did when he was here last month. Then, amid the clutter, half-concealed by a pamphlet listing hours for the local library, he spots it: a pink Post-It note carrying Lori's looping scrawl.

My Darling Boy.
　　Please don't be angry.
　　I've taken Dad's Pacific course.
　　I'll see you there, in the after place.
I love you,
Mum

It takes a few moments for Red to realise what he's reading. Her dad's Pacific course? Naturally the first thing that occurs to him is golf – and then it dawns on him. Bea's father. Lori's father. The father who, as the Huntington's chorea took hold, was unable to face what the future had in store and walked into the sea.

A knot fills Red's throat. He grabs the phone and hits Mada's number, the call tone ringing two, three, four, five, six times and then voicemail. He tries again. It's engaged. Red utters a string of profanities and tries again, panic rising.

This time Mada picks it up.

'I can't talk, Red, I'm driving.'

'Why don't you get a hands-free? Or better yet, a different car?'

'You can buy me one if you like.'

'Look, you'd better get back here.'

'I told you, Red. I'm taking a tutorial in fifteen minutes.'

'Well you're going to have to cancel it.'

'I can't. I need the money.'

'Mada, I'm serious. Get your fucking arse back here. Right now.'

'Wha— Hold on.' He listens to Mada swearing, the crank of the handbrake, then his voice comes back on the line. 'Okay, what's going on, Red?'

'Just get back here, mate. We'll talk about it then.'

'What is it, Red? Tell me.'

'Just get here.' Red hangs up.

When Mada gets out of the elevator there are two cops in the doorway and he can hear Red's voice from within, complimenting them on their quick response, managing to sound both sycophantic and patronising at the same time: 'That's under five minutes, fellas; good to see my tax dollars are doing their bit.'

'No problem,' says one of them. 'We were only next door.'

They have their backs to him, but the one on the left turns around and eyes Mada up and down. 'Is this your nephew?' he asks, turning back to Red.

'Yeah, that's him.'

'What is it, Redmond, what did you find?'

'She left … this.' Red holds out the note.

Lightbells
Chapter 12

Every time she hears that song, Lori remembers the feeling of being full. Because that was the song they played on the stereo, driving down Bangalow Road, on the way to the beach that day. 'Seabirds', the Triffids. Turning it up so the speakers crackled. How she's loved it ever since, the singer's voice so deep and resonant; the man's beside her too.

Music connects the dots that Lori can't figure out. Other art can do it, even the things she makes, though they're really just for her. But music does it best. Old summer music and playing it loud.

So where were you, my brown eyed boy? And where are you now?

Remembering how they'd cranked the radio, singing beach to beach. She had placed her hand there and known it for the very first time, turning onto Bay Street to buy a burger and chips, daydreaming of juice and vinegar and salt-crunch until her mouth was wet.

Yes, that was the day she realised.

The man beside her, singing, would be the father of her beautiful child; how happy he would be when she told him, when she was sure. And then he wasn't happy at all; he upped and ran. She had the baby, her sister by her side, her beautiful, perfect boy who didn't cry, not even a little, but gazed up at her with his old soul's eyes.

The second time she became full, she was so very sure she would have another baby. She could remember exactly the day she found out: the light-filled happiness overtaking her in the kitchen. She got the kit in its little white box and opened the flaps and pulled out the plastic stick, staring excitedly at the thin white strip. So *very* sure. Because she had made her angel that first time, and he was perfect, when she came home the second time and peed on the stick she put on the CD because it was the music of being full – that first time, and now.

'Seabirds', the Triffids.

She released a flow of urine on the little stick – there was a spritz on her fingertips but she didn't care. She sat at the kitchen bench when she came out of the toilet, staring at the instructions on their tiny folded square of paper, flattening them out as she waited to see about the stick, and she was listening to the song as she tried to read the pamphlet, with its teeny tiny writing, but all she could do was listen because the letters were so small and the song was so good.

It was eight weeks past her forty-seventh birthday, and she carried a gift that could not be wrapped. A gift that would never arrive. She'd felt it in there, its presence, like a small star growing. But she needed to be sure. And so sitting in the kitchen with the sun coming in, listening to old summer music from when she was young, she remembered the flapping air from the window as they drove, and how something back then felt the same as now, the times mixing together, the moments overlapping in the landscape of the song. This very apartment, this very spot, and she waited for the colour to change even though she already knew. Bea trying to interfere and the fight they had. Later in the hospital Bea said the flowing blood was probably for the best. For the best! What a thing to say!

Was the world so empty of love?

Was family not family?

Was life not made of life?

Well it wasn't, so she had learned. Life was made of death and there was nothing to be done. Oh, how was it possible to be so empty when she had been so full?

She had never forgotten his face and the heat and the sand that first time. How she had told him about the baby and the dark skin of his face had flushed pale, and the next morning he was gone gone gone, his friends smirking and shrugging and grinning, while she went on endless searches along the beach, haunting his favourite breaks – he rode goofy and would often surf apart from the other boys – but he wasn't there, and after endless desolate walks she had travelled south to Sydney, back to her sister, who sat her down and wiped her tears and made her hot tea, telling her everything would be all right, that he was just a stupid boy and they would go and find him, but that even if they couldn't they didn't need him anyway, and together they would find a way.

Lori isn't angry with him anymore. She wants him to know that she's not mad. Wants him to know about Mada, about his wonderful son. She doesn't need money, doesn't need a thing. It had just been too much for him, she understands that now, and she imagines his surprise at seeing her there, on his beach, imagines what he will say. Not that they will be together again, not like they were before. She is different, and he must be too. The whole world is changed, but she wants so much for him to know that it's all right, and to see him one more time, to walk on that same sand.

Lori listens to the final notes of the song erupt, and the afternoon sun reaches in through the balcony doors, touching every surface to unify the song, the moments of fullness, making the air bright and deep. The light and the music.

Lightbells.

That's what it is.

She thinks the word. Not to put a cage on it, just to point a way. How it was back then and how it is right now. With the light coming up from the water, the sun in the river and the river in the sun, those long afternoons coming back from the beach, singing along, all the windows down. The sun that summer, baking hot, so even before you parked the car you had to be careful on the vinyl.

The same bright sun as now.

She dreamed about him last night. John. With his broad forehead and deep eyes, wet hair kinky and wild with salt. Together they'd walked along the beach. Talked. Understood.

She will go and see him.

There is nothing else to do.

She will tell him that she forgives him. His son has grown into a man to be proud of: a man who is strong and clever and good; a man who has compassion, a man who wants to give.

Lori sighs happily.

She must do it properly, though. She needs all that money she got from the bank, money and clothes, if she's going to make it to Byron Bay and not have to worry. She can travel on the cheap, hitching, maybe the occasional bus, but she will need plenty of cash for hotels and food. Above all, she must be gone. She can feel the restlessness building – her toes are starting to itch. And she must not delay, not too long, for that awful man will see sooner or later that it is gone, and so far as he is concerned all the money in the world is his and he will not like it being taken.

With great care, she releases three drops of medicine into a glass of water: the medicine Mada's friend from the university dropped around. It has been a month now, and she really does feel better. But she must be careful: three drops, two times a day, to see if she can tolerate it, if she'll be okay. She puts the small bottle into a plastic bag and stores it snugly in her pack, the memory of what it was to be full returning to her, happy, in music and in light. Those days, down the beach. Swimming and then running, and kissing with salt-wet lips in the shade behind the rocks, John's thing getting bigger so she felt it against her belly, grabbing it with her hand so his eyes went wide. Wanting it so much, never wanting it to stop. Later she swam out to him, and he slipped off his board, easing into the rise and fall of the swell beyond the break. The boy and his hard shoulders, so strong beneath her hands. Holding the board and kissing. Rising and falling. Past the break. The secret, his secret, getting bigger so she feels it, and pulling aside her cossie so he can push it in. Holding the board. Heave of swell. Up and up. The feel of him shuddering as he squeezes out inside her, so his eyes close while she stares at him, joyously unblinking.

'Ahhh. *Wow.* You are one *wild* chick!'

The sun on her face, and it feels the same as now.

In light the life is carried. Carried from one to the next. We carry the life and give it, from one to the next. The boy who gave it to her. And the man she met, in the pub close by. So handsome – a carpenter – she led him home by the hand and he gave it to her as well, but in the end it didn't work, and she nearly died. And then, later, when it seemed there was no other way, walking to the water and knowing that she would surely drown. Striding until the water lifted her in its arms. The same water that flows out there now, flows out below the bridge and beneath the next bridge and all the way down to Bondi and up to Byron Bay.

The sun goes over the water and turns everything gold. Boats in floating fire. Life in the light.

Lightbells.

Life to me.

To me. How she had been blessed; he had carried it in him and put it inside her, and she had felt it stir there with the palm of her hand. Circling her hand on her belly. So empty now.

She will go and see him, there is nothing else to do.

First, she will head out to Wahroonga, because she can walk from there to the hitching spot, just like they used to do.

Hitching, all those years ago, when she first met him. The surfers the other day had made her think of his salty hair. How he'd pulled down his wetsuit and let it hang from his waist, all the muscles in lines together and his shoulders round and smooth.

She will get the bus then the train, then she will walk until she gets to the on-ramp, where the freeway starts north. There's a place where people stop, where they can see you and they're not going too fast. She won't get to Byron in just one night, but she doesn't need to hurry. The money from the bank is in her pack right here at the counter, and as she pats its surface she can feel the notes, lumpy and hard.

Her mobile phone is in her pocket, but she won't turn it on, not until she's ready. She doesn't want them calling her, interrupting when she's trying to make her way. She doesn't want them knowing at all, so better to leave it off. In her bag she puts her toothbrush and her warm jacket – the one that keeps the rain off, the one from her boy. There are a few T-shirts and a pair of jeans in there already. She can stay in motels, but she'll sleep on the sand if she has to.

But not around here.

North.

She will go north.

Down at the bus stop there are two women and a man, and the sun is bright and lovely and there are lots of cars. She loves how fast the cars go, how they whoosh with so much wind. What if you could capture that whoosh in the clay? What if you could make the clay into a shape that tells how fast they move? It's been too long since the clay found a form she likes, and it's exciting to think about shaping things again. Her thumbs start moulding without her realising it, shaping an invisible object from the air.

It all feels so exciting.

Making things! Adventure! Change!

She can see the bus coming, the driver high inside, and it puts on its indicator and pulls to the kerb, and she lifts her foot onto the step and then she is on her way. Her boy's face fills her mind as she gets off at Town Hall Station and walks underground, then boards a train, marvelling as it rocks her side to side, gentle and lulling. She thinks about the dream and whether it is real. She knows dreams are not real per se, but knows also that they are more than they appear, more than just a tired brain working out the knots. She knows that they show both the past and the future, that they have the power of augury if only you can read them.

In the dream she was at the place on the beach where they first met, and he was wearing what he wore then, his jeans hanging from the bones in his hips; how faded they were against his dark skin. And his frayed white Billabong shirt, the muscles in his arms making shapes beneath his skin. He saw her looking at him as she made her way along the beach, and she didn't stop looking and nor did he, and he put his arm about her waist, gently at first, until he was sure it was okay, and then gripping her tight to his side before she even knew his name, saying *Hey there girly* and she knew then he was special, that together they were special. That summer on the beach, living out of cars, having fires on the sand at night and taking off their clothes to swim, the water black, and all the while the surge of waves breaking open on the shore.

And when she woke that morning there was still the feeling of his hands on her. That's when she decided: she would go to find him. The sand on her back and his tongue in her mouth. Hands pushing. Down between her legs. The water black, and the white foam. The train rocks gently back and forth. Lori stares through the streaked glass and in every car there is a soul at the wheel. Someone always stops, after a while, if you wait. She will make her way north, to see what she can find.

Milk-Pro
Chapter 13

Mada is fidgeting at Bea's side. They're in the courtyard, as close to the grass as they can get. It's hot for August, the sun is beaming down, and if you only look at the grass, green with spring rain, you could be in the public park up the back of Bronte Beach. Outside. Having a picnic. A bunch of kids behind you playing cricket.

This is what Bea is thinking. About her and Lori playing cricket with their folks, up on the Central Coast before the disease took hold of their dad. There was a rental house they would always book, with a sandy trail behind it winding through the marram grass, and she and Lori would race to see who could be first in the water. It all seems so long ago, as though it's not even her life, but the memory of a movie, or a story she was told.

Beside her, Mada hangs his head in his hands, massaging his temples. She reaches out a hand and rubs his shoulders and he offers a tired smile.

'It's weird there's just … nothing,' he says eventually. 'If she really did *drown* herself,' he pushes out the word as though to give it distance from where he sits, 'there would have been a body. Clothes. Something. They spent three days with choppers scouring the coast.'

'I know. It is weird. And she didn't seem despondent when she came to visit me here. Angry. Unyielding as ever. But mood-wise she was better than she's been in ages.'

Mada nods his agreement.

'So … what do you think?' Bea asks gently. 'Did she really do it?'

'It seems,' Mada pauses, searching out the right word, 'impossible. That she's dead.'

'Doesn't it?' Bea hears her voice crack. She turns her face away from him: she must be strong, he cannot see her cry. She won't be able to stop, and there's no room for tears in prison.

'Zoe says death *always* seems impossible, to those who live, those left behind. But it just doesn't make sense,' says Mada. 'Why take the money, just to go drown yourself?'

'To give it away?'

'She's not that generous-hearted.'

Bea gives a snort of laughter despite herself. 'No. She's not.'

'And besides, like you said, she'd been happy lately. Happier, at any rate. Distant, but … better. These last months were the best I've seen her since the start of last year.' He stops, shakes his head. 'But if not, then why the note?'

'To get you off her back?'

'Charming.'

'I only mean that it's how she'd see it. Like she was doing you a favour.' Bea gives a shrug. 'She's been staging disappearances since she was five. There was *always* a note. That said, she never mentioned offing herself before.'

Mada crosses his arms. 'I'm not going to go searching for her if she doesn't want to be found.'

'Fair enough. If she's out there somewhere, it's probably best to let her be, let her come back when she's ready. She *can* look after herself when she has to. You know that. Or mostly, at any rate. But I can't tell you if she's alive, Mada. I always imagined that I'd be able to tell somehow, that I'd *know*. But …' Her voice trails out.

She leans back against the chair, pulling out her tobacco and papers. She does it almost shyly, knows it to be a new action for Mada to witness. His aunt. In the slammer. Rolling a durry. Just last year he was joining her at yoga classes. How it all turns on a pin.

'How's that girl of yours?' Bea asks.

'She's okay, I guess.'

'What do you mean?'

'I don't know,' says Mada. 'It's like we're in different worlds these days.' He glances at her, gives a sad smile. 'Still smoking?' he asks, as if casting around for a change of topic. His voice is neutral, lacking the nagging undertone with which the subject was addressed before she came inside. Considering everything else, the odd fag scarcely rates a mention.

'Still smoking,' she responds. 'It's the only pleasure that exists in this place. Besides, if I get lucky, it might bring an early death.'

'Don't *you* start.'

'You know, lung cancer doesn't seem so bad.' She's trying to be upbeat, silly even, but it comes out wrong, as if she's bragging. 'I've been thinking about it a lot, that's all,' she adds quietly.

'What?'

'Death.'

'Terrific.'

'You know it's different for Lori than it was for Dad. He always had problems. But we didn't know it was Huntington's. Late onset. He was one of the lucky ones. He was mostly fine through his working life, and then he got the shakes, stopped being able to remember where he'd put the wrench, stopped being able to fit it to the bolts. It made him so angry. He retired, sold the garage, and he'd lived for work, for his cars – the whole day all covered in grease. You know how your grandad was.'

'Kind of. I was pretty young when he—'

'Yeah. I guess you were about nine or ten. None of us knew what it was with Dad, but as he got older he was always on the edge of explosion, always muttering; this list of offences he kept against the world, growing by the day. We didn't know about Huntington's, not like now. But I always figured there was something, and then the diagnosis came, and he'd been getting worse and worse, and he saw what the end would be, and I guess he decided that he'd done his time. His Pacific course: that's what he called it in the note. Like he was going somewhere. Or playing a round of golf. Walking into the sea from the beach and trying to swim until he reached the far shore. He couldn't deal with it hanging over him. At least for most of his life it wasn't a question at the back of his mind, always blinking away, not like for Lori, for you. Not like it was for me, before the test results came back.

'Strange that Lori borrowed the words after all she said about Dad's departure. Because it's not a course,' she says, suddenly angry, 'it's not going somewhere. It's not elegant and beautiful. Life rattles out as messily as blood. If you're lucky you don't see it coming. You're here, and then gone. Maybe you're crossing the street, old, ready to go, and some woman like me isn't paying enough attention, or maybe she's pissed off, or maybe she's drunk, and she jumps the kerb and *smack*, your bottom half's an abattoir, caught between the car and the wall behind you. There's the shock of it, you're looking down and it's a mess, but you're already on your way, disconnected. Maybe there's not even any pain, not so you recognise it – you never get your breath back in, and that's that.'

Her hands are making fists in her lap, and with great effort she unclenches them and places them on her knees. 'And that's the lucky ones. If you're not it's slower, and the tremors start long before it takes you. You get to watch the whole sad show, swallowed by terror the whole fucking time.'

'Is this really what you want to talk about? The death that Mum may or may not have avoided. The way *I* might die?' Mada's had enough of her doom-laden intensity.

'No. Sorry.'

And she is. She doesn't want to let him know how dark she's turned, but a deep-seated resentment makes her want to grate against the world. Not the world in here: that world she needs to slip through, invisible as air. It's everything else, all that comes from beyond the walls, that's what she hates. All of it. Even the sunshine, as far as Bea is concerned, can piss right off, reminding her as it does of all the life she threw away, of all the pleasures of

171

basic existence disallowed by the fence wire and dysfunctional women, by the penal bureaucracy and the arsehole screws.

'It's not your fault,' Mada says with a sigh. 'This place is awful.'

She looks about, tries for upbeat. 'Oh, I don't know. A lick of paint. Some sprucing up here and there.'

'It feels,' he goes on, as though he hasn't heard her, 'like there's not enough oxygen. Like the sky is smaller.'

'The sky *is* smaller. Look at those walls.'

'I don't only mean that. More like it's smaller … everywhere. Like it gets inside you. I come in here and I can't even see properly.'

'It does get inside you,' Bea says quietly.

Mada takes off his glasses, rubbing his thumb and forefinger into the corners of his eyes.

'Mada, you must be disgusted with me.'

'Disgusted? Never! You don't owe me anything, Auntie. You're doing your penance.'

'What I did was fuckheaded. Someone is dead because of me.'

'I know. But look, we all do dumb things and mostly we get away with them. We sail on through. Because the roads are empty, because we bounce the right way. And then there are times we don't, and it all goes terribly wrong. Fate has a strange sense of humour.'

'Fate! Listen to my nephew, the scientist! Since when did you start talking superstition?'

He blushes, polishes the lenses of his glasses with his T-shirt. 'It's a metaphor. What you did was stupid, but you weren't trying to kill anyone. That's where fate comes in. Or bad luck, or whatever else you want to call it.'

'It's weird though, some part of it feels inevitable. Like I was willing it to happen. Like if it hadn't been that it would have been something else.' Bea glances at another prisoner, a dark-haired woman making out with her boyfriend on the grass. 'You think I was unlucky. My arse. University education. Good job. Father who didn't beat the shit out of me. Oh yes, it's been frightfully difficult. How could you not turn a life like that into an airline disaster.' She pauses, then says softly, 'Or a car accident.'

'Darling aunt, listen: you raised a son who was not your own, and did a good job of it, if I say so myself. Add a sibling who's been partway child most of the time, all of it in a family shuddering with disease, and a father who chose death instead. Just forgive yourself. We'll figure out the rest. Keep alive in here, until the time is done, then come back. You don't need *our* forgiveness.'

'I've had more good luck than bad, that's all I'm saying. But thank you. I'm an ingrate.'

'You mean an inmate?'

'Yeah, well. I'm so sorry, Mada. Sorry for everything.' She releases a sob that she can't hold in. Mada puts his arm over her shoulder and draws her into him, and Bea lowers her face to his shirt and tries not to cry.

'So am I,' he says. 'Just be safe. You'll get through this.'

That night it's Bea's turn to cook, and she's standing at the stove, watching for the pot to boil, when one of her housemates comes in. So far she has shared the house with twelve different women. At least now she has her own room.

'Whatcha cookin?'

'Rice.'

'Anything else?'

'Tomato and red beans.'

The woman comes over and sniffs at the pot. There's a sachet of chilli con carne mix empty next to the stove, and she picks it up to examine it. 'Ya know there's some chick lookin for ya?'

'What for?'

'Dunno. It's that skinny blonde who works the buy-up.'

'Good or bad?'

The woman shrugs. 'Could be bad, could be good. Says come see her when you pick up your stuff tomorrow.'

Steam is starting to vibrate the lid over the rice. Bea turns the stove down.

Could be bad, could be good.

She gets to the buy-up early the following day, but there's already a line. Maybe fifteen women, the shutter still closed. There was a fight last week, two women arguing over a bottle of shampoo, but the screws stopped it before it got nasty.

When the window swings open, the skinny blonde woman is there, as usual. Bea shuffles forward, waits, shuffles again. The only thing that happens fast in Club Fed is violence. Finally it's Bea's turn. She gives her name.

'You're Bea Campbell?' the blonde asks.

'Yeah. My housemate said you were looking for me.'

'Yep.' The woman fixes her with narrow eyes. 'You know anything about admin?'

'Computers and office work?' Bea isn't sure how such knowledge could work in her favour, but things are starting to look more on the good side.

'Yeah,' the woman says, waiting. She flicks back her hair. It's long, past her shoulders. She's kind of pretty, thinks Bea. Maybe twenty-five, even features, dark circles under her eyes.

'I know my way around Windows and accounting software. MYOB, you know?'

Her response gets a faint nod, a twitch of the woman's mouth that could almost be a smile. 'I might have a job for you at Milk-Pro,' she says.

Milk-Pro is the dairy processing facility adjacent to the prison. 'That'd be ace,' says Bea.

'Come find me Monday morning, after roll call. I reckon you'll do all right.'

The following week, Bea gets out of the transport van at the dairy processing facility. There's a farm. A few hundred cows. Most of the milking is done by prisoners, but the cows don't seem to mind. Almost the entire place, it turns out, is staffed by inmates. For Bea, it's like new air in her lungs. She is outside the prison and out of cuffs. No four-metre fence. No razor wire cutting every vista. She has made it out and through the gates, and after a year inside, the world beyond the fence is better, somehow more solid, than she remembers. The air feels different. There's a breeze: the wind of another world. She inhales the smell of cow manure, luscious and aromatic. There's something redemptive about the wholesome pungency of cowshit, she thinks. Its sweet earthiness.

Inside the factory it smells like custard flavouring. Synthetic and saccharine. It's loud, too. The conveyer belt of dairy products thuds and whirrs, so it's hard to hear what the woman giving her the grand tour is saying. She introduces herself as Rhino. Lab coat. Prison greens. Six foot tall, at least ninety kilos, most of it muscle. Bea gets her to repeat her name, just to be sure.

'Yeah, I know. Rhino. I earned it, and it stuck. Anyhow, I like it now.'

Rhino looks bulletproof. The story, she's told later, is that Rhino got her name after a well-placed head butt repositioned the nose of a long-term inmate, a woman who, in Rhino's words, 'tried it on'. Before entering Club Fed, she was a singer in a jazz club, but she'd lived, as she put it, a varied life, and she knew how to handle herself. As Bea watches, she hoists a full crate of milk from the floor to the top of one of the stacks.

Milk-Pro supplies dairy products to every prison in the state. Rhino points out the various stations along the production line, takes Bea to see the milking machines. There's a tall woman sweeping the floor. Very thin, short black hair, face covered in acne scarring.

'Keep clear of her,' says Rhino. 'Too much meth. She's still not right. You're in the office so you should be okay. I'll show you. Sweet job. Best pay on the compound.'

When they get to the office, there's another inmate sitting at a computer. There's no internet of course, but otherwise it seems like a normal factory office. It doesn't take Bea long to figure out how lucky she is to be there. Good work conditions. Pay of sixty-four dollars a week. It's better than most of the women get, and every workday she is allowed to wear a lab coat over her prison greens. Rhino is the office manager. She takes Bea through her responsibilities, which are mostly about ordering, ensuring the state's prisoners get their milk, yoghurt and custard.

'Think you can handle it?' Rhino asks.

Bea nods. Grins. She's run two offices with twenty-five employees, multimillion-dollar turnovers. But that was in another life. 'No worries,' she says.

'How old are you?' asks Rhino.

'Fifty. How old are you?'

'Twenty-five.'

'Twenty-five. How sweet it is.'

After her first shift, Bea takes off her lab coat at the end of the day and climbs into the van. She's on her way back to prison, but she feels a bit more human, a bit less afraid. Rhino is already in the van and makes some space beside her.

'What do you think?'

'It's great.' She means it, too. She can't help smiling. She had almost forgotten how.

'Yeah. Thought you'd do all right.'

Back at the prison, everyone lines up at the muster square. There's the siren, the roll call. Bea is thinking about all the things she can get from the buy-up with sixty-four dollars a week. Luxuries. A doona and cover. Shampoo. Chips and lollies. She has to order a week in advance, and she puts in a request for olives, anchovies, fettuccine, parmesan and a large tin of tomatoes, figuring to make a puttanesca. She's been too embarrassed to ask Red or Mada for money.

'What are you in for?' Bea asks Rhino the next day. They're in the office. It's loud, but not as bad as the factory floor. You can talk at least.

'Standing up for myself,' Rhino says.

'Yeah?'

'Yeah. One day, I caught this fuckhead meth-boy going out my window. I just got home, and he was lowering our TV through the big window in our lounge room. Little shit. So I pulled his legs out from under him. Dumb thing to do, I know – didn't even think what would happen to the telly. Sure enough it busted. Anyway, front part of him keeps going through the window, and the legs come back with me. Thing is, the window's deadlocked, so he's broken the glass to get in, and he hasn't cleared the glass from the bottom of the frame. Damn near cut him in two.' She shrugs. 'Judge got pissed off. I woulda got off with nothin if I didn't have a RAP sheet.'

'You had another run-in with a meth-head?'

'No. I swear for the first one I didn't do shit, just got lippy with this cop and one thing led to another. Fucker hit me first, as if that matters with the pigs. I didn't do any time for it – suspended sentence – but it was on the record. Anyway, they put me in here. Coulda been worse but, coulda been left in Silverwater. But it's bullshit all the same. Someone steals from you they should expect payback. My brothers and me used to wrestle, and I've boxed a bit. I got some skills.'

Bea believes her. 'What happened to the bloke?'

'It took the medics ages just to get him off the window. He was, like, mashed into the glass and frame. He lived all right, but the dumb prick still had a colostomy bag when they wheeled him into court.'

The Numbers
Chapter 14

Red celebrates the first quarter in the new building, the offices overlooking Darling Harbour, sending out the new secretary for cake and balloons: she buys a dozen metallic pink ones at twelve dollars a pop, but she does pretty well on the cake, and his relief at making it through the first quarter is sufficiently immense that he's inclined to be magnanimous. It had been a borderline operation for a while. Scraping by month to month as the cost of the move and new office space saw him haemorrhaging money. And that on top of the personal mortgage for the new house, which meant the bank pretty much had his balls in a safe deposit box.

The stress of it was almost too much to cope with. Day after day, the same worries, the same thought playing through his head: I'm almost there – I've only got to hold on until a few of the big commissions roll in. He was constantly on the edge of going broke, trying to stop it all from tumbling down, and the high rises and streets themselves had started to get under his skin. How hard did he have to try? Every day busting his gut to make a dollar. Every day thinking, fuck this city, with its six-dollar coffees. Fuck this city, with its hundred-dollar parking. And fuck this city, with its office space at a thousand dollars a square metre.

In what universe had he deemed a harbour view essential?

He could have found good space for half what he's paying.

But spend money to make money, that's what the logic had been.

And most days of the last three months it really seemed a ludicrous conceit. One month in, Min swung by the office, on the way to Golden Century with a couple of associates. Just a casual lunch to celebrate the first of the properties being signed. Min chatted as if the lunch was spontaneous, a great surprise, but of course he'd known they were coming, and no doubt they enjoyed the theatre of it as well. If smoke and mirrors were the way to get things done, then fire up the smoke machine, he was ready for whatever came his way. And, of course, yes! He would love to come to lunch! It was the informality of the restaurant, he supposed, that necessitated the ruse, although there were wines on the list that made him baulk, regardless of the client, and half of what was happening seemed to occur in a code that was beyond his reckoning.

It was meant to be celebratory, and everyone was very polite. Yet he felt like an alien. Terrified by a rising tsunami of debt. He sat at the table, watching the taxis on Dixon Street, looking through teeming fish tanks that walled off the restaurant from the street, the writhing seafood staring down on the diners, abalone suckered to the glass. Most of the conversation was in English, and the waiter brought an enormous mud crab to the table before they stuck it in the pot, and the bloody thing looked right at him, right through him. Beady eyes. Enormous pincers banded helplessly shut.

On the way to being boiled to death.

He'd read an article the previous week about how smart lobsters are: how they understand their environment, experience fear and pain. That meant that when placed in a cooking pot they were cognisant of the fact they were boiling to death, and felt every moment of their pain. Probably crabs were the same. I mean, what the fuck? thought Red. What kind of a twisted motherfucker is God? And it occurred to him that he understood that crab better than he understood his new business partners, and right at that moment it seemed he understood that crab better than he understood himself.

He worked to crack the hard outer shell, broke through the biggest of the pincers. An honour, Min later said, that it was presented to him. But he choked it down, and all the while his mind was filled with those beady eyes. Pleading. For god's sake, don't stick me in that fucking pot.

Well to hell with that, he now thinks. There are deals to be done, and if a few awkward lunches and tortured crabs are the price for making millions in the real estate market, he'll gladly pay it.

Christ, he'd boil the crabs himself.

And in the end, it was worth it to get space close to Chinatown; the view alone had paid off. Min Fang brought a couple of bankers and some other 'new friends' up to see him there, a couple from Hong Kong and some fair-haired press agent in killer stilettos and an impeccable suit who worked for the Libs, although she wasn't completely clear on what she did. He'd had a few deposits by then, and everyone sat in the conference room drinking San Pellegrino with the harbour below, talking about the sales spike in the last quarter, and it was a day like this, Sydney the gilded whore and everyone laughing at each other's jokes and Red at the head of the table in his new Brioni suit, the one Min had chosen for him.

A king at the head of his court.

And as it turns out, he won't lose the court!

Red eats his cake and offers a brief speech about keeping the sales coming, then takes a second piece and heads back into his office. He leans back in the Herman Miller desk chair, gazing through the spotless window at the spires of the Anzac Bridge, their crown of steel suspension cables, while below, if he leans into the glass, he can make out the tangle of roadways and tourist joints that wrap around the edge of the bright, cloudless bay, diamonds in the shifting water.

'You've done it, son.' He says the words out loud.

It is easily the best office he's had. Certainly one of the best he has even sat in. And he built it himself. His sweat. His guts. Red types the user ID into his online banking portal.

Next the password, typing the letters with slow care, using two fingers: M-0-N-e-Y-P-a-N-T-$-6-9. He gives a quiet chuckle.

The most significant settlement so far should be in today.

Red adjusts his tie. The atmosphere in the room is stuffy.

He'll talk to the new girl, get her to check the air-con.

He clicks on the Premier Care Business Account, the transaction records light up, and then Red isn't thinking about the air-conditioning anymore. Red isn't thinking about anything but profit: the numbers bright and clear before his eyes, leaving no space for him to do more than blink in their light. The latest payment is through and his account is looking sweet, sweet, sweet: multiple large deposits, one after the other.

He takes a gulp of air and grins maniacally out at the harbour, drumming his feet in celebration on the floor, then looks back at the screen. The settlement on the biggest yet of Min's deals has gone through, and he has generated two hundred and seventy-two thousand dollars commission, from just one sale. He stares at the numbers. Just. One. Sale. And there are more settling *this week*. Lots more. Total commission for the last three days will top seven hundred and eighty thousand. He has to pay the rent, pay his staff, and every week won't be like this. But he'll be nudging past the million for this week alone. There might be other agents who can top that, but he doesn't think so. Not at the residential end. Once the overheads come off the top, Min Fang's slice of the pie will be a solid chunk, but there's so much flowing in, that scarcely bothers him.

Angelo sure was right about that, she costs a hell of a lot. But Jesus, is she worth it. He picks up the phone and gives her a call before he can think of what he wants to say.

'Hello, Redmond. I trust you're well.'

Her voice is a combination of throaty English and melodic Chinese. He's never found Asian accents especially sexy, but hers is like smooth electricity, running from his ear right down to his crotch.

'The payment for the penthouse has cleared,' he blurts out.

'Okay,' she says. 'Good to have a short settlement, isn't it?'

'Good. It's better than good. It's almost three hundred K on that sale alone.'

'You're happy, then.'

'Happy? I'm ready to pop.'

'Then I'm happy.'

'Have dinner with me.'

The words surprise him as they come out of his mouth.

Silence. Then 'Why?'

'To celebrate.'

'Hmmm.'

'I'll take you to Tetsuya's.'

He knows it's her favourite restaurant. Min has no interest in the usual Sino-Japanese antagonisms: money has no race, or so she says, and good food is good food. Her breathing changes. Becomes deeper, more attentive. Like a music to which they are both attuned.

Finally, she says, 'You won't get a reservation at Tetsuya's. Not on a Friday night. Not a chance.'

'Maybe not.' He pauses. 'I bet *you* could, though.'

She offers a short laugh.

He can hear her stereo playing in the background. A weird instrument he doesn't know the name of.

'Is it correct that you're married?' she asks.

'Sort of.'

Until now, they've avoided all talk of personal circumstances. Until now, it's all been professional: a good laugh and a shared passion for golf. Red realises, right then, how much he's changed things with just a few words.

Min offers a snort of derision. 'You're not 'sort of' married, Redmond. You're married or you're not.'

'My wife's in prison.'

'Is that right?'

There is genuine surprise in her voice. Plus curiosity, even enthusiasm, as if he just got more interesting. Red is so used to his life being the subject of office gossip, he's started to feel as if he has a sign on his head saying, *Wife in Prison*. He finds it utterly refreshing that Min didn't know.

'How long has she been inside?' Min asks.

'Bit over a year,' he says haltingly. His euphoria begins to drain.

'And when does she come out?'

'Another year or so.' He can hear Min tapping a pen against her desk. The whole thing feels weird now, and he's about to tell her not to worry, that he'll see her next week, at the Finger Wharf property, when he hears the tapping stop.

'Okay,' she says. 'Tetsuya's. Tonight. Unless you hear from me, come at eight o'clock. I'll take care of the reservation. Don't be late.'

Min Fang is at the reception desk when he gets to Tetsuya's, and just touching his eyes on her, all doubts flee his mind. She's talking French with the *maître d'*, giving an easy laugh, owning the room. A couple of blokes in suits are waiting for a car and they can't take their eyes off her. It's seven fifty-nine, and she checks her Cartier, giving Red a nod of approval as she sashays over to greet him. A long dress, black and velvet, flows about her, and she has a scarlet shawl around her shoulders. There's something in the way she moves that stops Red mid-step. It's as if she really is a sorceress, or some kind of Franco-Chinese deity. She kisses him on both cheeks, French-style, and runs her fingers from the edge of his shoulders to the tops of his hands, a scent of sweet spice following her across the room.

Cinnamon. Clove.

Subtle and erotic.

An erection is pushing at the fabric of his pants before he even realises it's forming. Hard and sudden, beyond control, as if he's a teenager. Her eyes flick over his suit, and he is sure, in that instant, that she knows it's there, that she is the one who has summoned it.

Knowingly, deliberately, an act of conjuring.

They are shown to a corner table, overlooking the Zen garden, and she holds his arm as they walk over. All this is new. Every part of it. The way she speaks, the way she touches him. As the *maître d'* pulls out her chair, she hands him her shawl and orders sparkling water and a bottle of Cristal.

'You're hungry, I assume,' she says to Red, dropping her eyes to his pants, more obvious this time.

'Famished,' he says, taking his seat.

His cock is achingly solid.

She gives a light, throaty chuckle.

A brief spurt of laugher jets from his throat. He stifles it and rearranges his serviette. But Min only laughs again, as though she gets the joke, as though she knows what he's thinking even better than he does. Red feels giddy. His head is reeling and the champagne is yet to arrive.

All this, so utterly new.

Until now, she has been completely professional. Until now, she hasn't even touched him, except to shake his hand. No flirtation. Not even much in the way of cleavage. But in this moment, it feels like she's straddling him – without the merest brush of skin.

The waiter splashes mineral water into their glasses, then the champagne appears. There is a slow, luxurious pour, the colour straw-like, the liquid rising to the rim in foamy perfection, then settling to reveal a depth of fine, bright beads. Her mouth isn't moving, but for an instant he hears her speak within his mind: We will eat. We will drink. And then we will leave this place and strip off these clothes. And we will lick each other from shoulder to shin. And I will ride you, smooth, hard and long, beyond all tangible realms.

The following Friday, Red and Min share one perfect, smashing afternoon out at Rosebery. Red is feeling like he can't drop a shot, and Min tees off in black silk pants that, as she bends into the ball, so perfectly hug her arse that he can think about nothing but taking her. Fortunately, he's got his swing so deep in his bones it's as if the ball is a part of himself and he needs do little more than slap one hand to another to send it flying over the grass.

God, it feels good to be back.

He'd been so deep in the doldrums for so long – worried about money, worried about Bea. Well, screw being maudlin!

He's going places, and Min is helping him get there. It's business first and always, he tells himself – even Bea would agree with that; she wouldn't mind, really, if it makes them both rich.

And it's not hurting his swing any, that's for sure! Because Min loves golf more than Zeus loves lightning. She's constantly looking for an excuse to head to the course, and he's sure that it's his readiness to be persuaded that's caused her to fall into his bed. Ever since they had dinner, and she let him take her home, she's convinced him to meet her at Bonnie Doon, at Pymble, at the Lakes: a quick round at eleven, where she's 'made a little space'.

And it's not just the courses and lunches with this hyper-fuckable hyper-accountant cum lawyer; through Min, Red is meeting everyone. She takes him as her date to a dinner with a wealthy banker and philanthropist, an intimate affair with just a hundred of his closest friends, and the next weekend he's out on a boat that's bigger than his new house, owned by a Queensland coal magnate so ribald he and Red are the final crusaders propping up the bar at the end. He gives Red his card and lets it slip that he's searching out a few investment properties not too far from the harbour. Just by chance, the following week, he and Min pair up with two of Red's chums from school for an afternoon round at Moore Park; the fellas can't keep their eyes off Min. She and Red break eighty, Min on a clean seventy-one, and after a few hours of chit-chat on the course, and another few hours of problem-solving at the clubhouse, Red exchanges cards with them, both men confessing they'd been looking for someone decent to handle solid asset sales, a ritual which Min, explaining that she's 'out of cards', judiciously avoids, which only makes Red grow bolder. He decides to follow up with them the following Monday, even while he's shaking hands goodbye, and he can tell by the shades and YSL they play in his league.

The old boys leave Red and Min to prop up the bar, neither of them willing to let go of a round so splendid. Red is definitely half-cut, even he can tell, and Min is all but splayed on the carpet. It's the first time he's seen her even tipsy, regardless of what she's put down her throat. It's not so much that she's got clumsy, more like she's fresh out of fucks to give. She leans back in her chair like a gangster, her arm cocked on the backrest, her shoe under the table where it's slid off her foot.

'That's the best round I've hit this month.' Min lifts her glass again, gives him a big smile.

Red is taken aback. He's so accustomed to her excellence, he hadn't computed that, for her, this was something exceptional. 'Well,' he grins back at her, 'that's great.'

She lifts her foot and lets her toes gently massage his balls for a moment, then leans forward, her elbows wide on the table as she surveys Red. 'Maybe you're my lucky charm.'

'I think you're right,' he says. 'I was due some luck.'

'You know why we get on so well, Redmond? It's because you're an alien, just like me,' she says, 'and now you're *my* alien.'

'Bugger off,' he retorts.

'I'm serious,' she says, slurring.

'An alien? Whaddaya mean?'

'Ah Red, you're an alien, you are; it takes one to know one. Most people don't see it. Not those boys you know from school. They don't see anything but your Rolex and Hugo Boss. But some part of you doesn't fit. Not really. I'll tell you a secret: all my life I've been an alien. Ever since I was born. Too Chinese for the whites and too white for the Chinese. Too French for the British, too British for the French. Too Chinese or not Chinese enough. Always *baak gwai*. And there's my upbringing, such as it was. Raised by my mother's married sister, because of the shame my birth would bring to my mother. She was hidden when she had me. Hidden! My grandfather had threatened to kill the two of us, but eventually his anger drained away. My mother wrote to my father initially, but the letters were returned, and he refused to acknowledge me. Then, by chance, we met on the streets of Kowloon. I was with my aunt and mother, and my parents almost collided on a pedestrian crossing. I would have been about ten, and I remember they seemed stuck in a moment of silence for a very long time. All about them people were pushing, but neither of them moved or spoke. I asked my mother what was wrong, but my aunt said to hush. I could see they loved each other – she had never stared at a man like that, not that I saw. He looked from her to me, then back to her, and he began to cry. His wife had died the previous year; they had no children.

'After that, he would come and visit, bring me gifts, help me with my French, my English. He was an obsessive polyglot and passed his passion on to me. He created a fiction around the circumstances of my birth, paid for my tuition at Cheltenham. He was very well connected – he'd been with the French consulate for years – and as I got older, I travelled with him on consular business. Unofficially, but I met everyone important, or most of them.'

She takes another gulp of wine. Red is impressed – he'd ordered a final bottle of cabernet to see them home, and she's put away most of it. 'In business, all that's important is connection and money. Personal relationships are different, or they're not worth it. This is what I learned from my fucking psychopath ex-husband. Nothing like you. And that's why I like you, Redmond.' She runs her finger roughly over his cheek. 'You don't want to own me, you just want to fuck me.'

'Who was this guy,' asks Red, a stab of jealousy catching him unawares. 'Your ex-husband?'

'Don't worry,' she chuckles. 'He's dead now. A British bank executive, charming when he wanted to be, cruel as Satan when he didn't. He saw marriage in terms of property and finance, and I was just another asset, no more. From the day of the wedding he became a completely different man. He'd acquired the asset, it was won, and he'd treat it like any other. And when I say he was a psychopath, I don't mean that as a figure of speech. After I left him and took a lover, he tried to have us hacked up with a cleaver and dropped into Victoria Harbour.'

'A cleaver? What?' Suddenly Red feels almost sober.

'He approached a mutual acquaintance, Zhang Kuok-Koi, to do it. He was the incense master of a local triad, and expert at these things, but my ex didn't realise, until too late, that he'd approached one of my associates. When it comes to business, I play my cards close. You know this, eh? Zhang is a very hard man. He's seen and done much. But he's a man with a certain integrity. I'd reached out to Zhang after I left the psycho, as I was afraid of what he might do. As it turned out, Zhang was fond of me.' She smiles gently. 'He still is.'

She pokes a finger into her wine glass, then watches the liquid drip redly down her wrist. 'I had no idea of my husband's death until the police came knocking,' she says breathily. 'Had I seen my husband recently, they asked? I'd left him months before, hadn't seen him in nearly half a year. At first they refused to tell me why they were asking, pushed me for information, but in the end it came out that he'd been murdered. I'm sure, at first, I was a suspect, but the truth of my innocence couldn't be challenged. Perhaps eighteen months passed, and I was drinking with Zhang and some mainland officials after a big deal, when Zhang took me aside and told me what had happened. My ex was a pig, he said. So he'd killed him. Simple. He was unsure at first how I'd take it, but truth be told I was moved. No one had ever done anything like that for me before: literally saved my life and killed the man who threatened it.

'I've always been surrounded by strong men, Redmond. My father, his associates, my hideous ex. Now I make my own choices. I like you for your soft edges.'

'My edges are soft? And that's why you like me?' Red absent-mindedly makes his fingers into callipers to measure the fat on his gut. He doesn't know what to feel. The woman sitting across the table seems abruptly closer and more distant. A cold shiver passes down his spine.

'I want my life to be my own, Redmond, not some gift for which I must be thankful, for which I must seek the permission of a man who believes he owns me.'

'So that's why you took me to bed? Because I'm not a threat?'

'I fuck you, Redmond, because you make me laugh, because you're fun to share a round with, and because you so desperately like it. Don't you think that's enough?' She raises an eyebrow at him.

'That's good enough for me,' says Red quickly, offering his best real estate grin. Inside he's trying to figure out what he's got himself into.

'Good,' says Min. 'Now take me home and give me one of those fucks we both deserve.' She lifts her elbows from the table and gets to her feet with some difficulty. Red hurries round to help her, and both of them end up half on the carpet. Laughing, they grip one another and stagger towards the door, weaving shambolically through the carpark. Red clicks the remote and the Beamer lights up a few metres away.

'Are you sure you're okay to drive?' she asks as he opens the door for her.

'Yeah, no sweat,' says Red. 'I'm your lucky charm, remember?'

The Women of the Land

Chapter 15

Lori hitchhikes north, catching a series of short rides with locals, the suburbs giving way to bush. They cut through cliffs and over waterways, crossing bridges spanning estuaries and rivers, where the coast breaks into land. Over the Hawkesbury she's riding in a panel van, chatting away with two guys headed home to the Central Coast. Then she gets a short hop with a woman pushing ninety, who plays organ at the Gosford Anglican church: a friend of Father Bower, she says, who writes those wonderful signs. She gets dropped at a turn-off and walks back to the highway, waiting at the roadside less than ten minutes before her next ride: three girls in a Jeep, headed into work at Finnegan's Hotel after a blow-out in Sydney. They have to pull over at a rest stop, waiting ten minutes when one of them 'gets the spins', and once they get to Newcastle's outskirts, the four of them vote for McDonald's, where Lori shouts them lunch.

She spends her first night at a youth hostel on Main Street, in Newcastle, a huge, ramshackle terrace a few blocks from the beach. With the sun coming down it's idyllic: air gone luminous, young people everywhere. She takes a seat on the balcony, admires them milling about. She can make out the ocean at the end of the street, and she sits with her beer and orders chicken parmigiana and watches the light fade. Her meal's huge when it arrives, and Lori tucks in. She's full before she's halfway through and she pushes away her plate, still piled with chicken and chips, and heads down to the beach for a walk. In the peaceful saltspray air, the worries of departure ease away.

Next day, sun on the horizon and the ocean flowing gold. She goes down to the beach in her cossie and has a quick swim, then walks shoeless along the water's edge, watching the surfers, before heading back to the hostel and retrieving her pack. There's a café over the road doing baked beans and eggs for breakfast, and she polishes her plate clean with the last of the toast, then catches a bus to the edge of town so she can find a ride.

Without planning to, she turns her back on the sea for a while, heading inland on a whim in a rusted-out ute with an aged and weather-battered farmer. She likes the look of him, his sun-blasted authenticity, so when he says he's headed to Tamworth, Lori says, 'Great.' It's not clear to Lori exactly where or how far that might be, but so long as she keeps heading north she's on the right road.

He's got two kelpies in the tray, and they pass the time in companionable silence while she takes in the fields of crops, the desiccated remnant bushland, cattle gathered in slim eucalyptus shade under the sky's hard blue.

She's hungry by the time he drops her off in front of the big gold guitar. Lori casts a critical gaze over the peculiar stringless instrument, her sculptor's eye silently contemplating how it might be improved. Heat and dusty light shimmer in its curves.

No firm plan in mind, Lori finds herself strolling into a café near the visitors centre, to order a drink and decide on her next move. Tamworth's not a bad town, she reflects. Federation buildings lining the streets, friendly locals in thongs and singlets. Tourists everywhere. But the heat is oppressive, and she's come a long way in from the coast without really meaning to. Still, she thinks, all roads are correct when fate guides the journey, and she could do worse than spend what's left of the afternoon stretched out by the river. The waitress puts a glass of ice and a cold bottle of dry ginger ale in front of her. Tomorrow, Lori decides, she'll head coastwards first thing in the morning. She's got her backpack propped beside her chair, and she gives it a reassuring squeeze, feeling the stash of money right down the bottom, waiting to take her on, and on.

That night she sleeps beside an open window at the Stagecoach Inn Motel, the drone of air-conditioning units sounding long into the night. At first light she catches a ride to Bendemeer with an old woman in a Falcon, getting dropped off at the Walcha Road turn-off, heading towards the coast. She rides next with an Anglican minister travelling home to Kempsey, and they argue good-naturedly about the sin of pride as the landscape flies away. He starts to squirm when Lori turns the conversation to lust, arguing against its inclusion on the list of seven deadly sins, and by the time he drops her at a roadside motel on the highway north of town, he's sweaty and a little pink, and seems utterly relieved to be shot of her. The next morning, she's up and at it before the sun, spending a glorious hour by the highway in the expectant morning air. Time spent waiting by the bitumen doesn't bother her: wherever you are is the right place to be.

By the time she eventually reaches the Bangalow turn-off, still on the outskirts of Byron, she's taken about ten rides to get less than four hundred kilometres, the best of the day is gone, and her patience has expired. Lori slumps beside some graffiti in the concrete-walled grotto under the overpass, leaning against her pack. She could almost sleep here. Right here, plastic wrappers and bottles everywhere, but at least it's out of the heat. She gets up to scout around, assess the possibilities, but no sooner has she stood and glanced at the road than two blond Europeans in a rental camper pull over and motion her up.

Lori's spirits lift. She gives her biggest smile and clambers in the back. Together they ride up into the hills towards Byron, where the roadside scrub suddenly erupts into tropics, broad-leafed foliage spilling over the bitumen at every hairpin bend, flame trees exploding with vibrant red flowers, and when the lighthouse comes into view, the ocean flat and glowing behind it, she whoops and hollers and gesticulates so wholeheartedly that the driver pulls over to make sure she, and they, are okay.

'It's the lighthouse!' she says, pointing.

He stares at the edifice, and then at her, his brow furrowed. 'Yes, I see. It is very nice. But please stay in your seat and don't reach for the wheel while I'm driving. It isn't safe.'

'I only wanted to toot the horn.'

'Then please don't try to toot the horn while I'm driving.'

'Okay, Adolf,' quips Lori.

'What did you call me?'

Lori giggles.

'What?!'

He wants to throw her out of the van then and there, and only relents when his travelling companion won't allow it. The journey passes in silence until they merge with the coastal road; then the traffic stops with them still on the outskirts of town. Oddly, this seems to excite the driver.

'Ah yes, you see? Everybody's here! Didn't I tell you, Sofia? Look at all these people!'

They proceed in a stop-start fashion for a good twenty minutes; the closer they get to Byron Bay, the more kids in swimsuits there are walking between the cars, the more half-peeled wetsuits flapping beneath sculpted abs on tanned surfer boys.

'What's going on?' Lori asks.

'The party, of course,' says the driver.

'What party?'

He turns in his seat to stare at her, incredulous. 'Why, the music festival!' he says. 'Splendour in the Grass. Even in Germany we know of it. Surely this is why you're here?'

'Nope,' says Lori. She leans back in the seat and grips her pack to her leg, testing again for the wad of cash under the nylon.

They drop her at the roundabout on Lawson Street, every inch of pavement so full of people Lori can hardly move. Everywhere there are kids with ripped jeans and black T-shirts, girls with face paint, boys with singlets and muscles and tats, and everywhere there are No Vacancy signs. She checks the reception of every hostel she passes, and eventually, finding the yellow and blue sign of an information centre, steps into the air-conditioning for some help.

Inside the office it's even more packed than on the street, everyone talking loudly about the weekend to come. Lori waits in the ill-formed queue, tapping her foot irritably. When she eventually manages to talk to the guy behind the desk, inquiring about accommodation options, he asks for her reservation details.

'I don't have any details, that's why I'm here,' she responds.

'What hotel is the reservation for?' He asks without looking up, scowling at something on his computer with an air of patience tested.

'I don't have a reservation, that's what I'm saying.' No wonder she's waited twenty minutes to be served, thinks Lori, if this dotard is the best they can offer.

The man gives a short, dismissive laugh. 'And you're looking for accommodation?'

'Well of course I bloody am! I thought we'd been through that.'

'There hasn't been a spare bed in this town for weeks. You might have some luck in Mullum, try there.' He pulls a series of timetables from slots in his desk and hands them over to her.

Lori sifts through the pamphlets, which seem mostly to be bus timetables. 'Lennox Head? I don't want to go to Lennox Head, I want a place to sleep.'

'That's the best I can do,' he responds shortly, as though the thirty seconds he has expended on her is already too much by half. 'Why don't you have a seat?' He points to a plastic chair in the corner, through the throng of waiting legs. 'You can flick through these.'

Lori throws the papers back across the desk, harder than she intends. One of them loops up and hits the man in the glasses. 'I don't want to flick through bus timetables,' she says, 'I want somewhere to stay.'

Behind the counter, the man glares at her in shock.

'There are no availabilities,' he says after several beats.

All about them, voices turn muted. Everyone stares. Lori feels a flush of red on her face. She shoulders her pack, mutters an apology, and stumbles through the crowd towards the door. She turns down the street, walking on the road to avoid the worst of the pedestrian traffic, and heads into the nearest pub, her arms and legs jerking about of their own accord, leaping away from her as though to abandon ship mid-stride.

It's always worse when she's stressed.

Half an hour later, with a schooner of Tooheys New and a plate of calamari in her tummy, she's feeling a damn sight better. It's starting to cool, and she chases the last of the sun towards the beach. There seem, impossibly, to be even more kids about, restaurants and bars overflowing, buskers filling footpaths.

Everywhere music. It drifts under doors and out through windows, and by the time Lori hits Bay Street the music is a flood. From the pub on the corner people are spilling onto the roadway, a woman on stage singing her lungs out, while a guitarist in Jim Morrison pants, no shirt, goes down on his knees before the audience. Lori stops to watch for a spell, taking pleasure in the sea of young faces, the girls and the boys all half-naked, the girls with their perfect bouncy boobs spilling from their tops, all the boys shirtless, the buff ones at least, tattoos on smooth biceps, so much gorgeous young skin and muscle on display that Lori starts to tingle. Two men, their arms on each other's shoulders, are fist-pumping to the band. As she watches, a girl in a red bikini leaps from one of the wooden benches and wraps her legs about one of the shirtless boys, pashing him in earnest.

Lori can't stop grinning.

Singing out loud, she heads across the street, through the playground and down past the surf club, kicking off her thongs to wend a path over the grass, through the couples and families sitting drinking beer, standing about, talking, watching the water. Now she can see the ocean up close, she suddenly can't wait. Her foot nicks a plastic cup as she breaks into her awkward run. People stare at her rushing jerkily through the crowd. Lori doesn't care. She has to get into that surf this very moment, it's the only thing that counts. She gets to the steps, grabs the railing and trundles down, and then she's finally there, and the sun-warmed sand is soft and forgiving on her feet.

Without even thinking about it she drops her pack and strips off her T-shirt and shorts, then glances at her things a moment – the bag, with its hoard of cash hidden away – seeing them in a flash for the anchors that they truly are, nothing more than snags, she thinks, pulling at her, binding her to earth, all the things she owns only acting to make her heavier, and she resolutely turns her back and flees to the sea, picking up speed till she throws her arms out and launches herself into the ocean, plunging through an oncoming wave to break into that undersea world. The immaculate cold, tight and strong. Salt-blurred vision: rising and ducking through the shallows, swooping down on the next wave so she is almost sitting on the bottom beneath the churn, calm while it lifts sand from seafloor and writhing water all about, but she's too low to get drawn into it, and over the top of her a glistening shifting spire, and then it's the seafloor sifting up to swallow her toes. She stays ducked until it has swooped entirely overhead, and it's then she strikes out, underwater, to where the ocean deepens. The waves pull at her body in all directions at once, another piece of sea-drift awash in the endless current, and when the roll of it has passed Lori kicks up, breaks through the silver surface of air and into exploding blue light, sucking at the oxygen and not letting herself cough.

Sweet Jesus. That air!

From where she floats, rising in the next swell, she makes out the surfers lining up from the point, rising and falling. She will have to be careful, her stroke is not what it used to be.

Lori kicks with steady care, aiming to get far enough back from the break so as not to be surprised. She wants to be able to take her eyes from what's oncoming for a moment or two, and shifts into a version of her regular three-stroke freestyle, but it's too hard with the chop and her lungs are aching so she takes it down to two.

She's getting there though, through the sets.

She swims the last few strokes with her head above the water. There's a patch of calm, for the moment at least. Lori rolls onto her back, holds her arms wide and closes her eyes. Sun falls on her face like the vision of all the angels, washing her in its warmth.

When she opens her eyes again, she is floating out into the great dome of the sky, the rise and fall of swell lifting her up then away, up and away into the universe itself, as though she is a part of its breathing, this earth, this place, its breath passing through her and her own lungs but an echo of that same breath, and she feels the truth of it as surely as the saltwater gathers her aloft. She is of this world and they are built of the same stuff, the same materials and ecstasies, the same heartaches, the same light winding through her cells.

Back with the beach dry and warm beneath her she pulls out her towel, and laying her head to her arms she lets herself drip dry with the last rays of sun. Eyes mostly closed, filtering the brightness through her lashes. The beach running a lane of gold up to the edge of the sky. All about her people laugh and talk, and she feels beneath her the world in its endless turning. Lori lets her eyes droop, breathing deep of that world's breath, and all the while the sun is lush and gentle on her skin.

She wakes with the low boom of surf so close that it runs up beneath her; not water itself, but the feeling, the sound. Lori sits up, wraps the thin damp towel about her shoulders. The sound has shifted with the rising of the dark, and now, the ocean turned silver black, it speaks of shadows that prowl the waters, headland to headland in the molten break. The towel does little to keep her warm, and she pulls on a T-shirt, then rummages in her backpack for her jeans and a jumper. The wind is up. There's a change coming, the air spotted with rain.

The last surfer has paddled in, and he pauses at the shore to peel off the top half of his wetsuit, letting it dangle from his waist, so in the half light it could be skin dangling from a flayed torso, and the phrase comes back to Lori out of the gathering darkness: *Dance, Vitus, Dance.* She starts, a short circuit of electrical horror running through her, as though all the world's pain is lifting

203

from the mercury sea, ready to drown them all in a tsunami of death.

She gets to her feet and slips on her thongs. The sound of music comes distant from the pub, mangled by the boom of the surf. It's a different band now, thrashing their instruments. The anguish of the lead's wailing lament, as though he's torturing the guitar, sends a shudder of relief through her: it isn't the surf that has turned dark nor a world that's abandoned her; more that the band is rubbish. This place is still hers.

She considers, briefly, returning to Bay Street, looking again for a hotel to stay in, but then she remembers the information centre, the people, the man, and her head is so heavy she plonks herself back onto the sand and eats a handful of nuts, drawn from a pocket in her pack, then pulls out her extra jumper and her rain jacket, the one Mada gave her. Strength regained, she shoulders her backpack and stumbles along the beach, around the rocks, away from the surf club and into the shadows, where the low coastal shrubs might offer her shelter up beyond the tidemark, where she might dig a small place in the earth to protect her from the howl of the wind.

Soon she can't hear the pub at all, only the surf's plosive suck and boom – collapsing waves and the dull roar of a cosmos unceasing. She fashions for herself a kind of bed, in a hollow made from shrub roots, and, after wrapping herself in her waterproof jacket, she cradles her head on the towel. Closing her eyes, she pretends that she can sleep, and, in pretending, falls into a pattern where both sleep and waking are uncertain, bouncing through dimensions: dreams reaching into the landscape, landscape into dream, night and wind reaching into her soul. She dreams she is back there, at the bonfire on the sand so many years ago, and all John's friends are at the bonfire, but he is not. She tries to get up, tries to look for him, but her limbs are too numb to move, and, worse, some part of her knows that even were she able to rise there is nothing left to find.

She wakes abruptly, thrown into a darkness part composed of dream. The moon has disappeared, and the boom of surf is total, filling the air in wave after wave, filling in all the black. A fine mist of rain is falling. It feels to Lori as though she is inside the cloud of night itself, for there is no shoreline and no horizon and nothing but shadow on shadow, and the rain swirling up as much as down, as though gravity were confused. Only the surf comes through the black.

Boom. Boom. Boom.

She tries to forge a better bed, but the sand has hardened with the rain, so she digs into the hollow of the plants for solace, gripping a large paper-skinned root like a sailor on pitching seas. With grim resolve she holds tight, determined to ride it through or go down with the vessel, and for unknown hours she lies with the spray peppering her forehead, swirling as the wind flutes and shrieks in low branches, gripping herself fast to earth as she rides into the night.

A small black glistening sponge prods her about the face. Lori shoves it away. The sponge will not be cast off. It sticks in her eye socket, and, employing such leverage, attempts to lift her head from the sand.

Lori comes to aching wakefulness in the refusal of this last advance, thrusting the thing away and peering through sand-crusted lids. Reality forms in red-tinged shapes, a long beach with stretched morning shadows. Beneath her, pushing up, the cold, hard ground. There's an ache in her shoulder blades reminding her of a poem she once read. It's been there since before she remembers, but has turned to a dagger by the unyielding bed. In front of her, a scruffy terrier of indeterminate colour presses forward and once more attempts to lift her body by the application of its snout to her eye socket.

Lori forces the dog away. 'What's your caper, little one?'

Two women are standing between her and the water, knees covered in sand. They stop talking as she stirs and turn to gaze at her. One of them is rangy and white-haired. The other is shorter, darker, with wiry hair rising in a sandy kind of afro, high from her forehead. Both are lean and sinewy.

'He just wants to know that you're okay,' says the short one. 'He's not trying to eat you.'

The tall one gives a chuckle. 'Not yet anyway. He might give it a go if you can't get off the sand but, figuring you for a thing that's been washed up. You got any life in you? You travelling all right?'

Lori gets up on an elbow, fighting against the jacket which is caught around her body and will not release her arms. Oh, but her limbs feel tired. There's rough sand stuck to the back of her jeans.

'Yeah, I'm okay,' she says.

The sun remains low over the rocks and headland, the beach washed smooth by rain. The cloud has lifted and the coast is blue and long. She has slept late, for her at least. Probably about seven in the morning, she gauges. The dog is insistent, nosing her cheeks, and Lori pushes it back again and gives it a scratch. She finds the spot behind a matted ear that makes them instant friends, and it curls into her, adjusting its head on her thigh a few times before settling, mouth partly open and tongue dangling. A dog tag tells Lori its name is Olivia.

'Hey there, little girl,' she says. Olivia pants happily.

'Crappy night to be sleeping out,' says the short one.

'Tell me about it. Couldn't find a motel.'

'Splendour weekend. There's no spare bed in fifty k,' the woman says.

'I got that message.'

'Where you from?'

'Sydney.'

Lori sits up, releasing a groan.

'No offence, but you don't seem like Sydney. Plenty from Sydney here, but you not so much.'

'I dunno. Maybe it's a different part of Sydney. I hitched up through Tamworth and Kempsey. Only got here late yesterday.'

The woman offers a curious glance to her companion. 'Aren't you the traveller?'

She gazes up the beach a while, then turns to Lori, eyeing her up, a piece of flotsam of uncertain value, and deciding if she'll hand her in.

'We saw you here last night,' she says. 'You went by on the grass, out by the club. We watched you.'

'That right? Why did you watch *me*?'

A single gull walks along the beach, coming up behind them, poking at the sand. The dog sits up attentively.

'Well, you were different,' says the rangy one, casting an expectant eye at the dog. 'You took a dip. Looked like you were really ready for that water.'

'Yeah, really ready!' says the other, laughing. Then she stops, pulls her jacket around her. 'Why are you sleeping here?' she asks.

'I needed a place. It was just last night. I'm not sure about tomorrow.'

'Oh, you too, eh?' says the tall one.

The three of them laugh, although Lori isn't quite sure why. She decides she likes them. 'And what are you two doing?'

'Looking for pipis. Digging in the sand. Having a walk. We go back home today – we're not staying for the show. We couldn't get tickets even if we wanted them. We just came to see a friend get married, and we wanted to soak the last rays of all this up.' She opens her arms to take it in. The beach waking. There's a pack of surfers out back. Lori stares at them, mesmerised a moment: they sit on their boards, absolutely still, while all about the lines of ocean lift and fall, the resounding dump of rhythm pounding the horizon.

'We're going home today,' repeats the short one, as if this is significant.

'Where's your home?' asks Lori.

'Oh, out on the ridge, south a bit. So, what are you hitching about for?'

'To come here.'

'Why?'

'Just had to.'

'Had to?'

'Well, it's weird. Now I'm here ... I don't know. I wanted to see about a boy. I knew him here a long time ago, and then I had a dream about him, so I came, but when I got here, it kind of evaporated, and I'm just here, and it's colder than I thought it'd be. Who knows where he is now?'

The two women exchange a significant glance. 'So what's the plan now, sister?' asks the tall one with a grin.

'I'm just going to wing it,' says Lori courageously. 'It's good to have an adventure.'

'That it is, that it is.'

'You going to be sleeping here on the beach, then?'

'What if I am?' Lori gives a petulant stare.

'Just asking.'

'It's going to wear pretty thin with another night of rain.'

'Was wearing pretty thin last night, I'll tell you that.'

'The council will move you on as soon as they find you.'

'Well, I'm not real sure where else to go. With the music festival on. I figure I'll just hang around until a better idea arrives.'

'How about this for a better idea?' says the short one. 'Come to the Ridge for a bit. We live on a nice stretch of land. We've got space for you. For a while, at least. Who knows about tomorrow, eh?' She gives an easy laugh and bends to scoop up Lori's pack, as if it's already been decided.

'Come on, then,' says the other, taking Lori under the arm and raising her to her feet.

The three of them sing along to the radio, talking art, politics and patriarchy, heading south on the M1. The tall one is Jude.

She's an artist. She paints abstract landscapes, selling them in local galleries. The short one is Trish. She's a builder and a tradie, but these days it's mostly office work for a construction firm, about half an hour's drive inland from the coast.

'You'll like our place,' says Jude. 'Plenty of room. Might even be able to rustle you up some clay, there's a river close by. You ever sculpted with wild clay?'

'No,' says Lori excitedly. 'What's it like?'

'It's a bit of extra work, but it's … rich. You'll see.'

It's early afternoon as they turn off, following a rutted track forcing its way up towards the ridge top. Lori is in the back seat with Olivia, the dog having lifted her head from Lori's lap the instant they turned off the bitumen, sitting up quickly and staring attentively through the glass.

'Someone knows they're home,' says Lori, giving her a scratch.

Olivia offers her a distracted lick, not taking her eyes from the track. It's steep. More dirt and rock than gravel, half-buried boulders pushing through the dun earth. Trish stops to engage the AWD and revs high, the car complaining hard all the way up. They pass between two enormous eucalypts, either side of the track like gateposts, and then the house comes into view. Grey timber and a patchwork of rust on the corrugated roof, flushed in late sun.

Over the last thirty-five years, Trish explains, she's built the homestead and about half a dozen timber cabins. The cabins are mostly just one room, sometimes two, with sinks supplied by rainwater tanks. They're dotted about, further up the mountain from the homestead, with vistas to the valley and the steep falling ridgelines. The main house sits on a spire of rock, the land falling away and turning into waves of sandstone, butted to the eastern face of the mountain.

'Oh, it's brilliant,' Lori beams.

'Ta,' says Trish. 'Still no indoor dunnies, you've got to use the outhouse for that. But you'll like the bath. You can lie in the tub and watch the trees. She's rough, but she's home.'

They take her to one of the timber shacks on the edge of the forest, the furthest one from the house, and leave her to get settled. She drops her pack on the bed and walks about the room. All over the walls are photographs, old movie posters, stray objects nailed up: a snakeskin, an enormous leaf, a sculpture made of seashells and driftwood. There's a ukulele nailed up over the front door, half-consumed by a tangle of spiderwebs. The bed has a crocheted eiderdown, and the maker has omitted not a single colour from the universe's vast palette. Above the bed, stretching the length of the wall, is a hand-painted banner that reads *The Women of the Land*. There is dust everywhere, but the shack is otherwise clean, and Lori busies herself sweeping and tidying up, finding fresh sheets in a wardrobe and shaking them out. Everything carries the sweet residual pong of incense.

Her first morning, Lori wakes before the sun. She wanders down to the homestead, looking for company and a cup of tea, and finds Jude and Trish on the large timber deck, silently watching the early light lift stone escarpments from the misty valley floor. They drink tea and watch as the world takes form.

'So what are you running away from, Lori?' asks Jude eventually. 'You don't seem the battered wife type.'

'What makes you think I'm running?'

'No one hitches a thousand ks if they're happy where they are,' says Trish, leaning for the teapot.

'I suppose not.'

'So what is it? An ex? The cops maybe?'

'I wasn't running. I didn't leave Sydney because someone was after me, because I was unhappy. I mean, I was unhappy enough sometimes, but isn't everyone? I left to go and find … him. I told you. He's my boy's dad. Well, that's what I thought it was about. Then I got to Byron, and I kind of woke up.'

'Pretty impressive sleepwalking.'

'Thanks.'

'So what did you leave behind in Sydney, if you weren't running away?'

'My beautiful boy. My sister: they've got her locked up at Emu Plains. And her husband. The sponge. He's in real estate. Rakes in a lot of money but he doesn't *make* anything. He could never create something new. He just skims. Every time someone sells a house, he takes a little off the top.'

'Must be nice for him.'

'Yeah, sure,' says Lori, scowling.

She launches into a tirade – she has a lot of venting to do, and the women let her do it. Even she is surprised by how angry she is about Red, so he becomes the antecedent cause for every single bad thing that has ever happened to her, and to Bea, her poor sister now in prison – it's all Red's fault, it's all about the lack of love he showed her. The joy she finds in expressing this fury means the accuracy and fairness of her attack is neither here nor there. When she eventually grinds to a halt, she feels as if she has purged herself of bad residual energy. She lets her arms flop down by her sides and gazes from Trish to Jude.

'He makes me mad, that's all. Sorry, don't mean to be boring.'

'It's okay,' says Trish gently, 'We know what you mean. Why don't you go and have a bath. I always find a long soak in the tub helps wash away the stain of irritating men. Come with me, I'll grab you a towel.'

The bath is even better than Trish had said. It's in a sunroom on the side of the house, low walls made of rocks they've collected on site, with big glass windows, so you can stare all the way down into the valley as you lie in the suds. There are herbs growing in the windows, and a huge rosemary bush just beyond the glass. Lori spends what remains of the morning soaking away the past, watching the thin spirit of a distant fire trail into the sky. Her fingers have transformed into pale prunes by the time she lifts herself out, and she meanders contentedly back to her cabin to pull on fresh clothes.

Trish and Jude are still out back when she comes down to the house. There's a platter between them, piled with bread and cheese, a couple of small bowls of pickles and olives teetering at its edge. As Lori comes out, Jude gestures to the food and tells her to grab a plate. Most of the afternoon is spent like this, snacking, sipping tea, talking. Lori already feels like she has known these women for years, that they understand her, and she them. As the sun begins to fade they head off for a walk, following the trail that runs past Lori's cabin before climbing steeply into the hills. Olivia leads the way, head held high, and they loop the hill before heading home with the last of the light.

On the second morning, she befriends a colony of king parrots, employing a bag of seed she finds by her door. Down at the house, Jude has her easel set up, happily painting away with her eyes on the valley. Lori makes herself a piece of toast before joining her out on the deck. She spends most of the day exploring the surrounding bush, collecting stones that strike her eye, banksia pods, an irresistibly wizened stick. These treasures she arranges on the windowsill back in her cabin, small talismans to guide her way.

When her head hits the pillow that night, Lori sleeps a sleep so deep she becomes lucid in her dream, recognising the dreamscape and choosing to remain within it. She is there with the women, and the moon is full and bright, and all about them night beings wander the bush, floating down over the escarpment to cast themselves upon the coursing silver river.

Each day she dutifully takes her three drops of tincture, morning and night. The vial is about halfway done, and she considers contacting Carlos, but she knows that if she asks him to send up more it will get back to Mada, and she's not yet ready to be found. She isn't precisely sure why she wants to keep her location secret, but there is a sense of adventure in it and she's got elbow room, space.

After about a week, in the late afternoon, as the air is cooled by approaching cloud, she follows Jude's directions down to the river to scrape a few kilos of iron-coloured clay into an old ice-cream tub. Back in her cabin, she moulds a small pinch pot, just for a test. The clay is sticky, crumbling easily, but despite it being hard to work with, she finds great satisfaction in the new shapes forming under her fingers. The clay gathers around her cuticles, making dark half-moons beneath her nails, and it occurs to her that she is always happiest with her hands in the earth.

That night, as she's eating dinner out on the veranda with the women, she tells them about the pot and the tricky clay.

'Well,' Jude responds thoughtfully, 'we can soak it and screen it, mix it to make it even, increase the plasticity and get rid of all the crud in there. That would make it a lot easier to work with.'

'That'd be great,' says Lori, before she stops, crestfallen. 'But it's a lot of bother. I've got nowhere to fire them anyway.'

'Yes, you do,' says Trish. 'We can fire them in town. Jude used to do it all the time, when she went through her pottery phase. Besides, we can always light a fire and do them straight in the flames. That's the most basic, most ancient form of pottery there is.'

The following morning Lori forces a wad of bills into Trish's hand, causing her to ask whether Lori has robbed a bank. She tries to hand some of it back, but Lori pushes it away.

'No. Take it. We need to eat.'

Trish looks at the wad, then back at Lori. 'Looks like wine with our supper tonight,' she says.

Trish returns a few hours later carrying frayed canvas bags bulging with produce, and the back of the ute filled with building supplies. She's picked up the bottom half of an old copper boiler from the salvage yards, and in about two minutes she's working to get a PVC pipe screwed to the base while Jude stacks vegies into the fridge. 'Coupling's going to be a bit tricky,' Trish says, 'but I reckon we can reason with it.'

It takes her half an hour, and when she's done she stands back, cocking an appraising eyebrow before nodding in approval. 'Not so bad. We dump the clay in here' – she gestures to the top. 'We'll soak it for a while, then add water and mix until we get it to a slurry. Then we can screen it, drain off the excess water, and you'll be ready to go. It's going to take a little while, but it'll be worth it. We'll have to get it set up in the shed first, though – it'll be plenty heavy once the clay is in it.'

Lori and Trish lift the drum and carry it between them. Lori is so excited her fingers are tingling. Once they get the drum in place, she grabs Trish about the neck and hugs her effusively. 'How do you know all this?' she asks.

Trish blinks, flushed. 'From the internet. Where else?'

There are a million new ideas rushing about Lori's head. Where will she start? New forms take shape in her imagination, the things that meet her in her dreams. Beings of light and shape. Creatures. Spirits. What possibilities of new creation can she coax from the shyness of clay, a shyness that so loves to be touched?

'The best news though,' Jude says, as she comes into the shed and drops a calendar onto the work bench, 'is that it's full moon tomorrow.' She points to a small square with her finger. 'And moonrise is mid-afternoon.'

'What does that mean?' asks Lori. 'There's a season? For clay harvesting?'

'Well, I don't know what it means *exactly*. That's up to you. It's more, what do you want to make of it? It's your clay and your intention that you want to set into solid form. What imprint do you want to leave? What mark?'

'I never thought I'd make a mark,' says Lori in a small voice. 'It's, you know, only for me.'

'I don't mean it like that. More, if you're throwing a stone into a river, what do you want the ripples to be? What would you choose, if you could? What's your intention, in the throw? Art is an act. But it's also a thing. So it's weird, a bit of magic tossed into time's river. The full moon has power, that's all. Let's go down, grab some earth, and moonbathe a little.'

The following afternoon, the three of them and Olivia drive to a spot on the river that Jude knows about, further from the house. Trish turns off almost as soon as she hits the asphalt, and they follow a scrubby trail to park in the shade of a bridge. The river flows by, green and lazy, and they search along the bank until they find a pocket of earth that Jude and Lori agree is fit for purpose. Before they start to dig, Jude makes an offering, placing a few items from a picnic she has packed onto the edge of the riverbank and giving a small prayer of thanks for what they plan to take.

In less than two hours every container is filled. Olivia joins in, and by the time they're done she's become a small, animated golem, running from one spot to the next, barking and digging with joyous abandon.

There's a swimming hole a hundred or so metres up the bank, so the four of them traipse up the riverside, strip off their clothes and leap into the gently eddying water. Even in the heat, it's icy. Olivia is highly circumspect about the swim, and zig-zags along the bank until Trish climbs out, picks her up and collapses back into the water with the dog tight in her arms.

'She often needs a bit of encouragement,' she says, chuckling and dunking Olivia's head.

They remove the worst of the clay, and Jude lovingly combs the mud from Olivia's jowls with her fingernails.

After the swim they bask on a flat rock that hangs over the water. The stone glows in the late sun, and as Lori lies down, warmth arrives instantly. She settles on her back, light washing over her. A magpie warbles, melodic, distant, its call falling upon her as an offering and summons, an invitation – from the bird, from the great tree that rises over her, from all the cloudless sky.

'Look,' says Jude, pointing through the trees.

A perfect coin of moon, pale in the afternoon light, rises over the valley. Lori closes her eyes and gives in to the call, drifting into that bright beyond.

It's dark by the time they arrive back at the house. Together they dump the clay they've harvested into the metal drum, then fill it with water. 'We need to soak it for a bit. Then we'll mix it to liquid, screen it to get the crud out, and dry it on some old sheets. It'll take a couple of weeks, weather dependent, but it'll be worth it.'

Lori throws her arms around them both. 'You two are amazing.'

'Yeah,' says Trish, 'we are. But go easy, you're tweaking a vertebra.'

Lori releases them, standing back, abashed.

'You're all right, sister,' says Jude. She throws an arm over each of their shoulders and leads them out of the shed and back towards the house. 'Come on, we deserve a glass of vino.'

They soak the clay for three days before Lori's impatience takes over and she convinces them to start the mixing. Trish reappears minutes later with a power drill. It's got a paddle on its end, and soon she's got the wild clay whipped up like chocolate mousse. They screen out the rocks and roots and leave the slurry on sheets to dry.

After that, Jude and Lori head to the shed each afternoon to test the clay with their fingers. They make a ritual of it, Jude asking Lori about what she'll sculpt first, and all the new, exciting discoveries that await.

At the beginning of the third week, the clay is ready. They cut away a corner for Lori to work with and wrap the rest in plastic. Jude walks Lori back to her cabin, sets her up on an old, paint-spattered writing desk, and turns to leave her to it.

'You don't have to go,' says Lori.

Faced with this formless block, she's suddenly nervous.

Jude gives an understanding smile. 'You'll be okay,' she says. 'Just do what you normally do.'

'I don't really know what I normally do. I just kind of … look inside, until it starts to come out.'

'There you go. Art begins as a work on the self. What it becomes after that is up to you.' With that, she turns and walks back to the house, leaving Lori to sit before the moist, square block.

She pokes at it, driving in her finger. The texture is different from store-bought clay. Not just the coarseness, but also the way it grips, its elemental nature, its energy. Lori takes the piece of wire that Jude has left her and slices the block in half. Slowly, lovingly, she drives her thumbs into the pliant wet heart and starts to search inside the clay for what it wants to be.

***

From then on Lori rises each morning with a sense of purpose and hope. She conjures all manner of small creatures from the wild river clay: lizards she has spotted along the path, birds, even a wallaby. The birds don't turn out too well – so many tiny parts! – but all the same, to Lori it feels as though she has come home.

Some days she works on a rug in the sun, shaping with the help of a flat board on the grass between her cabin and the house, and Jude brings out her easel. Jude paints in pigments of moss and dirt. She leaches green tint out of old man's beard and applies it to the canvas, and powders the fresh, dry edges of bark, or golden lichens, incorporating elements of the landscape into her paints.

Entire weeks pass like this. A few nuts and a boiled egg for lunch, the two of them working side by side, coaxing new formulations from old materials, the birdsong and the creaking of the trees occasionally interrupted by an expletive of joy or frustration.

At some point, Lori stops marking time. Each day rises before her, rich with the promise of new creation, the rituals of tea and landscape. She sleeps, eats, talks with her new friends, fingers wrinkled and cracked with the constancy of clay, cuticles darkened with tan half-moons, her mind alight with newfound forms.

Sex, Robots, DNA
Chapter 16

It is two years since Carlos arrived in Australia, and no one from border security has shot him yet. And this despite the fact he's brown! His mid-morning tweet is a series of whooping emojis, thanking @AusBorderForce for their deference, and he's at the university early in the afternoon, determined to drag Mada and Paula to Café Bolívar, the Venezuelan place on Enmore Road, and crowing about his continued existence. His appeal for refugee status was rejected that morning, but his lawyer says they're not ready to deport him.

Not yet!

One avenue of appeal remains open, so the day is one to be celebrated: the government doesn't want him here, but they haven't shot him either. What a civilised country, this land of kangaroos! He is so determined to be upbeat despite the morning's setback that it is infectious. Paula pockets the keys to the office and the three of them march arm in arm through the gates, Paula singing '¡Ay Carmela!' all the way to the carpark, her resonant voice booming incomprehensible Spanish off the concrete and waiting cars.

'The time is come,' sings Carlos, 'to make some fun.'

They've been working on the preparations for some new trials, and it's good to get out. Too much lab work will drive you mad: this wisdom from Paula. Mada doesn't want to tell them, but he goes for his Huntington's result tomorrow, and it's all he's been able to think about. He hasn't glanced at a newspaper or watched TV in what seems like months, such is his anxiety about the impending result. He can feel himself shutting down, confined to a world of biochemical modification processes, drug pathways and membrane permeability, his entire energy poured into his work so there's no space left for anything else, absorbed by the research that just might save his life, the repetitive rituals of preparation filling his head every time he closes his eyes.

Heated glass. Solvents taking colour.

Zoe is so lost in her own research she scarcely even notices, and they have been passing each other like shadows at the breakfast table, incapable of connection, and squabbling over nothing. Yesterday they argued over the toilet seat, of all bloody things.

He sends her a text when Carlos turns up, to let her know where he'll be, but, as usual lately, there's no response. She's got the date of his test results, he's told her more than once, though he hasn't reminded her that it's coming up, and considering how deep she is in her own academic obsessions, he's sure that she's forgotten. He's doing his best not to be angry about this, not to judge her for it: he knows that all she sees is that he's staring at a screen, or a book, that if he doesn't tell her he is borderline losing it she can't be expected to know. All the same, he *did* give her the date.

The truth is, if the rest of his life were running more smoothly, this might not matter so much, but things at the university have deteriorated even further from the previous year. Not just his department but the whole place is busily going to hell, turning on the maelstrom of the widow's endowment. What started out as heated disagreement as to its best use has devolved into legal action and is becoming more bitter as the weeks progress. A not-for-profit has alleged misuse of the endowment, and as of that morning the university administration has counter-sued, alleging industrial espionage and the illegal acquisition of documents. The previous week, a band of lower level academics, with the help of the union, organised student marches on the administration offices and things quickly spiralled out of control, with the protests metastasising into broken bottles and spray-can vandalism, and discontent about pretty much *everything*: dispersed inequalities, academic standards, the climate crisis. The student union organisers banged on drums and carried placards decrying the death of education. Security officials panicked and called the police, who arrived with dogs and riot gear: a union organiser had her arm broken by an overzealous sergeant; broken glass rained down on the cops, and two bins were set on fire; a cop had his foot broken, run over by the History Chair who was impatient to exit the carpark. At the end of the night, four students were arrested on charges of possession after being discovered with an Orchy bong out the back of one of the colleges.

All of this ricochets about Mada's car as he drives the narrow streets of the inner west. Brandis has been especially painful today, and Paula is full of fury. While she's at the university, she tries to be fairly restrained when she talks with Mada about the mess that is their common workplace. But now, stuck in the stifling car with the traffic adding to her frustration, she is hammering on the dash and calling down judgment on everyone from Brandis to the dean. What a shit show! What a disaster! Mada finds a park on a side street and steps into the heat, relieved to be out of the firing line.

'No more shop talk,' he says firmly to Paula as she exits the car.

They hike up the street, red-brick walls covered in graffiti art, towards Enmore Road. The bar is half-full when they come in, and they find three seats in the corner, beneath a tiny stage. A sign hanging overhead reads: *He arado en el mar y he sembrado en el viento. Por lo tanto: yo bailo.*

'That's Simón Bolívar,' says Paula, noting Mada's gaze. 'Well, the first part anyway.'

'What's it mean?'

'I have ploughed the sea and sown in the wind. So, I dance.'

'Poetic bastard.'

'The second part is Kaysi's addition.' She indicates the woman behind the bar: dark-haired and willowy, tight black T-shirt.

A couple of musicians are playing, a woman on trumpet, a guy on guitar, the music way too loud. It's a cross between reggae and flamenco pop, a Venezuelan speciality, so says Carlos. The musicians are really giving it their all, leaping and spinning about the small stage, knowing all the edges without seeming to look. Traffic crawls past on Enmore Road, but they've found a different universe, a new atmosphere with a different fog, and to Mada it's a welcome relief.

'What'll you have?' he asks, getting up to go to the bar.

'No. Today is mine,' responds Carlos, leaping up and pushing him down by the shoulder. 'Today, my friend, we drink something real. Today you are Venezuelan. Time to toughen you up!'

He heads to the bar, crouching at the stage a moment, offering an apologising wave to the guitarist and fiddling with the dials on the amp. The guitar stops popping: it's still loud but at least there's no distortion. The guy doesn't seem to notice – he's locked eyes with the woman on trumpet, moving down the frets while she blows hard on the horn, her cheeks puffed. She blasts out one final ringing note, and the two of them arrive at a coordinated stop. Whoops and loud cheers. They bow to the crowd. Mada can still half hear the music, a ringing that shifts between his eardrums and his temples.

Carlos stops to talk to the trumpet player on the way back from the bar. She's sitting on the stage edge, sipping from a beer bottle. He's got three glasses in one hand and a bottle of brown spirits in the other, so dark that Mada can scarcely see through it. According to Carlos the Venezuelan publican imports it herself.

'Nothing too strong, Carlos,' Mada protests. 'I won't be able to think on your national poison.'

'Not all moments are for thinking,' Carlos retorts, waving the objection away. 'Some are for dancing. Some are for feeling. Pure intuition must have its place.'

'And this will do it?'

'Well, at least it's pure!'

Mada grins. He won't win this one. They toast Carlos's continued existence, and Mada shoots back the fiery liquid with a toss of his head. It burns all the way down.

Paula is amused. 'Look at him now, eh?'

Carlos is shaking his head. '*Hijo de puta*. This isn't medicine. Is there nothing you do slowly, just for the pleasure of it?'

Mada pauses, serious a moment. Right now he can't think of anything, other than Zoe. 'Isn't that how you drink tequila?'

Carlos puts his glass to his lips and sips the pale spirit, slowly, pointedly, before placing it gently back on the table. 'This is how you drink. And besides, this isn't tequila, it's rum.'

'It's all Greek to me.' Mada giggles, feeling slightly mad, and checks himself. Already it's gone to his head.

Carlos regards him fondly. 'You have strange ways, Australian,' he says, 'not to mention a strange name. I've met many nationalities, yet I've never met another Mada. Does it mean something – Mada – something beyond yourself?'

'It means my mother is a mad hippy.'

'Ah, the only ones for me are the mad ones.'

'She'd say the same. She once told me she found the name in a dream. Said it was the first man, riding back through time, back over his life. You are the first man, she told me, the first man, *backwards*.'

Mada's never told anyone this, aside from Zoe. It's not just the rum – he really likes these two. He cleans his glasses on his T-shirt and perches them back on his nose. Everything is still pleasantly smeared.

An hour later and the bar's so loud they've got their heads clustered low over the table so as not to have to yell. Mada has made the mistake of asking Carlos why Venezuela is a basket case – Carlos doesn't much like his wording. He's cursing solidly, calling down damnation on all sides of politics with spectacular enthusiasm. Chávez, Maduro, the Chavistas, La Mesa de la Unidad Democrática. Plus the American Empire and the IMF for good measure.

Mada, searching out safer ground, asks the two of them how they met.

'I was on the Orinoco,' says Paula, smiling wistfully at Carlos, 'doing research for the university, when I saw this madman dive from the edge of one of the Warao settlements, dive straight into a river that was far too swift to swim. He disappeared into the brown water and didn't emerge. I was sure I was watching a man drown – one complete minute went by while we steered the boat over to where we'd seen him go in, lifting the motor so as not to slice him up. We drifted down twice, circled back. The forest people lined the bank, watching. There'd been a lot of rain, and the water was fast and full of mud. And then he emerged with a victorious yell, clasping above his head this shining thing, as proud as if he was bearing the flame of Olympus. I thought he was some *tonto* tourist and told him so, but he only grinned and called me *guapa*.'

'We met properly that night,' says Carlos, picking up the story, 'sitting around a fire. As it turned out, we were there for the very same purpose: to learn the botanical lore of those remarkable people. From that time onwards we've never been far apart. I followed her, transferred to the university where she was teaching. She tries to escape me from time to time – this last attempt, coming here, is certainly the most impressive –

but I won't let her go. There's no woman in the world like Paula.'

'And there's no man in the world like you, my love.' They exchange a kiss.

Mada supposes the rum is finding its mark with them as well. The abrupt turn to intimacy reminds him of Zoe, and he checks his phone to see if she'll be joining them. No response, and he dwells a little on her lack of interest in his test results coming back. 'So did you ever return to the tribes along the river?' he asks, dragging himself back to the present.

'Yes,' says Carlos. 'Most years we go, or went, before things became impossible and we came here.'

'And what were you diving for?' asks Mada, 'that first time?'

Carlos grins. 'My Zippo.' He retrieves a silver lighter from the pocket of his jeans, giving it a flick, and a low flame burns as he places it on the table. 'It was my father's. He saved the life of an American serviceman at the end of the war, and it's one of the few objects of his that I possess. I'd dropped it as we disembarked that morning. I'd already gone in a dozen times when Paula appeared on the river, diving in, sifting that mud and trying to hold fast against the current. I would have gone in twenty dozen times more, but I emerged victorious that very moment.'

'Are you still in touch with the river tribes?'

Carlos tilts his head, his expression grave. 'Some, others not. The year before we left, a group of *puta madre* prospectors machine-gunned an entire village, higher up the river, near the Colombian border. They were mining illegally. I had friends in that community,' he glances at Paula, 'we both did. There's no possibility they were there without government knowledge.

The mining camp was far too large. I did some investigating, wrote about what I discovered, named names: this is the reason I'm very unpopular with certain politicians. You can dive into the Orinoco and emerge unscathed, but don't attempt to pause the flow of gold, not when it flows upstream.'

'It's hard to see a future for these people,' says Paula sombrely.

'The illegal mining is so bad?'

'The mining, yes, it's bad enough, but the damage caused by the interruption of their culture is far worse,' she says. 'The young are drawn into the city from the villages, lured by gadgets that ten years ago could not have been dreamed of. Imagine,' she says, 'that you've never seen a television, and then, over perhaps ten years, you enter the internet age. Even in the heart of the Orinoco what they want to buy is a flat-screen TV. The attraction of these devices is so new and sudden. Like a drug. The flashing lights, the smell of new plastic – like something pheromonal to robots. This, even more than mining and machine guns, is what's destroying those people.'

'*Sí!*' exclaims Carlos, clapping his hands. He switches between Spanish and English, rolling out deep Venezuelan 'r's as he warms to his topic. '*Putos robots con amil nitrados.* This is what it is. You can imagine the smell of robot pussy? *Es esto, el capitalismo.* Plastic pheromone pussy. There's no word in the Piaroan dialects for *robot*, of course. None in any Yanomami dialect. But there are many words for *pussy*. Oh yes—'

'No, *es falso*,' says Paula, wagging a finger before his face in a small, seductive dance. 'Capitalism may promise robot pussy, but what it delivers is robot dick. A robotic dildo, drilling the world for resources.' She sits back and drains her glass, then leans in conspiratorially, eyeing the surrounding tables as though assessing them for potential spies. 'We live, we walk these streets, we think we know a city's systems. But its assumptions, its programs, take hold of us. Some of it we see. Much we don't. There's so much behind the mirror, beyond recognition, beyond conscious knowing. That's what creates the tension inside us. Winds us up in ways we can't understand.'

'And the other ways of thinking,' says Carlos, 'of the forest, of nature, of the tribe. The ways of the spirit. They get wound up too. But the tension is wrong, they cannot survive it. And when all the young of the village have decamped to the city? When their gears have been broken as thoroughly as by sickness? There's nothing to be done. They'll die out, those people. It won't be the new diseases, the mining or the cattle. Oh, they'll do their damage, destroy the forest, kill those who stand opposed. But the drug of capital will finish everything off. With the young lured away, the old ways will vanish. A way of knowing that has great beauty, great importance, will disappear. The spirit realm of the jungle will shrivel up, and then it will be gone. We are perhaps the last generation to share the world with such people, to have the privilege of knowing them and learning their ways. You can't even imagine what knowledge they hold, the knowledge that will be lost.

'Perhaps one-quarter of the world's medicines are derived from plants of the Amazon and Orinoco, and we've assayed but a fraction of what's there. And yet we bulldoze and burn it down, to plant soybeans and dig for gold.'

'So you appreciate the urgency of our project with the jungle plants,' says Paula. 'In the forest, the body of knowledge is written in the people. The village headman has a knowing that is both communal and distinct. He passes down what he knows to his sons, but the apprenticeship is long. When the villages are gone, what is known will go with them. There are few books that record this lore and fewer still that scratch the surface. And that's to say nothing of the innate value of these cultures, the rights of these people to exist on their own land.'

Carlos shakes his head wearily, as if having heard and made the argument many times before. 'Enough of this!' He waves a dismissive hand. 'We're here to celebrate.' He grabs the rum bottle and refills their glasses, just as the music stops abruptly.

All eyes turn to the performers, but the guitarist is shrugging, pointing with the neck of his instrument to the bar. The trumpeter dangles her instrument at the end of her hand. The two of them step back and clear a small space as the bar owner clambers onto the stage. She stares out at the patrons, all silent, expectant.

'Today is the anniversary of the death of Hugo Chávez,' she says. 'Well, we think it is.' She shrugs. 'There's debate over the date. But each year, we who have escaped to this unlikely corner of purgatory give a toast.' She raises her glass. '*A la mierda los dictadores. Libertad o muerte.*'

A cheer rings out. A guy in a baseball cap and a muscle shirt is celebrating the death of the despot, says they should have shot him in 2002, says that the country has still not recovered.

A clamour fills the bar.

Paula is up from her seat, screaming across the table at the musclehead in rapid-fire Spanish: '*Papeado idio. Mostrar respeto por los muertos, culo. Mírate, un títere de Estados Unidos, con sus bombeados hasta los músculos y sombrero estúpido, Mírate …*'

Her voice rises above the bar's manic din, but now the musclehead's mate is yelling back in English – the murder rate, food, inflation through the roof. Chávez driving the country into a ditch and Maduro unable to drive it out but refusing to let go of the wheel.

'Yes, sure,' shouts Paula. 'Because the free market has been such a great success! The great tentacles of the G7 siphoning our wealth into American coffers. It's a wonder Venezuela didn't implode years ago. But we didn't! We're strong!'

Half the bar erupts into cheers. The other half calls, '*Mierda!*'

'Of course we are,' one man yells back. 'It's survival of the fittest since Chávez died. Only the strong are left! What are you doing over here if you're so fond of him?'

'Finding a way to live,' she retorts.

'*¡Cállate, puta!*' yells the musclehead at Paula.

Paula tosses her drink so that it arcs across the room, a thin flying stream of liquid, its accuracy surprising. The rum catches him full across the chest and face. For an awful second Mada thinks the bloke is going to kill her, leap the tables and beat her to death. But then the entire bar is into it, everyone yelling, and the guy in the cap is still standing there, undecided whether he should cop it, an awkward statue with its arms splayed.

From the end of the counter, by the coffee machine, the owner has taken out a length of timber and slaps it hard to the bar, the noise enormous in the small space. Everyone shuts up.

'*¡Tranquilo, amigos!*' she says. 'Tomorrow we argue. Today is for remembering, honouring those who could not get out. Andrea, pick up that trumpet and blow us a song. Fast and happy, sad and slow, whatever takes your mood. Not for Chávez. He's dead, he can't hear it, and fuck him for being dead and leaving us in this mess. Blow it for those we left behind. Blow it for us. We're all in this *cagada* together.'

The bar goes quiet. Beyond her, through the doors and past the footpath, the traffic is a parking lot. Idling motors, fumes and heat. Then the trumpet starts up, one long note filling the air. The other musician picks up the tune, the trumpet's blow turned mournful and long, lamenting all that never will be. In the bar's stillness, Paula sits heavily and leans back in her chair.

'So it goes,' she says, raising her glass. '*El Comendante. He arado en el mar y he sembrado en el viento.* One day, let it be enough.'

By the time Mada wakes the next morning, Zoe is already on her way out the door. 'You were in late,' she says accusingly.

He massages his temples. 'Paula and Carlos,' he manages to utter.

'Mmm. I got your message. Looks like you had fun. I've gotta go, see you tonight.'

Mada pushes himself up on one elbow, gazing at her bleary-eyed. 'Okay.'

She kisses him lightly on the forehead and turns for the door.

Mada considers staying silent, but he has to tell her, it's too important, and blaming her for forgetting isn't helping him feel better.

'I go for my results today,' he blurts out. 'At Westmead.'

Zoe stops, her hand on the doorknob. 'Bugger! I'm so sorry, I completely forgot.'

Mada grunts and rolls over. 'Doesn't matter. I'll see you later.'

'It matters!' She comes up behind him and lays a hand on his shoulder. 'I'm sorry. I have to run, I have a meeting, but please call me when you know.' She plants another kiss and heads for the door.

He buries his head beneath the pillow, but once he's heard the dull roar that he's sure is the sound of her bus, Mada drags himself out of bed, turns on the shower, and blasts himself with water while his eyelids glow red.

By the time Mada parks outside the apartment block that afternoon, everything has changed. His footfalls as he walks the staircase from the street, the echoed slam of the fire door in the stairwell — all of it seems a kind of speech, the rhythm of his steps sounding it out: to live, to die; life and health, sickness and sorrow. So much weight. He stops outside the door of the apartment, jostling his keys, and somehow he can tell that Zoe is home, that she's waiting for him. She'll be mad with him for leaving his phone at home, for not calling as soon as he had the result, leaving her to stew while he battled the traffic home from the hospital. Did he do it deliberately, he wonders, a subliminal punishment for her forgetfulness? He can't tell. He's sure that she won't complain, though, because everything, *everything*, is so much more important, and both of them know it.

And then he opens the door and finds her at the end of the hall, the very place he imagined her, expectant and very still, as though she might be trying to divine from the way he's stopped on the mat the nature of the result, watching him but not meeting his eyes. Mada closes the door, feeling numb, but still she stares weirdly off kilter, as if her neck is stuck, as if she's half watching the television in the lounge room, aware of what she's doing, of her body, all of it, but not able to change, because she's thinking about the enormity of the future that may or may not be.

To be sick. To be well.

How all trails of what is to come lead into and out of this same place.

And it's as if he can see hope playing about her head, an awareness of the moment not only as it is, but of all that lies outside it, before and behind, all that relies on it. But none of this she wants to show, because to wish too much of the future is to invite its destruction, to reveal how much it matters. The extravagance of care. This mountain of what will be, which he sweeps away with his eyes, with the sudden spread of his grin, and so she sees the precise nature of his thought, of how much it matters to both of them and what their future might be. And before he can say it's okay, it's negative, I'm going to be fine, she has caught it in his mood, his smile, in the atmosphere itself, and suddenly the moment overspills the air that carries it. All the preparation she has harboured since the morning, the way she has steeled herself to be strong for him (and what would she do? Would she stay? He would not allow it, but all the same …), leaving her in a breath, so that suddenly it is destiny come calling with the last of the day, the sun just a bit off setting, a beam of mellow warmth, precise and diffuse in the same instant, the light of an entire future stretching out before them: their future, which they will share, and a resounding *yes* to life, to possibility; a sudden happiness arriving through the door like Lotto come with the postman.

She puts her arms around his neck and kisses him deeply.

'It's negative, isn't it?'

'Yes.'

Her eyes turn up and both of them are in tears, oxygen and the universe remade in fine new brightness. She kisses him again, everything she has within her coming out in that kiss, her body cupping into his, ravenous for each other's salt. She grabs her purse from the hallstand and pulls him back towards the door even as she wipes her eyes with the back of her hand, pulling at him, gripping his fingers and yanking so hard he cries out with the shock of her ferocious, insatiable happiness.

'Come on, you're taking me dancing.'

'It's only 6.30.'

'Then we'll go for dinner. Just come on.'

'Can I change my shirt? I've been sitting in traffic for an hour and a half.' He lifts his arm sleeve and takes a cautionary whiff.

'Sure. But no shower, I like how you smell, and your jeans and shoes are fine.' She grins, twirls, lifts her arms. 'Just hurry up! All of a sudden, I'm famished.'

They walk to a Spanish place on Cleveland Street, both of them basking in the other. Once she's extracted every ounce of information she can – how it went at the hospital, the certainty of the result, how he's feeling – Zoe starts happily dissecting an essay she's been reading. Mada lets her babble, knowing it for the release that it is and overjoyed to have her back. Cars glide past, the air a smoke haze filled with twilight and possibility. There's a table for them right there in the front window, and they order a bottle of tempranillo and gulp down a glass before they've even ordered food, she staring at him unblinking, then leaning across the table and kissing him, a kiss full of hope from her wine-red lips.

They're halfway back to the apartment, on the walk home, when she pulls him into the garden of a terrace house and shoves her hand down his pants. It's been so long since they made love, his hunger for her is instant, and before he realises fully what she has in mind she's hitched up her skirt, undone his belt, and pushed him down onto a bed of ivy behind a thin hedge, embedding him inside her with a fierce joy. They both cry out with the force of it. There's a noise from above, a light coming on in the window over their heads. Zoe presses herself flat, her knees beneath his arms, and places her finger over his lips. Then, pulling down her finger, she kisses him slowly, rocking back and forth, her lips wet and inviting, throatily whispering into his ear, the pheromonal candy of their bodies in the air, pushing him deeper.

She gives a slight 'Oh', almost of surprise, and a great wave of orgasm passes through them both as they clutch each other in immaculate spasms.

Moments pass. A breeze. Entangled in each other's shadow.

Zoe is pressed to his chest, breathing deeply, rejuvenated and emptied in one. Mada stares up, marvelling at her. A couple is approaching on their side of the street: they can hear the click of the woman's heels, the man's voice. He's talking about real estate, how the neighbourhood is gentrifying, how their property value has increased ten percent this last year alone. The lovers exchange silent eyes. Zoe mimes vomiting, and the two pass metres from where they lie, clicking off up the street while Mada and Zoe stifle giggles. Zoe rubs herself against his skin, running her nose up and down his neck, drawing him in. With one last kiss she slides from him and gets to her feet.

Sisters
Chapter 17

It feels like the best day of Bea's life, the day she gets a transfer to Stacey and Rhino's house. Rhino is the one who manages it. She's got pull with the screws, although it's not clear to Bea why, and she won't say beyond a wink. Suddenly, though, it's as if they're in it together, and Bea's going to get out alive. The brooding violence of the corridors doesn't disappear, but Bea has a crew, and they know the gaps and shadows of the place, know how to survive.

The first night together, they all pitch in on dinner. Stacey chops the onions, laughing at her tears, running unchecked down her cheeks, and it's as if she loves them, those tears, as if they're helping her along. Rhino is squeezing garlic into the pan, the oil smoking hot so the garlic burns before the onions are diced, and Stacey calls her a drongo whitie – doesn't even know how to make spaghetti: 'Ya *never* put the garlic in before the onions' – and Rhino says she's half Italian and she'll be damned if she'll take advice on spaghetti from a Koori: she'll let *her* know when the wallaby shanks go on the barbie. But the argument's already won, because it's Rhino who has to clean out the pan and mince fresh garlic, both of them laughing and grinning as if their faces might split.

Bea sets the table like it's Christmas dinner, getting loo roll and tucking it under the forks to serve as napkins, and they all think this is funny and fine and posh, and there's a great mound of pasta in the middle of the table, covered, completely covered, in parmesan – that's Bea's buy-up cash at work – and Rhino snatches the spoons off the table and puts them away, because spoons with pasta are for kids, and this is how the wogs do it, and we wogs invented spaghetti so we should fucken know. Bea sits down and looks at the two of them and it hits her that she's happy. Not happy, considering everything. More, this is what happiness feels like and at some point she forgot, long before she came inside. She hasn't had fun like this with Red since forever, and even then it would have required three hundred bucks in food and five cocktails apiece. A weird feeling of gratitude flows along her spine, buzzing electric at the base of her skull. Bea is struck by the sense, from nowhere, that she's here for a reason. That things will, eventually, get better. That she's lucky, just lucky.

'I need to say grace,' says Stacey.

The other two exchange glances, but say okay, if she has to.

'Dear God,' she intones, 'thanks for the grub, and for me mates. But tell me: why did you make men so stupid?'

'Ha–ha! Yeah!'

Rhino loves this, she's laughing and clapping her head off. 'While you're at it, tell us why you made the director such a cunt.'

'And if Mary was a virgin,' chimes in Bea, 'doesn't that make it non-consensual?'

'And if you really do exist, what about mosquitos?'

'And genetic disease?'

'And this place?'

That quietens things down a bit.

They sit for a second, grinning sheepishly at one another.

'Any more questions?' asks Rhino, squaring her shoulders.

'Nope,' says Bea.

'Good,' says Stacey. 'Bog in.'

Rhino jumps from her chair to get at the food, and picking up Bea's plate dollops on great forkfuls of pasta, then does Stacey and herself. It tastes about as good as anything Bea ever ate, and they all gulp it down appreciatively.

'So that screw doesn't like you much, does he?' says Stacey, lifting her head from her plate, mouth still half full, poking her fork at Bea. 'You know, the one with the shaved head.'

'Nope. He's the knob jockey my sister pushed over. He's made me piss in a cup twice this week.'

'Yeah, he's a deadset fuckwit, that one.'

'Keep clear of him,' says Rhino, warningly. 'He's got a vicious side.'

'I'm doing my best,' says Bea. 'But he's always staring at me. He's as bad as that enormous blonde chick. At least she's upfront: she tells me she's going to jump on my head as soon as she gets the chance.'

'She'll have to go through me first,' says Rhino.

'Me too,' says Stacey. 'I'd fuck that chick up plenty before she lays a finger on you. I might be small, but I could bust that bitch's nose so good she couldn't see to swing. Anyway, enough of this place. I want to hear about the junky you were put away for. Tell me the nitty-gritty: did you see his guts spill out; can he still walk?'

Rhino lets her draw out the details, until she's amping up the gross bits, giving a blow by blow, the horror in the bloke's eyes, the paramedics trying to figure out the best way to extract him, all the while him hanging there, half in the house, half out. The two of them start a madcap routine of dancing intestines with the long red threads of pasta.

The spaghetti is starting to look less appetising, so Bea changes the subject. 'How about you, Stace? You never told me how you ended up here.'

'Long story, mate.'

'We got time,' says Rhino.

'I got plenty,' says Stacey. 'But you're up for parole in six months.'

'Ain't life sweet,' says Rhino.

'Lucky you,' says Bea.

It comes out more sour than she intended. She feels deflated, but works at not showing it. There's a wish, quickly suppressed, that the parole board will say no. She doesn't want to face the idea of going through her final months without her friend.

Rhino is watching, not unkindly. 'Come on, Stace, tell us ya story,' she says, still with her eyes on Bea.

'Well. Me and the law, we never saw eye to eye,' she says. 'White law never liked my people much. We have our own law, but the pigs never give a shit about that. I grew up in Cootamundra. They took Mum away from Gran when she was small, put her in the Cootamundra Girls' Home. Thing was, Mum was from the coast, where there's lots of trees, the ocean. Coota was dry as. Cold in winter, hot as fuck in summer. I was born there, and I still hate it. Wasn't our place. She must of run away twenty times. At first she was too small to know how to get back to country, but she found a way. She was in and out of that hole until she and Ned hooked up, and then they had me. Lucky them, eh! My lawyer said in court that I'm a victim of Social Darwinism. Like it's from a textbook, a disease or something.'

'I guess it is, in a way,' says Bea.

'No way. Me and Mum are survivors, not victims. Two centuries of dumb white arseholes shooting us and poisoning us and treating us like dogshit. We're still here, we're still strong. Fuck em, we're alive. Some of us, anyway. They tried to make blackfellas die out, but we're too tough, too smart for em. Wanted to train Mum to be a servant for white folks, figured our mob were dumb cos we're nothin like them. Always been like that, they didn't understand us at all. The cops were always out to get us. We'd be drivin along, wouldn't matter where, and they'd pull us to the side, give the car a once-over. Ned had a good job, nice car, but that didn't matter, just made em mad. He was a mechanic. Bloody smart, too.'

'He still about?'

'Nah.'

'Sorry.'

'Yeah. He didn't touch drink, didn't do nothin, but they'd lock him up anyways. Mostly cos he wouldn't take shit from shaved-head coppers. Then, the last time, this highway patrol pulls us over. Real dick, he was. You could see it in his sunglasses, big reflective things like he figured he was on TV. Ned couldn't find the rego papers, and the pig started goin on about the car bein stolen. It was Ned's car, a sweet Valiant he done up himself. So he loses his patience, starts mouthin off, just under his breath, not like he was ravin or anything, bout how it was his country that got stolen, not this effing car, how the copper was standin on Wiradjuri land. Not aggressive, but so the pig could still hear. Course the cop just up and takes him in. No papers. Suspected stolen car. And we turn up to the cop shop in the morning, and, yeah – said he hung himself.'

Bea drops her fork.

'Total load a bullshit,' says Stacey. 'Wouldn't even let us see the body. After that, me and Mum ended up in Sydney. Mum's still here, but she's pretty crook. And I've been in and out of Silverwater a bunch of times already, mostly cos I won't take shit from cops either. Fucken hate that place. What a hole.'

'How old are you, Stace?' asks Bea after a while. There's a wobble in her voice.

'Thirty,' says Stacey.

'Damn. I thought you were twenty, tops.'

'Must be all them trips to the salon,' she says with a grin.

'So why are you in here now?' asks Rhino.

'Manslaughter.'

'Geez.'

'Me boyfriend. He was a whitie. Pale as a ghost. Had the most beautiful tattoos. Birds. Tribal bands. Not Aussie blackfella stuff, but swirly, like ya see on the footy players. And this big cross on his back, Jesus on it and everything. Blood coming out of the hands, where the nails went in. Fuck, it was beautiful.'

'What happened?'

'We were walkin home from the pub. Arguin. He'd given me a few hits before, but this is the first time he goes like he straight up wants to hurt me, to break somethin. He'd had a fight with his dad, about datin me. Old prick called me a fucken Abo, like I wasn't even in the room. Miserable old turd. So we went out and got pissed. I don't even remember how it started, we were totally maggot, but he busted up my eye real good. So as I'm gettin up from the ground, I pick up a brick and I let him have it. Like hard. He goes over and lands with his skull on the step of a terrace, and I watched the light shrink in his eyes, holdin im.

'Anyways, it goes to court, and I'm sayin I was just defendin meself, and I didn't mean it, but I've got a record, and the cops say I've been abusin him. Poor little white kid getting smashed up by the Koori. Jury buys it. Twelve white pricks in different shades of blue, ya better fucken bet they do. Now it's four and six in this dump.'

'Shit.'

'Yeah.'

'Could be worse, but.' She cracks out her trademark grin. 'I was lucky to get minimum security. I could be in a house with a bunch of psychos. Could of never met you lot, could be out at Broken Hill.'

Bea wakes in the night, unsure at first, in the dazing sleep-edged twilight, where she is. She stares through the window, shaking the vision out of her head. She'd been dreaming about the dog, Henry, of the day they found him in the shop and how happy

Lori was: how, for a brief moment, it was like being sisters again, real sisters, like when they were young, rather than how it was later – Lori playing the half child, and Bea playing mother. She remembers bringing home the dog, and how the two of them laughed away Red's howls of protest. How they were in it together.

All that love was still there, despite the history and angry words.

That's what the dream was about. Being sisters again.

Of course, the dog arrived in the middle of it all; it was towards the end of the previous year when the events that led her here had really started. It was then that Bea had noticed her sister was plumping out. She didn't get much exercise and she ate well, not having developed the difficulty swallowing that overcomes those who live long enough with the Huntington's curse, so Lori's mildly expanding gut didn't seem significant at first, not something Bea needed to concern herself with. But Lori's attitude was puzzling; she seemed to like her middle-aged spread, running her hands over her newfound girth with the faraway smile that she wore so often back then. Bea would find her standing on the patio, humming quietly and staring at a tree, patting her belly contentedly.

Bea was more concerned with her own body, which, from the point of view afforded by sensuality or other markers of singular selfhood, she would have been just as happy to be done with. How often did she and Red make love that last year or two before she was locked away? Once a month? Once every two? She can remember the last time clearly, although no doubt it had faded from Red's mind before even settling there. He had come back from the golf course: it was late, and he woke her as he fell into bed, clumsily stroking her hair, his breath like metho, and rolling onto her he gave a kind of grunt by way of requesting consent. Too tired to refuse him, she shifted her hips a little and waited it out, which didn't take long. He tried talking sexy, slurring and stinking, and not two minutes later as she got up for a shower he rolled into his own bed-divot and was snoringly asleep. That didn't count, except in the most technical sense. No. The last time they had made love was years before.

Early on, when they were trying for a baby, they'd had sex to a rigorous schedule that kept at least some of the pleasure alive. When they 'succeeded', and she became pregnant, the joy had lasted for about six weeks. Then the chest pain started. She had miscarried, the doctor had run tests, and a list of reproductive problems were revealed, as well as some previously undiagnosed heart issues in Bea, including a right bundle branch block. Sounds like a traffic problem, said Red, before the reality sank home. Further pregnancies, they were told, could be extremely dangerous, possibly life-threatening, and the doctor advised right then and there, with all the bedside manner of a rugby coach, that Red have a vasectomy and that they look into adoption.

A chasm opened in the floor, both of them staring into it. Bea felt shock clench her brain and body, could sense Red's severed dreams draining away.

What would become of them?

Nothing was the same after that.

She'd shared none of this with anybody. Bea wasn't the type to spill her secrets. Problems were to be endured: hunker down and wait for them to pass. It takes time to learn the way things fester, the way they become a part of you, so that they're no longer a problem; rather, it's that *you* are different, disappointment has burrowed inside you and made a home. Lori, by contrast, would share personal information with utter nonchalance. Constipation, vaginal mucus, a bladder infection – it was all reported in such detail as to be disturbing, and frequently in the most inappropriate situations. And yet there was a kind of relief in it, making Bea feel she had a good grip on things herself.

She, after all, knew when to shut up.

And this, no doubt, was part of the problem: the illusion of knowledge, of control, for although there were certain changes happening in her sister, at the time Bea had been too pushed to think about anything other than work.

It wasn't until December, with the adrenaline of an office in crisis subsiding, that Lori's obvious shortness of breath, her deepening dreaminess, and at last her firming belly became impossible not to see. On her lunch break, Bea guided her sister to the doctor's office. Lori followed unquestioningly, and they waited amid piles of magazines and midday television banality, which Lori scowled at unblinkingly, while Bea tapped away on her laptop and did her best not to freak out.

Dr Cohen was very serious, very competent if not exactly speedy, and not far from retirement. He ushered them into his office, sitting down at his desk, the wall behind him covered with images of his children (at least half of them in doctor's garb) and grandchildren (two of whom, under five, held toy stethoscopes), and asked with his usual graveness what the problem was. He knew about the Huntington's – he'd been the one to line up the tests for the two of them a decade or so earlier, after their father's symptoms were, finally, correctly identified, and six months before he walked into the sea and made an exit of his own time and choosing.

When it first came, Lori's diagnosis appeared to affect Bea more than it did Lori, who by that stage had already begun to fade into gradual withdrawal, although then, as now, the chorea was mostly limited to a general clumsiness. The two sisters had been close growing up, and in comparison to those early years, Lori, then so filled with life and joy, now seemed hollowed. With hindsight it was clear that Lori's diagnosis had been a wrecking ball through their relationship, and they had never quite recovered. In the end, Bea had come out of the depression her sister's illness inspired by throwing herself into her career. Any attempt to talk about the future with Lori was met by a wall of what seemed like indifference. 'I don't really think about it,' was all Lori would say, and Bea wouldn't push her, and that would be that. In this way they had gradually, relentlessly, grown apart.

It was his knowledge of Lori's diagnosis, and the fact that she had escaped the same fate, that Bea saw play across Dr Cohen's face that day, along with an unwavering certainty as to the nature of her sister's 'condition'.

So while Lori went into the bathroom, carrying a clear plastic jar with a bright yellow lid, smiling dreamily – as if she was quite as sure of the result as the doctor – Cohen took Bea to task.

'Such matters should be more carefully managed,' he said drily.

'She's forty-seven years old, for god's sake,' said Bea.

'It's statistically unusual,' Cohen responded, 'although certainly not unknown.' He seemed genuinely annoyed with her, thought Bea, as though her sister were a teenager, pregnant from a fumbling night in the back of a boyfriend's panel van when Bea was meant to be playing chaperone. He handed Bea a referral for an imaging centre and a family planning brochure.

'I'll send you along for an ultrasound, but from my initial examination it's entirely possible she's outside the window in which termination is generally encouraged.'

In the stifling antiseptic air of the office, Bea felt a small spasm of vomit rise in her throat. 'Ugh.'

'Sorry?'

She swallowed it down for the acid it was. 'Nothing,' she said.

'You need to think this through, Bea.'

The sour-acid taste grew in her mouth. 'Could I have a glass of water?' she said.

Cohen got up slowly from his desk and went to the sink, coming back with a plastic cup, placing it on the desk before her. He took Bea by the arm. 'Let's start with the ultrasound,' he said, gentle now. 'We can see where we stand after that.'

Bea dropped Lori back at the apartment and drove straight home. She poured a large glass of chardonnay, threw salts into the bath and opened the taps, discarding garments as she went. The reflection that greeted her in the mirror seemed at that moment to be some kind of foreign object: her belly, not swollen but slightly dimpled with the accumulating weight of middle age; her heavy breasts, breasts she had always been rather proud of – yet none of it was capable of producing a child.

Who was she? She felt unsettled, muddled. What of her sister, with this new life growing inside her? And what did it mean for her, the person now gazing back through the steaming haze of the mirror. She took a sip of the wine, turned off the taps, and slipped into the heat. When she had finished the wine and scrubbed herself raw, she pulled the plug, and walked through to the bedroom.

She felt, almost, okay.

She hunted through her purse for the details of the imaging centre, and made an appointment for the following Monday. This was a problem that could be solved and all things would find their place.

When she got back to the office an hour or so later, she didn't tell Red, not straightaway. The only person she shared the news with was Gina, who had been with them from the start, and even then it was more accident than plan, Bea blurting out the story before the words had traversed her brain.

'I've got to admit, I had my suspicions,' was Gina's response.

'Well I bloody didn't. I wish you'd shared them.'

'I mean … look at her. At her age and everything.' She glanced quickly at Bea. 'Sorry, I didn't mean it like that. But, you know, it's amazing!'

'Yes. We're very proud of her,' said Bea sourly.

When Monday came, she picked up Lori and drove her to the imaging centre. In contrast to her recent dream-like state, Lori was focused and seemed to brighten in tandem with the shifting pixels on the sonographer's screen, her eyes widening excitedly with the emergence of the unmistakable human form of her baby.

Bea, however, was transfixed by a different emotion, a hard lump forming in her stomach, the feeling increasing as she too stared at the screen. You didn't need to be a bloody sonographer to know the pregnancy was well along; the viability of the foetal heartbeat only proved what they knew.

How could she have missed it?

After the ultrasound she took Lori home and went back to the office. It was time to tell Red. She had put it off long enough. She tucked her head around the door and found him bent over his desk, frowning at his desktop keyboard, massaging his brow.

'Got a minute?'

'My head's pounding. Can you grab a few pills from the cabinet?'

She came back brandishing a foil pack and placed it on his desk. He popped a few, threw them down with a gulp of water, and looked up expectantly.

'What is it? You've got your worried face on.'

Bea stood there a moment, trying to find a way to frame it. No matter the terminology – up the duff, in trouble, in the family way – the reality was the same. Eventually she took a breath and said, 'Lori's pregnant.' The words came out flat and irritated, laden with inconvenience.

'Oh shit. How did that happen?'

'In the usual way, I expect.'

'Don't be sarky.'

Bea put her hands on her hips and glared at him.

'Didn't you get the pill for her?' he asked.

Bea nodded. 'Of course I did. You know that. Years ago. But she has to take them. I policed it, checking the packs in her bathroom, making sure she was on track and reminding her when she wasn't. This last year or two it didn't seem necessary anymore.'

'It didn't, eh?'

'She's forty-seven. She spends all her time in her apartment. I didn't think …' Bea's voice trailed out.

'You figured she was all dried up and too old to tango?'

'You've got a real way with words, Red.'

He grunted. 'So, who was it?'

'No idea. She won't say anything. When I question her about it, all she does is smile at me and gaze into the distance like a Jane Austen heroine.'

'Huh.' They shared a smile, despite it all. That was one thing about Red. Even when you were stuck in Shitsville, he knew how to ride it out. 'She'll have a termination, of course.'

'Of course. But I'm not even sure if it's legal. It's far along.'

'Well … that's dandy.'

Bea slumped onto the black leather visitors chair, for the first time looking, really looking, at the painting over Red's desk.

'Who's that painting by?'

'Boccioni. And it's not a painting. It's a photograph of a painting. Your sister gave it to me, remember? To be honest, I thought you'd selected it yourself. That's half the reason I put it up.'

'No. I hate it.'

'Great. Why don't you let her know?'

'Ha ha.'

'Look, love, there's something else.'

'Yes?' she asked tiredly.

'Regardless of all this, it's time for Lori to, you know, work from home.' He held up a hand to forestall objection. 'I know she's your sister and you love her, but she's become a liability to the company. I don't mind paying her …'

'Oh. It's you that's paying her?'

'I didn't mean it like that. Don't think I don't recognise the contribution you've made to the business.'

'Not just me, Red. My family, which means Lori too. Which means you want to fire someone who, by rights, owns thirty-three and one-third percent of the company from which you propose to remove her.'

'Honey, please. Her attention's all over the place. She can't focus to save herself … It looks bad to clients.'

'She's organising stationery cupboards, doing the photocopying. How much focus does she need?'

'Enough so that she doesn't email clients confidential in-house communications every time, no, you're right' – he held up a hand again – '*almost* every time she happens to come across an unmanned PC. Enough so she doesn't pour unwanted cups of tea into the paper recycling, or attempt to replace printer toner with coffee. What can I say? We can't Lori-proof the entire office. We've tried. You know how we've tried. You're the one who's done it all. But every day it's something else. She's getting worse, honey.'

Bea lowered her head into her hands. She knew that he was right, and she hated it, oh she *hated* it, when he was right.

'Okay, yes. So she goes. Regardless.' Bea grabbed the foil pack of pills and popped out two for herself. 'God, what a day.' She stared out the window, playing absentmindedly with the chrome bauble of his desk toy. 'The thing is, I don't know what is her, and what part of this is the Huntington's. I went to cut some fruit for her the other day and she was yelling at me. I mean, she's always had a bit of a temper, been a bit off with the pixies. Maybe she's just getting a bit more stroppy and internal as she ages, like the rest of us. Or maybe it's more. I can't figure out what's her and what's the disease.'

'Is there a line? Does it matter?'

'No. I suppose not.'

Red expelled a breath, rolled back his shoulders. Clearly that had gone better than he was expecting. Bea could see his mind shift to other things. Work, golf, she couldn't tell. He checked his watch, then his phone, before looking back at her, as though surprised she was still there. 'When will they do the operation?' he asked distractedly.

'I don't know, Red,' she said, abruptly feverous. 'I've just come from the cunting ultrasound.'

'Okay, okay, don't get your blood up.'

'Gee, I'm ever so sorry, but it's kind of a big deal.'

'I'm sorry, honey, but it's not my fault.'

'Who's saying anything about it being your fault?'

Red shuffled through a stack of papers. 'Just let me know how it goes.' He picked up the phone and put it to his ear and looked at the door expectantly.

Fuck it, thought Bea, I'm going home. I'm going to pour myself an enormous glass of wine and take the afternoon off. She texted Gina from the car that she'd be out the rest of the day, and slipped away without Red seeing.

Not that he'd care enough to ask questions.

***

The heat outside was rising in waves from the street, warping the air above the car-clogged tarmac. It took Bea fifteen minutes to drive back to Lori's Rozelle one-bedroom. Weaving through the traffic, and driving, as she liked to say, whenever Red told her to slow down, not *too* fast, just bloody *fast enough*.

She found Lori shirtless in the bright heat, the swollen roundness of her belly and breasts glistening with perspiration. As Bea came in, she offered a smile and turned back to her work.

The sculpting table was covered with a collection of clay figurines, vaguely humanoid forms with rounded little torsos and thin, stumpy legs. It had been a long time since Bea had looked at the collection of figures, really looked at them, and finally doing so, noting their air of obvious pregnant fecundity, she castigated herself for missing the obviousness of it all. How could she have overlooked this shape obsession too? It had taken over from Lori's previous favourite sculptural form just months ago, the tiny geometrically printed rectangles that represented the Iron Cove Bridge, visible below through the western window, and before that it had been small, sculpted waves, and before that, tiny boats, or maybe it was the boats and then the waves. Whatever, these clay models occupied almost every corner of the apartment, and just a few months ago the focus had shifted to these obviously pregnant avocados. How on god's earth could the symbolism of this shift *and* Lori's swollen midsection have eluded her? She dropped her handbag and regarded her sister, working hard at pushing down her anger, levelling herself out.

'It's like a sauna in here, Lori. Mind if I close the balcony door and turn on the air-con?'

'I'd rather have the door open. You know I hate that thing. It's so unnatural. I like the sound of the cars. They make me think of travel, time.'

'How about the fan? You'll still hear them with the fan going.'

'If you like.' Lori shrugged and worked her thumbs over a spherical moulding of clay before standing it on the table and staring at it, her head tilted to the side. She picked it back up and worked her thumbs rapidly over the base.

'I don't suppose you know who the father is?' Bea asked.

'Oh yes.' Lori turned to offer an enormous grin, still holding the figurine in her fingers.

'I mean where he is. His name. What he does.'

'He's a carpenter. So handsome. Young too!'

'What's his name?'

'Daniel. I think. Or was it Damien?'

'I was hoping you'd be the one to know.'

'Daniel. I think it was Daniel.'

'Don't suppose you have a number for him?'

But Bea knew what the answer to this query would be before she asked it, and sure enough Lori gave that same infuriating smile. Turning back to her work she started humming, as though still lost in the sensual reverie of post-coital bliss.

Bea breathed deep, clenching and unclenching her fists, telling herself over and over that it wasn't her sister's fault, not the sex or the pregnancy, not any of it. Lori did not understand the implications, the complications, she told herself. Yelling was not going to help and what she had to do was stay calm. She took

Lori by the clay-stained hands, removed the small sculpture and placed it back on the table, and in the calmest, most loving voice she could muster, told her they would see a doctor together, that it would all be taken care of, that she didn't have to worry about a thing. Then she turned, while her composure was intact, and made for the door, and she was halfway out to the landing and already managing the crisis in her head, planning the necessary medical visits, telephone calls, therapists, so they were already almost out the other side, Lori happily vacant in hospital greens in the recovery room, sad but accepting of all that had passed, when her sister's quiet voice came floating to her, carrying above the sounds of the traffic. 'I know. I'm going to have a baby.' Melodious, happy, detached.

Bea stopped, turned and, after walking back inside, firmly closed the door, before resting a moment with her hand on the knob, eyes closed, deep breathing.

'Lori, you're not going to have a baby.'

'But I am.' She lifted her shirt and ran her hand around the circumference of her belly. 'I can feel her.'

'You can't look after a baby, Lori.'

'Yes I can.' Her voice quiet, insistent.

Bea knew that voice, and for an instant she felt breathless panic. 'No, you are not. It's impossible.'

'I know,' said Lori, animated, joyous. 'It's a miracle! You told me I couldn't. Not again!'

'And I meant it.'

'But I can. I can feel it growing here.' Lori placed her hands over her navel, smiling – no, positively beaming – with the joy of it. 'See? You see?'

'Lori. You're sick.'

'I'm not sick. It's a baby. You keep saying that but I'm not.'

'We are terminating this pregnancy and that's the end of the conversation.'

'No,' said Lori loudly. 'No. It's beautiful. All of it.' Her eyes filling with tears. 'What does some disease have to do with me? With my baby? I can look after her. I will.'

'How, Lori?'

'Mada was my first baby. He's an angel. She will be my other baby.'

'If he *is* an angel, it's because I bloody raised him. I'm not doing it again, Lori. I am not.'

'Good. This is my baby and I'm going to have it.'

There was no argument or compulsion that would convince Lori to terminate the pregnancy, and although Bea, for some years now, had assumed something of a role as her sister's guardian, there was no legal framework for this arrangement – nothing that could, with the force of the law, place her sister's will beneath her own. Although she did not admit it to Red, she felt weirdly relieved by this, as the idea of dragging her sister, screaming, into an operating theatre was like something from a horror film. Yet so was the alternative. Once again, Bea would be the one to pick up the pieces. She'd have to raise a child that wasn't her own, because her sister was in many ways a child herself.

And so it was decided that, in the months leading up to the delivery, Lori would come and live with Red and Bea, that Bea would have a few months away from the office to help her sister, and that a solution to the day-to-day care of a child would be

found. There was a party for Lori and Bea on their last day at
work, some two weeks before Lori was due. She sat in the office
kitchen with a cake in front of her, her belly like a smuggled
basketball beneath her dress.

'You'll be back in no time,' Gina said to them both, not
knowing then that this was the final moment of Lori's 'career'.
Everyone was very nice about it, very excited, although there were
a few raised eyebrows as to how a woman of Lori's 'quirkiness'
might cope with a child, for neither her Huntington's diagnosis
nor the matter of her moving in with Red and Bea had become
office knowledge.

Two days later, waddling pregnant through a shopping mall,
Lori spied the puppy. And much to her own surprise, Bea said
yes, she could have it. It wasn't exactly that she wanted to please
Lori or even rescue the dog. More that, examining the animal's
bewildered face, its eyes following every passer-by in the hope
of salvation, she felt she understood it. Understood the look. The
world enormous and brightly lit and forever beyond the glass.

Three days later, as Lori was sitting in front of the TV on
Red's favourite chair, she began wailing. Bea turned to her sister
to find her dress and the chair covered in blood. Lori stood,
gripping herself at the base of that broad belly, attempting
to staunch what seemed an endless flow. On and on it came,
Lori's wailing gaining in pitch, until she finally collapsed,
hugging herself and crying inconsolably while Bea called for an
ambulance.

In the end, rather than mothering a new child, Bea found
herself caring for her younger sister, for the collision between
Lori's miscarriage and the increasingly manifesting Huntington's

sent her into the worst spiral Bea had witnessed. Truth be told, it was payback. Bea was guilty, for as soon as she was sure that her bleeding sister wouldn't die, the certainty that she would lose the baby had filled her with relief.

Relief!

That didn't make her a bad person, but it made her, at the least, morally suspect. She deserved what she got, and this was her penance. To play nursemaid to her sister, to leave her career behind.

At first, Gina called her regularly. They needed her to tell them how to manage the photocopier, temperamental beast that it was, or how to handle some client or other. Even at home, she felt indispensable, and sometimes Gina would call just to moan about politics and the general state of play. How it wasn't the same without Bea there each day, how everyone else was too dull or too loopy. So when was Bea coming back?

She really wasn't sure. It would only be a few months, wouldn't it, until Lori settled and returned to her apartment. Surely they could get by until then? Besides, Bea herself felt utterly lost inside the haze of Lori's mourning. Even as she hated, at the same time, her ongoing unemployment, there was something so *easy*, so seductive, about it.

Then Gina stopped phoning, and Bea was the one who made the calls, until one morning she got the new receptionist – since when did they need a second receptionist? – and the woman, Lindy was her name, or Linda, said, 'Please hold,' without any recognition, and then a minute later came back on the line and said, 'Sorry, she hasn't come in yet,' leaving Bea to wonder why

Red had gone ahead and hired someone new, even though he claimed they couldn't afford it. Cash flow was, as Red put it, tighter than a fish's arse, and that's waterproof.

The woman's voice confirmed the lie, and Bea imagined the conversation, Gina at her desk, saying, 'No, not now, I need to prepare for the legals meeting, just tell her I'm not in.' So when Red called later that morning, Bea answered the phone in a state of despondent irritation.

'Honey, I'm not going to be home for dinner,' he said. 'Something has come up.'

'That's the third night in a row.'

'Can't be helped. They're new clients.' He sighed theatrically down the line, as though drinking cabernet with a bunch of out-of-towners was a terrible chore. 'This is how the Germans do business.'

'Can't someone else go?'

'Like who?'

'What about Gina?'

'Gina? She can't close a deal like this. If I don't go myself, they'll take it as an insult.'

'It doesn't seem like you want to be home very much.'

'You know that's not true.'

'No I don't.'

'Darling, I've got to go, there's a lot to do before the meeting.'

'Fine.' She hung up the phone, not waiting for his response, and went to the fridge. There was a time when she would have been the one having work dinners, making excuses.

The clock read eleven thirty-seven.

Each day she was drinking earlier.

Henry was nosing at her ankles. She reached down and gave him a scratch. Red had moved all the hard booze to the garage the week before. It was just gone when she went to pour a brandy. She knew he wouldn't have tossed it – he drank as much as she did, albeit with different consumption patterns – and she'd soon found the hiding place. Besides which, he hadn't moved the wine from the cellar under the stairs: that would be half a day's work and he was far too lazy.

It was so like Red not to make a scene about her drinking, or even ask her if she was struggling, and at the same time not to do things properly. No, he wouldn't give the alcohol away, take it to the office or pour it down the sink. His halfway measure summed up her husband perfectly. Somehow, Bea realised of a sudden, she had become a housewife who drank during the day. All that work, her career, no kids of her own: still it had happened. For people like her, housewifery was an alcoholic profession. And she knew, as part of this new knowledge, that when the glass in her hand was empty, she would pour herself another. Because she deserved it. What was she saving herself for?

How very entitled she'd been in her misery: that's the thought that strikes her, thinking on it now. She could have changed things if she'd wanted to; could have made other – better – choices. Out in the night, the prison is still as death, as though the whole place is empty. She imagines the corridors deserted, the entire facility throbbing with its savage concrete energy, its steel and bitumen, the emptiness of all those who've passed through its gates: all that history of misery, all that personal pain, breathing in and out.

Bea blinks up at the ceiling's stark shadows. She can't tell how many of the last few hours she's passed sleeping. The real world hovers invisibly beyond the wire. Is her sister out there, alive still, somewhere in that anonymous dark? Or is she gone, rejoined with the cosmos, whatever that means, her body already turned skeletal by fish? Bea tries to imagine it, Lori, dead. Just to see if it's possible: hoping for a message, a feeling, a sign. But there is only the room's shadow. Muffled voices. Crickets in the grass. A distant truck accelerating along Old Bathurst Road. She listens as it roars through the gears and fades into the night.

Mondays
Chapter 18

Red catches the eye of the new receptionist through the glass of the lobby. Staring daggers at him. He'd chosen her for her photo, but no sooner had she started answering the phone than he could tell she had attitude. There's no wit, though, none of the verbal razorblades Bea would throw down. Just her judgment, delivered in disdainful eyeball rolls. And now, every morning, there she is when he gets to work.

Bloody Mondays.

He gives her a 'Good morning' that he hopes reminds her who writes the pay cheques. She isn't looking at him, though, just holding up an ugly stack of mail that he knows he doesn't want to read.

'Ms Fang is waiting in your office. I asked her to wait out here but she walked through anyway. Quite a few calls. The list is there.' Her gaze never leaves her monitor.

In his office, Min Fang is propped up on his desk, half sitting on it, leaning back, the split of her black skirt riding up on her exquisite pale skin, so her suspenders are visible at the lace edges of her stocking. The woman has powers, Red'll give her that. A charm hangs about her neck, suspended between her boobs – which are small, but, he notes yet again, with great satisfaction, perfectly shaped.

She gives him a hard look. 'Do you arrive so late every day?'

'I come in when I'm good and ready. That's the advantage of being the boss.'

'That sort of attitude doesn't encourage loyalty from staff.'

'What do I care?'

'It shows. That's all.'

'What do you mean?'

'The girl out the front. She hates you.'

'How do you know?'

'It's obvious. The way her mouth moves when she says your name.'

'She should be thankful she's got a job.'

Min is twirling a letter opener as she speaks, expertly, as if she could throw it and make it thunk into the wall, but she stops and abruptly points the thick chrome blade at his chest.

'You didn't find my earring, did you? I lost a stud. I only noticed after you dropped me in Woollahra the other morning.'

'No. You want me to call the restaurant?'

'I did.' She pauses. 'You okay? You look … sick.'

'Traffic was awful. I think my ulcer is back.'

'You should take better care of yourself. Eat more vegetables. Play more golf. Drink less. Especially whisky.'

'What would I live for, if not whisky?'

Min snorts. 'Golf. Sex. Golf. Money. Golf. Real estate. The Lord Jesus. Golf. That's what you get to decide, Redmond. Make it anything you want, plus golf.'

'What are you, my cheer squad?'

'Why are you always so maudlin? Get it together, we need to talk.'

If any other woman said that to him, he'd tell them to bugger off, but something about Min Fang saying it makes him like her more. She really knows him. God, she looks hot, too, perched on the edge of the desk with her tits sticking out. He can feel a boner forming as his eyes linger on the outline of her nipples, profiled in the sheer fabric of her blouse. Two weeks earlier, after a competitive auction on a garden apartment with extensive harbour views, she'd dropped the louvres, latched the door, and reclined on the freshly sold-off kitchen bench, all six square metres of single-slab granite. Slowly she'd pulled back her dress to reveal suspenders, no panties, and ordered him to lick her pussy until she told him he could stop. Even now, he can feel in his shoulder blades where the heels of her Manolo Blahniks had dug in. There were still angry welts there, he had glimpsed them just that morning. Knees on the floor and the harbour shining in, gleaming in the stainless steel, while her stilettos clutched his back like the talons of an enormous bird.

The memory of it has not left his mind for more than seconds since.

Red locks the door. 'You're right, as usual,' he says.

Her eyes widen and she slides from the desk.

'Redmond, no, I'm not here for that. We need to talk.'

'We will. We are.'

'It's important.'

'I know.' He walks her back so her arse is against the wood, and then it's his wood she's pushing against, and he's making the joke in his head even as he hitches her skirt up and goes to work on his fly.

'Red, listen!' She pushes his head back and locks eyes. 'You want to hear this.'

'You're not here for business. Just *the* business.'

'Redmond.'

'Then why did you wear those things?'

'They're just stockings, for god's sake.'

'Yes, business.'

She palms either side of his skull and glares into his eyes, but even so he can tell she's warming to the idea. He pushes her panties aside and prods ungently. She's dry and uninviting, not even close to ready for him. The angle isn't good either. He adjusts. Tries again. Fails. She seems half-annoyed, half-amused, but she's not complaining anymore, not making him stop.

'Maybe you need to turn around,' says Red.

'Redmond, you need to—' She shifts a little. 'Oh!'

'Mmmm.'

'I'm serious.'

'Me too.'

He works to get a rhythm going.

Min shuffles along the desk, pulling him with her, then shifting sideways she flicks her foot at the back of his knee, so the two of them fall heavily onto the couch. Not losing contact, both crying out as his arse hits the cushions.

They cast an eye at the door.

'Jesus,' says Min. 'You've maybe split my cervix.'

'Don't blame me. It was you with the kung fu move. Could have broken my – Ouch! Careful! – dick.'

'I think maybe it's already broken.'

'Working … well … enough.'

He still can't tell if she's angry or horny.

As if to clarify, she pulls up her knees and grips the back of the couch, properly working away, flexing the fine muscles of her legs, eyes closed and giving in to it. His groans begin to speed up. It is then, with her blouse open, the small perfection of her breasts pale against the black silk, that she pushes back his head to stare him full in the face and say, 'You are going to be audited, Redmond.'

Hearing, but not. Not comprehending, or mostly not wanting to.

Min stills her motion as he jolts beneath her.

Almost immediately, Red's cock starts to shrivel. Still inside her, but only just. The worst possibilities play out in fast forward, like an eggbeater inside his skull. Red fights to maintain solidity, closing his eyes, refocusing, trying a few more thrusts but not finding the friction, the feeling, the thought of the tax office bubbling up in his head, the death of all erotica.

The battle is lost.

She clenches her thighs and his deflated dick slides from her like an empty sausage casing. It rests wetly on his leg between them as he glares into her amused eyes.

'Jesus, Min.' He pushes her off irritably. 'You could have bloody told me.'

'I just did tell you. Next time maybe you'll listen when I say stop.'

'You're a witch.' He stands and pulls his pants up from his ankles.

'Pity my powers don't work on the tax office.'

A spike of fear slides into his temple. Min waves at his crotch while he does up his belt. 'Maybe you need to eat more ginger. Purifies the blood, keeps the parts that matter working.'

Red sits back into the couch, sullen, watching her readjust her knickers and skirt. 'What do I see in you?'

'Discount facilitator.'

'Discount? The regular fees must be through the roof.'

'They are. Now, you need to hold onto your shit, Redmond.'

'I do have hold of it. But will they find anything?'

'We'll see. I'm very careful, but nothing's foolproof.'

'You're full of reassurance.'

She purses her lips, sits back on the desk, sliding the silk up her leg to reveal the suspenders, her smile a challenge. 'You want to finish what you started?'

Red frowns, gazes out the window. Cars stream endlessly across the Anzac Bridge, and under that bridge, his beautiful house: the house on which he owes the bank two million dollars.

'I feel sick.'

She gives a shrug. 'Too bad. I'll send you a jar of pickled ginger. My sister makes her own. Maybe it'll help?'

'You really are a witch.' He walks over to the door and opens it, motioning her out. 'Come back when you've got some good news.'

As he turns back into his office, the receptionist is typing with the speed and force she reserves for moments of the greatest disapproval. Red feels a twinge of something like pleasure, but it's gone before the door clicks closed.

Red meets Min a week later at a tapas place in the back streets of Circular Quay, the walls covered in wine bottles, posters of matadors working the cape. She's already there when Red arrives, sitting upstairs, at a table by the window, looking up Pitt Street with a plate of cured ham in front of her, a rolled tube of pink flesh between her fingers as she greets him. She puts the cured meat into her mouth, halfway, so it sits there on her lips, and she stares at him, her impossible legs crossed at the ankles. Luxuriating in her own body.

Red asks the waiter for a double Stoli on the rocks as he collapses into the chair opposite her. 'Jesus, it's hot out there. I swear it's got so humid it may as well be raining. My shoes were sticking to the asphalt. My underpants are drenched with sweat.'

'Charming.'

He squirms about on the seat, working to unstick his scrotum from the side of his leg, releasing a small but audible fart in the process. He feels it coming and still lets it go, figuring it will rub her the wrong way, as he's not sure he's forgiven her and wants to needle. She raises both finely pencilled eyebrows, as though in disbelief, and, crinkling her nose, pushes over the plate of ham.

'When did you get squeamish?' Red wipes his brow with his serviette; he needs to get fit, go back to that trainer. The guy is a fascist, but does he ever get results. An image of him and the trainer, busting a gut together, doing circuits in the park, buff and sweating, lifts itself into his mind like an answer to all his problems. He examines her again, contemplates going the grope, but gives it fifty-fifty odds she'll slug him.

The waiter puts his drink on the table. Red scowls. He picks it up and examines the level critically, holding the glass in front of his nose, before glaring at the departing server. 'Double, my arse.' He holds the glass towards her. 'Does that look like a double to you?'

Min shrugs. 'You should be an accountant.'

'What's that supposed to mean?'

'Nothing. It looks, maybe, one and three-quarters.'

'Don't start with me. Not now. I still haven't forgiven you for last week.'

'Why do I need forgiving?' She is being playful, partly at least, but he can tell that he's found a spot under her skin. He makes the decision, conscious or otherwise, to push at it for a little more leverage.

'You could have broken something,' he says.

'I thought I did. I haven't seen evidence to the contrary.'

He ignores this and pushes on. 'Given me long-term damage. You know how sensitive my system is.'

'So you keep telling me.'

'I've had a lot of stress,' he says. The conversation is not going as well as he had hoped. 'My wife gets out of prison in less than three months.'

Her eyebrows form into a single knotted line. 'I know. You tell me every time we meet. I haven't forgotten. I know when she comes out. I can count.'

'Not that well, apparently.'

'Don't push me, Redmond.'

Red tosses back the rest of his drink. 'You said you'd be careful. You said you'd be *very* careful. All transactions would go through residents.'

'I was very careful. And they did. 'All documents were prepared with great care. All are legal. But the ATO follows money trails. It's their job. They have people who are good at it. Not as good as me,' she smirks, 'so I think we'll be okay. But they're well resourced.'

'This was all meant to be above board.'

'Don't be a baby. You knew what you were getting into, Redmond. Don't play the kiddy dumbfuck with me. I *was* very careful. But this is political. The government wants to put trophy homes on the wall. Show how tough they are. Show the Hansonites they don't like Chinese people either. Show they can tackle the housing crisis. Maybe they'll find something, maybe they won't. I can't turn water into wine.'

'You've no problems drinking it, though,' Red shoots back sourly.

'Shut up. You shut up right now, or I swear—' Her face goes scarlet. 'I brought you clients. I brought you many clients. Just like you wanted. Really, you're such a little boy sometimes. You didn't do it. You didn't know. When was the last time something happened that you *did* know about?'

Red places the palm of his hand on his forehead, trying to drown out her voice. His head is aching. 'The last time I didn't hire someone to make sure things weren't fucked up,' he says.

'Aargh!' Min tosses her serviette at him, pushes back her chair and struts over to the stairs. Red listens to the strike of her heels on the wood as she descends to the street, watches her walk up the footpath, hand raised for a cab, resisting the urge to go after her. As she gets into a taxi she throws him a fierce glance, and a jolt goes through him. He has that sinking feeling of having overplayed it, as if it was there in his hands and he knew what he was doing, but now it's shot right by him.

The urge to run after her rises in him, stronger this time, and he stands at the table, pauses, sees her taxi stopped at roadworks, maybe fifty metres up the street, and he quickly throws three bills on the table, equivocates on another twenty – he's looked at the menu already, read the prices and done the maths, but did she get a glass of wine in before he got there? It drives him half-insane for a quarter of a second to have to lay the other twenty down, but he has to assume yes – and then he's running up the street, coming alongside the cab and opening the door and climbing in, so he's got the seatbelt on before she can utter a complaint.

The taxi driver takes stock of him, then offers Min a questioning glance. She stares out the window, as if she hasn't heard him get in. He knows how angry she is by the muscles in her jaw, swollen and twitching as if she's come down with glandular fever. He can hear her teeth working away, cracking against one another, above the sound of the traffic.

Next morning, by some perverse miracle, the two of them are side by side in bed. Well, almost. She's a step ahead, an absent presence. After the fight, she screwed him with abandon, as if she really was trying to break his dick, or fuck him in two. Even so, she's said about three words since the restaurant. Her jaw is still doing the talking, and in the night her teeth sounded like the grinding of granite blocks. Red slept terribly, spending half the night jittery, making a list of things in his head, the 'Before Bea Gets Back' list. Part of it covering his tracks, concealing the mess; part of it about making things nice for her. He was still taking mental notes as the light came up, and he listened to Min wake beside him.

Normally, in the mornings, Min would nestle close. Like a cat in so many ways. Sharp, retractable claws. A love of affection. But this morning she wiped her face with her hands and got out of bed without a word or glance. He watches as she stands before the bathroom mirror, marvels at the muscles of her neck. She runs her index fingers beneath her eyes, tracing the dark beneath. Then, seeing his gaze, she slams the door between them, and he listens to her on the phone, talking to her PA while she waits for the shower to heat up.

He'll drop her at her office, then come back and get ready for work. There's still time. His first meeting isn't until ten. That'll give him the chance to smooth things over. He'll tell her he's sorry, take her out to lunch later. He'll say he's been stupid, that he's had his head up his arse. But listening to the hard edge to her voice, it starts to feel like he's utterly done his dough.

He calls through the door, tells her that he'll run her in, then listens for a reply but there's only the sound of the shower. Red pulls on some shorts and a polo shirt, and goes into the spare bathroom.

On the street, the sky is so low and flat overhead he can almost reach up and touch it. Grey and thick like an underfloor of cement. He can hear the traffic from the Anzac Bridge, the hissing skein of tyres on asphalt, and he turns to look at the water as he opens the car door, his gaze carrying the hope that the view will cheer him up, a hope which he knows rides less in the beauty of it, the light, the harbour, than in their proximity: how close to it all he has managed to purchase this rarely available five-bedroom, three-bathroom plus off-street parking with classic federation windows and facade. That it's *his*. This point of pride, this symbol of what he's managed to do, that no one can diminish. This house. Big, classy, right on the water.

Pretty good. Pretty effing good.

But looking into the underbelly of the bridge, the light is empty, depleted, and a wash of plastic bottles is visible on the water. It's only when he turns back and slides into the car that he realises Min is halfway up the street, walking up towards Glebe Point Road, her shoes dangling from her hand and her phone at her ear. She raises a hand to an approaching taxi.

Red gets out, calls to her, one foot still expectantly on the rail of the car door. 'Min, come on, I'll drive you. Don't be like that.'

She doesn't look back, just crosses the street to the taxi, climbs in the back and slams the door. Red stands there, halfway in the car as the taxi drives towards him. She sits in the back, refusing his glance. The taxi turns in the neighbour's drive and creeps back up the street. Red gets behind the wheel of the BMW, turns on his phone and tries her, but it goes straight to voicemail. He sits there a good five minutes with the car idling, the radio mumbling through morning drivel: a shock jock raving about immigrants and the Labor Party and how the ABC should be abolished. He switches off the ignition, gets out of the car, and walks back into the house.

Steal Big
Chapter 19

Not long after Bea was transferred to Emu Plains, almost two years ago now, Red sent her advertising material about their new house, before he made the purchase. He even asked if she liked it, and if she agreed to it, though what was she going to say? After the sale settled, he sent her photographs of their furniture and things inside and more shots of the view. He was obviously over the moon about it, and in truth she liked the idea and the photos. It made her feel as if her life was moving forward – her whole world hadn't fallen apart just because she had. The photographs separated her from the poverty and general brokenness of the lives of the other inmates: the beautifully restored house, with its multimillion-dollar view, offered a point of difference that wasn't about the luck of the draw.

She wasn't like them. No way. *She* had a beautiful house, worth more money than any of them would ever see. *She* would go and live there, with her husband, when she got out. Her husband, who, despite his faults, hadn't bashed her head against a door frame, who didn't deal drugs and wasn't a junky. That difference wasn't about good luck or bad, she thought. That difference was categorical.

On Tuesday morning, after roll call, Bea is told to report to the office. It's one of the screws who tells her, one of the more vicious of the bunch, and Bea doesn't ask for details. She knows how the place works now, and a call to the office is unlikely to be good. She imagines a falsified urine test; perhaps an inmate has stitched her up for something, is in it with the guards. By the time she makes the office, she's already anticipating a return to the hell of Silverwater, with time added to her sentence for some minor infraction of the penal code.

She is ushered into a small office and told to sit down, and after a few minutes two men come in and sit down across the desk.

'Hello Mrs Campbell,' says the man on the right. He has dark hair and tinted glasses. He picks up a manila envelope and taps it significantly on the desk. The one on the left is tall and thickset. He gives her a nod.

'Hello,' she says. She glances from one to the other.

'Do you know why we're here today?' asks the tall one.

'No.' She hears her voice get tight and high. She works to bring it back to normal. To be calm. To breathe.

'We're here on behalf of the ATO.'

'The what?'

'The Australian Taxation Office.'

Beneath her chair, the floor opens. What has she done? Would they do her for unpaid taxes? While she's in this place? What would that mean?

'We have some questions with regards to your husband's real estate dealings.'

A wave of something like relief goes through her. 'I haven't been involved with the company for two years. I mean, I've been in here. You know that, right?'

'Yes, Mrs Campbell. We know that. We've read your file. But there are certain,' he pauses, 'irregularities in your husband's business practices. Your cooperation could reflect positively on any parole hearings.'

'Well,' she says, 'I'll tell you what I know, but I don't think it'll be much.'

'Just be straightforward and open with us and we'll figure out the rest.'

'Right.'

The two men sit, watching her. Neither says anything more. They seem to be waiting for her to spill the beans.

'So, what?' she asks. 'What do you want me to say?'

'We were hoping you'd know that.'

'Know what?'

'Well, that's the thing, isn't it?'

'Sorry?'

'Just be open with us.'

'Open about what?'

'About your husband.'

'What about him?'

'His business dealings, Mrs Campbell.'

'Oh, for the love of god – what about them?'

The two exchange a glance. The one with the glasses gives a very slight nod.

'Mrs Campbell, has your husband spoken with you about recent property sales?' asks the tall man.

'No. Not really. I mean, we have a new house. Or kind of new.'

'The one in Glebe.'

'Yes.' She glances sharply at him. 'He said things have been going well. That he's shifted some major properties. That's about it.'

'Did he mention who they were shifted to?'

'No.'

'And has he mentioned any foreign investors he may have been dealing with?'

'No. Why? What's this about?'

'Some of your husband's transactions have attracted attention. We're investigating, that's all.'

'Why? Which ones?'

They gaze at her without comment. The one on the right releases a sigh.

'How often do you talk to your husband?' the one on the left asks.

'Every few weeks.'

'That's not particularly often, considering he's your husband.' This from the glasses man, with a sneer.

'He's not a particularly good husband,' Bea says. 'Perhaps you should let him know.'

This shuts them up.

She would never dare dish out sarcasm like that to the screws. If she did, she'd end up squatting over a mirror. Or worse. She glares from one to the other. The room is short of air. Dried out. She leans back in her chair and fills her lungs. It's going to be okay. It's not about her. It's something stupid Red has done. She lifts her hands from her lap and spreads her fingers, flexing them, working to get her breath and blood flow under control.

'We don't talk much, and he tells me bugger all about what's happening at the office,' she says. 'That's the truth. Please, can you tell me? What's this about?'

The one on the right stands and goes to the door. 'We'll be in touch, Mrs Campbell,' he says. He motions her into the corridor. 'Thanks, for your' – he pauses, gives the word space to land – 'time.'

A week and a half later, Saturday afternoon, her name is one of the first over the loudspeakers when the afternoon visits are announced. Red is coming in, as they'd organised. His first visit in five weeks, and she knows he's only coming because she told him he had to. He tried making excuses. The weekend is when they do most of their inspections. It's a busy time. But she doesn't want to ask him about the ATO visit over the phone. Inmates' conversations are routinely recorded, and if he's forgotten, she's afraid he'll say something stupid, something that will get him – them – into trouble.

She passes through security, and sees him leaning with slightly awkward casualness against the old piano in the prefab. He has a new suit on. A darker shade than his usual, so it moves from black to blue as he shifts about. She can tell by the cut and the sheen that it's expensive. Some designer brand. He probably paid more for it than the screws spend on their cars. He's fiddling with a cufflink, lifting his right shoulder to adjust the fall of his sleeve, stretching out his arm. It's one of his tells. Shows he's nervous. A memory comes to her – so distant it's almost a dream – of watching him adjusting his cuffs prior to an auction. They were in the lounge room. A huge place. Views out over the harbour. She can't remember the suburb, just the water glinting, and the boats.

Another lifetime.

There's a screw grabbing at one of the inmates, and she can see Red watching with undisguised contempt. She knows well enough by now how much he hates this place. It's only when the guard has gone that she sees that it's Rhino there, talking with her brother. Their heads huddled together as they watch the departing officer.

The brother's lips form the word 'pig'.

He's done time too, if the neck tats are anything to go by.

'What was that about?' she asks Red.

'That chick took something from her boyfriend. That bloke checked it out, thought it might be drugs. But it was only a bag of change for the machines. You should keep an eye on her, though,' he adds under his breath, indicating Rhino. 'She looks pretty dodgy.'

A needle of anger pushes into Bea's temple. 'You want to start telling me who to look out for?'

'She's a real unit,' he says defensively. 'Just look at her.'

'You can be a real deadshit sometimes, Red.'

'Jesus. Settle down. Have a look; I mean she's got forearms thicker than mine. And her—' He catches Bea's expression and shuts his mouth.

'Good thing, too. She's saved my arse more than once in here.'

'Sorry. I didn't realise she was your friend.'

'Whatever.' She takes him by the elbow and guides him to an empty bench outside. 'Just tell me why the ATO is coming in here to grill me about property sales?' she hisses.

'Grilling you? Oh fuck, I didn't—'

'Just tell me.'

'We've been doing well lately, that's all. You know how resentful people get when you're successful. It's the tall poppy syndrome. The new office has made a big difference. We've built up a better client list, managed to attract some high-wealth individuals.'

'How did we manage that?'

'Well, like I said, the new office is really something, and I've had a consultant on board. So …'

'So?'

He shoots a quick glance about, takes a visible breath. 'It's a group of international clients,' he says. 'Businessmen. Big family money, and I mean big. Party connections in China. Some out of HK. A few Americans. But the money is beyond anything. Thirty million is nothing to them, they just need us to help them spend it. One of them took me out on his boat. It was a cruise ship. Bloody enormous. Swimming pool and everything. You would have loved it, honey.'

'I don't doubt it. But if you're just selling them real estate, why did I get a visit from federal investigators?'

'It's a beat-up. We've been selling property to rich internationals for decades, and it's never been a problem. I mean, the government hasn't been over-keen to investigate. It's all investment, after all. Now the bastards want a scapegoat. They can blame a few rich Chinese for a housing market that's out of reach of the poor. I mean, when were the poor meant to own houses anyway? Isn't that why we call them *the poor*? The government doesn't want to trim their own income streams, the bastards don't want to take a hit with their own investment portfolios ... I mean, politicians are so stupid. The other day—'

'Red.'

He stops. 'What?'

'Were these legal purchases or not?'

'Yes, of course they were. I mean, on paper.'

'On paper.'

'They weren't breaking the law, not exactly.'

'And you knew.'

'Well, it was all fine—'

'On paper.'

'It's really not *our* problem. The purchases were made for valid entities. If they have to be resold that's too bad, but our commissions were validly obtained. I mean, if they had proof we knew, if ...'

'You knew,' she says flatly.

'It's not like I did anything wrong. It's not my fault if these guys weren't honest.'

'Fuck you, Redmond.' Bea can feel her face redden. 'Half the chicks I meet in this place, you know what they've done? What they stole to end up here?'

'I only sold them property. Come on, honey. You don't mean that. What would be the point of sticking me in here? I haven't *stolen* anything.'

'Yeah, you're right. What would be the point?'

'I did this for us.'

'You did this for you.'

'Come on, babe, we both want a bigger slice of the pie.'

From the look on his face, this isn't going how he thought it would. He probably figured she'd be up for anything now she was a hardened crim. His lips are moving but the words aren't getting air. It's like watching someone drowning, that's the thought that comes to Bea. His lips, treading water. All his life. Treading water. Fuck him. Fuck all of them. Fuck all the bullies of the yard. Fuck the ATO and all the whoring suit-clad automatons she watches on the nightly news.

'You think you can make deals with crooks, but still you're not a crook?'

'Steady on, love.'

'Steady on, my arse. Let's not pretend these arseholes you're in business with have done any less than the people in here. What are they like, your new associates? You think they'd have your head beaten in if you threatened their interests? Like the women in here got smashed up because they said the wrong thing or didn't have dinner ready.'

The pallor in his face, the momentary panic, tells her she may have hit on an unlikely truth. She lets out a chuckle.

'Petty crime,' she says quietly. 'Stealing someone's shoes, or their phone. That's what'll get you locked up. But the white-collar deals? For that shit, nobody goes to prison. Pull that shit, you're too rich to fail. Fuck you, Red. If I have to spend another day in this place because of you, I swear to God—'

'It won't come to that. I did this for us, honey. I did it so—'

'No,' she cuts him off. 'You did this to win the game. You did it for the new car. You think it's not stealing because you don't have to point a gun, or get in through a window. But if you're doing deals with crooks, Red, it means you're a crook. We promised each other we'd do it right.' Her throat tightens.

Bea glares out beyond the yard, beyond the wire, out where the city writhes about, glorying in itself. The sky is blue and dry and clear. No clouds. Just heat, blasting through the evacuated air. Jesus, she needs a drink of water. Sun bakes the concrete, radiating from the ground and the metal awnings. She makes herself breathe, pulling it back together. Red goes to stand and she reaches out a hand and pushes him back onto the bench. He gapes at her in shock.

'These women in here, half of them were raped by the time they were ten. Alco dads, junky mums, pedo uncles. What do you think the judge said? *Oh, don't worry about a little break and enter, you only stole six hundred bucks worth; we know you've had a rough trot.* Steal a TV and get busted, you'll be in and out of prison till you're dead. But steal big and you're an entrepreneur. That's the ticket. Steal too big to fail.'

By the time Red gets to his feet, Bea is already halfway across the grass, heading back in, back to a world she hates a fraction less than she did at the morning siren. She spins about, hollering back at him across the baking yard.

'Thanks for the visit, Red. You know what? I think this time it really helped.'

The days pass, and she tries not to think about Red, because every time she does, she feels the anger rise again. She's not even sure why she's so angry. It's less, she ponders, what he's done, than the way he wants to wriggle out of it. So she distracts herself with television, avoids shadows and corners, and in this way the hours slide by.

One stifling afternoon she realises it's been a week since she spoke to Mada. He would talk to her every day if he could, but she's come to hate the calls. Just as he has, she can tell. She's incapable of talking about the place she's in, and short of anything else to say. She can hear his discomfort down the line, how he blathers on about his life, trying to drain his descriptions of colour, so the thought of his good times doesn't leave her depressed.

Today, though, she has the sudden urge to talk to someone beyond the fences, to connect to some kind of normal life, and she shuffles over to stand by the telephone. Not too close, but close enough so it's clear she's making a claim.

There's a woman there already, talking, but no one else, and Bea leans back against the wall and keeps watch up and down the corridor. A group of women have been sizing her up the last few days. Giving her shit. She doesn't want to offer them any chances, and she runs her finger along the brickwork, nonchalant and watchful, listening to the conversation without appearing to, without trying to.

'Someone's here. Hold on a sec,' the woman on the phone says. Then louder, 'Eh, sis!'

Bea looks up. The woman has taken the phone from her ear and is staring at her.

'Oh, sorry.' She starts to move away.

'No. Don't effing wander off. Come ere.'

Bea fires a glance to where cameras and guards might be, then takes a few steps towards the woman. 'Yeah?'

'You much good at writing?'

'I guess.'

The woman holds a piece of paper out, along with the receiver. 'I hurt me hand. Write this down, will ya?' It's only then that Bea sees the arm. A flesh-coloured bandage over her hand. Maybe a splint under there as well, but she has it tucked up like a broken wing. Bea takes the phone and holds it to her ear. 'Hello?'

'Hello love. You got the pen and paper?'

'Yes,' she says.

The woman leans against the wall, unsmiling, watchful.

'Okay. His prisoner number's 100217.'

Bea scribbles the number onto the paper. 'Okay, I got it. Whose number is it?'

'Lucy's husband's.'

Bea glances at the woman. Lucy. There's a fresh scar leading up her cheek into her left eye. Pink sensitive flesh beneath. Residual dark of bruising. Lucy. Her mum and dad named her Lucy. The light bearer. An optimistic name, bestowed, no doubt, with the usual hopes and dreams. She hands the woman the slip of paper and walks off without a word.

A few days later, Rhino is granted parole. She says goodbye before Bea goes off to Milk-Pro, wishes her good luck.

'What are you going to do?' Bea asks.

'I'll live with Dad for a bit. Then we'll see. I want to sing, you know. We'll do a bit of busking, try to score some gigs. I've spoken with the others. They've got their own projects, but they're keen to jam.'

'Sounds good,' says Bea. 'Sounds *really* good.'

'Don't worry, babe, you'll get outta here in a bit. Then you can get back to your huge fucking house and your dipshit husband, and the two of you can drive about all day in your Beamer, being rich and white and free.'

'After this place, I'll take what I can get.'

'Too right.'

'I like the idea of getting the band back together.'

'Yeah,' says Rhino, her face flushed with longing. 'Sounds all right, doesn't it?'

The Brownshirts
Chapter 20

Leading up to his final appeal to remain in the country, Carlos becomes terse and dark. He withdraws inside a depth of gloom, so that most of what Mada says to him goes without response, registered with no more than a nod. He *knows* it will go badly, and offers a grim countdown to deportation. *Today is eleven days ... Today is ten ...* He puts in long hours at the lab, arriving at seven, not leaving until well after dark. He is obsessed with a new tincture he's been working on, as if it's the answer to everything. His notes fill page upon page in his journals, and sometimes Mada will find him in the office that joins the lab, his eyes bloodshot, deliriously tired. Paula is worried, of course – just saying his name her voice contracts – but he dismisses her concerns.

Mada is approaching Paula's office one afternoon when he spies Carlos in the doorway.

'Oh stop it,' he overhears the Venezuelan say. 'Enough with the fussing and worry. I get plenty of that from my own head.'

'Just promise me you'll sleep tonight,' Paula pleads. 'You go out to the bar, crawl home or hide in the lab, smoke yourself comatose every night. My love, you've got to sleep. And I mean real sleep, not this mania followed by collapse.'

'*A la mierda.* Enough. You're not my—' He registers Mada's presence and offers a curt nod.

'Hey, Carlos.'

'*Hola.*' He hoists his pack onto his shoulder.

'You okay?'

Carlos stares at him a moment. 'Yes. Of course.' He turns on a heel and strides to the fire stairs.

Paula catches Mada's gaze and rolls her eyes.

Every day that creeps by, his melancholy deepens. The three of them are in the lab together the following week, and when a burner hose gets tangled, Carlos hurls the implement against the wall with such force its base breaks free and pings across the room. It smashes a glass flask on a shelf, the shards raining down to land with a tinkle on the floor.

'*¡Bien hecho!*' says Paula sardonically.

Carlos grunts.

Even his lawyer doesn't hold much hope. Indeed, it is the matter-of-fact assessment of his counsel that has Carlos so despondent: 'You should make your preparations. If they decide you're an unlawful non-citizen, Home Affairs will put you in immigration detention until they can get you on a plane; best thing is to go voluntarily before they put you in – you won't enjoy it in there, and it will likely mean restrictions on your right to return.'

They go out to Café Bolívar the day before his hearing, aiming to find some cheer with camaraderie and music, but Carlos will only speak sorrow and riddles. He inhales rum with absolute purpose and an absence of joy, not drunk so much as elsewhere, in an expatriate world too distant for the others to reach. At one point after ten minutes of largely incomprehensible Spanish, he abruptly grabs Mada's arm. 'Something is there, at the heart of the universe,' he says, his grip tightening.

'Is there?' asks Mada, nonplussed.

Paula reaches out and gently strokes Carlos's face.

'If you search it out, you can feel it,' he says emphatically. There's a glint in his eye that's almost maniacal. Mada shoots an inquisitive glance at Paula, but her eyes are on her lover.

'It is there, inviting you forward, invisible, indivisible, distinct. Gaia, God, Hecate. All the names and none. Joy. Creation. The essence of fuck. You can feel her in your fingertips – the energy of this world dwells within your skin.' He holds out his hand as though half expecting it to crackle with electricity. 'Even here, right now, she will come, if you ask with an open heart, with meaning.'

He's gripping Mada's arm so tight it hurts. Mada puts his hand over that of the Venezuelan. 'Sounds good, my friend. All my fingertips seem to feel these days are laptop keys.'

Carlos stares down at the hand for an instant, as if waking and trying to remember where he is. He straightens up, refills his glass and tosses back another shot of rum.

'Enough,' says Paula, pushing back her chair. 'Let's go.'

'*Tu vas, yo me quedo,*' responds Carlos. He pours another shot without looking up.

'No. You're coming, my friend. Tomorrow you must be in court. We can't have you turning up like a half-dead thing.'

She grabs him under the arm and tries to drag him from his chair, and, failing, signals Mada to grab the other arm.

Together they heave him onto the street.

Getting outside brings Carlos to, at least a little. Mada gives the two of them a bit of space as they slouch towards Paula's place, hoping she can pull him out of his malaise. The street is hot, unsettled, a storm front's approaching. They walk into a blustering wind, bearing into it as the traffic rushes past, the air moist, thick with exhaust and on the edge of rain.

As they come up to the rail bridge and turn onto King Street Mada sees the cops. Four of them. The one in front is broad-chested under his gear vest and uniform, his peaked cap pulled low. He's got a leashed dog and he's walking towards them on the footpath that spans the bridge. The other three walk behind him, two thickset men, one very tall, and a woman with a blonde ponytail.

'Eyes up,' says Paula. 'Here come the Brownshirts.'

She says it lightly, playfully, as though trying to lift the mood.

Mada gives a forced laugh. He's staring at the dog but it doesn't seem funny. For one thing, the animal is huge, a black German shepherd. And it's true – the cops carry a paramilitary air: boots over their cargo pants, holstered guns, vests loaded up with gear. The dog scarcely glances at Mada. It really is enormous, with a dark, furry mane. It pulls at its lead as he passes, so the handler jerks forward, and Mada turns to see it make a beeline for Carlos, sniffing at his hands and jeans. It attempts to stand up on his chest but the handler pulls it back. The animal plants its butt firmly on the ground and stares from the handler to Carlos, its tongue lolling. Carlos tries to keep walking, but another officer takes his arm and pushes him back against the steel of the bridge railing.

Carlos recoils, staring confusedly, not yet understanding what they want. Pauls tries to step in but the ponytail blocks her way. The cop in front of Carlos gets out a pair of gloves.

'The dog has alerted, sir. We have reason to believe you are carrying illicit substances. We are required to conduct a search.'

'*¿Qué?*' says Carlos, squinting at him.

'Drugs, sir. Would you please turn out your pockets?'

'My pockets?'

'As I said, sir. The dog has alerted.'

'Alerted? What?'

'All right, mate.' The cop exchanges a long-suffering glance with his colleagues. 'Just face towards the railing, if you wouldn't mind. I'm going to conduct a search of your person.'

Carlos gets it then. He pushes at the man's hands and starts backing away, not looking scared so much as angry. 'You're not sticking your finger in my arsehole because the dog knows how to sit.'

The cop exchanges another glance with his mates, not friendly now. He grabs at Carlos's arm, but Carlos is having none of it. He bats the hand away forcibly, so the cop stumbles into the barrier that divides them from the tracks. The cop glares at Carlos. He pulls a canister from his vest, then lunges, red-faced, grabbing the collar of the Venezuelan's shirt and twisting it in his fist. Carlos pulls back, glancing down at the canister, then at the cop, eyes darting wildly, taking in the steel bridge, the wind, the traffic. Abruptly he contorts his body, writhing his arms, so the cop is suddenly clutching a dangling shirt without Carlos inside it. The female cop has to work hard to hold Paula back, who's calling, 'Calma, calma', her arms outstretched. Mada reaches towards Paula but the guy with the dog shoves him back. The cop blasts a squirt of aerosol towards Carlos's face – a neon-white jet of gas bright and fleeting in the headlights. The Venezuelan swings away and most of it goes wide, the wind whipping it out over the railway tracks. The air is filled with an eye-burning astringency. The cop swears, leaning against the railing while he wipes his eyes with the back of his hand, then, looking down and finding Carlos's shirt, he pushes it into each of his eye sockets. He does it twice then glares red-eyed at Carlos, who grins at him, wiping his own face lightly, mockingly, with the back of his hand.

'¡Viban los compañeros!' he taunts.

'Right, wog, you're done,' says the cop. He throws the shirt to the ground, shoving the canister in his vest, and draws his sidearm. His mates retreat a few steps.

'Take it easy, Barry,' says the guy holding the dog.

Carlos stares at the weapon, then at the man's face. He takes a step back, beyond the kerb, his foot coming down onto air where he'd expected firm pavement. Abruptly stiff-legged on the road surface, he jerks away from the cop, away from them all, staggering backwards. He rights himself, staring at each in turn, and finally at Paula, straight-backed and fierce. The wind is whipping about his hair, his breath heaving.

It is at this moment that the car comes tightly round the bend, moving very fast, hugging the kerb as it chases the last orange blink of signal. A dark blue ute with fat chrome mags. There is an instant in which Carlos registers it and lifts a hand, open-palmed, heralding the vehicle to stop. It hits and his body folds double, his face smacking the bonnet, loud, metal and organ, metal and bone, then bounces up, rolling over the windshield to hang in the air an instant before he drops to the bitumen with a sick, wet slap.

Paula screams.

Mada leaps towards Carlos but his arm is wrenched back, searing pain where the dog has taken hold. The car skids to a halt. Smoke billowing. The acrid stink of rubber.

Everything ringing. The gurgling V8.

The cop yells 'Release!' and Mada drops to his knees, a pulsebeat of red surging between his fingers. Two of the cops start running for the car as a cropped head appears, gawking through the passenger window, taking in the cops, the dog, then searching out the crumpled shadow of Carlos on the street.

Shirtless, bloodied. Lit dark in the yellow streetlight.

The head disappears.

There's a Southern Cross on the rear window of the cab, and through the glass Mada glimpses the two men inside turn to each other. The stereo stops. Blue duco shining. Mada on his knees, gripping his bloody arm. He hears a man shout from within, voice full of panic: 'GO! FUCK'S SAKE GO! JUST GO!'

The tall cop is first to the car and pulls open the passenger door, but there's a screech of tyres and he's yanked face-forward to the bitumen as the car roars off. The other runs in useless pursuit. The tall one picks himself up and starts to run after the car as well, but it blasts though a red light, narrowly missing an SUV, and thunders up King Street, the engine growling up the gears, veering through traffic until it is gone from sight.

The two cops stop in the middle of the road, staring after it. They turn to face the oncoming traffic, holding up their hands.

The street in the wake of it.

Carlos.

A shadow with weight. His body shifting in small, jerking twitches, giving his last energy to try to sit, to offer one final thought before he is unable. Then breath leaves him and he slumps, legs splayed, a mute dark pool expanding into the night.

Paula has pushed past the female cop and kneels at his side, hands on his cheeks, cradling his head with delicate fingers and kissing his face as the officer with the dog waves a torch into oncoming traffic, walking to the centre of the intersection, the dog pulling at the leash, straining for the place where Carlos lies, and the woman calling for an ambulance on her VHF saying 'Code red, code red, corner King Street and Enmore Road, Newtown, code red, pedestrian down. Hit and run. Vehicle licence ...'

When they leave the hospital it is after 4am. Through the glass doors and into the night. Windless now, still. A group of students, meandering back from the pub, pass the line of ambulances parked rear to kerb – waiting, expectant. Two police cars are parked in front, an officer sitting in the first with the window open. He gives them a nod, opening the car door and signalling them to stop.

'It just came over the radio,' he says. 'They got them, south of Wollongong.' He sounds excited, eager to share the news.

Paula puts her arm through Mada's. 'Piss off, *pendejo*,' she says. 'You think you're bringing us some great prize?'

He gives her a confused glance, and moves forward, as though to comfort her, but Paula recoils, hissing, and pulling Mada by the arm she marches up to Missenden Road. Ahead of them, the students walk towards the university, their laughter subsiding into a murmur of voices. Jacaranda blossoms shine blue in the college floodlights. A single car cruises past, silent as a shark, and then the road is darkly lit and on they walk through the emptiness.

When they get in the front door, Paula goes into the kitchen and pours several fingers of rum into a couple of highballs, pushing one across to Mada without glancing up. Her shirt is mottled in tinted patches of black and her face is scratched and tear-streaked. A bandage wraps about Mada's arm, thirteen stitches beneath it.

Mada is searching for some word of comfort, but there is nothing to say and he reaches out to touch her on the shoulder. She brushes him off, mumbling about a shower, fresh clothes, and trudges up the stairs. The spirit burns in his throat as he gulps, a fire reaching inside his lungs. He coughs and throws what remains in the sink, then fills the glass with water and walks out to the patio. The night hums, faintly luminous. A truck in the distance. Somewhere a yell, a man's voice, whether pained or celebratory Mada cannot tell. He walks back inside and picks up one of the journals that Carlos has written in so obsessively, still on the table where he'd dumped his pack not twelve hours earlier. An image burns in Mada's mind: blood seeping red through a white starched sheet. The outline of a face below.

What does it mean, all this death? First Lori, now Carlos. Have they found peace? Death is the end of suffering; there must be a kind of peace in it. At least it is the end of regret, the end of all the pent-up worry we carry day on day. It is final, absolute. Dying is the one thing we can't do by halves, regardless of how we try to escape it. Carlos's great-hearted laugh will sound no more. Yet he can't escape the feeling that some part of him lingers, refuses to depart. What does that mean? What is it, that part that remains? What is it that does not abrade, that stays with those left with the burden of care?

As much to drive out these black ruminations, drive out the image of Lori swimming to infinity, of Carlos broken beneath a sheet, he sits outside, opens to a random page of the journal and starts to read. Is he hoping to find a secret of resurrection, a reversal of time? He turns through page on page, his head bent over the minuscule, precise handwriting.

And it does help, a little.

Carlos, at least, is alive within. It feels oddly profound to be reading his friend's script. The shape of each letter as distinctive as a face. Punnett squares with spiralling decorated edges, a formula written at the top of a page, crossed out, corrected, rewritten with new inclusions and new results. The developing story Carlos was telling deepens with every page, and the more Mada reads, the more he enters the Venezuelan's way of thinking.

Mada traces the evolution of the tincture – Carlos's last obsession – ratios recalculated and reworked over and over again. Light is advancing unhurriedly through cloud, diffuse, insubstantial, when something arrests the movement of the pages, lodging in his mind as he flips forward, so he turns the page back to stare, not yet comprehending, at a ghost in the ink. A particular letter with an ornate shape sits underlined above a page of tightly knitted notes:

Patient L: Female. 49 y/o. 59kg.

Dose: 3 drops, twice daily.

Side effects: Increased pulse (3–5bpm)

Observation: First consult. Early stage chorea, increasing with agitation.

Self-reported: Diminished 'wobbles'. {? placebo} Increased creative desire. Strangeness. Elation. Connection. Visual distortion. Colour/light sensitivity.

Another meeting is recorded. More details of the patient: her diet (including bananas and avocado), the times of day the dose was taken, her exercise patterns, all kinds of personal habits. The more he reads the more certain he is that the subject is his mother, and the more certain he is that the list of patients is not, as he first thought, drawn from established clinical trials, but rather reflects Carlos's own experiments. He flicks back through the journal with a mounting sense of discomfort, then anger. What if Carlos's tincture is what took his mother over the edge? What had he been thinking, handing her an unproven medication with psychoactive effects? There are six other research subjects, each identified only by a single letter. Three appear to be using the same tincture as his mother;

three are on a placebo concentrate of alcohol. How had Carlos managed to identify and contact sufferers? How had all this work been possible, right under Mada's nose? Right under Brandis's obsessive gaze?

The idea makes Mada feel physically sick. He glares mutinous from the journal to the sky. Had Carlos's actions been discovered, Mada's position at the university would have been in jeopardy by dint of association alone. It could have cost him his scholarship, his entire academic future.

He sits a long time, staring out at the sky. There are clouds massing, pushing in from the coast. The wind is picking up again, a sharp, sudden drop in the air. The clouds are thick, bloated with darkness, low and vast. They look so close. As if he only needs to reach out and prod a finger to burst them, drench the entire city. Part of Mada wishes he could: wash the place clean, wash it all away. The last twenty-four hours have brought the only rain-bearing cloud they've seen in months. So what does it matter, he thinks, when there's nothing left to grow? What does it matter, rain, on this concrete wasteland? He picks up the journal, stares at the cover and throws it, hard, so it sails out over the fence before flopping down out of view. He focuses resentfully on the spot where it disappeared, but even as he looks, he feels the lie of it: the garden all about him full of living things, opening itself upwards in hopeful anticipation of long withheld rain.

A flash comes from the roiling cloud, a deep rumbling of thunder. Without thinking about it, Mada is up, running to the fence, where he props a chair against the edge to climb over the timber slats and drop into the yard beyond. He retrieves the journal and brushes it down. The first drops of rain start to fall, and he hoists himself back over the fence and retreats beneath the awning, a sporadic percussion already hammering the tin overhead, until it opens up in earnest, a stampede now, thundering, building, painting its own drowned world, sucking the air like a hurricane. Mada grips the journal close and lets the air and rain whip about his face, his bare arms, the spray like the ocean, the drops enormous.

Then it stops, and the first rays of sun blink in and out, the wind cycling the storm south, so he can see the clouds moving bodily overhead, a whole city of weather stretching into the sky. With a peculiar sense of shock, Mada realises that he's not angry anymore. Not about Carlos. Not about any of it. The university. His mother. Bea. The need to take Zoe in his arms rises so forcefully in him that he feels it as physical pain, an ache behind his sternum as though a stone is lodged there.

The sun is well into the blue by the time Paula comes downstairs. Her face is blank, dark shadows hollowing her eyes. She has showered, changed into a plain black dress and combed her dark hair so it lies flat against her scalp. Mada is unsure how much time has passed since they came in. Four hours? Five? He catches his reflection in the glass doors – his hair tousled, dark splotches of blood against the white of his T-shirt. He holds out Carlos's journal, open at the page describing Patient L.

'Did you know what he was doing in here?' he asks.

'Yes, of course.'

'And you didn't try to stop him?'

'Naturally, when I discovered what he was doing, I advised against it. But have you ever tried to stop Carlos from doing exactly what he wanted?'

'Fair enough. But you might have told me. It's my mum, Paula. My mum!'

'That I didn't know. Clearly he wasn't bringing patients into the university.'

Mada pauses, looking down at the journal, flicking through the pages. 'Paula,' he says eventually, 'this work is good. I mean, I understand now what it was he was doing. The sample size is tiny, but there's the start of something here.'

'Of course,' she says dully. 'What were you expecting?'

'It's just that so much of what he says—'

'Isn't "science"?' She makes quotation marks in the air.

'Yes, I suppose.' Mada feels his face redden.

Paula takes his hand in hers. 'It's okay. I know. His sense of the world was ever his own. He and I shared some of those same arguments which I overheard from the two of you. Yet there are few who met him whose lives weren't made richer by it.'

She opens the freezer, pulls from a container a small ziplock bag of seeds. These she holds out to Mada. He takes the bag to examine its contents, each individual seed rolling about like a tiny green egg. 'I can't take them all back with me, and he'd want you to have some, if you believe you can do anything with them.'

'You're going back?'

'Yes. I must take him home. He'd want to be returned to the forest that he loved.'

'But you'll come back to Australia?'

She shrugs. 'I don't know. What is there for me here? Then again, what remains of my homeland that's worth returning to? My father has gone to Peru. My friends have fled wherever they can. What kind of life is possible there now? The future before me is one that I never considered. So we shall see, my friend, we shall see.'

Mada nods slowly. 'But are you sure about me keeping these? They meant a lot to him.'

'Yes, I'm sure. You should store them in the freezer until you're ready to begin. He made considerable notes on breeding,' she says, indicating the journal. 'I'll have this scanned before I depart. Then you can have a copy. His other notebooks too, and the files from his laptop: there's a decade of field notes from the Amazon and Orinoco. Let's see what you're able to make of them.'

'I can copy them if you like. You must have so much else to do. I can go down to Fisher now.'

'Yes,' she says, smiling sadly. 'Thank you. That's a good idea.'

She hands him Carlos's faded knapsack, her touch reverential.

'Will you be okay, Paula?' he asks. 'I can stick about as long as you like.'

She gives a dejected shrug. 'What to do, when you outlive those you love the most? Even the young ones. It's a bitter pill to swallow.' She looks him over appraisingly. 'How about you? You look half ghost yourself, Mada. Have you eaten anything?'

Mada reflects. It takes an inordinate amount of time for him to figure out the last time he ate. The previous twelve hours are a blur – only feeling, no time. 'I don't think so,' he says eventually.

'There are *arepas* in the fridge. Have them with some cheese.'

'I don't know if I can eat.'

'If you don't know, then you can. You look ready to collapse. Lie down if you need to.'

'No. I want to get this done. And I have to see Zoe.'

'Okay. But first, eat.'

She takes the pastries and cheese from the fridge and Mada's stomach churns noisily. The flavour is rich and delicious, and they eat in silence until Paula says quietly, 'Carlos made them.'

Mada glances at the pastry in his hand, then at Paula. Tears are streaming down his cheeks before he knows they're there, and when he looks at Paula her face has crumpled. They fall into each other, sobbing, Mada still holding the half-eaten pastry.

'Come,' she says after a time, 'you must return to your wonderful girlfriend and find a way to heal. You will make your own path, Mada, find your own way. Even if I don't return to Australia, our futures will entwine again. I feel it.'

'It seems like we've travelled so far, only to end up at the beginning again.'

'No, that's not true. We're like Newton, just children on the seashore, diverted with pebbles and shells. While all the time a great ocean of truth lies before us undiscovered. You think this, now, is where you started?'

'In some ways.'

'*He arado en el mar y he sembrado en el viento.* We must have no regrets, Mada. We must try, always, to shape a better world, for in our trying we make it so.'

Mada walks the block to King Street and takes a right down the hill to Sydney University. One foot before the next along City Road and through the thicket of Thai restaurants, bookshops, pubs. The strangeness of the streets, people going about their lives. He keeps his head down, waits for the lights without impatience or thought. The streets are skeined in run-off from the storm, the sun pushing away the last clouds and surging in blinding flashes. Mada avoids every eye, and when he makes the campus it is mercifully empty, thanks to the inter-semester break. He enters Fisher Library and starts on his task.

It takes over two hours, and when he is finished, and he's returned the final journal to the knapsack, he stumbles through the door and down the steps into the day's bright sun.

Mada doubles back through the park on his way to City Road, meandering among the vast buttress roots of the Moreton Bay figs, when something makes him pause. Or not so much something, but everything. A sense of the pulsing world, running from leaf to branch and stem, stopping him in his tracks. Since before sun-up he has swum in the strange waters of Carlos's writing and formulations, and now a sense of it permeates each living thing. As though a coloured light runs from one plant to another. Plants are speaking to us constantly, Carlos had said, if only we would listen. Not just in the jungle, but everywhere. Mada gazes along a root, up the trunk of one of those magnificent trees, up and out through the branches. All you need to do is figure out the language, said Carlos: there is a grammar to healing, a grammar which the forest wants to reveal. A language of forest, a language of sky. Physics and philosophy have the same root, yet it is a lesson he is endlessly forgetting.

The day has grown hot, and he finds a place dried by the sun, partly shaded by the broad, green leaves, and stretches out on the grass. A vine drapes along a fence, its flowers amplified green trumpets. Mada lays his head on the pack, resting his eyes a moment as the sun strobes in and out, in and out through leaf and stem, in through the redness and darkness of part-vision, in the mind and through and out. A number, a word, a pattern of colour in the light. And within every colour, the names. Each name overlapping and folding into the other. Veins of every leaf, nervure, a model of the whole, the universe entire, each minute structure a fraction of what is. Thin pollen-dusted fronds, their nebulous speech, one to the next. Whatever understanding there is between trees, birds, rivers, rock. What speech there is within that rock, guiding roots into what they seek. The scent of minerals within the earth. The iron drawn into those roots. That is the language: a blood and sap of living things. Of cells and the secret speakings of earth and twig. It's as if he can write the formula from which his body is formed, write out his neurones and muscle and blood, all the names turning solid and connecting back to the things they speak of, back to him, that he might connect to their essence and render it on the page.

There is a vine trailing from the tree, waving in the wind, but when he blinks that vine is not a vine at all but a snake, a serpent spiralling about the branches, enormous, vibrant, shifting colour. It winds its way along tendrils of light, hanging down to speak of that for which he has longed and hunted. The mouth moves but he cannot discern one word from the next, so Mada reaches out a hand, tries to still the air so that he might better listen, and again there are the words at the far edge of hearing, secret names of all the seen and unseen things, the seven thousand names of earth, the shadow places between divinity and physics, offering them forth as a secret to be shared.

The names, the names.

They lie at the tip of his tongue as he wakes, the edge of the seen, but although he grasps for them, stretches his arm up into the sun, the outline of what he saw moves away – palpable, present, yet fading before his fingers, sifting from his mind even as some remnant shape endures.

Red Counts Down

Chapter 21

Red spends a day being grilled by the tax office and comes home in a state. They sat him down and filled him with shitty coffee and endless questions: about his knowledge of this corporation and that corporation and of a Hong Kong national going by the name of Min Fang Boucher, and he, in all stupidity, denied he even knew her. When they pointed out that she was listed as a financial contractor employed by his agency, he made an unconvincing backtrack: 'Oh, *that* woman. Yes, she helped us with our accounts from time to time', and the two tax agents exchanged a glance, as if they'd got him, and it made him feel sick in the stomach. It was at that point he started shaking from caffeine, from all the coffee combined with lack of food, and just when he thought he couldn't stand another minute they abruptly stood up and said the interview was over.

The feeling of it, though, hasn't left him.

All his work, kissing arse with politicians, bankers and clients, scraping together every dollar he could. None of it meant shit. End of the day, these bureaucratic wankers could snap their fingers and make it all disappear.

'Doomy fucken doomsday,' he says out loud.

His voice makes the room feel very empty.

Red repeats the phrase, savouring the expletives.

He feels slightly better, but not a lot.

As the days tick down to Bea's return home, one and then the next, Red feels increasingly wretched. Every time his phone rings it makes him jump. He's back to scraping by at the office, watching the accounts on an hourly basis, sneering at his staff when they can't close a sale. To make matters worse, it's been hot as hell. Dry and endless heat for weeks. The fires are on the news all day; all day a gloom of smoke haze assembled loosely to the west. The sunsets are crimson. He spends his nights staring numbly at TV news, or binge-watching golf videos when he can stand no more of it. His swing, so loose and free just weeks before, has abandoned him entirely, all his flow gone. In bed he stares at the ceiling, gritty-eyed and sleepless.

It's the last Saturday before Bea is due to be released and he's dozing on the couch, when banging reverberates through the house. Someone is hammering on the front knocker with the insistence of law enforcement. When Red opens the door, there is his nephew's girlfriend. Her hair is cropped short, and most of her face is concealed behind black-framed sunglasses that are way too big for her head. She could be pretty, he reflects, if she wasn't so annoying. Clean herself up a bit, get rid of the piercings and motorcycle boots. Wear a dress occasionally and let her hair grow.

'Good morning, Zoe,' he says. He's pleased with the authoritative fatherliness of his voice.

'Hello, Redmond,' says Zoe, half smiling, softening the 'd' as if she knows what's in his head. 'Sorry to come to the house, Saturday morning and all. But we couldn't get you on your mobile.'

'It's fine. Yeah, think my phone died.'

He absently goes to pat his pocket, then remembers he has his robe on. 'What can I do for you?'

'There's a problem with Mada's flight back from Melbourne,' she says. 'You know, the one that was supposed to come in tonight. Mada's having a fit about not getting back in time – they're saying it could be days. He wanted me to make sure you were going to be on hand on Tuesday, just in case.'

'Yeah, I'll be about. I told him I'm good to pick her up – he was the one that was insistent that he should go. What's he doing in Melbourne anyway?'

'Talking to Monash about their doctoral program. He didn't mention it?'

'Maybe he did,' says Red. 'I've been ... busy. What happened with the flight?'

'The fires grounded it.'

'Shit. Terrific. So when will he be back?'

'It depends on the fires, on the winds. The airport's closed – didn't you see the news?'

'Yeah. I saw it. I just didn't realise he'd be needing to fly.'

Zoe steps back, looks Red up and down, as if she's figuring

him out. 'Bea is still scheduled for release on Tuesday, isn't she? Mada wants to sort out a plan B for the collection arrangements. He was getting antsy because he couldn't get through to you, that's all. You know how he is when he hasn't got things locked down.'

Red shifts uncomfortably. He is suddenly hyper-aware of the fact that he hasn't showered. 'Yeah, it's Tuesday.'

'You must be excited,' she says.

'Of course.' Red swallows.

'Have you seen her lately?'

He clears his throat. 'Recently enough.'

'Mada says she's coming here.'

'That's the plan, but we'll have to see.'

'See what?'

'What she wants,' he says drily. 'Why? You want to interview me as well?' The girl has a nose on her all right.

He thinks about Bea, rotting away in that hole, filled with ferals and druggies and dipshits. Who knows indeed if she'll come back to him, hardened woman that she's become. He prefers to picture her the day they opened their first office, how proud and fine she looked in her Gucci dress, how they really thought the two of them could take over the world. Make millions. Do it right. Red works to regulate his breathing: negatives turn back upon the self and are best discarded – this is what the therapist has drummed into him. This week, more than any other, it is important he follows his shrink's advice.

'I'm going to see her tomorrow,' says Zoe.

'You? Why?'

'Mada asked me to.'

'Why would he ask you?'

'Because he couldn't get through to you and it looks like he isn't going to get there himself. Sounds like the airport's a total mess. She's expecting a visit. She's about to come out and he thought she might go a bit nuts if no one turns up two days before the release date. Just figured she might lose the plot, you know; must be tense in the days before you're due to come out.'

'Yes, I suppose.' The words fall flatly from his mouth.

'She's had a rough time of it,' Zoe says.

'Well, it's not a holiday camp. If they make it too much fun, everyone will start stealing, just to get inside.'

'I'm sure,' Zoe says sourly. 'So Mada said the parole board was going to come by. To make sure the house was acceptable.'

'You *are* well informed.'

'That must have been weird.'

'Weird? Yeah, it was weird all right. Asking me how much I work, when I get up and when I go to bed, my drinking habits. Everything but when I take my morning dump.'

'Strange they'd let that detail slip.'

He gives a snort. 'Ya reckon?'

As she walks back up the drive a few minutes later, he watches the perfect curves of her arse in her tight jeans and for a moment envies his nephew. That girl, he thinks, what a piece of tail. A pain in the cahones, sure, but all the same. He stands in the doorway, watching as she struts off, then realises he's scratching his nuts as she gives him a final look. No matter what he does, he always cedes her the upper hand. A stab of guilt drives in sharp under his ribs. Red discards it with a short 'fuck it' and walks upstairs for a shower.

* * *

The more time that passes, the more Red thinks about the past. Not just *the past*. More *that past*. The year when it all went to hell. What he might have done differently. How everything can change so fast. The charges. The verdict. The cops arriving to tell him that she's in hospital. And the trial. He keeps coming back to the trial. That, more than anything. And it's not just the humiliation of having a wife in the dock, but more the whole affair, how absolute and inescapable it all felt, despite the utter randomness of the event itself.

Two years, three months in the slammer. And that was a good result. Sentencing could have been worse. Way worse. But the lawyer did his job, amplified the 'circumstances'. Still, it's an image he can't get rid of: a guard leading Bea from the dock in handcuffs, her desperate glances through the gallery. Uncertain. Scared. Sweeping the throng and finding Red, staring back at her, already halfway to the exit.

He remembers holding her gaze for a moment; he could see well enough she was looking for a modicum of hope, of forgiveness, anything which might say it's okay, you'll get through this, we'll get through this, I love you, despite all else. But he had stared back empty, embarrassed, and had trudged up the stairs to where security guards flanked the entrance of the emptying gallery. They weren't looking at him, just gazing from one thing to the next – the light fixtures, the dock, the bench – as if that was their job: making sure each thing remained in its place to prevent the whole illusion from flying into space. Justice. Immutable truth. Right and wrong. You've got to tie that shit to the floor. Mada had nodded and mumbled an apology and already made his way up the steps, and by the time Red was outside he was long gone.

Red had gone over the road to Kinselas, and that's where he'd stayed until he'd thrown enough money at the bar to become persona non grata. Drinking double Johnny Blacks, neat, focused on the sharp amber circling in the glass. Not thinking about the trial. Not thinking about her. Not thinking one iota, lest he could help it. Just working towards numb as fast as his arm could carry him. At some point he'd tipped back enough Scotch to lose count, and having held up a note and gestured to the barman, been ignored and tried again, before realising that the guy was some kind of hero, looking at Red and shaking his head, and he wasn't even sure what he said to the bloke, something like don't be a prick, mate, just get me a fucken drink. And the guy not saying anything, just that same pissant shake of the head, and Red slid his glass over the bar with a flick of his finger, so it sailed off the other side, the barman watching it slide over the timber and into empty air, not trying to stop it, just following it with his eyes, arms folded, as though he was watching fate work, and Red's mild surprise at not hearing it break, and then there was the bouncer already behind him, holding Red's arm as though to keep him steady, but already dragging him out, and he was thinking: when did that bastard turn up? Then abruptly sideways through the door, legs wobbling, just staying vertical as he was shoved onto the street.

Going downhill.

Because it was easier.

The Hollywood Hotel! The idea lighting up like an aircraft beacon. A haunt of his youth. Maybe the owner, old Doris, was still holding court, propping up the bar beside the rows of her studio portraits.

Red stumbled across the park beside the police HQ. Surry Hills. No cabs, but it wasn't much of a walk, and then, from across the square, he caught the glance. He wasn't even meaning to, but the woman clocked him, made it known in the jut of hip that she was whoring. Her silhouette. That's what he'd noticed. The sun low behind her, between the high rises, and it wasn't as if he was looking for it, not really. He only wanted total anaesthetic, to get lost in the night, somewhere, anywhere. But he was still walking across that grass, looking at her, and a part of him wasn't going to be the one to blink. Halfway across. Going slow. Steady. Undrunken. Two police dismounting bikes up by the cop shop, a woman sliding out of a taxi and crossing the road to an apartment block, the driver stepping onto the street and lighting a cigarette, and Red, walking, all horror pushed so far back by the Reverend Johnny Walker he's feeling almost happy, suddenly swinging his body with it and thinking that he could, how he might, and then before he knew it she was there in front of him. Did he walk to her or did she go to him? And he felt himself sway back. Gravity. Space. Her legs stretching down to platform heels and they're damn fine legs, with the sun behind and cheekbones assuming for an instant a perfect line, some fantasy from Pornhub catching in her face. Now he was starting to think about it, but he's not that guy, or hasn't been, not really. Kings Court maybe, after a night with Angelo, a big-end client and he's too polite to say no, but certainly not a pickup from the park by the cop shop. But then he thinks: what would it matter? The fuck it matters! And just as his body gets the idea, a small ache somewhere between his balls and his gut, spreading out so warm and urgent it's as if he's already inside her, she turned so her face caught the sun at a new angle and smiled at him, saying, 'Hey there, hunk,' or some such marketing, and it was an instant before his eyes got the whole of it, that big wide smile, so when he saw the dark space where a front tooth should be, a small black hole sucking at the light, he recoiled and stumbled to the edge of the footpath, and the woman saw, knew it was her, the realisation plain even in Red's double vision, and she telling him to go fuck himself, he wasn't man enough, probably couldn't get it up anyway, dumb old cunt, and she could barely stand in her heels herself, but she flung about and strutted back across the park, back to whatever scraggy orange hell she was inhabiting, and Red thinking she deserved it, whatever it was – her life, her fate – that things might be rubbish but he wasn't a mess like *that*. Then the sign for the Hollywood Hotel up ahead, and there was no bouncer, so he walked right on in and sat at the bar and lifted his chin to the barman, nice, polite, and ordered double Johnny B with a Coopers Green chaser, and he was looking about for Doris, checking out the black-and-white glams, and for a minute he felt all right, or if not exactly *all right*, then good enough so as not to give a shit one way or the other.

He stumbled home sometime in the morning; still pitch black, but maybe not for long. Fumbling with the keys. Finding the lock like trying to roger a snail, and it was extra hard to see as he'd left the prick of a porch light off and the sensor was on the blink. He kicked a pot plant in the dark and then kicked it

dunny, the whole house, calling 'Henry, Henry, where are ya, mate?', but the stubby little shit knew better, smart dog, then discovering the goddamn waste of space asleep in the laundry and shutting the door – 'You're not going anywhere!' – and heading back to pour the well-deserved, the ice landing like glass on glass, and tipping in three fingers, maybe four, then knocking it back and going through to the bedroom, and there was another one in there, at the doorway, a dollop of demonic Mr Whippy, perfectly dank on the cream carpet. Then striding back to open the laundry door to find the dog still sleeping in a cardboard box tipped on its side, and flipping it up so the hairy flesh of the thing slid to the bottom with a pulpy thump and a yelp, and as he picked it up it already knew, its claws scraping away on the cardboard base as it tried to keep its balance, tried to run up the box, but nowhere to go you fucker, nowhere to go, and Red grabbed the keys from the floor, went out the front and shoved the box behind the BMW's bumper so the twin exhausts were flush against the cardboard, his hands shaking as he punctured the cardboard at the meeting point of box and exhaust then shoving his fingers in there, tearing a hole, not too large and not too small, butting the outlet, making sure it was flush, folding the flaps in so it wasn't exactly airtight, but close enough, and then he sat back in the car, catching his reflection in the rearview and nothing there but rage – how the universe owed him; how it would pay – and pressing the button and there came the low, jet-like firing of ignition, subsided purring, a brief thought of the salesman's face at the dealership, that grin of recognition: you may be middle-aged but you can still have fun; think of all the pussy you'll get and don't you deserve it with the money you earned. Then the upped tempo of the dog's scrapings and the box bumping about as Red went back inside, skirting the footprints but conscious not to breathe much, not looking, not thinking. He picked up the glass where he'd left it and filled it again with whisky and drank most of it in one hit, but as he lowered the glass from his lips the sickness pushed up in him so it was overpowering, the shit smell existential, as if the air itself had gone putrid, as if what he was smelling hadn't come from the dog, but was the stink of existence, the death that life feeds on to keep its spark burning bright, the death that permeates all life and can't be escaped, not just this life, his life, but all of it. Forcing himself to sit still, he worked it back down, then when he couldn't stand it anymore, he careened through the hall to the nearest dunny, a burning retch of Scotch and acid blasting out, half in the toilet, half in the lead-up. Collapsing to the floor, panting, covered in filth but past the act of caring.

Minutes passed.

Red was aware, abruptly, that the rage had leached away, and he was sitting there emptied, stinking, looking at a smear on his tie, puke running down the lapel of his jacket. He could feel the wetness of it on his pants, sticky and revolting. He pushed up from the floor, decided to get a hotel – the cleaners were coming tomorrow so he wouldn't have to deal with any of it – then the sound of the dog came back, the tooth-edged scrabbling of claws on cardboard, but now the rage was gone gone gone and what was left was loathing, not of hound but self, and he staggered off the floor and stumbled down the corridor, hoping there was still time, desperate suddenly for anything, a sign of life.

Finding the engine purring, quiet and unhurried, the parking lights on, the night utterly dark beyond the car's glow, he cut the engine and went to the box, opened the flaps and peered inside. Blinking through the cloud of exhaust, he saw a darker shape in the hollow. A motionless smudge. Red dragged it out and squeezed its chest, trying to fill those tiny lungs and trying again, before he sank to the gravel with his back to the wheel, closing his eyes and holding tight. Eyelids strobing behind the lids, Bea's face departing the dock, her fear, then the hooker, and the world's a giant swamp and he's but one fucker wading through it, and this is how the light runs down, sucking in vision to a fine black dot.

When he woke he was shaking and the dog was cold and hard in his arms. The car door was open. He nearly brained himself on the sharp metal as he pushed up from the concrete, dazed, into the morning dark. Sun-up maybe an hour off, the sky splotched grey. From his jacket came the stink of sick, the smell alone enough to exit what remained of his stomach lining, bent over sideways by the rear wheel with the dog still in his arms. With great effort, he got to his feet and leaned shakily against the car.

The box was behind the boot with the top half-open, and he went over and pulled back the flap to drop the stiff shape of the dog inside. Then he sank back to the ground, rocking there and staring, his lips giving out an ill-defined lament as the cold grew deeper in his bones.

First Lunch, Then Prison
Chapter 22

Zoe is still asleep when the landline rings, and she stumbles through the apartment to the phone, sending a sleep-stained hello down the line. It's Sunday morning, not *so* early, but early enough that she's not impressed. She doesn't even know who has the landline number. There are smoke-filled clouds through the window, hanging above the street. Even here, distant from the fires, the scent of burning eucalyptus is thick in the air.

'Hey Zoe! It's a beautiful morning, babe!'

'*It is?*'

'Course it is!'

Zoe picks up the kettle, and, discovering it full enough for a cuppa, flicks on the switch. 'Who is this?' she says.

'It's Lori, ya drongo.'

'Lori?' She pauses a moment. '*Lori?!*'

'Of course. Who else?'

'Just about anyone. Where are you? My god, we thought you were dead!'

'No way. Alive and kicking. I've been living with some chicks I met on my travels, that's all. South of Byron, inland. They're awesome, you'd love em, I've learned heaps.'

'I mean, that's good, Lori, but it's been a year, Mada was worried sick.'

'I didn't mean to worry him. It's only … is he there?'

'No, he's in Melbourne for some interviews. He'd really want to hear from you though. Did you try his mobile?'

'My phone died; I couldn't find his number. Remembered this one, but! Doesn't matter. I want to find out about Bea. Does she really get out next week?'

'There's meant to be a review or something, but it looks pretty sure.'

'Is my boy picking her up?'

'Yeah, the two of us will go get her. At least, he will if he ever gets back from Melbourne. He should have been back last night.'

'What do you mean?'

'His flight was delayed. With the fires. It's a total mess, but yeah, she's out this Tuesday all right.'

'Tuesday! Oh, I miss her! Where's she going? I want to meet up, surprise her.'

'You'll be a surprise all right. She's going to Redmond's new place. Well, it's *their* new place, I guess. But it's a different house. Still in Glebe, but down by the water. Got a pen? I'll give you the address.'

'Thanks.' A pause while she scribbles it down. 'Hey Zoe, I've had a great idea. Promise me you won't tell Mada I called. I want it to be a surprise for him too.'

'No way, I can't do that.'

'Why not?'

'You told him you were dead, Lori.'

'No I didn't!'

'You left a note.'

'I did *not!*' She sounds genuinely offended. Then she says, 'I mean ...' The thought trails out.

'We held a memorial for you. Down at Bondi where your dad ...' Zoe stops, unsure what to say.

'The note wasn't what he thought,' Lori says eventually.

'I read it, Lori. It wasn't that vague.'

'But it was from before. I mean, I did write it. I even tried to do it. But it didn't work. Maybe that's why I left. I don't know.'

'It's been a year,' Zoe says again.

'I just wanted to be free,' she says. 'I wanted Mada to be free.'

'You're his mum, Lori; he doesn't want to be free from you.'

'Doesn't he?' she asks. 'Really?'

'Of course not.'

Lori sniffs down the line. 'Thanks,' she says thickly. 'Guess I'll see you on Tuesday.'

The conversation plays in and out of Zoe's head as she heads into the library. The really crazy part is that Mada half suspected as much, suspected that Lori was still alive, that she'd disappeared on a quest of her own and would reappear when she was ready. When she called him to say his mum was alive and on her way, not two minutes after hanging up from Lori, he didn't even

323

sound surprised. Sure enough, as far as Lori was concerned, the whole thing was a misunderstanding, almost a joke. Zoe tries to throw it aside. Isn't family always half-mad? But she can't stop thinking about how Mada reacted. He sounded almost numb. Admittedly, he was about to step into a meeting with a bunch of professors when she called, a meeting which could reshape the course of his life, but all the same she was worried about him, worried about them. Zoe has her own big news, which she's kept from him for almost two weeks.

The thing is, now that Mada's having trouble getting back, Zoe can think of almost nothing but his return, and Lori's call has only made it worse. Mada has been so hunkered down inside himself since Carlos was killed that she feels a need to keep him constantly in sight, to make sure he's safe, from himself as much as anything. Being in the library doesn't help at all. His presence is everywhere: she even met him there, so that in saying 'Fisher Library, Sydney University' she is in fact saying 'Fisher Library, Point Alpha: Mada/Zoe', as though all fields of knowledge combined within the walls unite under the fact of their love. It doesn't matter that he is a candidate at a different university. Indeed, that he has, just this week, conducted interviews at two Melbourne institutions. Fisher Library is theirs. And so Zoe walks down the book-lined aisles, thinking of Mada as she tracks down an aberrant volume. Then, finding her favourite desk free, she pulls out a stack of books from her bag, opens her laptop, and attempts to hunker down for the morning.

Two hours later, having skimmed over a couple of relevant journals and dropped a few choice endnotes into her dissertation – making sure to reference her examiners now that she knows which three women are going to be marking it – Zoe steps from the library's air-conditioned cool into the violent brightness of the day. She submits her thesis next month. She's so close to being finished she can almost taste the freedom. She's really doing the final touches at this stage, and it is, she's not afraid to say, a damn fine piece of scholarship. Zoe is already eyeing a post-doctoral position at Monash, and considering her publication record is already significant she can't help but feel that the odds are leaning her way.

Haze from the fires gives the sky a white-brown glow, but now she's outside, the heat doesn't seem so bad. There's a bit of breeze coming in from the park, and the sky, shining blue even through the smoke, offers a kind of promise: a promise that Mada will be okay as he negotiates the mess of the airport, the loss of his friend, the shock return of his mum, and that he will come home to her in one piece, still in love, his future open. A promise that her thesis will be passed without correction then published to wild critical acclaim, and that she will write her own history and find her place, and that students will in due time emerge into this same Gondwanaland sunshine, having basked in the brilliance of her work in the paper-scented library, the same library from which she has just emerged, and feel in themselves the overflowing compulsion to wade into the cultural swamp which is this 'specific sociopolitical Australian moment', as her doctoral supervisor termed it in their most recent meeting. For what Zoe wants, beyond Mada and some kind of liveable life together, beyond her personal career-oriented ambitions, is to rile up those who follow in the footsteps of her work. To make them critical of the manifest injustices of this world, not for any other reason than the fact that she is *right*, and as such it is up to her to make them angry, so angry they'll want to change the world, so angry they'll fight for justice for the custodians of the land she walks on, so angry they'll blast a space open in which women can lead. In short, what matters to Zoe is that she have an impact and get a message through.

The message of the moment, though, her theory-laden, PhD-riddled brain has to concede, is mostly about lunch, and after that, prison. And after that ... well, one thing at a time. Right now, she will focus on lunch, which although in possession of a certain cultural significance, is chiefly concerned with proportions of ingredients such as rice and sugar and salt, textural combinations rather than textual ones. She gives a giggle. Playing with ideas always makes her feel better.

She'll call her folks tonight, she decides. They're up north, in the land of her grandmother, and her grandmother before. They raised her in Sydney, her mum and dad – her mum having received a fragment of academic acknowledgement herself, after her dad left the church: the university had, at least, put some of her writing on the curriculum, even if they hadn't invited her to teach. Her mum and dad had high-tailed it for the bush a week after Zoe turned eighteen. It's been too long since she went back to the land, but her folks understand. They're proud of her, and not afraid to say it.

She crosses the bitumen of Parramatta Road and walks into Glebe, deciding against tofu in general and tofu burgers in particular, reasoning that meat is brain food, and turning into Sappho Books, partly because she can read in the courtyard out the back, partly because her current thought of chorizo tapas seems a wisdom beyond compare, and partly because, of late, the bookshop has become a meeting place for the politically sane of the area, and she has a good chance of running into someone with whom to have a rave.

Two and a half hours later, blasting The Saints at full volume, Zoe pulls in to Emu Plains Correctional. She parks behind a beaten-up Holden and pulls the keys from the ignition. She doesn't get out though, just stares blankly at the clock instead. She knows it's the right thing that she agreed to do this, but all the same she feels pretty odd about it. She's never visited a prison before. This fact seems normal in the scheme of things, but she finds herself mulling over what the statistics might be. The percentage of Australians who have visited a jail; the percentage of those who've been incarcerated. She knows the percentage of Aboriginal people in Australian prisons, she's devoted a chapter of her thesis to it, and she lets her mind go off on this tangent, sitting in the car, deciding if she's going in or not.

She, at least, has a choice.

But she's here now. And she promised.

Collecting the tobacco Mada asked her to bring and grabbing her purse and keys, she takes a deep breath and opens the door, stepping into the stiff wind and white summer haze.

Bea is expecting Mada to turn up, so her eyes drift over Zoe, not clicking at first. There is a V-shaped scar over her lip. Zoe takes off her bug-eye sunnies and comes on over, slowly, as if Bea's a nervous animal and she doesn't want to spook her.

'Bea?'

'Yeah? Oh, it's you, Zoe. Where's Mada?'

'He's at some interviews, for Monash, trying to restart his doctorate. His flight was cancelled because of the fires. He should be back tomorrow.'

'Okay,' Bea says with little reaction. 'He's okay, right?'

'Yeah, I think so. Bea, what happened? Your mouth …'

Bea raises a hand to her lip, absently tracing out the scar. 'I slipped in the shower,' she says, looking away.

Zoe frowns. 'Do you want to walk a bit? The guards said we can go around the courtyard.'

Bea glances over at the guards, swaying nervously, shifting her weight from one leg to the other. A few seats along, another inmate is trying to get her hand beneath the stretched denim of her visitor's jeans. 'Come on. We can talk in the courtyard. And don't stare. These chicks've got tempers on em.'

It's bright and stiflingly hot outside. There's no wind, not here inside the compound, just haze-bright air and the burning sun. Bea makes her way slowly to a bench beneath an awning, then rolls a cigarette and sticks its end in her mouth. Methodical. Detached.

'You'll never guess who called this morning,' says Zoe.

Bea flicks ash off the cigarette and offers a shrug.

'Lori,' Zoe says quietly.

'She called?' says Bea blankly.

'Yes. Called our place, in Redfern.'

'Well—' Bea starts, then gives an exasperated guffaw. 'What did she say?'

'Not much. She's been travelling. She needed some space.'

'Well,' Bea says again, shaking her head and smiling. 'Well. I can't say I'm shocked, but all the same …'

They sit in silence for a time while Bea finishes her smoke.

'You must be pretty desperate to get out of here,' says Zoe eventually.

'I can't even talk about it,' she says.

Zoe realises she's still clasping the tobacco, and hands it over. 'Thanks.'

'No worries. So … what happened to your face? Really.'

Bea checks over her shoulder and lowers her voice. 'One of my housemates is a total psycho. Fine one minute, friendly even, then she snaps. She thought I was trying to get out of the housework, so she jumped on my back and slammed my face into the bedhead. The screws came by right then. Good thing, or she might have killed me. She hops up and pretends it's a joke, like we're laughing our arses off. They do the inspection and I'm holding my mouth. Told them I slipped on the tiles.'

'What? You should have said what happened!'

'Fuck no. Then I'd really be in the shit.'

'But there's a duty of care—'

Bea laughs: sharp, sudden, bitter. 'Don't start. If I paper her and I don't make parole, I'm fucked. Even if they put me in protective, even if I get a transfer. Maybe her sentence gets extended. Maybe they put her in management cells, maybe solitary. Sooner or later, either she gets out, or it's someone else. If I rat, I may as well stick my head in a door. There's no protection in here, no more than you can sort out for yourself.' She stops talking suddenly, staring across the yard, running her tongue over a the chip in her tooth, poking at it with grim fascination. 'I want to get out in two days. That's what counts. They should have moved me to Jacaranda by now, across the road, or even Parramatta Transitional. I applied, but it didn't go through.'

'You should be cleared for parole, though? You're out on Tuesday?'

'There's no *for sure* in this place, not until I'm on the other side of the wire.'

'How was the hearing? Did it go okay? It would've been hard, after everything ...'

'Yeah, it was hard all right. You know, they asked if I regretted my actions. Honestly. *Do you regret what you did?* Remorse is important, they said. Bloody hell, it made me so fucking mad. I said that yes, of course I do. I mean, I'm in here, aren't I? Wouldn't *you* regret being here? They said that this wasn't what they meant. I said yes, I know, but it's a weird question, as who in their right mind would say no?'

She looks down at her hands, as if they were unaccountable or newly formed. 'They were such a condescending bunch of arsewipes they got under my skin. But my lawyer smoothed things over and now I'm pretty sure I'm coming out. They went to see Red, and I guess he managed not to say anything too stupid.'

'Will you be okay? Going there?' asks Zoe.

'Glebe?'

'Yeah.'

'Why not?'

'Well, you know. Are you and Red okay? I mean, I know it's not my business or anything, but ...'

'You think he's dangerous?'

'It's not that ...'

Bea offers a droll grin. The V-shaped wound on her lip widens, but she doesn't seem to feel it. 'I've survived Silverwater Correctional, I think I can handle Redmond. After all, he is my husband.'

Between a Hummer and a Mole
Chapter 23

It's pretty much impossible, thinks Bea, should you have done something stupid, really stupid, not to return to it again and again, replay it continuously like parochial morning radio on *Groundhog Day*, stuck in a time glitch you lack the key to escape. This is especially true if the mistake you made had serious consequences, and it is deeply, fundamentally, inescapably true, if that mistake ends with you having completely fucked your life, or ruined the lives of others, so that all there is to do is turn over the 'what ifs', stuck in a shithole as miserable as Emu Plains Correctional, running a daily gauntlet of broken lives, people with stories even more off-journey than your own.

Hell, Bea concedes, she used to rehash even minor mistakes *before* she got locked up. It was a part of her makeup. Something she seemed unable to discard, a pathology that left her forever dissatisfied with whatever present she found herself in, incapable of making peace with her past regardless of how innocuous her slip-ups: a slighted friend, a moment of rudeness, an act of non-compassion that might have been avoided. Even in childhood, Bea would loop together all her worst-wrought moments, playing a near-constant cacophony of dissatisfaction, one she could rarely escape.

It was hard enough before, in the outside world. A career, shopping, dinners with friends – you can eventually forgive yourself anything if you're busy enough. Even Christ said it: you can't give alms to all of them.

But here in prison, where most days it's a Roman seesaw between monotony and violence, there's no place to look but within. So Bea returns day on day to the months preceding her big mistake. This is what Mada likes to call it: *your mistake.* She doesn't know whether the nomenclature helps. Its lightness. Its sense of equivocation. All she knows is that the moments are arrayed as if they are the jigsaw pieces of a past she can't rearrange.

It was after Lori haemorrhaged in front of the television and lost the baby. That's when it really started. Bea hadn't blamed herself so much for that, not like now. But she had spiralled into her own darkness so deep and so long she couldn't find a way out. Pushing away all offers of help, so in the end, with hindsight, there was no possibility but ruin.

Wasn't that always true of hindsight?

What mattered was to maintain the illusion of sobriety. To hide her 'problem' from her friends.

And so on the day that it happened, she had barely left the house for weeks, except for grog-shop runs and corner-store groceries. Even so, she'd let her attention wane. She had stopped listening for the slam of the door, had taken a nap at the wrong moment, been too tired to notice the signs, and so Lori had disappeared.

Oh, her sister had wandered off frequently enough.

I mean, was she her sister's keeper? She never went far, never for too long at least. They would find her at the neighbours, or down at the park on the corner. If she couldn't be located it was never more than an hour or two before she came dawdling back. But on the day it all fell apart, Bea had searched half the day without a sign or word. She had noticed Lori gone early in the morning and thought little of it at first. But then the hours passed, and she got worried, and after walking the streets, talking to neighbours and shop owners (which she almost never did), she'd taken up a spot in front of the telly and guzzled wine (which she almost always did), waiting for her sister to reappear. Late in the afternoon, the call had come through.

There had been an incident, and this time it was serious. At least so announced the voice down the line. Some cop, somewhere, and her sister was locked up. Bea had offered a quiet expletive to do with Jesus and copulation, and then in her most polite voice she said, 'I love my sister but she has some mental health challenges. How can I help?'

A young officer, she was told, had suffered a fractured wrist. There had been an altercation. It was possible it was accidental. It was possible Lori hadn't intended to hurt the officer, but she had been overly forceful, and very strong considering how frail she seemed, and now they were holding her in Parramatta and they would talk through potential charges when Bea came to the station.

'Parramatta?' said Bea. 'How the hell did she get to Parramatta?'

'Perhaps you can discuss that with her when you arrive,' said the voice, smooth as silk. 'As I say, it is possible she didn't intend to hurt Constable Knott, but this situation is serious ...'

'Yes,' said Bea, 'I'm sure that's it. I'm sure she didn't mean to hurt anyone.'

But in the same breath, she was thinking: Oh, it was deliberate all right. Everything she does is deliberate, even the things that appear the most random. And obviously there's no choice but to go and talk it out, nothing for it, and she screwed the cap on the pinot gris and put it back in the fridge, and immediately took it out again and poured a quick slug to fortify herself, tossing it back in one tip of the hand, because god knows she would need it. She could park around the corner and march her sister out, so even if the coppers *did* smell booze on her breath, so far as they knew she would be getting a cab.

The wine helped, at least a bit, and Bea started feeling that things might turn out okay: maybe her sister would smarten up a bit – a few hours in a cell could be just what she needed to get her head together. The last time Lori had been in trouble with the cops, she was as quiet as a lamb for weeks. So Bea would have to get there and smooth things over, and she could still be back for evening cocktails, just a dram or two before Red got home and started getting paternal.

Turning out of the driveway, she accelerated hard through the lights, feeling better, more confident, making the green and veering around the corner, driving west as fast as the bitumen would carry her.

The traffic went to hell when she hit Parramatta Road. Just like it always did. The evening peak heaving and honking, despite the fact it wasn't yet five. School mums collecting kids after soccer. Tradies knocking off later than they wanted to, judging by all the utes. All the same, now she was on the road she was feeling less traumatised by her sister's stupidities. Because what were the cops going to do? Stick her in prison? They had protocols, methods, ways of dealing with stroppy women with psychological complaints and borderline dementia. It was the Huntington's muddling the connection between one moment and the next, dissolving resistance to her temper, as it had from the beginning. That, combined with the shock of loss. It was a lot to deal with. Still, her sister normally got by pretty well, considering everything. Or she had, before she lost the baby.

Her sister could still think, so long as her blood wasn't up. But if her temper *was* up, things could get bad. With this thought at the front of her mind, Bea planted her foot, finding a fraction of amber before the light went red, feeling the car surge, shooting across two lanes and up the inside.

Sure enough she could still drive like a demon.

She loved the way wine made her drive: as if she was free, as if the roads belonged to her. She stopped worrying. She weaved through the car horns – she could outdrive the lot of them; she had a *feel* for the car. She blasted up the inside, some joker in the right lane doing forty kilometres, and Bea thinking: Fuck you, buddy! You want to go slower, you'll need to find reverse! Nearly touching, then across the lines and back in front, accelerating into a turn, flanking some oversize chromed-to-glory piece of junk. Good Jesus, it was a Hummer. She might have even said it out

still deep in her private rant, half trying to get the guy's attention just so she could flip him the bird, and now she'd finally got a glimpse of the dickhead behind the wheel and sure enough the guy was fucking *huge*. Not some muscle Mary after all, but rather an enormous burden of a man, like one of those freaks from the lifestyle channel who's too big to leave their bed, some kind of lipid-based Hindenburg, and she was staring at this guy, happy to have her prejudice confirmed, happy to have a place where her mania might be directed, to have somewhere else to look, that's what it was, somewhere to throw her blame and spit out hate, vent at all the foulness and botching of genetics, nature's cruelties, the waiting cops. Then, in her peripheral vision, she saw it. It was almost as if she felt its presence there, in her chest, before her eyes had taken it in, and she swung her head back but couldn't turn fast enough, jamming her foot onto the brake while up ahead the car, creeping onto the road from a side street like a nearsighted mole, an ancient, ill-shaped brick of a car, brown and squat, nosing into her lane, the right lane blocked by that goddamn Yank behemoth and she was hard on the brakes so she heard the screech and the anti-skid kicked in as she tried to slide behind the Hummer, squeeze the gap, so close she might make it, if she could just squeak through that fraction of a— And then slam, the airbag, emptied of breath; she collected the mole's nose and the screaming crunch as if she'd left the car and been stopped by a wall, and something snapped, blinding and sharp, like hitting concrete not air, and then the car was sideways and the screech of it against the Hummer and a spinning leap off the median strip, and she, the vehicle, the road itself or so it seemed, jumping from the bitumen, spinning into oncoming traffic, and

the sound of a car horn swinging past – so close she could have
touched it – and her foot jamming the brake pedal so it felt as if
her leg would snap, and through the windshield an oncoming
car locked up, flying towards her, so she saw the driver's face,
frozen in an instant of wide-eyed panic, then it slammed her
forward in an explosion of glass and a ringing in her ears that
carried on and on.

Lori Goes Home

Chapter 24

Even insomniac sparrows aren't farting yet, just pushing out the zzzs, it's that early, but you can tell the time of morning if there's any kind of light. Same as when they were little girls: she would always be the one waking Bea, convincing her to slip out into the pre-dawn stillness – that expectant dark. You have to know the country, the time of year, but the brightness of the sky is a language if you know how to read it; you can even feel the passage of time as you sleep. That's what Mada's father used to say: as good an alarm clock as ever you need. He'd be up and throwing on frayed shorts, ready for a surf, irrepressible as he grabbed his board and wettie and headed to the door.

Lori judges it's around 5am, then pulls the clock from her knapsack.

Four forty-seven, not bad at all.

Lack of sleep doesn't bother her. Never has. A woman does what she has to do, no matter if she's been going all night and all day. Plenty of time for sleep when she's dead, and she has the address in her pocket and she knows that her sister is coming home, knows that it's today, and she pushes her things into the backpack and leaves the motel room.

Outside, on the street, the sun's not up, but getting closer. A faint red glow lifting from the east, a few stars visible at the sky's edge, the cool of early morning. Cars parked black on driveways, footpaths empty, shadowy foliage of ferns and bushes. With all the smoke, she hadn't seen any stars for days: the wind must have moved onshore. Still, that incense of burning bushland is thick in the air. She followed fire trucks along the highway for hours yesterday, even tried hitching from one, just as a joke – they gave her a good-natured blast of their airhorns.

When she left the Ridge, Trish and Jude were in full emergency mode, mowing every blade of grass, filling the guttering with water, even felling a couple of eucalyptus saplings that were sprouting too close to the house, all the while watching the smoke advance along the valley, fire creeping up the rocky walls.

It was so dry they'd had to truck in water at the end of spring, but now the tanks are charged, connected to sprinklers around the roofline, the diesel-powered pump ready and primed. Lori has a moment of worry for them, but dismisses it with a smile. They're strong, and they know what they're doing. Trish drove her to the highway yesterday morning, clad in cotton overalls and work boots, embracing Lori warmly and wishing her godspeed, before tearing back to the house to continue with the preparations.

Almost all of Lori's new creations are behind her now, having remained at the Ridge. As she prepared to leave they were straying about the room, staring hopefully at her as she pushed things into her rucksack. But there was no space to take them along, and anyway the joy is in the genesis, not the possession.

All the same, it stung to let them go.

Before she walked out the door, she held them in her hands, picking up one and then the next, farewelling each in turn. She felt so grateful for what they'd given, such pleasure and connection. She has just one of her new pieces stowed away; she decorated it with Trish and Jude the week before and could not let it go. A huge, beautiful mug for tea, glaze shining like living algae bubbling over its sides, breaking into patterns of fossil and ancient fern. No doubt her goodbye with the women would have seen all of them balling, had it not been for all the smoke and the fires bearing down. As it was, they were all distracted. It wasn't just the fire, it was Lori too: a new open road before her. The mug is there though, snug as a bug, deep in her pack. She's got it wrapped tight in the jacket from her boy. Her boy, who she will see again so soon!

It's a good thing she left with an extra day up her sleeve, as with all the road closures and banked-up traffic it took her a full day just to get to Gosford. The highway was completely closed for part of the afternoon. Now to get to Sydney. She goes through what there is to remember: telephone number for a taxi and Bea's new address. Number and address ... and what else? There's one more thing, and then it comes to her: cash, has she got the cash? She gave Trish and Jude most of it, but hopes she kept enough for a taxi and the payphone. There's a frantic moment when she's thrusting both hands into her robe pockets, pulling out everything, dollar coins for the phone and a couple of tissues, and sure enough there are a few scrunched-up bills – she remembers stuffing them in there, the memory of it like a light going on – and then she can see the phone booth she spotted yesterday, another thirty metres down the road, and she knows she'll make it, that it'll all work out. She's been figuring it out for days: Bea is getting out and heading to the house, and they'll make a party of it, that's what they'll do. She'll see her beautiful boy again; it'll be a family reunion! A taxi to the freeway and she'll hitch the rest of the way.

She pulls open the door to the phone booth, smacking herself against the pane on the way in, swearing at the glass and the phone box and all phones in general, then lifts the receiver from the cradle and drops a dollar in the slot, probably more money than is needed, but she isn't going to fumble about with change. She waits for the dial tone. Nothing. Puts her finger to the cradle and waits for the dollar to be returned. Again, nothing. It comes to her that the phone is kaput, that the government can't even keep a public phone working, and she smashes the receiver against the phone casing and leaves it dangling pathetically on its metal cord.

God, but she's tired of a sudden.

There is a chill to the early morning air. She lowers herself shakily to the gutter by the phone box to wait for a ride, a taxi to come past, realising then, too late, that she has left her jumper in the motel room, and that she still has her bathrobe on. Oh, for the love of all that's holy, she has her bathrobe on! What is she doing? She became so used to wearing it in her cabin at the Ridge. She hunts about in her pack, but everything is stuffed so tight in there she can't be bothered extracting her jacket and repacking her load. What does she care anyway? It's just a bathrobe. It doesn't mean she's a degenerate. Doesn't mean she's dropped the bundle.

'A taxi,' she says out loud, then repeats 'taxi taxi taxi' under her breath.

She has a place to go. Her sister is getting out of prison today. She knows the date. She knows what it means. This point of her inner vision so crystalline, while so much else is shifting, blurring. Yes, plenty is a blur now, she can admit that much. But this is not. Today is the day Bea comes out. Bea. Bringer of happiness, that's what her mum said the name meant. But for Lori it always meant her sister was a little bee. Black and yellow, like happiness, like honey. Tough. Loyal. Plenty of sting. Tough as her mum herself had been. And her dad! No self-pity. Not wretched. Just grabbing fate by the horns and knowing when it had you beat. Plenty of pride in him too; even when he walked into the sea he did it with guts, made sure the rest of them were well set up.

Lori looks up. A car is coming. How long has she been sitting here? Her legs are cramped and hold little feeling. She bashes her hands on them, watching as they shift about, numb and needled. The car slows as it sees her, but it isn't a cab and it keeps on driving. She raises herself stiffly and begins to shuffle in the direction of the highway. She will have to walk, that's all. Walk until she finds a taxi. The sky is glowing deep red now with the rising sun and smoke. Fires burning along the coast: she'll be lucky if they haven't closed the highway again.

An hour later, she thrusts her right hand into the pocket of her robe, groping in the soft cottony lint of it, as though to determine the limits of the space. Nothing in there at all. Where is it, the damn— The damn ... thing she's hunting for? What is it she's missing? And then it comes to her: paper? Paper! Yeah, that's it. The address. She hasn't been there before, and her memory isn't to be completely trusted. She knows this. The address for the new place the Sponge has sucked up, a new mansion down on the water. That's the thing she needs.

She comes to an intersection. There are more cars here, a few pedestrians. Lori searches about for a cab. A middle-aged woman has slowed on the street in front of her, looking her up and down then averting her gaze, as if she's some sort of leper. And this woman is ... what? A bourgeoise bimbo? Some religious nut headed to a meeting at six in the bloody morning? White suit, a scarf half covering her head. Lori is talking out loud again. It's only now that she realises it. And so what? No crime in that. She shuts her mouth and hardens her jaw, pushing away the burn of shame. Her mind is starting to let go of her, she knows this to be true, although it isn't that business everyone keeps talking about, her *condition*. It isn't that. She's just getting tired is all. And isn't life tiring? Doesn't it wear you down? And where is that damn, ahh, where is the damn thing? She gropes about until she's sure that the pocket is bare, bare except for a few stray threads, and as she has her left fist clenched in the emptiness of the other pocket she recognises this as an ill omen boding poorly for the day. But right then and there the thought comes to her: the breast pocket, yes yes, she knows it, so her right hand fights its way free of that lower pocket and pats down her chest, and sure enough there's the lump of coins, the curled paper of the address, and the memory returning in that moment, putting each thing, itemised, into the pocket after she found the bills.

She leans out, over the gutter, swaying at the road's edge in the wind-rush of all the speeding metal, vehicles like UFOs as she stares into the smoke and streaming light. She waves at the bright top lamp of a taxi, but the bastard doesn't even slow. Behind the cab a truck, and it thunders by so fast and close it nearly has her, and the driver hits the airhorn the moment he's level, so between the horn and the rush of the thing, Lori is thrown to her back foot and almost over, swinging out in a wild, unsteady orbit, a trembling slow-motion turn until she gets hold of gravity again, and raising herself with resilient pride she once again lifts a hand, a cab to see it, or not – she can't make out a jolly thing in the headlights, and so she stands there, determined, her arm waving into the melee and the changing pitch of engine noise, tyres on the roadbase, but there's a cab there all right, the driver signalling from the other side of the road, he's pulled into the bus lane and he's yelling, pointing, calling out 'taxi stand', gesturing to some alleged place through the lightening smog. Lori lets slip a stream of profanities and casts an eye down the road, into whatever ill fortune of traffic might be oncoming, a kind of challenge to the blurring grey, the milky red of sun-up, then turns her eyes back to the dirty white sheen of the taxi. There are no bright oncoming beams to hold her, and she steps slowly onto the blacktop and shambles across the four lanes towards the cab, making the centreline without incident before squinting left towards the sun and bitumen horizon, a sliver above the broken facade of a fish and chip shop, the closed pub on the other corner, the blinding dispersal of it, and she can hear something coming but she can't see it, not yet, and the taxi driver is yelling at her, pointing down the road at the traffic lights, and she can see the guy now, hyperventilating, screaming blue murder at her, and she stands on the centreline and feels herself sway out, car horn, rush of wind as it passes, and with a kind of resignation she holds the robe tight with her left hand, her right hand flailing before her to part the sea of cars, out into the noise and traffic, to where the driver gestures wildly to the truck she missed by inches. 'Ya crazy woman, ya nearly got yaself killed. Get off the road before you're squashed flat.'

But dawn is upon them, and she must be on her way. No rosy fingers, but a bloom of rising red above the black smear of asphalt, awake in the fire of all that is to come.

Byron Bay

Chapter 25

Red is in the lift, on the way up to the office, when an unfamiliar number lights the screen of his phone. He lets it go through to voicemail. It could be a genuine client, but Red is highly suspicious of numbers he doesn't recognise, and logs every seller into his contacts as soon as he's sure they're moneyed and serious. This information is generally accompanied by the caller's suburb and a rough estimate of value, the latter to ensure the correct level of grovelling from Red and his staff.

And right now, who knows who the hell it might be. The ATO again, or even, God forbid, some dodgy-arsed goon that Min has sicced on to him as retribution.

Still, those guys probably wouldn't bother calling first. They'd just drop around the house one day. Red gives an involuntary shudder. But surely she wouldn't, it wasn't his fault. Min's voice rings in his head: *Nothing is ever your fault.* He pushes it aside, straightens his back, and exits the lift.

His snooty receptionist isn't in yet, so he unlocks the office door and hangs his jacket on the coat-stand. A Victorian number. Cast iron. Solid as a rock. He has a thing for antiques, does Red. Min told him about ten times that it looked out of place in the office, with its Herman Miller chair and Carlo Mollino Cavour desk. She said the weight was all wrong, the feng shui or some crap like that. But he held his ground, and now he's glad of it. Fuck her. A red dot lights up the message bank of his phone. Red gives it a tap and hits the speaker button, putting the phone on his desk and pulling up the office blinds. Darling Harbour materialises briefly through the smoke below, a combination of glinting water and construction work, before being swallowed again.

Good morning, Mr Campbell, this is Detective Page from the New South Wales police force. Please call me urgently.

Oh Jesus. If anything could be worse than the ATO ... Is he about to be arrested?

Red drops into his chair, staring at the phone. His heart is beating so goddamn fast it's going to rip his ribs apart. For a moment it's hard for him to draw breath. He undoes the top button of his shirt and yanks at his tie. Min had given him strict instructions not to talk to anyone but his lawyer after the ATO debacle – he'd pleaded with her for help, and she'd finally taken his call – and then she'd jumped on the next flight out.

Red stares over the harbour. Normally this is one of his favourite activities. It is his city. He owns it. Everywhere he looks there are properties that he has sold, which means, in a way, that he owns them too. It's Red and his kind who control Sydney's most important resource, he reminds himself. No cop on 85K pa is going to change that. This city belongs to men with money. Men like him. For men like him, the rules are malleable. What was it Min said? *We use the laws in the countries in which we operate.* *Use* the laws. Not obey them. The law is just another instrument. Red is not one of those subject to the law, not in any plebeian sense. No, he's one of those who manage it, who make the law their own. But right then Red's phone lights up again, and that same number, Detective What's-his-Face's, is spread across the screen. The cop doesn't leave a message this time.

It's nine thirty-six. Red's stomach is off. No symptoms as yet, but he can feel it starting to churn. Maybe it's the heat, the smoke. It's all he can do to rush from one climate-controlled space to another. Who was that theologian who believed Satan to have possessed his bowels? They were talking about it on the radio as Red was driving into work one morning. Martin Luther, that was it. The DJs had made jokes about it. Ha ha, crazy old Luther, so constipated the devil had taken up residence in his bum. But Red understands. If the devil is going to make a home anywhere, it would be in your guts, and if anyone has the devil curled about his innards, surely it's Red. He rises, picks up his putter and tries to send a golf ball into the auto-return cup at the far corner of the office. This often calms him down when things are turning godawful. The force of effort, the concentration. Red is good on the green – more consistent with putts than his drives, that's for sure. But the ball goes wide by some centimetres and his insides give another churn. He closes the louvres and slumps back into his chair.

By the time the cop has tried twice again within fifteen minutes, neither of which calls Red picks up, he's a mess. An agency guy is trying to get him to finalise the artwork on some print advertising, and Red is staring at the email with its luxe kitchens and harbour views and price guides and it's as if the whole thing is in a foreign code, as if he's forgotten how to read, and the only thing he can think of is goddamn Detective So-and-So. It's past ten when that same number lights up, and yet again Red watches the phone ring out. This time the cop leaves a message, and Red turns to make sure the office door is closed before he hits the play button.

Yes, hello Mr Campbell. It's Detective Page again, from the missing persons unit. Could you please call me back at your earliest convenience. Red sits bolt upright, staring at the phone. *Missing persons unit? What the—?* Then it comes to him. Lori. Of course, they're calling about his goddamn sister-in-law. It's nothing to do with the ATO investigation. It isn't anything to do with him at all. Not really. Only that he gave them his number when she disappeared, so he's the first port of call. A wave of relief passes through him. He squares his shoulders, picks up the phone, and dials the cop's number, sparing a quick thought for Bea. Has her sister's body finally been found, just as she's to be released from jail? He hopes, almost despite himself, that this isn't the news that will greet her when that hellhole finally spits her out.

It turns out the cops found Lori meandering by the highway, alive and kicking and then some. She seemed confused, that was all; she hasn't been charged with anything, and the welfare bloke has recommended she be released into someone's care. They fill

Red in on her story, what she's told them about her time away, which isn't much.

She scarcely says a word when Red picks her up from the station – in her bathrobe no less – just trots behind him and gets into the car. 'Oohhh,' she says then, clicking her seatbelt and running her hand over the dash. 'So smooth. What kind of car is this?'

'An M4 BMW,' says Red proudly.

'Gosh, it must have cost a lot.'

'Yeah.' Red glances across at her. 'It cost a lot all right.' He works to keep his voice level, but the weight of everything is on him so thick he can't hold it back. 'Why did you go away, Lori? Bea's been worried, Mada too. They thought you were dead.'

She glances over, her face impish. 'I wanted an adventure. But I decided to come back, to see my sister. She gets out of jail today, you know.'

'Yes, I know.' Red takes a deep breath. 'But where in god's earth have you been? You've been gone over a year.'

'Really? It doesn't seem that long.'

'Well it is.'

Lori sighs, staring beatifically out the window. 'So beautiful,' she says.

It's unclear whether she's talking about her time away, or the passing shops of Parramatta Road, or the sky with its smoke haze and fumes. At this, Red gives up entirely, and they conduct the rest of the journey in silence, his teeth grinding away until he has backed the car into the drive and stopped the engine.

Lori opens the car door and gives a sudden exclamation. 'Oh, so shiny!' She bends down and retrieves something from the footwell. 'Look,' she says.

She's holding up an earring, a single diamond stud, gleaming brightly. 'Isn't that pretty. I wonder where it came from?' She fires a glance at Red. He feels the blood rise in his cheeks, but then, without another word, she clambers out and wanders off down the cul-de-sac and into Blackwattle Bay Park, oohhing and aahhing over the water, the trees, even the cars hammering over the Anzac Bridge. Red brings her back and guides her into the house, sits her on the lounge and gets her a cup of tea, all the time eyeing the pocket into which he has seen the earring disappear. Lori is glancing this way and that, searching the house for god knows what, and no sooner has he got her settled than she's up again, hunting about.

Red follows three steps behind. 'What are you looking for, Lori?'

'Where's Henrietta?' she asks.

'Out the back.'

'Oh, I can't imagine she likes that very much. Let's bring her in.'

'She's coping.'

'Go and bring her in. I want to see her,' she says. She sits down again, eyeing him, and starts to dunk her tea bag up and down. Again and again. The bag lifts then drops to the water, lifts then drops, lifts then drops, as though intended as a form of torture. She glances at him pointedly, dunking the bag, lifting and dropping it back into the cup. His head is vibrating with the unbearable slow uselessness of it. Time stretches. Red's mind is fertile with fantasies of throwing her from the roof, witnessing her slow-motion descent to the grass.

'Okay, sure, whatever,' he says, abruptly getting up to slide open the patio door.

Lori lifts the bag over the saucer, dangles it there, and lets it splat.

Red hunts about. Where's the dog? He calls its name, then sees it waking dozily in the shade beneath the outdoor table. 'Come on,' he says.

Unsteadily, the mutt rises to its paws and shambles into the house. That should shut her up. Red closes the door to take a moment outside before he has to face her again, and sits on a deckchair to soak up the filtered morning sun. All about him the air is white, thick and cloying,

Ten minutes later, back inside, the dog is already snoring at Lori's side. Lori gets up as Red comes in. She gazes intently over his shoulder and rushes to the back door with an excited exclamation. Red spins, half expecting to see a tribe of hippies streaming in, but Lori only makes her way to the mat, steadying herself against the wall, then bends to pick up one of her squat sculptures that Bea had forbidden him from throwing out.

'Oh no! It's broken!' she says.

'Jesus.' He strides over and plucks it from her hands. Half an arm is missing. Big deal. He must have stumbled over it some night during a session with Min. 'Why didn't you tell anyone where you'd gone, Lori?'

'I didn't want Mada to worry.'

'No concern about worrying me then?'

'Nope.'

Red takes a gulp of air. 'You didn't want him to worry, so you told him you were dead?'

'That was a mistake ...' Lori rubs her eyes, looking, briefly, as though she might cry. She'd better not, thinks Red, he simply couldn't cope with that, but abruptly she spins about and commences meandering through the house. She reaches the front door, pulls it open, and strolls with jerking purpose up the drive.

Already Red can feel the sweat gathering beneath the armpits of his Armani shirt. 'Now where are you going?'

'To wait,' she calls over her shoulder.

'Not on this street, not looking like a vagrant in that bloody robe. I've got neighbours here.'

'You're not the boss of me, Redmon,' she yells. She stops at the end of the driveway, scarcely visible through the haze, leaning back against the bonnet of the car. 'I'll just wait for them here.'

Red strides after her, feeling his anger starting to bubble over. He grips her by the shoulders, willing her to see sense.

'Stop it,' she says, glowering in alarm, as though his fingers are tarantula legs digging into her arms. Red releases her. Patting down her robe and taking a step back, she fixes him with a scowl. 'Bully.'

'For the love of all that's holy: what's got into you, Lori? You can't wait in the gutter in a bathrobe!'

Lori's scowl deepens. 'Byron Bay,' she says abruptly.

'What?' Red feels an immense weariness overtake his body. 'What about it?' he says pleadingly.

'That's where I was going. To see a boy.'

'What *boy* do you know in Byron?'

Lori's jaw juts out, trembling. 'Mada's, of course,' she says.

'Mada doesn't have any boys. What are you talking about?'

'Mada's daddy, you clot. You think you're very clever, Redmon. Frankly, I don't see it.'

Red wants to claw out his eyes. 'That was twenty-five years ago. You think he's been waiting on the beach in Byron for twenty-five years? We tried to find him at the time. Don't you remember?'

'I had a dream about him. I thought he was meant to be there. But it turns out the dream was only to get me travelling. To meet the Women of the Land.'

'Are you really as crazy as you make out?'

'Not half as crazy as you,' she says.

'I'm going to put you in a home. I swear to god, I'm going to do it.'

'Why do you swear so much? And anyway,' she adds dismissively, 'you're not. Not for one second.'

'I am too,' he says. 'There are places in Byron, you know. Nice places.' He's grinning now, talking gently, warming to the idea. He takes her hand in his. It has genuine possibilities. If that's where she wants to be, who is he to deny her? She'd be locked away, so long as the bills were paid. He drops her hand. The bills ... those places are expensive.

'Pish!' says Lori emphatically.

'What?'

'I said *pish*. My sister won't let you. Put me in a home. She's coming home today, I know she is.'

'I thought you never wanted to see her again. That's what you said before you moved out.'

'No I didn't.'

This blatant lie has Red fuming. His ears begin to burn, so he can feel the heat of them above the collar of his shirt.

Lori continues to prattle on. 'You know what the Women of the Land called you?' she asks.

'I've never met these Women of the Land,' Red snarls.

'I told them about you. Do you know what they said? They said you're just another bullying man. They said they know your type' – Lori nods with every word – 'said they've seen it lots of times. Your type. *Just. Another. Bullying. Man.*' She pokes her finger into his chest, hard, accentuating each word.

'I told you: I've never met them,' growls Red, louder this time.

'Doesn't matter,' she yells into his face. 'I told them everything.'

He wipes droplets of spittle off his cheek with the back of his hand. His head is throbbing. He wants to reach out and throttle her, take her by the neck and squeeze. He glances about: nobody would see him, not with all the smoke. Jesus, he could probably drop her in the harbour and nobody would find a hair of her before the bull sharks had cleaned her up. Red forces the feeling down, walking tight circles, massaging his temples with the balls of his fists.

And still she won't shut up. 'Look at you!' she yells. 'With your fancy car and fancy house. Not enough to keep my sister out of jail, but. Not enough to do any good.' She moves up the drive in an ungainly rush, stooping to pick up a terracotta pot and launching it at him with surprising speed. Red leaps aside, and the pot lands on the bonnet of the car with a thud, spilling earth and scratching the paint.

'Fuck. Now look what you've done,' Red says angrily.

'Oh, I see. That's the problem, is it? That's what matters?' Lori bends down and seizes another pot. He goes to grab it, but she lurches out of reach, waving her free arm erratically. 'You think that's what's important, you really do! You sad bastard!' She hurls the pot at the car with all the force she possesses, spinning herself off balance and tumbling into the garden.

As the pot lands, the windshield gives a high-pitched click, and a dirt-strewn silver star appears at its centre.

'You crazy bitch!' screams Red.

Lori pushes herself up on an elbow, laughing. 'Ha ha!' she yells.

Red glares in disbelief from her to the car. 'You're insane,' he finally says. 'You're actually insane.'

'Piffle,' says Lori. She climbs to her feet and peers at the windshield, assaying her handiwork. 'Yes,' she says, satisfied, 'now we're getting somewhere.'

Inbound

Chapter 26

Mada ends up spending a total of forty-three hours at the airport, waiting for the resumption of travel after the closure of airspace along the east coast. All week, fires burned around Sydney, at Holsworthy, Illawong and Kurnell, with westerly winds driving flames and smoke. Half the city was swallowed white. An ember storm sent a glowing rain on the airport and homes of the eastern suburbs, sparking grassfires that raced all the way to the edge of the runway. Melbourne wasn't faring much better: a fire in bushland near the Thunderdome jumped the M79 into trees at Organ Pipes National Park; westerlies were blowing at eighty-five kilometres an hour.

At eleven o'clock on Saturday night, Mada found himself in an airport hotel, where he spent eye-glazed hours between wakefulness and sleep, unable to stop himself from watching the endless stream of disaster footage: slow, close reportage of homes in flames, bereaved siblings, burned pets. Montages of crews and water-bombers valiantly battling impossible flames.

Less than eight hours later he was back at the check-in, and the bedlam was even worse. Flights resumed early morning before being suspended again. The backlog kept growing. The departure hall was crammed with suits and families, almost everyone in masks, the air borderline unbreathable, even inside. No faces, only eyes; jostling, tight. There were thousands of people, pumping any member of ground staff they could grab for non-existent information.

The chaos intensified as the backlog extended. People pushed through the doors from the overflowing footpath. Mada stood inside the terminal entrance, where the crowd broke into roped lanes. A few spots ahead in the queue that snaked towards the Qantas desk, an exhausted woman in a blue floral dress tried to control three kids. The youngest was in a pram, the other two both under five, and for hours they took it in turns to scream.

At midday flights resumed. Airport security opened up a new line and the crowd sheared apart. Mada watched as the woman's oldest boy, who had been playing with one of the bollards, was pulled away by the crowd: she, clinging to her son and pram, called out in the direction of the boy's screams. A guy in a leather jacket with a bandanna over his mouth dived into the throng, lifted the kid over his head and carried him against the tide back to his mother. Half an hour later an elderly woman was carried off by paramedics; a little later a man in a suit was arrested for assaulting a Qantas steward. Mada's feet were aching and his throat was parched and cracked.

TV newsreels on screens inside the terminal, mounted above the chaos, showed fire crews spraying jets of water into walls of flame. Thin liquid ribbons bent and fractured by wind. The fire swallowed it all. Sydney flights were suspended again, then reopened, then suspended, as the winds hid, then revealed, then hid the airport. Another night at the hotel passed much like the first. At four in the morning, Mada decided he would rent a car and drive north. But when he looked up routes on the net it didn't seem possible. Up and down the eastern seaboard sections of highway were closed to non-essential traffic. There was no guarantee he wouldn't get stuck somewhere south of Wodonga. He sat back heavily on the bed and turned on the television. He couldn't eat: his stomach was in knots, and the hotel food tasted of ash. Eventually he dropped off to sleep, falling immediately into a dream in which Bea was released from prison. She exited the razor wire to wait for him in a field, while all about her a scrubfire closed in.

He woke, packed his meagre possessions, and headed back to the airport: already the crush was so bad he couldn't get inside the terminal, and he joined a snaking line of faceless passengers, some with T-shirts over their noses and mouths, others in surgical masks. The illusion of order had been returned in the night: there were cordons, cops, airline staff outside funnelling people into endless lines. They re-announced information that Mada had already learned and gave nothing by way of comfort. At one o'clock that afternoon, a police officer drove beside the line, announcing that easterly winds had driven the fires back on themselves, and had pushed the choking clouds inland with enough force to allow full departures to resume. Finally, with the wind turned onshore, there was enough visibility for the flight crews to see what they were doing.

He wasn't home yet, but slowly, inexorably, the line began to move.

Mada finally takes off at six thirty on Tuesday morning, having waited almost three days for the smoke to clear and a new seat to be allocated. If all goes well, his mother is scheduled to be released from prison in approximately four hours. He hasn't been able to eat for over two days, but as the aircraft thrusts skywards he feels his spirits rise. They lift out of Melbourne and into clouds of smoke, so it's only flashes of bush and dry pasture below, breaking through intermittent gaps in the haze. His stomach gurgles loudly as the stewardess holds out a tray. There's an upturned mug and a plastic-covered sandwich. Mada swallows the first half sandwich in three quick bites, and he's wolfed down the other half before she's finished serving his row. She tells him that the next steward will be along in a minute with coffee.

The coastline passes beneath them in red-tinged early morning sun. In places he can make out the fire fronts, long lines of flame and smoke dividing life from death, great grey curtains rising from the earth and streaking inland. Remnants of the fires are visible too, blackened trunks and charred earth, the land but a black skeletal memory of itself. But it isn't until they start their descent into Sydney that Mada sees the full extent of the destruction. North of Wollongong, sections of the Royal National Park are burned all the way down to the beach, as if the entire continent has been consumed to the very edge.

Then his eye is drawn northwards and he catches his breath. The landmark towers on University Drive are untouched, the road empty but for a single red truck, lights flashing. But on the northern side of the road, the bushland bordering the campus has been cratered black and, even as he watches, smoke is rising from various buildings about the grounds. The library, with its high roof now collapsed, has opened up like a burned insect. Little remains where the Faculty of Science was: scorched concrete columns and the ever-rising smoke. Long clouds billow forth and stretch into the sky, trailing high over that white supposition of a city, the city built of smoke on smoke.

Mada feels a lurch in his chest that has nothing to do with the plane's loss in altitude. It looks as though half the university is gone.

As they come in to the runway, fire crews are stationed in readiness. There's little left to burn, but still they stream jets of water at the blackened earth, waiting to see what fresh emergency will greet them next.

When Mada enters the terminal, Zoe's is the first face he sees, and in his gratitude to find her there, to have got through, he forgets the blackened earth. There is only the shape of her lips, her cheekbones, her bright, bright eyes, the smoothness of where her shirt clings to her body and the way she is standing, connected more securely to the earth than anyone about her. She's gazing back at him, unblinking, and he has the peculiar idea that the two of them are sharing the same thought, that they are both finally present in a moment together again. That he lost her without quite realising it, and what a fool he must have been. He drops his backpack and puts his arms around her, and he knows by the precise firm softness of her waist, the way she curves into him, that this is his home, and if he has his way he will never leave again, and the enormous weight of all that has happened, all that he has seen, lifts, at least a little.

'I thought you were never going to come through.'

'So did I. We flew over the university …'

'I saw it on the news.' She hugs him tighter a moment.

Mada breathes deep. Swallows. He has to hold it together; the day is a long way from done.

'How's the traffic looking?' he asks.

Zoe pulls away a fraction. 'How's the traffic?'

'I just mean … Oh fuck, Zo.'

'It's okay.' She grips him about the middle, squeezing him with her palms to his ribs. 'How did you get so skinny?' she asks lightly. 'You weren't away much more than a week. Melburnians are always going on about having the best food in the world.'

'Not at the airport they don't.'

Mada lets himself fall into the feel of her, the sweet spice of her perfume and sweat. He can't wait to lie by her side, to tell her everything, and even as they stand there he starts to explain it all. The madness of the airport, the plumes of smoke, how good the meetings with Monash were, how sane the staff appeared compared to the dysfunction he's accustomed to at UES.

Zoe takes Mada's hand in hers and draws away. 'Just a moment,' she says. She takes a deep breath, searching out a place to begin. It is the wrong moment, she knows it, but it's not getting any better right now. She had confirmed her suspicions a few days before he left and she was damned if she'd weight him with it just before the interviews, so she curled it inside, dropping him at the airport as she forced it down, and all morning now she has felt it growing closer and closer – the need to speak – for she has to tell him face to face, and she is sure that Mada has taken her withdrawal these last weeks to be rooted in the same causes as his own: the university, his doctorate, Carlos, his mum. For weeks he has been trying to convince her to move to Melbourne with him. It's not a terrible idea, even if it is at least partly motivated by his need to escape his family, escape the disaster of the university, at least for a while, and he starts trying to sell her on the relocation yet again, babbling at three hundred words a minute, as he does when he's nervous, when he feels there's something wrong which he might be able to fix.

'You know, maybe it's a long shot, but maybe it's not. What's out there is enormous and we've scarcely touched it. I mean, sure, we've found a lot, categorised. It's a miracle what's been achieved up to now. But as far as sequencing? Testing? We haven't even touched it. Your postdoc applications should be coming back soon, and the philosophy department at Monash is terrific. I'm sure Mum will be okay, she survived without me for long enough. It's Melbourne, not Siberia, I won't be so far away. And anyway—'

'It's complicated, Mada.' She touches him, lightly, on the cheek. 'We need to talk.'

'Please, Zoe – if they say yes, I need to take it. To do something. It's not just that I have to get out of this place. I can feel an edge to what's hidden, what's just out of reach. If I close my eyes, the chemical shape of an answer already has an outline. For everything that exists in nature, there is its opposite. Carlos wrote that in his journal, and I can't help but think that he's right. There's always a way for the scales to balance. There must be. It's the only way the maths of the universe makes sense. There's a plant. An element. The mould growing on the scat of some Tanzanian goat. Something! Something's there. I just have to touch it with my mind. I know it, Zoe. I know it.'

'Mada,' she says insistently.

But now he's desperate for her to understand, to convert her to his cause. 'Gene therapy is another thing. But there are ways to neutralise the protein, slow the cell damage so it's virtually negligible; so it doesn't become symptomatic until you're a hundred and twenty-three. I know it with a certainty, Zo. I can feel it in my spine. We only have to keep on looking until we find it. We could go together, start afresh. Melbourne's gorgeous. I couldn't leave you behind. Honestly, it would kill me. I can't give up, but I know there's an answer. I know it.'

'Mada!' she says loudly, irritation creeping into her voice. 'I need to talk to you.'

He stops abruptly, caught off guard by her vehemence. 'Aren't we talking now?'

'*You're* talking.'

'Well, yes. It's only …' He trails off.

She watches. Quiet for a time, waiting for him to start breathing again, to be present to what she has to say.

'I'm sorry,' he says. 'What is it?'

Zoe takes a deep breath, inhaling the airport air. Steels herself. 'You can't get mad. I waited until now to tell you because of everything that's happened: with Melbourne, after Carlos,

Paula, the university, your mum. It's been a crazy time. Also, I wanted to be sure.'

Mada is staring confusedly at her. 'Sure of what? What do you mean, *waited*?'

'Mada, I'm late. Actually, I'm *really* late.'

'Then let's get going,' he says, exasperated.

Zoe smiles, takes his right hand into hers, and curls his fingers in her own, placing a light kiss to his fingertips and linking their hands before her.

'Do you love me?' she asks.

'Yeah, Zo. You know I do. We're going to grow old and incontinent together. I love you like crazy.'

'That's good,' she says. 'That's really good.'

She puts his hand to her belly, to that slight lump of a beginning. 'Mada,' she says, watching the light go on. 'You're going to be a dadda, Mada.'

'I'm what? You're not—'

'I am. I'm pregnant.'

Mada's mouth opens, closes, then opens again. Slowly, by increments, a smile begins to form. 'You're not joking, are you?'

'Nope. Now,' she says, suddenly businesslike, 'we'd better get a move on, or we'll have to get Red to pick her up – she's due to be released soon.'

Mada shoulders his pack. He puts his arm about Zoe's waist and together they walk to the exit. Neither of them speaking, but basking in the sensation of their bodies side by side, together again, as they should be, a secret knowledge in the air between them.

***

They exit the carpark, turning into the heat and traffic, and Mada grips Zoe's leg as she steers them nimbly through the gap between two trucks and accelerates along the right-hand lane. They don't get far. The motorway is jammed worse than usual, bumper to bumper, smoke so thick they can scarcely see more than two cars ahead. They drive on through the corridor of concrete sound barriers, suburbs and warehouses shifting in and out of view. The smoke thickens and lightens, as though they're flying in and out of clouds. Mada stares fixedly at the clock.

Zoe can feel the anxiety building in him. The air-conditioning isn't coping, and it sounds as though the transmission is giving out, flicking up and down between the gears. Long grassed edges shift brown beside the motorway, billowing in the hot wind. Mada glares at the traffic, inwardly fuming. She can almost hear the gears of his mind turning.

'It'll be okay, we're nearly at the turn-off.'

'I know. It's not just that, it's, you know … a baby. What do I know about looking after a baby?'

'What does anyone know before they have one?'

'But what if we fuck it up?' he blurts out. 'What if we can't do it, if we're not enough. What if we're rubbish parents, if we can't afford to feed it. What if …' His voice trails off.

'What if everything? Of course we'll fuck it up, Mada. At least a little bit. But we'll have plenty of successes and some glorious adventures along the way. You're the scientist. Isn't that what you were saying last week? That all we can do as humans is to fuck up a little better each time. If we need our answers to be absolute, new knowledge is impossible. Those are your words. I mean, there's only one way this whole thing ends, and spoiler alert: none of us gets out alive. So let's just make it, I don't know ...'

'As great as it can be.'

'Yeah. As great as it can be.'

It's twenty-five minutes from the M4 off-ramp into Emu Plains, the traffic reduced to a single lane as they drive past black twisted trees and stubble. They finally get to the sign for the Department of Corrective Services, taking the corner as sun breaks through the haze, air-con utterly dead and blowing naught but heat. Then they see her: a solitary figure striding towards them along the road's edge. A herd of cows watches through wire fencing, grouped at the centre of a dust-brown field. There is an overnight bag in her hand, and even from this distance they can tell she is walking very quickly, her long stride almost breaking into a run. She doesn't seem to recollect the car at first, and as they stop she stares through the glass with neither hope nor recognition.

To Mada, Bea seems smaller and wirier than he remembers, although it's been less than a month since his last visit, and she can't have changed so much. Still, she's thinner, her face chiselled, stripped of fat and all soft edges. Zoe yanks on the handbrake and says, 'You get out. I'll give you time to have your moment. Your aunt can sit up front; you drive home.'

The door is already open. Mada steps out onto the pale straw verge, and the two of them stop, staring at one another in the dreary heat. They stand uncertain for a moment, Bea's stare blank, unsure if he might be some kind of mirage, a false dream of freedom. Then she drops the bag and throws herself at his chest, gripping him like she'll never let go, the sun beating down on his face.

'Great Southern Land' comes over the radio, and Zoe turns it up, winding down the window, the opening chords an eerie accompaniment to the sweltering tableau.

'Come on, Auntie,' Mada says, taking her arm. 'Let's get you home.'

Freedom
Chapter 27

Bea's hands are on the dash. Leaning forward, straining against the seatbelt unaware until she feels it cutting into her clavicle. She's trying to push aside the panic, the feeling that she shouldn't be here. That at any moment someone will spot her, cuff her, take her back inside. There's something unsettling about the busy bookshops and cafés, how crowded the footpaths are. She thought it would be the reverse, that driving familiar ground would give her the sense she'd done her time. Instead she feels an edge of terror, a thug or a cop on each street corner, ready to take revenge.

Mada puts his hand on her leg, giving her his version of a reassuring squeeze. He's stopped shooting her quick, nervous glances, stopped asking if she's all right. They weren't even five minutes from the prison gates when, in response to his third query, his worried glance taking in the state of her, she switched off the radio and said, 'Yes, I'm fucking dandy. Just watch the road, okay? I've spent two years in prison so I'm a bit on edge!'

Zoe reaches over from the back seat to place a hand on their shoulders. It's meant to be reassuring, Bea knows, but they have to stop touching her or she's going to lose it. She takes a long slow breath as Zoe gives her a pat.

She breathes again, as deeply as she can, as if the whole atmosphere might be drawn into her lungs. The world just there, and she's now allowed to join it. On they drive, quietly through the white air, past the fire trucks, through all the forbidden suburbs, all that ordinary, quotidian life. Other people driving cars, walking along the street. Ignoring one another. Handbags luxuriating on café tables. Wallets in the back pockets of jeans. Mobile phones in hands. What lives they lead, these everyday people. Do they know how easy it is to lose it all? How fragile life is?

A right turn into Leichhardt Street. She looks at the sign. It's new, shiny. The road narrows, cars parked, a couple up ahead wandering slowly along the footpath, young and fit, the man's left hand tucked into the woman's back pocket, and the sight of this commonplace affection cracks her shell, so the freedom of the place suddenly shines and what a miracle it all seems. Not them, not their bags of groceries, but the entire human parade. To stroll up the road. To say hello to the shopkeeper and buy the fresh stalks of silverbeet she can see sticking out of a bag, grown on a farm and transported through the streets, refrigerated, handed over for a few dollars to anyone who wants some. The absolute miracle of modern urban existence, its mechanisms and structures. The beauty of it. She feels a tear slide down her cheek. She wipes it away quickly and glances over at Mada, to make sure he hasn't seen. She's not going to let herself go or she'll never stop.

Mada slows the car to walking pace as they turn onto Oxley Street. She notices the street sign, this one bent out of shape as if a garbage truck's collected it, and knows they're getting close. She manages to return Mada's smile then closes her eyes and winds down the window to feel the air coming in, the hot air of freedom. She can smell the harbour over the smoke, the dampness of it, a faint waft of fish and salt.

Pure and free.

It is then, breathing in that free air, the sun's strobing brightness, that she hears Mada's 'What the—', his intake of breath, and she opens her eyes to see him fixed on some point at the road's end. The car accelerates and she feels the terror come, quickly, breathless, in a rush.

A white prison van parked out the front.

A group of cops.

This is what she conjures. Because she would rather self-immolate than go back inside. She can't do it. Can't. And as they pass a line of cars she sees her sister, for so many months thought lost to her, standing near the edge of the road, cloud and bridge behind her. The water blazing, burnished with the long flare of late morning light, and as Bea watches, Lori bends to pick something up, a terracotta pot of all things, and jerks it haltingly over her head. The scene is surreal, too strange to be true. Red has his arms stretched out towards her, and as she comes forward he wrestles the object from her and holds it out of reach. The dog is running between their feet, barking madly. Lori lunges at him, her whole body in the thrust and, as Red stumbles, the pot wavers unsteadily at the end of his fingertips before coming down on the bonnet of the car. The pot cracks, not smashing but rolling over the duco, roots showing pale through the jagged break. The car is a mess of dirt.

As Mada jams on the brakes, Lori is turning, looking for something else to throw, but Bea and Mada leap out, catching the end of a long run of expletives as Mada grabs his mother's arm, urgently shouting, 'Mum!'

Lori jolts back, gawking at him, as if surprised to find herself on the street, with the child she hasn't seen in – how long? – amid the carnage of broken pots, black splotches of dirt, a long garden stake, a twisted wiper protruding from the vehicle like the snapped wing of a bird. Her jaw firms and she spins and rewarms to her task, bending to a large pot, a massive thing that stands just inside the gate, reaching out her arms to encircle its girth. But the weight of it is tremendous and she can't make it budge, and she is squatting like that, heaving at the thing, when Mada gets his arms around her again.

As Bea approaches cautiously, she sees black lines streaking her sister's dirt-smeared face. Surely Lori will do her back in trying to lift the thing, for she's steadfastly shrugging Mada off and refusing to let go of her intended missile. Lori stops, staring at Bea, utterly still for a moment. Then she raises a thin arm shakily towards her as her face slackens into bewilderment.

'It's okay, sis, it's me.' Bea takes her sister's outstretched hand.

Mada slowly releases her. Lori straightens up, shifting and swaying in the bright sun. She stares from one to the other, her eyes darting from sister to son, as if she's woken from a dream, meaningless and obscene at the same time, and she's not sure if she's still in it, not sure what the world might mean.

Red stands next to the car, a shadow beneath his eye. At first it looks like a wound, and there are dark marks on his clothes as if blood has dripped onto his shirt, but then Bea realises that it's earth and potting mix, black humus dotted with green fertiliser granules. She lets out a laugh, a sharp, gritty cackle. A prison laugh. The hardness in it. The lack of pathos, lack of giving. It spurts out again and she can't help it, the ridiculousness overwhelming. That her sphere of physical danger might be reduced to this: a husband who can't manage a confrontation with her sister and some potting mix. Red walks towards her, stopping a few feet away. Lori, hearing his footfall, rounds on him, and with a strangled cry she stumbles forward, her hands outstretched, as though to throttle him, so that Bea and Mada are forced to grab at her arms, and the three of them struggle in a blind, awkward dance until Lori quietens.

Bea grips Lori's shoulders, shaking them gently – 'Sis, that's enough, come on' – so after a time her anger seems to quieten.

The five of them in the vibrant day, wordless, blinking; a car cruises slowly down the street and turns at the cul-de-sac that marks the harbour's edge. Across the water, a ceaseless drum of road noise from the Anzac Bridge. Lori has her arms spread from her sides, her dressing gown gaping, shifting from one foot to another like a ragged bird.

'Are you okay?' Bea asks Red. She lifts a hand to his eye, then stops herself before the gesture becomes a touch. Red completes the movement, touching her hand briefly then wiping dirt from his face.

'Yeah, I'm right. She's pretty strong, considering.'

Bea eyes Lori up and down. She can see Mada doing the same, ready to grab her and hold on, as if he's expecting his mother to start swinging at any moment. Red stands a few feet away, out of arm's reach.

Lori turns to Bea. 'He's fucking about on you,' she says with decisive clarity. A vengeful resurrected angel. 'I found an earring in the car. A real one.'

'Sis, please stop,' Bea says. She doesn't even listen at first, doesn't want to hear.

'He is, I bet it's true,' says Lori sullenly. Earthbound once more. She's fossicking in her pockets and releases a triumphant exclamation before pulling out a small stud, holding it stoutly before her with thumb and forefinger. It glints diamond bright.

Red glares wildly at her, wide-eyed and murderous.

Good fucking Christ, Bea thinks: it is true, and even her sister knows it. Isn't the humiliation of prison enough? She is too exhausted for this. Tired to the bones. There's nothing left inside, nothing in the tank. Not hope, not even disappointment. Just nothing. It's obvious that Red's anger at his sister-in-law is an admission: not guilt, or not only guilt, which would be bad enough. It's his intention to keep the secret, that's what Bea reads in his face. They hold each other's eyes, both of them drawn to this one certainty: that Red has no space for denials. That he's got nothing in the tank as well, no fuel for another trip, for the creation of a new story. When he sees this realisation take her he tries to speak and only half succeeds, so his anger is replaced in an instant with a kind of desperation, his words coming out as a half-strangled plea, and there is something pathetic about it, the inconsequence of it, the way it mumbles out into what may or may not be denial, but it's convincing no one, coming out so weakly that even Red seems unimpressed by his defence, unsure even what it is he wants to say.

He shuts his mouth and stares at Bea pleadingly.

Bea wants to be sick. She wants to punch Red in the face. Hit him like a girl. The way the chicks in prison punch a face. It's not the infidelity, so much. Two years in prison, she's not even surprised. It's the look he gives. He's not upset about the discovery, not afraid he might lose her. It's more that his principal mode is embarrassment once his deception has been uncovered. That's what gets her. His head wobbling tremulously from side to side, as though he's struggling to comprehend that he's not as smart as he thinks, that perhaps Lori is right.

What is she even doing here? Why doesn't she book into a hotel, find a fragment of peace? But then Red catches her eye, and his face collapses and he's saying that he's an idiot, that he loves her, blubbering away until she can bear no more of it.

'Oh, shut up, Redmond,' she says.

It comes out in her prison voice, the one she cultivated to keep herself alive, with its promise of pain, its pretence that brutality will be paid in kind. Red looks shocked, as if he has seen a part of her he didn't know existed.

'Look … we've got plenty of time to figure it all out,' she says more gently. She takes a gulp of air, gazes about. Broken pots over the drive and steps. One of the house windows cracked. And the car half-covered with ceramic and earth. 'Nice place you got here. I'm surprised the neighbours didn't call the cops. Hell, I'm surprised you didn't.'

'I figured she'd exhaust herself eventually.'

'Figured wrong, didn't you?' jeers Lori.

'Give it a rest, Mum.'

The dog nuzzles Bea's ankle.

Bea picks it up, and is scratching it absentmindedly behind an ear when a realisation strikes her. 'This isn't Henry,' she says.

The colour drains from Red's face. 'No. That's Henrietta.'

'What happened to Henry?'

'He's dead,' says Red tonelessly. 'I would have told you … but you had enough to worry about.'

'Oh. Poor Henry.'

'He's buried in your veggie garden, back at the old place,' Red offers, his tone faintly unctuous. 'I'm sure we could go for a visit if you want.'

'It's okay. I have enough graves to tend. What happened? I hope it was quick.'

Red winces. 'I don't think he suffered much,' he says.

'Well. Thanks for not calling the cops, Red,' says Bea, her eyes softening a touch. 'I know she's my sister and all, but I'm well aware what a handful she can be.'

'It was impossible. You turning up to the police. Not here. Not today.' He takes Bea's hand lightly in his own. Lori is walking in tight, unsteady circles, muttering to herself. Red glances at her balefully and turns his attention to the car. He picks off a large shard of terracotta, brushing dirt from the windshield with his hand.

'Besides,' he says, the man Bea knows returning, 'it was an insurance job after the first pot hit the duco. This way I'll blame it on the local hooligans.'

'Local hooligans? *Here?*' Bea's gesture takes in the water and the street, all the smoky suburban perfection.

Red shrugs.

Mada and Zoe have come to Bea's side, and for a few seconds the three of them embrace, so that Bea feels a part of herself unlock, and she basks in the redemption of human touch, gripping them both to her, burrowing her face into Mada's shirt.

At that moment, as she lifts her head from Mada's shoulder, Bea sees the terracotta pot rise into the air. Lori has hefted it bodily from the garden, and, using their moment of affection as cover, swung it straight-armed at the BMW with all the force that she and gravity can muster.

'Quit it,' Red growls, lunging forward with his arms outstretched. There's a squeak from the dog, Red stumbles, and the pot sails between his two hands to land smack centre of his face. The ceramic edge strikes with a sickening crunch. Red staggers and falls to his knees, blood gushing from his nose, then topples sideways, curling up on the concrete driveway with a wail of pain. Bea sinks to her knees beside him, instinctively shielding his head with her body, one arm waving in Lori's direction to ward off any further blows.

'Mum, stop!' exclaims Mada.

'Ha!' Lori is hopping in circles like a demented crow, throwing her arms triumphantly into the air. 'That's enough, all right. That's enough. Can't buy your way out of that one!'

Mada and Zoe have her then, but she is not trying to push past them. Rather, apparently struck by the realisation of her success, she stills herself, gazing down at Red wide-eyed, half-exulted, half-disturbed by what she has wrought. Mada grips her tightly to him while her expression turns to horror. Red has pulled his hands from his face and is trying to open his eyes, but the dirt and blood are making it impossible.

Lori points. 'Did I do that?' she asks timidly.

Mada, his arms still encircling his mum, stares down at Red. 'Yes Mum, that's all you. Can you hear me, Red? Are you okay?'

Red offers a weak grunt.

Bea takes the corner of her shirt and wipes away the worst of the muck, then, lifting his tie, she places the fabric in his hands and presses them over the bridge of his nose.

Red gasps.

'Close your eyes and keep pressure on that,' she says. 'Not too much, though, I think your nose is broken. Zoe, would you go inside and grab a few towels from the bathroom? Bring fresh ones, and wet one down. We'll try to clean him up a bit.' She is surprised to hear how steady her voice is. Red is mumbling incomprehensibly, a blend of invective directed at his sister-in-law and directions to the linen closet, something about the second door to the right.

Bea quiets him. 'She'll find it.'

Zoe leaps up the steps, emerging moments later with two towels in one hand and a bottle of vodka in the other. 'Multiple therapeutic uses,' she says, holding up the bottle of clear spirit. Mada takes it from her, unscrews the cap, and tosses back a decisive swig. Zoe's eyes go wide. 'What happened to the man I knew?'

'He's been hanging with a bad scene.'

'Pass that here,' Lori demands.

'No. Sorry, Mum.'

'Come on. I don't want to drink it. I want to sterilise his face; it must be hurting.' She wags a finger at Red.

They all look at Red. His eyes are closed. He waves one hand vaguely over his head, as though shooing away an imaginary mosquito.

'No. Fucking. Chance,' he says slowly.

'That'll sting plenty,' says Zoe, frowning.

'Yes,' says Lori. A grin pulls at the corners of her mouth. She's trying to keep it in check but can't quite do it, and she lurches, one arm outstretched, straight at the bottle.

'Probably kinder to let a nurse at A and E sort it out,' says Zoe.

Mada passes the bottle back, and turning his mother to face him, accentuates each word so she can't mistake his meaning. 'Stop it. That's enough.' Finally Lori stills. She stares into his eyes, lighting up a moment as though surprised at finding him there. Mada draws her to him and steers her away, sitting her down in the gutter by the car's front wheel. Her anger seems to drain away, and soon she's peering down the street towards the bay, where the thickening haze has swallowed the bridge, then gazing up at him and telling him about driving past the fires on her route home, heading south to Sydney through the Central Coast.

'You know,' she says to him pensively, 'I had the strangest dream the other day. It was about your father.'

'Oh yeah?' Mada sits on the kerb beside her, putting his arm around her shoulders. 'What happened?'

'Well, we were on the beach,' says Lori. 'We met there, in Byron Bay, and I told him about you.'

'Is that right?' Mada asks. 'What did he say?'

'He said he liked your name.'

'I see what you mean. That is strange.'

'That is *not* the strange bit,' She glares at him irritably. 'It was strange because he was old. Really old. I think maybe I'll see him again. Some day. Just not yet.'

'That's nice, Mum.'

'Isn't it.'

'So … Mum?'

'Yes?'

'How would you feel about being a grandma?'

'How would I feel? How? I'd feel amazing!'

'Good. Because it looks like you will be.'

'Whaaaat?'

All eyes shift from Mada to Zoe and back again. Even Red is squinting over. They're both grinning fit to burst. Lori grips her son tight, gazing up at him, starry-eyed.

Bea joins them both in an enormous hug, then drops to her knees beside Red. 'What do you say to that? You think you felt old before.'

Red groans.

Bea pulls his hands away from his face, where they're cupping a towel over his injuries. The angle of his nose is wrong, and there's a deep gash on his cheek beneath his eye. Blood flows down his cheek, pooling in his ear.

'Jesus,' says Mada, looking over. 'We'd better get him to a hospital. Come on, Red. I'll drive you. RPA's not far.'

But Red doesn't move: he's lying back on the concrete holding the towel over his face again. 'Give me a minute.'

Bea takes it all in. Her husband and their scene of broken domestic life, with its detritus of soil and shards, the smashed car, the smoke hanging low on the water. Her sister, diminishing mentally and bodily, being comforted by Mada after assaulting her husband. There are sirens out towards Broadway.

And yet a wave of relief passes through her with such force she gasps for air. She has survived. They've all survived. Not forever. But for now, they're going to get through. And there is a certainty, sharp, sudden, rising in her, that no matter what else she faces, she will see it through. That she will face it without lying to herself, without turning away. That for all the tragedy and mess, she's one of the lucky ones. And this word repeats itself inside her head. Lucky. Lucky. Lucky. She feels the truth of it, her immense good fortune, gratitude pulsing through her in waves, so that she staggers, shuddering with the immensity of it. I am so very lucky, she thinks, and here I am in the lucky country. And the madness of it makes her laugh out loud.

We of the lucky country. Burning to a crisp.

Ha! She'll take it, though. You bet she'll take it.

A nice car. A bed with clean sheets. No one waiting to bash her unconscious. She'll take it in a heartbeat. And it's so funny, because it's so real, and yet so unaccountable, so strange. This life that she has earned with her stupidities and the life she has been given, what is written in the stars – all of it foreign beyond reckoning, yet so completely *her*, so entirely her. This life that is the whole of her, all she has. And she is one of the lucky ones.

Even with everything. Especially with everything.

It's ridiculous, she thinks. The complete impossibility of it, everything hanging on a thread, all of us, dangling like paper dolls, not knowing whether we'll ride out the wind or tear and fall. Utterly ridiculous. The entire thing. Yet here we are, no choice but to live it out. Another snort of laughter escapes, and then it has hold of her and there is no chance of keeping it at bay, so it erupts in an unhinged convulsion: all that she has escaped, all that she has not, all the stupid turns of self and fate. And here she is, husband taken down by a pot plant, a sister in decline now arriving back from death, half the country on fire, and she is one of the lucky ones, and she can't help but laugh at the idiocy of it, the sheer mundane impossibility, and then it all comes out, everything she's pushed down, for years, for decades even, and suddenly tears are gushing down her face and she's not even sure if she's laughing or crying.

It is this thought, the muddling of joy and anguish, that starts to bring her back. Bea gives one last snort, wiping her nose with the back of her hand.

They're all staring at her with concern. Zoe is holding her arm with both hands.

'Auntie, are you all right?' asks Mada.

Bea tries to answer, but her throat is tight and dry.

Red lifts the towel from his face. 'Thanks,' he says, his voice flat, nasal. 'Thanks a lot.'

'I'm sorry, Red. I'm not laughing at you. It's only … it's all so mad.'

'What is?' He asks tiredly, delicately re-lowering the towel.

'Life. All of it. We're jetting through and it seems so normal. Most of the time, when you're in the thick of it, there's nothing to do but just get on. I've had such fantasies of the simplest things: getting up to have strawberries for breakfast, picking up food from the supermarket, going to work even. How small the stuff of daydreams. They're extraordinary though. Extraordinary. And so fragile. All of it.' She waves at the street, the water, the smoke-wreathed bridge. 'It's normal, everyday, ho-hum. But it's mad and unstable and none of it certain. And what else can you do but laugh?' She releases a sob, and shrugs. 'Or cry?'

Tears stream down her face.

She takes a tissue from Zoe and blows into it noisily. The tears don't stop, but she doesn't care.

Zoe grips her shoulders. 'You know, it's going to be all right,' she says, 'you're going to be all right.' Bea grins at her and nods, and Zoe hugs her so tightly her ribs might crack, their faces pulled together, wet.

Mada chuckles grimly. 'Hasn't this all just worked out nicely? Welcome home, Auntie.'

Red offers something incomprehensible. It might be 'Yeah! Welcome home,' but the towel swallows most of it, and it could just as well be 'Fresh hell, in the bones.' Bea pulls back his protesting hands so she can continue to mop his face with a corner of damp towel. He gives a whimper as she wipes muck from his nose. A tear runs from her chin and lands on his temple.

'So,' she says, wrestling back control, batting away his hand and determinedly wiping the blood and dirt from his ears, even

Acknowledgments

The opening citation, *Those the gods would torment, they first let glimpse the future,* borrows heavily from Sophocles' Antigone: 'τὸ κακὸν δοκεῖν ποτ' ἐσθλὸν τῷδ' ἔμμεν' ὅτῳ φρένας θεὸς ἄγει πρὸς ἄταν'. *'Il faut être absolument metamoderne!'* is from Arthur Rimbaud, *Une saison en enfer:* 'One must be absolutely modern.' The line *'He arado en el mar y he sembrado en el viento'* is from Simón Bolívar: 'I have ploughed the sea and sown in the wind.' *'¡Viban los compañeros!'* is from César Vallejo's poem 'Pedro Rojas'.

At the time of working through the final drafts of this manuscript, we inch ever closer to a cure for Huntington's disease. This book offers an account of some of the disease's history and the ongoing research for a cure. A novel, however, has its own needs: at times the science is stretched, or has ended up on the cutting-room floor, and for this I seek the readers' indulgence. I would like to extend enormous gratitude to all those who contributed interviews to this project, but should emphasise that this is entirely a work of fiction, and all of its failures are my own.

This book is dedicated to my mother, Dorothy Sellheim (née Inkpen), and to my sister, Annelies. Thank you both for the love and exuberance with which you navigate the world, and thank you for shoving books into my hand before I ever wanted to hold them. I am blessed to have two such strong, compassionate women guiding my life.

Thank you to my agent, Selwa Anthony, for all of her advice and care. Selwa did not give up on this manuscript, and considering how long it took to complete, that is a marvel. Thanks to Brian Dennis, for his steadiness and good humour. Thanks also to the team at HarperCollins Australia, whose patience has been monumental, especially Catherine Milne, Scott Forbes and Amanda O'Connell.

Thanks are due to Professor Clement Loy, of the Faculty of Medicine and Health, University of Sydney, and Director of the Huntington Disease (HD) Service at Westmead Hospital. I would also like to acknowledge the pioneering work of Nancy Wexler and her family. Thank you to Adam Mada, literally a magician, and a fine friend, for allowing me to steal his name, and for his Venezuelan anecdotes. Thanks also to Amelia du Randt, for her many stories and insights, which were so key to some aspects of this novel. Thanks to my newest brother, Wayne England, for helping me to understand golf – 'It's a game, not a sport!' – and to my newest sister, Jackie, for her encouragement and support.

The chapter 'The Women of the Land' is offered as homage to Zoe and Amber Jackson, and to Trish Crick, without whom this book, as it is written, would not have been possible. The Women of the Land was the self-given name of a group of women who set up a commune in coastal New South Wales in the early seventies, where Zoe Jackson raised her daughter, Amber. Trish, who died as I was finding the final words for this manuscript, did indeed build a sprawling house, with an enormous veranda, high on a ridge, living there off-grid with Zoe for decades. Trish, both builder and philosopher, built huts too, which often ended up being used by women who needed them, one- or two-room affairs which look to the escarpment and out along the valley. Trish's insights into Huntington's disease were vital in the telling of this story. Zoe, a visual artist and as unique and pure a creative soul as I have known, has fought her own long Huntington's fight, and I have tried to bring something of her spirit into this book. Thanks to Amber Jackson for trusting me to write this story, for being a wonderful dog mama to Leroy, and a true friend.

This book was written over a strange and unstable period, both globally and personally. To those friends who helped to keep me sane(ish) through an insane time, thank you and enormous love: Alison Urquhart, Kieran Adair, Stuart Cooke, Jason Childs, David Ritter, Zok Nyste, Robert Malherbe, the ever-inspiring Rizo and Nick, Josh Murray, Andy Quan, Sharelyn and Kane, Erica and Steve, Deb Lennie, Nigel Bullen, Pete Tually, and Morgan Boehringer. I would also like to thank Mathew Kuppe and Dan-O Tigchelaar, both for the late-night restless-minded whisky-fuelled chats and for making much of this last year liveable.